Jonathan Pembroke

RUMBLE
IN
WOODHOLLOW

Book 1 of *The Holly Sisters*

Kaytlyn –
Thanks for reading
and welcome to Woodhollow!
Cheers!
Jonit Pembroke

QUICK BIRD PRESS

To Mom and Dad
Thanks for everything

Note: A glossary of the mystical races populating Woodhollow can be found at the end of the book.

ACT ONE

ARRIVAL

Chapter One

The young faery paused at the north edge of the plaza. *Huh,* she thought. *The Log isn't what I expected.*

The other buildings lining the perimeter of Bayberry Square were shops of stone and mortar, with broad glass windows displaying their wares. Occupying the entire western edge of the square, The Log appeared exactly as its name implied: a great fallen oak with a tangle of roots at the north end and a collection of shorn branches at the other. A wall of red bricks sealed the end of what would have been the tree's base. Rows of wide windows had been carved in the trunk and the top leveled, providing a flat roof bound by a waist-high brick wall. A painted sign proclaiming the tavern's name hung over stout double doors.

I guess I didn't think it was an actual log. Sydney furrowed her eyebrows. *Still, it's not much of a hideout.*

A trio of goblins shouldered past her. Sydney said, "Hey."

The three stopped and stared at her. Each wore a frown on their green-skinned faces. Like most goblins, they were shorter than her own five-and-half feet and broader in the shoulders. All three wore spark-scarred leather aprons over their tunics and trousers.

The nearest goblin narrowed his eyes. "Whadda ya want?"

"What do you know about that tavern?"

"The Log?"

She nodded.

The goblin snorted. "You're a faery, you tell me."

"I'm new to town, so I don't know. Have you been in there?"

"You stupid? Of course we've been in there. Everyone who's anyone has been in there." He flicked his eyes up and down her frame. "You going to work there? On stage?"

"No."

"Just as well. You're not bad but with that knockout they have singing, if the audience had to put up with you instead, they'd get bored and leave. Maybe they can put you to work doing dishes or something."

The goblins laughed and walked away.

A nearby trow and dark elf strode past. By the amused looks on their faces, Sydney could tell they heard every word. The trow said, "Think she'll last long?"

"Maybe Marla will take pity on her." The elf laughed. "If not, I give her a week."

She glared at them and muttered under her breath. "Assholes."

"Well, then. You must be Sydney."

She turned to the source of the voice.

A faery leaned against the corner of a nearby lightstone post, his arms folded. He was close to six feet tall and slender, though his arms rippled with muscle and sinew. He wore a sleeveless white tunic over scarlet calf-length breeches. A wide black silk sash circled his waist, giving him a somewhat piratical look—the thought of which would have brought a smile to her face if she hadn't been so annoyed.

"Yeah, I'm Sydney. Who the hell are you?"

He smiled, took a few steps towards her, then bowed. "Markus."

She glanced at his wings as he straightened, which were pale yellow with streaks of blue. "Thistle Clan?"

"Of course. And you're Holly Clan."

"Holly Clan has pink wings with dark red highlights."

Markus nodded. "Even though your colors are random, you were born into the Holly Clan, weren't you?"

"How do you—"

"How do you think?"

Sydney hesitated. "Marla told you?"

"She described you to a tee. Medium height, blue eyes, auburn hair you normally wear in a ponytail, like you have it now. Cute face. And the same blue-dotted gray wings your father had." He paused. "Not too many faeries arriving in Woodhollow today match that description."

"She had you waiting for me out here? Why?"

"You'll have to ask her."

Markus extended his hand for her worn-floral print suitcase but Sydney shook her head. "I got it."

"If you say so. Come on inside."

Sydney fell in next to him. She stole a couple of sidelong glances at Markus, noting his strong jawline, collar-length curly black hair, and sparkling green eyes. He moved with confidence and purpose. The more she looked at him, the more Sydney's irritation dwindled. A trickle of desire leaked into her thoughts.

Okay, Sydney: he's hot. And it's been a while since I broke things off with Jacob. I wonder.... She glanced at him again as a second notion occurred. *But if he and Marla—*

She pushed the thought from her mind.

Markus led her to the double doors at the tavern's entrance. She said, "What's the deal with this tree? Seems kind of...."

"Odd?"

"Shabby."

"The Log has been here in Woodhollow forever. It's changed hands a lot over the centuries and even though it looks a little run-down, it's one of the strongest buildings in town. It carries quite a bit of prestige for whoever holds it."

"That's perfect. Hiding a gang headquarters in a building where everyone knows about it. Marla's not as bright as I thought."

"Are you going to say that to her face?" Markus laughed when Sydney looked away. "Besides, it doesn't matter if a gang operates in the open when most everyone is afraid to move against it. And even if folks weren't intimidated we have other assets."

A pair of drunken dwarves emerged from The Log and staggered past them. Markus held the door for her.

Tables and benches, filled with drunken creatures, crammed the long tavern room. Brownies and *landvaettir* drank together at one table, dryads and wood elves at another, *vilas* and trows at a third. Patrons careened in various directions, slopping ale and wine on one another. Odd verses of drinking songs filled the air.

A faery of perhaps forty years, with a pair of blonde braids, a lined, scowling face, wide hips, and wearing a barmaid's dress, nearly collided with them. She made an exaggerated motion of hefting a tray lined with empty mugs out their way. Her wings—similar in color to Markus's—quivered in exasperation. "Damn it, Markus, watch where you're going."

"Sorry, Robin."

The waitress eyed Sydney. "Who's this?"

"Sydney. She's the one Marla was waiting for."

"Hmph. Not what I expected. From the way Marla talked, I figured she'd be ten feet tall and breathing fire." Before Sydney could say anything, Robin whirled into the crowd, snatching up empty mugs and slapping away wandering hands from the folds of her dress.

Sydney snorted. "She's a real peach."

"Don't mind Robin." Markus closed the outer doors behind them. "She's always crabby when she's working. It's the only way she can deal with getting groped all the time."

"You guys allow that in here?"

He shrugged. "I think the regulars do it more to get under her skin than to actually cop a feel. Of course, sometimes they take it too far and she ends up decking one of them."

"She's also Thistle Clan. You related?"

"Distant cousins. Her and her brother Garth—" He motioned to another middle-aged faery behind the bar. "—handle the day-to-day drink service in the tavern."

The lightstones about the room dimmed, save for the handful at the far end over a small stage. The crowd cheered and banged their mugs on tabletops.

A buxom faery with long dark hair and wearing a low-cut red-sequined dress with a thigh-high slit sauntered onto the stage.

She waved and simpered to the crowd, bending low to give them plenty of looks at her deep cleavage. Sydney wasn't sure it was possible but the roar of the mob grew even louder.

The woman opened her mouth and out came the most beautifully melodious voice Sydney had ever heard. As if someone had thrown a switch, the crowd went quiet. Sydney considered herself a bit tone-deaf but even she had to admit the singer's lush body was only half the draw. The faery's voice was almost hypnotic in its purity. The rapt faces of the tavern patrons suggested they wouldn't move if the building itself were on fire.

Markus took Sydney by the elbow and steered her through the mob, to an unassuming door in the back corner. She noted the sword-armed fairies—one man and one woman—lounging to either side. Their alert eyes never stopped scanning the crowd.

The woman gave them a brief nod and stepped aside as Markus reached for the door's handle. The eyes of both guards lingered on Sydney, though they said nothing. Markus motioned her through, came in behind, and closed the door.

The space beyond was a short hallway, leading to a door. To their left, a wooden staircase ascended to the next floor. Another stout door lay to their right.

Markus rapped the door on their right. "Storeroom, also leads to the kitchen, if you get hungry and don't want to go through the main room."

"Okay."

He motioned to the door at the end of the hallway. "Down here."

Sydney followed him. "Who's your singer?"

"Natasha. You'll meet her later."

"Is she one of those assets you talked about?"

Markus grinned. "She is, actually."

"Nice body and that voice is heavenly. Between the two, I bet she really draws the crowds."

"Yeah, she's a regular sex kitten on stage but don't piss her off. She's a crack shot with a crossbow."

He pulled open the door to reveal a long, well-lit workshop. Faeries clustered in various groups. In one corner, a trio huddled over a table laden with dissimilar trinkets Sydney suspected were stolen. At another counter, a pair of fairies picked at a series of mocked-up door locks, under the eye of a third. A set of identical twins stood next to a table laden with tubes and glass beakers. One hefted a beaker and glanced at the other. The other nodded and the first poured the contents of the beaker into a jar.

Markus pointed another door on the far side of the room. "Over there." Without waiting for a response, he walked to the fairies sorting through the stolen goods.

Sydney ignored a few questioning glances from the room's gang members. She strode to the door and pushed it open without knocking.

The room beyond was plain and square. A young faery sat sideways behind a wooden desk. Her hands fiddled in the open drawer of a file cabinet. A couple of bulging folders piled on the desk and a neat stack of papers lay off to one side.

The seated faery took in Sydney's appearance at a glance. "Can I help you?"

"Here to see Marla."

"Ah, you must be Sydney." She stood and Sydney realized the faery was probably as old as her, though her tiny body made her appear younger. The loose ringlets of the faery's chocolate-brown hair flowed over her shoulders. Her amber-accented forest-green wings marked her as a member of the Dandelion Clan.

The woman extended her hand. "I'm Lila."

Sydney took the offered hand with her own and pumped it once. "Marla's secretary?"

"Executive assistant."

Sydney stared at her and Lila blushed. "All right, secretary. I hate that word."

"Is she in?"

"Yes, she said for you to come in whenever you arrived."

Sydney opened the door to the interior office. The acrid reek of burning tobacco washed over her. She wrinkled her nose and stepped inside.

The office was the same size as the exterior one. A narrow desk occupied the center of the room. A tall window spanned the breadth of the far wall. Sydney blinked; the window appeared to be a view of the square in front of The Log but the room's location was all wrong for that orientation. She decided it must be some form of magic.

A faery about the same size as Sydney sat behind the desk. Her wings were pink darkening to red at the edges and were folded behind her. She wore her dark hair in a tight braid draped over one collarbone. The remains of a stubby cigar hung from her lips. She wore a tight-fitting gray tunic and simple black trousers.

The faery scowled as she read a sheet of paper clutched in both hands. She did not look up when Sydney entered.

Lila pulled the office door closed, leaving Sydney and the other in silence.

"Hello, Marla."

"Did you bring them?"

Sydney dropped her bag and flopped in a chair in front of the desk. "Hello to you too. 'Nice to see you, Sydney.' 'Did you have a hard trip?' 'How is Aunt Brigid?' Those are the kinds of questions someone might ask their baby sister whom they hadn't seen in seven years. But no, you still go straight for the jugular."

Marla dropped the sheet on the desk. She plucked the cigar from her mouth, and set it in an ashtray. "I see you're still the same whiner you were when I left."

"Not quite. I realized a long time ago I don't have to put up with any shit from anyone. Including you."

"Well, at least you learned something, Syd."

"Nobody's called me 'Syd' for a long time."

Marla cocked her head. "No?"

"You were the only one I ever let get away with it."

"You need to loosen up. Now, can I have the designs, please?"

Sydney sighed. She hefted her bag, unbuttoned the top, and fished out a bound sheaf of parchment. "Here you go."

Marla snatched the papers. "This is all of them?"

"Everything that was in Mom's footlocker."

"Hmm, I thought there were more."

"Maybe there were at some point but this all I found."

"Okay."

Marla untied the pages of designs and started flipping through them. Sydney waited a moment before saying, "You're welcome."

"What?"

"You're welcome."

Marla's shoulders slumped. "Thank you. You're right and I'm sorry. I just have a lot on my mind."

"Such as?"

"Gang business."

"Yeah, about that. You're the boss of this crew? Seems like you've done quite well for yourself."

"Not too bad," Marla said with a smile. "We've pretty much cornered the market on the stimulant trade."

"Drugs? How'd you do that?"

"Shroom."

Sydney blinked. "Shroom?"

"Albino mushrooms. The twins figured out a way to soak dried mushroom powder in alcohol and cook it back down. Works like a psychedelic and aphrodisiac rolled into one, without any harmful hangovers. It's been profitable."

"You do know that albino mushrooms are toxic to almost every race but faeries, right?"

"That's why we cut it."

"Isn't that dangerous?"

Marla shrugged. "Hasn't killed anyone yet."

Sydney shifted her weight. "The clan chiefs would be horrified and outraged that you're perverting the source of our magic—not to mention that Aunt Brigid would be disappointed you used her herbalism lessons to give losers a high."

"The clan chiefs never come to Woodhollow, so they won't learn unless some snitch runs and tells them." Marla gave Sydney a pointed glance.

"Doesn't bother me."

"As for Brigid," Marla said, "I doubt she'd care what I'm doing since she ran me out of Holly Grove."

"That's not how I remember it, Marla."

"Whatever. Besides, it's not like we're raiding the 'sacred'—" Marla hooked her fingers in the air. "—harvesting grounds in Sylvan Valley. We set up our own fields in the woods outside town."

"Who's farming them?"

"Sprites."

Sydney frowned. "And you trust those half-wits?"

"Oh, hell no. They try to steal from us all the time. It's like dealing with children." Marla paused. "How is Brigid?"

"Angry."

"At me?"

Sydney shook her head. "No, me. She was against me coming to see you here in Woodhollow. She said you would be, and I quote, 'An awful influence.' " A smirk crossed her face. "Tell me she's wrong."

Marla snorted. "Brigid never liked me."

"No, Marla, she loves you very much. She's just worried about us."

"Well, I'm fine."

"Are you?" Sydney leaned forward. "You said there's trouble here."

"Nothing we can't handle."

They were silent for a moment. Sydney stared at the stack of papers she'd brought. "What did you want with these things, anyway?"

"None of your business."

A thought occurred. "Oh, Marla. You're not planning on weaponizing these, are you? Mom said that was incredibly dangerous."

"Mom and Dad lost the right to tell us what to do when they went and got killed, Syd. Besides, I've done a little research. I think we'll be all right."

Marla hefted the cigar and took a long drag. She blew a perfect smoke ring. "So I suppose you'll be heading back to Sylvan Valley."

"I hadn't thought about it yet."

"You're welcome to stay for a few days if you keep out of the way. I don't know how much time I can spare, but—"

"Okay."

"Okay, what?"

Sydney smiled. "I'll hang out a few days. Maybe we can have some time to catch up. If not, I'll wander around Woodhollow a bit and check it out. Is there anything I should know? Is there any danger out there?"

Marla slowly nodded. "All kinds, Syd. All kinds."

Chapter Two

"So, you're Marla's baby sister?" Lila said as they tromped up the stairs.

"Yeah, by four years."

Lila opened the door. "Okay, this is it. I don't snore, so you should be all right."

Sydney glanced around the small chamber. There were two beds, each with a wooden chest at the foot, and a small bedside table bearing a lightstone lamp. The room was otherwise devoid of furnishings.

"Sorry, Lila, I don't mean to crowd you here."

"It's fine."

"Not much in the way of furniture."

Lila shrugged. "I don't spend much time here unless I'm sleeping."

A muffled cheer echoed from below and Sydney winced; the thin floorboards did little to dampen the commotion from the tavern.

Gonna be fun trying to sleep through that.

"Honestly, I didn't know what to expect." Lila flopped on one of the beds. She kicked off her boots and folded her legs beneath herself. "I mean, Marla's talked about you and your aunt but she never got into a lot of detail. She's pretty quiet about her past."

"She was always kind of reserved. Unless she's mad. Then she's loud."

Lila snickered. "Well, that hasn't changed."

Sydney sat on the other bed. The sheets felt clean and fresh, and the stuffed mattress was surprisingly comfortable. "How old are you, Lila?"

"Nineteen. You?"

"Twenty-two." Sydney pointed at Lila's wings. "Dandelion Clan, right? How'd they feel about you running off to join a criminal gang"

"They barely noticed I was gone. Neither of my folks was in the family succession line and I'm their seventh child. You know how that goes; those facts alone put me on the outskirts of the Clan."

"Yeah, I get that," Sydney said, repressing a snarl. *Boy, do I ever.* "Sorry, go on."

"I didn't have a lot of prospects in Sylvan Valley so I ran away when I was sixteen, came to Woodhollow. I spent a month begging on the streets before Markus lassoed me into the gang." Lila paused and peered over Sydney's shoulder. "I'm sorry but I thought you were part of the Holly Clan, like Marla. I'm not familiar with those marks."

"I am Holly Clan, sort of. My dad was a freebooter and adventurer, without affiliation. He and Mom didn't cast the clan binding spell when I was in the womb." Sydney thrust her thumb at her blue and gray wings. "So I got these. Random coloring, as fate intended."

"But Marla has the clan wings."

Sydney hesitated. "The circumstances around her birth were a little different."

"I see."

"So tell me: how did Marla end up in control of this outfit?"

"She beat the crap out of the last boss."

"Marla did that?"

"Yeah, she did. Tripp was a drunk and the gang was falling apart but he was big. And experienced. He was forty-something and had been in a lot of fights. No one would challenge him until Marla did. She put up with his incompetence for two years before she couldn't take it anymore, right after—" Lila clamped her mouth shut.

"Right after what?"

"Nothing." Lila stared at her hands for a few seconds. Then she raised her gaze to Sydney's again. "Marla could have killed Tripp. She probably should have but she settled for chasing him off."

"And he just went?"

"He didn't have a choice. It was leave or be killed. He swore revenge and all that as he ran off."

"That sounds like the plot from a bad book, Lila."

Lila grinned. "I know. Marla is savvy enough to not get killed by a cliche—you know, such as sparing his life only to have him show up later with an army in tow. She kept tabs on him after he left town. He ended up in Tharsis in Kroven, doing mercenary work for some dwarven outfit. He died in a skirmish between two of the merchant houses."

"That seems convenient."

"Marla thought so too but one of our members, Will, saw Tripp's body. Anyways, that's ancient history now. Marla's in charge and we're doing great." Lila stood and stretched her hands over her head. "So do you want me to walk the streets of Woodhollow with you? Show you around?"

"No, I'll be all right. I'm sure Marla has stuff for you to do."

"She does but she told me to look out for you, at least for today."

"On that note, is there anything I need to know?" Sydney scowled, remembering her arrival at The Log. "Other than to watch out for smart-mouthed goblins?"

"Well...."

"Well, what? Spit it out, Lila."

The younger faery took a deep breath. "There's some tension out there in Woodhollow."

"With the authorities?"

"No, with some of the other gangs." Lila pursed her lips into a thin line. "When the faeries were a small factor in the underworld, nobody paid us any mind, except to ridicule and mock us. But when Marla got the Shroom business up and running, some of them took notice, and started leaning on us."

"Like who?"

"The Cons, mostly."

Sydney blinked. "The who?"

"The Cons." Sydney's face must have betrayed her confusion, since Lila continued. "The Leprechauns. They're easily the strongest gang in Woodhollow. They see what we've got going with Shroom and they want in on it. And, uh, we have history."

"Go on."

Lila looked for a moment as if she didn't want to say anything. Then she took a deep breath. "The rivalry has gone on for years. From what the old members told me, it was mostly one-sided. They bullied us because they could. Then Tripp got in a fight with one of the Cons over this wood elf at Belles. That led to a little...altercation."

"How little?"

"They ambushed an entire party late one night, on Bell Street. Twelve faeries, a third of our gang at the time, got caught in a crossfire. Because Tripp had never placed any priority on us keeping our magic active, none of the gang were able to access ours, while the Cons were overcharged with theirs."

Lila sniffed. Her eyes filled with tears. "I had only been in the gang a few months but I knew them all. All twelve of them were friendly to me. Quentin, an old faery from the Poppy Clan, taught me how to pick pockets. He was so nice. Every one of them were cut down like dogs."

"Shit."

"Yeah." Lila wiped her eyes. "After that, the word came down from Lord Burnside."

Sydney raised her eyebrows. "The ruler of Woodhollow, right?"

"Yeah."

"Burnside's ogre Enforcers started cracking down on street fighting. There haven't been any major incidents since the Massacre but the damage was done. We lost our mojo. The Cons edged into our territory and we surrendered a lot of power and prestige. We barely managed to hang onto The Log. Eventually, the Cons eased off and just started berating and humiliating us in public. Seeing how weak we were, the other gangs joined in but no one else got hurt. That status kind of hung there until Marla blew her top."

"Tell me what happened."

"After Bell Street, Tripp got smashed every night—like, incoherent drunk."

"Out of guilt, I assume."

"Right, but it made things worse. The whole gang started to unravel. That was when Marla stepped in. I remember it clearly. After watching Tripp get loaded every night for a month and after begging with him to make some changes, she stormed out of the office, went to the main tavern room, drained two beers one after the other, slammed her mug on table, said, 'No more,' and went right back to Tripp and beat his ass."

Sydney scratched her arm. "Knowing Marla, I am sure she has a grudge against the Cons too."

"Yeah. She thinks about the Bell Street Massacre every day and sometimes, I think everything she does is designed to prevent that from ever happening again."

Lila looked so unhappy that Sydney tried to force a little levity into her voice. "Avoid leprechauns. Okay, got it. Anything else?"

Lila sat up. "Oh, yes. Whatever you do, don't fly inside the walls of the city, or even nearby if you're outside."

"Reason?"

"Lord Burnside's drake patrols. Nobody is allowed to fly inside the city without a permit. Anyone who does, they'll force to land and give a hefty fine."

"I'm kind of poor, Lila. If you can't pay do they put you in jail?"

"If you're lucky. If not, they might rip you apart and eat you on the spot. Or flame-roast you. But that doesn't happen very often—usually only if you give them a bunch of lip and they lose their tempers."

Sydney sighed. "Okay, the Cons and no flying. Anything else?"

"There's the other gangs: the Dryads, the Hobs, the Browns, the Rats. They've backed off since we got the Shroom going and haven't picked sides, so in theory, they shouldn't be a threat."

"In theory?"

"It looks that way, but we're never one hundred percent sure what they're doing. They have their own aims and I am sure some of those go against ours."

"Okay."

Lila nodded. "Burnside's ogres patrol the streets but unless you do something stupid or provoke them, they won't pick a fight."

Sydney snorted. "I suspect their definitions of 'stupid' and 'provoke' are a little different than ours."

"Quite a bit. Even so, they do tend to leave us alone."

"They don't move against the gangs, then?"

"Not as long as we keep the ruckus to a dull roar."

"Fair enough." Sydney stood. "I'll be back in a bit."

*   *   *   *   *

"Hey, Missy! Move yer ass!"

Sydney dodged to the side, just in time. The wagon, pulled by a massive six-legged and green-scaled lizard, trundled past. The dark-skinned trow driver glared at Sydney, who slapped her left hand into the crook of her right elbow and thrust her upturned arm at him.

"Up yours!"

Ignoring chuckles from nearby pedestrians, Sydney resumed her walk. The Log lay on the east edge of the city, so she had not seen much of Woodhollow while getting to it. She gazed at the tightly-packed buildings. Unlike the airy, spacious clan villages of Sylvan Valley, which were built into the branches and trunks of great trees, the stone buildings of Woodhollow often left no space between them at all. Most of the shops and homes rose two or three stories. The eaves of the red-tiled roofs jutted a few feet from the walls, casting long shadows over the streets. Here and there, narrow alleys separated the shops and homes. She half-expected to see glowing eyes staring out of the alleyways in hungry anticipation but the darkened lanes were still.

The cobblestone lane opened into another wide square, this one lined with wooden stalls and wagons loaded with goods. All manner of creatures called out, hawking everything from boots to pickled fish. A swirling mass of shoppers moved through the wagons and at times, she had to shove her way through.

She grabbed the money purse from her pocket, hooked the thong around her neck, and tucked it beneath her shirt.

I'm sure faeries aren't the only thieves in this town.

An ornate building dominated the south side of the plaza. Each of its three stories contained a full row of windows. From about half the windows, scantily-dressed ladies called out to those below and beckoned seductively. A wide assortment of men—and not a few women—trod in and out the wide double doors, under the watchful eyes of a quartet of burly goblins. The sign over the door read Belles. There was no symbol or depiction on the sign but to Sydney, the establishment's purpose was readily apparent.

I wonder if Marla has her hands in the hooker racket too.

She picked a random street and left the square. Her thoughts drifted to when she had received Marla's letter a week before. Her sister's request had arrived at a fortuitous time.

Sydney had been on the verge of leaving Sylvan Valley anyway.

Marla took nothing from their parents' belongings when she'd left seven years before, so due to guilt and sibling obligation, Sydney felt she owed it to her sister to bring her the one thing Marla *did* finally ask for.

She hadn't thought much about the magical device designs over the years. Their parents spent five years collecting the plans. She remembered her father specifically saying he and Sydney's mother wanted to open a forge for small magical items when they retired from their adventuring lifestyle. Most of the plans detailed small, harmless trinkets that were capable of minor magical feats, and of limited value.

Does Marla really want to turn them into weapons?

Sydney shrugged to herself. Whatever Marla planned to do, it was out of Sydney's hands.

What about me? Do I dare place myself in Marla's hands?

She could return to Sylvan Valley at any time. Aunt Brigid would welcome her; Sydney could resume work in her aunt's small apothecary shop in Holly Grove, where Sydney assisted Brigid in grinding plants and mixing concoctions and healing potions. She could easily go back.

Go back to what? she asked herself.

The Holly Clan had never truly accepted her. With her wings marking her lineage, she always felt like an outsider and had been treated as such. The clan was rarely outright rude but they were always distant and reserved, as far as Sydney was concerned. She had no friends and only one family member remaining there.

Brigid had loved her younger sister Jenna and had been distraught when Jenna died. Brigid also loved her nieces and had taken in Sydney and Marla without reservation. Brigid had always treated them well and Sydney thought her aunt had shown her and her sister nothing but affection and kindness. But Brigid was also strict, and the work in the shop was smelly, repetitive, and tedious.

Face it, Sydney. You're bored.

She *was* bored; bored with mixing potions, bored with dealing with jerkoff customers. She had toyed with the idea of leaving several times and striking out on her own. Sydney knew that was why she'd leaped at the chance to deliver the designs to Marla and left Sylvan Valley, over Brigid's objections. She wanted some excitement, some....

Purpose. I want some purpose.

Well, that and the wanderlust comes into play.

Sydney curled her lip at the thought. Many faeries lived their entire lives in Sylvan Valley, not leaving a single time. Most faeries were homebodies, who felt safe and relaxed amid their own kin. Her parents had been anomalies and Sydney knew that over their lives, both she and Marla felt the urge to get out and see the world.

But did she want to be caught up in something as dangerous as Marla hinted at?

I can return to that drudgery. Or I can stay here, and see what my big sister is really getting into—and knowing how Marla invites trouble, probably get killed in the process.

Sydney shook her head. She didn't have to decide anything right away.

She came to an intersection and paused, gazing in each direction. As with the other streets she'd seen in the city, they were crammed with pedestrians and lizard-drawn wagons.

"Hey, winger!"

The two of them lounged by the lightstone lamp. Both stood at six feet and were broad through the shoulders. They were all but identical in their similarities, having ivory white skin, red hair, and equally-red trimmed beards. Each bore a green jacket over their black vest and white shirts, with green knee-length pants, and green-and-white-striped hose. Black shoes with silver buckles clad their feet and each man wore a lime-colored top hat.

Sydney looked around to find the target of their address. Only after a moment did she realize that both men glared at *her*.

"Yes, I meant you, winger." The slightly-larger of the two men grabbed his corncob pipe from his mouth and jabbed it in her direction. "What are you, deaf?"

"No, I'm not deaf. What's your problem?"

"You are, winger." The second man chuckled. The first regarded Sydney with a nasty sneer. "But it's a problem we can solve."

They spread to either side of her. Sydney backpedaled, suddenly wishing she'd brought a weapon. She held her hands up, with palms out. "Look, boys—"

"We'll be lookin' at your guts in a moment!"

"Hold it, hold it."

The two froze at the new voice. The crowd parted and a squad of muscle-bound ogres tromped into view. The new arrivals wore chain hauberks over their leather jerkins and breeches and carried crossbows. Heavy swords and maces hung from their belts. Most of them appeared to Sydney as simple-minded brutes but the one in the front had a look of crafty intelligence and calm, implacable eyes.

Sydney swallowed uncomfortably. He was also the biggest ogre she had ever seen, easily half-again as tall as her.

The lead ogre took in the situation at a glance. He pointed at her two aggressors. "Seamus, Henry. You know better than to start a fight on the street in broad daylight."

The one with the pipe raised his hands. A mock grin painted his face. "A slight misunderstanding, Crol. We were just welcoming the young lady to Woodhollow."

"Uh-huh. Go do your welcoming somewhere else."

Seamus slapped Henry in the chest with the back of his hand. The two sauntered into the crowd.

The ogre turned his gaze on Sydney. "I haven't seen you before. You part of Marla's crew? Or just new to town?"

"Uh, yes, to both questions."

"And Marla let you on the streets by yourself? You all getting suicidal now?"

"I don't know what you mean."

Crol waved his hand at her. "Scamper back to The Log, before you run into more trouble. And make sure Marla fills you in before you get yourself skinned alive by some other gang."

Sydney nodded and backtracked the way she'd come. Crol and his ogre squad watched her until she was out of sight. She kept looking over her shoulder, to see if anyone followed but spotted no one. She wondered if Marla should have warned her the situation was that dire. The longer she walked, the more annoyed she got. Then angry. Then enraged.

By the time she reached The Log, Sydney was ready to ignite.

She stormed through the front doors, almost bowling over a pair of gnomes. They yelled at her but she scarcely noticed. The guards to the back rooms were not the same two that been there before but they didn't react when she stomped past. She guessed that since Markus had brought her through earlier, she was now a "permitted" person.

Let's see how permitted I am five minutes from now.

She pushed open the interior door and stalked across the workroom to Marla's office.

Lila looked up, startled, as the door banged into the far wall. She half-stood. "Sydney?"

"Out of my way."

Marla glanced at Sydney when the latter burst in. "Hello, Syd. Bad day?"

Sydney lunged across the floor. She grabbed Marla by the tunic, hoisted her from her chair, and slammed her against the wall. Sydney pressed her face into her sister's. "You fucking jerk! Why didn't you warn me?"

Marla's eyes narrowed. Before Sydney even knew what was happening, she hurled backward. Her head slammed against the floor. Her mind went foggy.

In the haze of her thoughts, she heard Marla yell. "Lila!"

Soft hands helped her to her feet. Woozy, she let the hands guide her to a chair. "What...what happened?"

Lila's voice was just a whisper in her ear. "I think you made her mad."

Sydney's senses slowly came into focus. Lila stood hunched over her, a look of concern on her young face. Beyond her stood Marla, her arms folded and face a thundercloud. She clenched an unlit cigar in her teeth.

"Marla—"

"Syd, I don't care what your reason is. Don't ever come into my office and attack me again. Is that clear?"

"Yeah."

"Good. Now, what hell is wrong with you?"

"Two of those...what did you call them? Cons? They came after me on the street."

Lila's eyes widened. "In full view of the public?"

"Yes." Sydney sat up. The back of her head throbbed. "I take it that's not normal."

"No." Marla's face was grim. "Lila."

Lila stood straighter at the change in Marla's tone. "Yes?"

"No faery leaves The Log alone. Minimum of two per party and every group will personally inform either Markus, Dana, or Gordon of where they're going and when they expect to return. Is that absolutely clear?"

"Yes, ma'am." Lila scuttled out.

Marla returned to her seat. Her face lost some of its grim nature and her eyes grew distant.

Sydney said, "Well?"

"Tell me about it."

"Not much to tell. I was walking down the street, minding my own business when these two guys tried to start trouble. By the way, what is with them calling us, 'wingers?' "

"Cons use it as a slur for us. Just part of them being assholes. The worst thing is, other races are starting to pick up on it and use it too."

"Are they all just dicks, or what?"

"Yeah, they are. Arrogant, pushy creeps, with a handful of sadists thrown in for good measure. Go on."

"Things were getting dicey. I was lucky a group of ogres showed up. From what Lila told me, I take it they're the local peacekeepers."

Marla nodded. "Lord Burnside's personal shock troops. They're called Enforcers."

"One of them was the biggest ogre I've ever seen, including the mercs Brigid used to patch up at Fort Bloodwell. I think one of the Cons called him Crol."

"He's the chief of the Enforcers. Be careful with that one, Syd. He's much smarter than an average ogre and I've seen him throw a hobgoblin twenty-five feet. Not someone to screw with."

"Drakes and ogres." Sydney frowned. "They all work for this Lord Burnside. What the hell is he, anyway? A dwarf or something?"

"No." Marla hesitated.

"What?"

"A wingless worm."

Cold engulfed Sydney. "You mean, like the one that—"

Marla raised her hand. "That's what they say. I've never seen him. He never comes out of his compound. Just his dictates. Whether Lord Burnside is a worm or not, it doesn't matter. The ogres and drakes do whatever he says without hesitation, so I don't ask a lot of questions. Now speaking of ogres, you were saying? About Crol?"

"Oh yeah. This Crol guy chased off the Cons and told me to hightail it back here. I did, mostly because I was scared shitless. Of course the longer I thought about it, the madder I got that you hung me out there to dry without so much as a warning."

"It wasn't on purpose." Marla pointed at the tip of her cigar. A tiny spark flashed from her finger, lighting the wrapped tobacco leaves. "There's been a lot of pressure from the Cons for us to knuckle under and let them into the Shroom trade but they've never actually attacked someone before. I have to figure out if McGee is upping the stakes on us or if those two idiots were acting on their own."

"They assumed I was in the gang. Why?"

"Who knows? There are dozens of faeries in Woodhollow that aren't in the gang." Marla scowled. "Unless they are watching The Log and saw you come in. If that's the case...well, I'll deal with that in a bit."

"Either that or just bad luck on my part. Story of my life." Sydney rubbed her head. "By the way, what did you do to me? I didn't even feel you touch your magic."

"I didn't. I've learned how to fight since I've been here."

"I can tell."

Marla's blue eyes focused on Sydney. "It helped keep me alive. You stick around, you'll learn too. If you survive long enough, that is."

Chapter Three

The sisters sat in silence for a moment before Marla said, "How are you set for crumble?"

"I'm not. Why would I have any?"

Marla's face suggested disbelief. "Brigid used to have stacks of the stuff."

"Of course she did but she could only legally sell it for coming-of-age rituals, marriages, and stuff like that. Don't you remember how restricted magic use is in Sylvan Valley?"

"Yes but I thought maybe you got a little light-fingered with Brigid's inventory."

"She still keeps an iron grip on her ledgers. I couldn't have cooked the books and walked with some if I'd tried." Sydney smirked. "You should remember that."

"Yeah, I still feel the welts on my ass from when she caught me." Marla inhaled, birthing an orange glow on the tip of her cigar. She tapped out the ash. "But we're not at home anymore. You need to keep crumble on you day and night. You don't want to be caught out there without your magic available."

Sydney recalled what Lila had said about the Massacre and Marla's obsession with it. "You probably should have told me that before you let me go wandering in the city without it."

"Probably. I figured you would have had some on you before you left Sylvan Valley. Wide, dangerous world out there and it doesn't pay to go unprepared. I guess I overestimated your wisdom. Sorry."

Sydney glowered, conceding the round of barbs to her sister. "Is using crumble illegal, like flying?"

"Nah, magic is fine to use in the city, as long as you don't use it to hurt or swindle anyone. Flying is only illegal because Burnside charges for the permits." Marla gave Sydney a pointed look. "Do you still want to hang out here for a few days?"

"If I do, are you going to kick my ass again?"

"Only if you need it."

Sydney hesitated but nodded.

"Okay," Marla said. "Then you need to earn your keep."

"How so?"

"You need to contribute to the gang's prosperity, even if you just help us straighten up after the tavern empties out at night."

"I hate cleaning. Don't you remember that?"

"We'll find something for you to do."

A sneer crawled onto Sydney's face. "You want me to put on a slut outfit and shake my tits at the crowd like the other tramp?"

"One, you don't have the tits for that." Marla's eyes narrowed. "And two, that's a low blow at Natasha. She's not a whore, she's an entertainer. She dresses that way to reel in the rubes but all she does is sing. If you want to audition for the whorehouse, we can make that happen."

"No, thank you."

"Besides, I think you'd like Natasha. She's a sweet girl. I know she'd like you."

"How so?"

Marla smiled. "You're her type. She likes 'em pretty and innocent."

"Oh." Sydney's eyes widened as Marla's insinuation hit home. "Oh! I'm not gay, Marla."

"Really?" Marla seemed genuinely surprised. "Never mind then."

"You thought I was? Why?"

"You never showed any interest in boys."

"I never showed any interest in girls, either."

Marla nodded. "Okay, that's fair. You don't get any...urges?"

Sydney flushed. "Once in a while. But I rarely felt like it was worth the effort."

"So you never...."

"There was a guy in the Poppy Clan. Jacob. I used to see him when Aunt Brigid and I would go to Poppydale to pick up certain ingredients for the shop. We'd, uh, hook up about every six months."

"Just to take the edge off?" Marla said with a laugh.

Sydney's face burned. "I don't really want to discuss it."

"Prude. Anyway, as I was saying, there are no freeloaders allowed here. Everyone in this gang works, everyone contributes."

"What do you want me to do?"

"Go out there and find Dana. She should have something you can help us with. Make sure you ask her for some crumble. She'll set you up."

"Which one is Dana?"

"Older, long gray hair. She's the only faery in the gang from the Foxglove Clan. She tends to wear gowns, not pants. Should be easy to find."

Sydney stood. Her neck was stiff and she felt a quiver of resentment towards her sister, for knocking her senseless. "She one of your underlings?"

"One of my lieutenants. She's our treasurer, coordinates with our fences, and supervises the Shroom production. Gordon handles our Shroom distributions and collections. Markus runs our operations and fighting training."

"Operations. By that, you mean raids and theft."

"For the most part, yes. Markus is a natural." Marla grinned. "I think he was quite struck by you."

"Why?"

"He hasn't stopped yapping about you since you got here—though considering what you just said, about your lack of enthusiasm for getting laid, bad luck for him. If you see him around, he can set you up with something productive too." The smile slid off Marla's face. She waved a hand at the door. "Now go on, I've got crap to do. I'll talk to you later." She shuffled a pile of papers, picked up a quill, and started making notations on the top sheet.

Sydney sighed and left the room.

She ran into Lila on the way out. The secretary gave Sydney an intent look. "You okay?"

"Yeah, I'll be fine. I have a hard head. Marla told me to find Markus or Dana and do something useful."

"Markus is out on a job—"

"Stealing or dealing?"

Lila smiled. "One of those. But Dana was just out there with the twins."

"Thanks."

Sydney went into the workroom and angled towards the alchemical set-up she'd seen earlier. Three faeries stood about the table. Two of them were thirty-ish men and identical as a pair of oak leaves, right down to the downturned corners of their mouths as they bent over the table with a collective frown. Their golden wings rimmed with purple marked them as members of the Lilac Clan.

The third was a slender, older woman. Sydney guessed she might have been fifty-five or sixty. Her waist-length hair was an iron-gray color and hung straight between her silvery wings.

The old faery eyed Sydney as the latter approached. "Let me guess. Sydney?"

"That's me."

"Dana." The old faery extended her hand. Sydney shook it.

"Marla sent me out here to help out. She said you might have something I could do."

"I do, actually. Marla tells me you know something about alchemy."

"A bit, yes. I helped our aunt run her apothecary shop for years. I mixed potions, ground ingredients...stuff like that."

Dana tapped her chin with her forefinger. "Okay. The twins here could use a hand. We're trying to get this batch of Shroom done before the next shipment of raw mushrooms arrives from the outlands. We're tinkering with the formula and it isn't coming out quite right. Think you can help?"

"I'll try."

"Good. I'll leave you to it, then." Dana nodded to them and strode away.

The twins gave Sydney an identical gaze. She blushed. "Uhm, hi."

"Hello," they said in unison.

The one on the left touched his chest. "Lucas."

The other duplicated the first's gesture. "Lucian. And you're Sydney, Marla's sister?"

"Yeah."

"Well, hope you can help us out here," Lucas said with a grin. As he smiled, a duplicate smile spread on Lucian's face.

She stared at the ingredients strewn across the table. *Great. I come all this way to escape mixing potions and find myself...mixing potions.*

Sydney squared her shoulders. "Okay, guys. Let's get started."

*   *   *   *   *

Sydney dragged herself up the steps to the room she shared with Lila. Her shoulders and wrists ached from hours of stirring the shroom solutions. Rainbow hues stained her fingers. Her hair hung in sweaty strands and in her fatigue, it was all she could do to place one foot in front of the other. It had been hot, sweaty, grueling work, just like what she'd left behind.

I hate my life.

They'd soaked the mushroom powder in alcohol until it formed a pale white slurry, which had to be stirred continually, then slow-cooked it back to a solid form, infused with some raw magical power to leech out the last of its toxicity, ground to powder, dyed, and bottled. She'd stared at the vials of red, green, blue, and yellow. "Why all the dyes?"

Together, the twins said, "Colors have more commercial appeal."

Lucian—at least she *thought* it was Lucian—said, "Some claim the different colors taste different."

"Nonsense," Lucas added, "but whatever sells better—"

"—that's what we run with," Lucian finished.

She'd been too tired to ask further questions.

Lila lay on her bed, nose buried in a book, but popped up as soon as Sydney opened the door. When she saw it was Sydney, Lila sighed. Her wings drooped. "Oh, it's you."

Sydney eyed Lila's midriff-baring shirt and short skirt. "Expecting someone else?"

"Err, no," Lila said, her cheeks turning pink. She wrinkled her nose. "You stink, lady."

"I can't imagine why."

Lila opened her footlocker and tossed a folded cloth at Sydney. "Showers are down the hall."

"I don't feel like going through the trouble of heating up a kettle of water."

"Summoning a rain cloud is a pretty simple spell."

The memory flashed through Sydney's mind of when she'd been trained in the rudiments of magic. Calling a small raincloud into being was one of the ceremonial rituals all young faeries were taught—more to learn the basics than anything. "Well, yes, but—"

Lila handed Sydney a tiny paper packet. "There's enough crumble there to power that spell. Ask Dana or Markus about it tomorrow. They'll give you a whole handful of those. You can get as much as you want, within reason. There are more clean towels in the laundry, off the left end of the workshop."

Sydney's stomach growled. "Any protocol about getting something to eat here?"

"Nah. Just go down to the common room after you're clean and see Garth, the bartender. Mid-forties, Thistle Clan."

"Yeah, I saw him on my way in."

"He and his sister Robin run the bar and kitchens. They'll feed you."

Sydney scowled. "This all would have been nice to know earlier."

"We're all pretty independent here, Sydney." Lila grinned.

"If you have questions or want help, you'll need to ask first."

"Why are you helping me, then?"

"Marla told me to. You probably ought to learn where the kitchens are, anyway. And the laundry. We all take turns with the cooking and washing." Lila glanced at the door. "Now, go take your shower and get some food. Make sure you take a change of clothes with you and take your time."

"In other words—"

"An hour, Sydney. At least an hour."

Sydney grumbled all the way down the hall. On the doorway at the far end hung a sign which read, "Showers." She pushed her way inside.

The long, narrow room was lined with eight small stalls, each with walls about neck-high and a swinging wooden door. In each stall, the tiled floor gently sloped towards a small drain.

Faeries, one male and one female, occupied two of the stalls. Both of them were naked as the day they were born. A tiny dark cloud hovered over each one, pouring a steaming flow of water into their stall. Neither paid her any attention.

Sydney slung her towel over the door, stepped into the stall, and peeled off her grimy tunic and trousers. A chill washed over her skin. Sydney stared at the packet, unsure of what to do.

"Pop it in your mouth."

Sydney looked up. "Huh?"

The female faery two stalls over motioned at the packet in Sydney's hand. Her voice was soft and throaty. "Put it right on your tongue. The paper will dissolve in about a second. The crumble dose will give you enough power to run a raincloud for ten minutes or so, depending on how hot you make it."

Sydney blinked. She recognized the woman.

"Thanks. You're Natasha, right?"

"Yes. And you're Sydney?"

"You got it. I heard you sing earlier. Your voice is amazing."

"Thank you." Natasha smiled and Sydney was struck by the blend of innocence and seductiveness in the singer's features.

Natasha's teal wings were broken with white lightning-like streaks, which meant Natasha was a member of the Poppy Clan.

I wonder if she knows Jacob.

Sydney placed the packet onto her tongue. In an instant, the flimsy paper containing the flakes of mushroom dissolved. The insides of her cheeks tingled. Tendrils of energy bolted down her arms and legs. Sydney concentrated.

A dark cloud appeared over her head. It shuddered and a miniature lightning bolt cracked to the ceiling. An instant later, the cloud opened and a torrent of hot water poured loose.

Sydney groaned as the warmth cascaded over her skin. She ran her hands through her hair, trying to shake loose some of the filth.

Natasha ran her hand across her scalp. "Feels good, doesn't it?"

"Yes. I never thought about using the training clouds for bathing. If this is what we can do, I wish they'd let us use more crumble in Sylvan Valley."

"You know how the clan elders are. They'd consider this a frivolous use of sacred mushrooms." Natasha's voice carried a note of amusement. "War and ceremony only, remember?"

"That sounds right."

The man exited his shower stall, dried himself off, fixed the towel about his waist and left the showers without so much as a backward glance.

"Modesty isn't a strong point around here, is it?"

"Not really, no." Natasha stretched her arms over her head, bringing her breasts into view. Sydney averted her eyes and Natasha laughed. "You'll get used to it."

"I'm sure I will. You don't have to shove those things in my face to make the point."

"Aww, where's the fun in that?"

Sydney washed the grit and sweat from her body. Natasha terminated her rain cloud, stepped out of her stall and dried herself. She donned a wispy robe that did little to hide her curves. Natasha winked at Sydney and left the room.

Sydney placed her palms on the stall wall and leaned against it. Water poured over her face.

This just keeps getting better.

Chapter Four

Sydney fumbled and the lockpick slipped. A spark leaped from the lock and struck her palm. Sydney yelped and yanked her hand to her chest. She inspected it but like every other time, there was no blemish on her skin and no pain, save a lingering tingle. Frustration brought angry words to her lips. "Damn it." She shoved the lock away and stood.

Dana shook her head. "Well, that's ten tries."

Markus sat down across the bench from them. "And ten failures."

Sydney rubbed her hand. "You could have started me on the easy lock."

Dana snorted. "That *is* the easy one."

"All right, I am not going to be picking locks anytime soon. Maybe I can do something else useful. I can be the muscle for the operation, keep an eye out for the ogres while you all burgle."

Markus sighed. "Sydney we've faced off on the mats three times. In all three, I disarmed you in less than five seconds. You dropped your sword twice and gave yourself a nice slice to the arm."

She resisted the urge to finger the light stitches just below her left elbow. "I was getting used to the grip."

"If you say so."

"So much for talking about me nonstop," Sydney muttered.

"What's that?"

"Nothing. There has to be something I can do." Sydney put her hands on her hips. "I'm not completely useless, am I?"

Neither Markus nor Dana responded. Sydney waited a moment. Her eyes narrowed. "Am I?"

Markus took a deep breath. "Sydney, I don't want to lie to you—"

"Hang on. If you're going to tell me how much I suck, go ahead and lie to me instead."

He refused to meet her gaze. "Well...."

"Enough, you two." Dana waved them to silence. "Marla made the decision. She wants Sydney to go on the run tonight. So we better figure something out."

Markus folded his arms. "Still not in favor."

"Nor am I, Markus. But Marla's the boss. I already tried to talk her out of this. Do you want to take a crack at it?"

"Not really." He sighed again. "I hate going on a mission with one hand tied behind my back."

"Uhm, I'm right here," Sydney said.

Dana pointed at the lock. "Again, Sydney. You need all the practice you can get."

"I think I should stop now."

"No, your sister insisted."

"Maybe I don't want to go with you tonight."

"That doesn't have a lot to do with it," Dana replied. "You're going."

Sydney's temper flared. "Says you. If I am such a bleeding incompetent, you won't want me slowing you down. Besides, you can't force me to go."

Nearby gang members stopped their activities and stared at her. Sydney glanced at the somber faces and wondered if she had put her foot in it.

"That's fine," Dana said, her tone cool. "We won't force you, but understand something. Every faery here is part of our team of their own free will and no one is forced to stay. But every single one of us does our part of the dirty work, and that includes risking ourselves for the gang's prosperity. Those are Marla's orders, and she leads by example. She works in the kitchen, she hauls firewood. She's shed blood on our behalf and earned the right to command us. So if you're going to stay here, you are going to follow her lead too—especially until you prove yourself. No one slacks. I don't care if you are her sister, and I wager Marla doesn't either. If you don't want to even attempt to work outside The Log, we can put you to work full-time in the kitchen or laundry and free up a more capable faery to hit the streets."

Dana grinned at her. "And Marla told me how much you enjoy cleaning."

Sydney opened her mouth to reply but thought better of it.

Dana's smile faded. She pointed at the door that led to the common room of the tavern. "Your other option is to walk out of here and return to Sylvan Valley or wherever it is you choose to go. Stay or go; whatever you choose, understand that it's your choice."

It hung there a moment. Finally, Sydney snatched up the lockpick. "Fine."

She caught the slight smile pass between Dana and Markus She ignored it.

*   *   *   *   *

Sydney knelt in the mouth of the alley. Her black tunic and trousers hugged her like a second skin and her auburn hair was bound in a bun and covered a black knit cap. Lila had dabbed soot on her cheeks and forehead for the evening's expedition. She'd tied her wings down and draped a lightweight black cloak across them. The cloak placed an uncomfortable amount of tension on her wings but her anxiety kept her mind from the pressure.

Sydney fingered the sword belt hanging on her waist. She wasn't used to the weight and even though the short sword wasn't heavy, it dragged at her stride. The bottom of the scabbard attached to a loop around her lower thigh, meaning the weapon didn't jiggle or rattle when she moved. She touched the handle of the long knife on the other side of her waist.

Hope I don't have to use these. I'll end up cutting myself for sure.

Her lip curled. *Cut myself again!*

Markus crouched next to her, with two other faeries—Patrice and Gordon—close behind. They were dressed similar to Sydney. All three bore expressions of grim confidence.

They waited in the dark depths of the narrow space between buildings for the Enforcer patrol to stumble past. The ogres were deep in their cups and even as they trod the deserted street, they passed several bottles of wine between them. Gutteral laughs and snorts drifted in their wake as the ogres shoved and slapped each other.

Sydney shook her head, wondering how such obvious buffoons kept any kind of peace. Her thoughts drifted back to Markus's words when they set out.

"It's not the ogre patrols that worry us, Sydney," he had said. "With a few exceptions, they're all muscle and no brains. They're damn strong in a straight-up fight but are pretty easy to avoid. It's the drakes that could throw a kink in our plans."

"Do they fly at night?"

"Not every night but they don't announce when they do and there doesn't seem to be any pattern to their night flights. We just have to keep our eyes open."

At the thought. Sydney glanced skyward but could see little of the darkened sky from their narrow vantage point.

Drakes. A few had passed through Sylvan Valley, some coming to Brigid's shop. Even though they weren't full-blown dragons, every drake had still been too large to enter the building, so Brigid had gone outside to deal with them. The memory of her aunt standing nervous before those hulking fire-breathing reptiles, each twice the bulk of an eight-foot cart lizard, sent a bolt of unease down Sydney's spine. Not one of the drakes done anything but deal with Brigid honestly but Sydney thought they could have just as easily killed her. And Sydney. And everyone in Holly Grove, had they been of a mind to.

And this Lord Burnside. Marla says he's a worm, a wingless worm. She paused. *I wonder if he's related to the one—*

Tears clouded her eyes. Sydney jammed her lids shut and fought to control her breathing. A detached part of her mind reflected on how the thoughts and memories could still be so painful.

Get it together, you idiot.

She took a deep breath and wiped the moisture from her eyes. Sydney glanced at Markus, wondering how much of her weakness he'd seen.

He wasn't looking at her. His gaze was fixed on the retreating ogres. Gordon scanned the direction from which the ogres had come. Patrice eyed the deeper part of the alley, guarding their rear.

They're all watching something. I wonder if Markus didn't give me an assignment because he wants me to learn...or thinks I'll blow it?

The deeper part of her conscious answered. *The latter. What would these waterworks while you're on the job make him think?*

Sydney brushed away the last of her tears. She peered at Markus, watching for a cue on what to do next.

His transformation had been remarkable. Gone was the cheery, happy-go-lucky faery that greeted her on arrival. Markus wore a look of business-like determination. His orders to Sydney and the others were terse and direct.

He's all job now. I wonder if I can get to that point?

Markus flicked his eyes at her. He winked, though his cheeks and mouth never twitched.

A tickle spread through her abdomen.

"All right." Markus's voice was just above a whisper. "Patrol's gone. Crumble."

Sydney pulled one of the paper packets from a pocket in her trousers. She put it in her mouth, feeling the immediate tingle of energy racing through her. It would give her just enough to power a couple of small spells or one big one in an emergency. If she didn't use the energy, it would gradually fade over an hour.

Markus nodded. "Gordon, go."

With the agility of a spider, Gordon skittered across the street to the storefront facing the mouth of the alley.

Sydney mentally reviewed the briefing on their target. It was a jewelry shop, run by a pair of husband-and-wife gnomes. While Markus acknowledged the faery gang was not above running a protection racket, he had said this particular couple had borrowed money from the gang—at staggering interest, of course —and had not repaid it, or even begun to. Polite but firm reminders had been rebuffed with threats, so Marla had ordered the shop to be "closed," as she put it.

Sydney didn't know if she believed all those justifications. It felt like a robbery. She did know that she was eager to prove her worth to Markus and the others. The alternative was to go back to Sylvan Valley.

Sydney pressed her lips into a thin line. *No, not that. Not yet.*

She revisited the plan. Though none were expected, Gordon would check the entrance for magical wards and pick the lock. She, Gordon, and Markus would then enter the shop and make off with everything valuable they could carry. Patrice would stay outside and provide overwatch and warning, and, if the need arose, a distraction to allow the others to escape.

Sydney glanced at her. Patrice carried a two-handed crossbow with an oak stock and springy steel limbs. The brown-haired fairy held the loaded weapon half-raised. The look on her face suggested she'd be happy to use it.

Sydney herself was just to follow Markus's lead. He'd assured her that he wouldn't be putting her in a position to fail.

She hoped he was right.

Since the proprietors lived in the room above the shop, silence was of the utmost importance. Once inside, they were to take five minutes, no more. If they made off with enough uncut gems, rings, and the gnome's tools, it would probably break the shop. Marla would claim the spoils as repayment of the loan and the jeweler could stay in business or not; the heist would conclude their affairs with him.

"Unless he comes after us," Markus had said with a shrug. "Then we'll put him down."

At the time of the briefing, Sydney wondered how often it came to that. As she crouched in the alley, she realized once was going to be too much for her.

Gordon peered into the window, then pressed his left ear against the door. Without lifting his head, he raised his right hand with fingers extended.

"Sydney, go."

She glanced to either side. The cobblestone lane was still empty. Hazy light surrounded the post-mounted lightstones at each distant intersection. It was dark enough, she thought, and—

"Sydney!" Markus hissed. "Haul ass!"

She darted across the street. Her heartbeat pounded in her ears and her breath came in a few ragged pants. Before she knew it, she was next to Gordon. He frowned at her but said nothing. A moment later, Markus fell in beside them.

Gordon placed all ten fingertips on the door and closed his eyes. He murmured something under his breath. He withdrew his hands and gave them a curt nod.

Sydney nodded in return. *No magical wards.*

Gordon fished a long, narrow metal rod from the folds of his cloak. He inserted it into the lock and rotated it a half-turn. There was a click as the bolt gave way.

Sydney winced. In the silence, the sound of the latch sliding open was horribly loud.

The door swung inward with a soft *creak*.

Markus drew his fore and middle fingers across his lips. Sydney nodded, understanding that meant no further words until they exited the shop. The three of them paused and listened. There was no sound save a steady *click* that repeated at regular intervals. Sydney supposed the gnomes kept a metronome in the shop to act as a clock.

Markus handed her a burlap sack and pointed to a bench on the west wall, just beneath the stairs to the upstairs room. Sydney took the bag and crept towards the bench. Behind her, Markus and Gordon dispersed to their tasks.

On the bench lay a variety of uncut gems and half-finished jewelry. Sydney had no idea what was valuable and what wasn't, so she concentrated on volume, grabbing as many pieces as could, as quietly as she could. She grimaced every time something clinked together in the bag.

A soft moan drifted from the second floor. Sydney froze. Her eyes flicked to the stairs. Sweat broke out on her forehead.

Another moan followed, then another. It was only then that Sydney realized what she'd thought was a metronome was the soft squeak of a bed rocking back and forth.

You've got to be shitting me.

She grabbed the last few things she could, tied off the drawstring, and sought the others. Gordon slipped out the door. Markus pointed, indicating she should follow. Sydney nodded and shuffled towards the exit.

Blinding light stabbed her sight. Her night vision gone, Sydney threw up her hand to shield her face.

"What the hell is this?"

Sydney blinked away the spots. The first thing she saw was the front face of a loaded crossbow.

The tip of the bolt pointed directly at the spot between her eyes.

The light source receded and an enraged face moved into view: a round face, with beady eyes behind wire-rimmed glasses and bearing a pug nose. Long whiskers formed mutton chops on both sides of the jawline. The mouth twisted in a snarl of anger.

The man shifted and the light fell over his body. Sydney noted he was scarcely three feet tall. She also noted that he was buck naked and his erect manhood bobbed in the uneven light. If it had not been for the weapon aimed at her face, she would have burst out laughing at the sight.

"A faery!" The gnome thrust forward the one-handed crossbow until it was six inches away from the bridge of her nose. "You treacherous sack of dragon shit! Invade my home? I'm going to send you back to Marla in a box!"

"Wait, wait." Sydney's mind raced. "I'm not with the faeries."

"My ass, you're not!"

"No, I'm freelance from out of town. I mean, you've never seen me with the faery gang, have you?"

The gnome blinked, then spit on the floor. "That doesn't mean anything."

"Look, I didn't sign up for this. It was the Cons who sent me."

'Why the hell would the Cons come after me?"

"They knew about your debt. It was a quick score because they knew that you'd blame the faeries. That's why they hired me."

"What?" The gnome's face betrayed his confusion. "I don't —"

Markus was nothing but a shadow. He slipped one arm under the gnome's and levered his weapon upward. The crossbow *twanged.* A puff of air slapped her forehead as the miniature arrow arced a hairsbreadth over her skin.

With his other arm, Markus brought down a truncheon on the jeweler's head. The gnome collapsed in a limp heap.

Sydney stared at the bolt lodged in the low ceiling.

"Heinro?" A soft voice drifted from above. "Are you talking to someone? Come on back, lover. We're not done yet."

Markus swiped his hand at the exit.

Sydney bolted out the door. Only when she was halfway across the street did she consider that she should have checked to see if it was clear. Fortunately, the lane was still empty. She dove into the alley and collided with Patrice and Gordon.

Patrice shoved her aside as Markus joined them. He said, "Split."

Patrice and Gordon nodded and melted into the shadows.

Sydney's legs trembled with sudden realization. She placed her hands on her knees to stay upright.

Inches. Two inches lower and I would have earned myself a new sphincter right in the center of my forehead.

Markus nudged her. "No time for that, Sydney. Move."

She stumbled along the alley until they emerged at the far end. Markus put his hand on her shoulder and gave a pat of encouragement.

"Where are Patrice and Gordon?"

"I sent them on ahead. 'Split' means for the team to split up and take separate routes to The Log." He chuckled. "Though with Patrice and Gordon, they may stop to knock off a quick one before they head back."

Sydney's mouth dropped open. "Quick one? You mean have sex?"

"They both get a rush out of the danger. They've been at it for months. Every time they're on a mission together, they end up banging in a back alley somewhere."

"Isn't that against the rules or something?"

Markus shrugged. "They're both highly competent and it's always after we hit the target. Gordon's just in it to get laid. I think Patrice...." He shook his head. "Never mind. Now come on."

Sydney scarcely remembered the run back to The Log. Markus brought them to the side entrance, nestled in the brick wall behind the tangle of roots at the unearthed end of the fallen tree. He rapped on the door twice. A few seconds later, she heard a *thud* as a bolt slid back and the panel swung inward on silent hinges.

"I see you made it."

"Dana." Markus sounded surprised. "I thought Anders was on watch tonight."

"I relieved him. I wanted to see how our protegee did."

"She lived."

"Barely," Sydney croaked. "Gordon and Patrice?"

"They made it back a few minutes ago. Come on, Sydney."

Dana offered a steadying hand and guided Sydney down a long hallway. Even at this late hour, the raucous noise from the common room filtered through the walls.

The hallway exited in the main workshop, off to the side of the laundry room. Dana led them directly to Marla's office.

Sydney said, "Is she still up?"

"She never sleeps while we have an operation going."

Lila sat limp at her desk. Her bloodshot eyes indicated she had not slept much either. "Go in. Patrice and Gordon are already in there."

Marla reclined in the chair behind her desk, while Patrice and Gordon stood to the side. Gordon's brow was furrowed and his arms folded. Patrice appeared calm and unruffled. Sydney looked them both over but aside from Patrice's flushed glow, nothing appeared amiss.

If Markus hadn't said something, I'd have no idea. You gotta get more observant, Sydney.

Marla rolled the cigar from one side of her mouth to the other. "Okay, Markus. I heard a little bit from Gordon and Patrice but why don't you tell me what happened?" She did not take her eyes from her sister.

Sydney's stomach wrenched. Even if Markus recited the facts, it was sure to paint her in the worst possible light.

I guess the only question is she going to just send me home, or kick the crap out of me first?

He glanced at Sydney then focused on Marla. "Everything went according to plan, up until the moment for us to withdraw. We were almost done. I had just sent Gordon out and was getting ready to move Sydney when the shopkeep slunk down from the top floor. I'm not sure what tipped him off. None of us made any noise as near I could tell. Maybe he just had a premonition. Anyway, I think he was in the middle of banging his wife since he came down the stairs with his pecker out."

He paused. "He saw Sydney first. He had a handbow. I thought he was going to drill her but she started talking and kept him distracted. Before he could pull the trigger, I clubbed him."

"Heinro knows you, Markus. Did he see you?"

"No, only Sydney."

Sydney kept her face still. She didn't know if Markus omitted the gnome's shot into the ceiling for his benefit, or for her own.

"Did he get a good look at her?"

Markus shrugged. "It was dark, her face is covered in soot, and I'm sure half his mind was still on getting his rocks off. He knew she was a faery but Sydney spun some story about the Cons hiring her as a freelance contractor. I don't know if he bought it all but he sure looked confused. His wife never came downstairs, so she didn't see us at all."

Marla stared at the ceiling a moment. "Did you get enough to settle his debt?"

Dana hefted a bag. "I haven't had a chance to see what Sydney and Markus are carrying but what Gordon had was a good step in the right direction. We should be fine."

"Good job, guys. Go get some sleep. No, Sydney, you stay a second."

The others filed out. Dana gave Sydney a wry smile. Markus departed last and winked at her again as he shut the door.

Marla watched Sydney stand nervously by the door for a moment before she let out an exasperated grunt. "Oh, sit down, Syd. This isn't an execution."

"Convince me otherwise."

Marla motioned to the seat and Sydney took it.

The gang leader exhaled a puff of smoke. "Where'd you get that garbage about the Cons?"

"Just came to me. To be honest, I was just saying anything I could think of to keep him spilling my brains on the floor."

"Why the Cons, though?"

Sydney spread her hands. "I pulled it out of my butt. Sorry."

Marla cocked her head. "Sorry? Why should you be sorry?"

"You're not mad at me?"

"No. Why?"

Sydney looked at her hands. "I got the impression Markus thought I fucked up."

"Not at all." Marla stood and walked around the desk. She hopped up on it next to Sydney. "You thought fast on your feet. You kept Heinro distracted and from figuring out that Markus and the others were there. You planted a seed of doubt in his mind."

"Meaning?"

Marla snorted. "Heinro's a worm but even a worm can crawl to the ogres and tell them what happened. Now, he won't be sure of what really did happen. He only saw one dirty-faced faery he didn't know and would have a hard time identifying. He'll get laughed out of the Woodhollow Jail if he tells that tale. He'll probably just suck it up. We'll keep an eye on him to make sure. Best of all, we didn't have to kill him, which would have created its own problems."

"So you think we got away with it?"

"I do." She reached out and tousled Sydney's hair. "You did good, kid."

"Really? I pretty much begged like a coward."

"Valor gets you killed. This isn't a storybook. Survival is more important than bravado."

"Aren't you worried about the Cons throwing a fit for taking the blame?"

"They'll just deny it and with no proof, no one will be the wiser. Besides, tossing some poor bastard's shop when they can pin it on someone else is something they would do, and have done. So they can hardly rely on a reputation as upstanding citizens to defend themselves. No, I think they'll just ignore it if that becomes the official story."

Sydney exhaled. It was so much to take in when she'd expected to be chastised, or worse. "I...I don't know what to say, Marla."

"I do. Say you're going to go get some rest. Since you're all back here safely, that's exactly what I'm going to do."

"Okay." Sydney stood. "Where do you sleep, anyway?"

"Down the hall from you."

"Alone?"

"Most nights." Marla returned to her side of the desk and ground out the stub of the cigar. "Lila!"

The secretary appeared at the doorway.

"We're good. Go to bed."

Lila slumped. "Will do. Sydney, don't wake me up when you come in."

Chapter Five

Sydney dunked the handful of mugs into the warm, soapy water. Her arms ached and the hours of immersion wrinkled her fingers. Her back and shoulders hurt, and she stunk of sweat and ale.

I don't care if I have to crawl in a stall with someone else. I am getting a shower tonight.

Lila nudged open the door to the kitchen and entered. The hoots and cheers from the tavern swelled, then faded as the door swung shut. The younger faery staggered under the weight of her burden of plates and mugs. She reached Sydney and dumped the crockery in the washbasin. A bit of soapsud splashed on Sydney's tunic.

Lila giggled. "Sorry."

"I'm so dirty I don't even care anymore. What time is it?"

"Sometime after two. If it makes you feel better, it looks like the crowd is about done drinking. There's only a few tables left. Robin is collecting the last of the dishes now."

Sydney's wrinkled her nose. "If there's only a few of them, why are they so damn loud?"

"Anders is doing his juggling routine again. They're all drunk, so they're shouting and laughing a lot." Lila laughed. "Plus a dark elf got a little extra grabby and Robin laid him out with one punch. The rest of them thought that was downright hysterical."

"Good for Robin." Sydney rotated her shoulder. The joint cracked. "If that's what left, we should be able to finish pretty soon."

"Yeah." Lila stretched her arms over her head. The tips of her wings quivered. "You coulda got out of this if you had taken Thom's turn at preparing dinner. He hates that."

"So do I." Sydney dunked a plate several times in a row and scrubbed the surface with a wire brush. Once she was satisfied all the food bits and grease were gone, she rinsed it in the hot water and placed it on a stack of clean plates. "I burn everything and people get pissed. Donovan didn't talk to me for two days after last time."

"He's a big guy, he likes to eat."

"Does Marla ever take her turn down here?" Sydney hefted another plate. "I've never seen her on crap detail."

"On occasion. She's usually busy."

"I bet."

"Sydney, the important thing is that she's willing to come down and do this work, even if she doesn't have time very often. She doesn't think she's too good to get her hands dirty— figuratively, or literally. That's one thing that always separated her from Tripp, the old leader. He thought he was above all this. Marla doesn't."

Lila's voice was almost reverent and Sydney made a mental note to pay special attention to how to the other faeries spoke about her sister.

She'd been in Woodhollow for a few weeks. Her days had been split between training and performing various menial tasks around The Log. She knew the forty or so gang members by sight now, if she struggled with names at times. She'd been out on several day trips with Dana to buy supplies but had not been on a run since that night the gnome shoved a crossbow in her face.

At first, Sydney resented it; despite Marla's encouraging words, she felt as though she was being kept on the sidelines like she was some sort of liability. But as she observed, Sydney noted that none of the faeries were used on jobs more than once every few days, and often less than that. When she asked Marla why that was, her sister merely said it was a good way to keep everyone fresh and rested.

Sydney understood that. But a burning need festered in her gut. She was eager to show the first night had not been a fluke.

She was eager to prove herself again

The thought came back to the front of her mind: *I could forget about all this, go home.*

The idea of returning to the drudgery of the shop filled her mind with dread—not dread of death but of terminal boredom.

At least here, it's something different every day, even if the work sucks.

As if reading her mind, Lila said, "You're anxious to go out again, aren't you?"

"Is it that obvious?"

"Yeah, you seem a little antsy."

"Maybe I just need to get laid."

The younger faery smiled. "I wasn't going to say that."

Sydney snorted. "Why not? Marla tells me about every other day."

"Well, Markus likes you. I could make myself scarce in the room."

"No, Lila." Sydney sighed. "I was being facetious. He's attractive but way too uptight."

"Only when his mind is on business."

"Yeah and then he's a bit too casual about it, like he just wants to score, you know?" Sydney shook her head. "Not quite what I'm looking for."

Lila grinned suddenly. "Natasha likes you too."

"Let's not discuss that."

Robin stuck her head in the kitchen. "Dishes piling up out here, ladies."

"Okay, coming." Lila moved to the exit. "How's your hand?"

The barmaid laughed. "Better than his face. Next time he'll keep his paws to himself."

"You have a wicked punch. How'd you do that without breaking your wrist?"

"It's not too hard." Robin took Lila by the arm and pulled her into the tavern. She held out her fist and pointed with her other arm. "You just have to make sure your wrist and fist aren't bent but lined up properly like this. See? Then you—"

The door swung shut behind them.

Sydney rinsed a mug and let her thoughts wander to Markus. She admitted to herself that he was strong, handsome, and her heart beat a little faster every time she looked at him. She caught him staring at her several times.

She could hop in bed with him. No one in the gang would care—not much, anyway. A number of the members tangled between the sheets and few of them displayed much jealousy or possessiveness. She recalled that it was hardly different back in Sylvan Valley, where many faeries rotated between sexual partners with an almost routine frequency.

So why don't I?

It was the memory of her parents, she was sure.

Sydney recalled right up until the last time she saw them, just how much love her mother Jenna and her father Max had shown each other. They had been together for sixteen years and according to what her Aunt Brigid told Sydney, neither of them had ever so much as looked at anyone else. Sydney remembered how her parents would smile at one another, take every opportunity to touch each other's arms and stand close whenever they could. Sydney had taken for granted that was the way it was supposed to be, between all couples.

And Sydney wanted that.

Markus. Was there any future there? It was too soon to tell but she doubted it; she just hadn't felt that kind of spark.

She thought of Jacob, the strapping young faery from the Poppy Clan, with whom she'd shared a bed a few times. It had been satisfying in the moment but on further reflection, Sydney found the memory hollow and mechanical—mere physical release as opposed to some deeper connection. She'd deferred his advances on her last visit.

Then there was Natasha. Sydney shook her head, unsure what to even do there. The singer was beautiful and intelligent. She also seemed kind and had a wicked sense of humor. Natasha's attention elicited some feelings in Sydney she didn't understand.

Not quite attraction, but maybe curiosity. She shied away from the thought.

Lila returned with the last of the dishes, allowing Sydney to put aside further thoughts of romance. She finished washing up, trudged to the showers, cleaned up, then collapsed in bed.

*   *   *   *   *

Sydney woke to a soft but insistent knocking. She glanced across the room but Lila's bed was empty. She stood, shuffled to the door and opened it.

"Good morning, Sydney."

"Dana? What time is it?"

"Sometime around nine."

"By the time Lila and I got finished and I had a shower, it was past four. It's too early for you to be bugging me."

"Be that as it may, we need to go down to the docks and deal with a little issue."

Sydney groaned. She could tell Dana to get lost and hide in bed but in the end, Sydney knew she would do what she was told to do. Her answering sigh shook her whole body. "Let me get dressed."

She made to close the door but Dana elbowed her way inside. She leaned against the wall and folded her arms. "Go on, I'll tell you about it while you put on some clothes."

Sydney peeled off her short nightgown and grabbed a pair of trousers. She glanced at Dana and noted for the first time that the older faery wore a crimson-dyed leather vest, matching pants, and hobnailed boots. Her iron-gray hair was bound in an elaborate coil behind her head and a wide belt lined with knives hung around her narrow waist. It was the first time she had seen Dana in anything other than a dress and slippers.

Sydney donned a fresh tunic. "You're dressed differently. First time I haven't seen you in a gown."

"I always dress for the business at hand. When I'm dealing with fences and suppliers, I have to put the gang's best foot forward."

"Nobody else here wears nice dresses."

Dana scoffed. "And that's what I get for hanging around a bunch of uncouth, ill-mannered youngsters. No sense of decorum. Marla told me your aunt ran an apothecary. Didn't she wear a dress or a suit at work?"

"Yes but that was a business."

"So is this, Sydney."

"All right. So why the change now? Expecting trouble?"

"Pretty much." Dana frowned. "We've been getting ale from Sunbolt Shipping for years, at a consistent price. They just told us they're upping the price per keg."

"How much?"

"Double."

"Double?" Sydney yanked a boot on. "Marla can't be happy with that."

"She's not. She smells Con involvement and I agree. Sturm Sunbolt has been a consistent vendor but like most dwarves, he'd bend us over if there was money involved."

"I've only met a few dwarves, so I'll take your word for it." Sydney picked up her other boot. "Is this going to shut down the tavern?"

"No. The tavern operation is self-sustaining and even turns a profit. At least, it did. With higher ale prices, it may not. If need be, we can supplement its cash flow from other activities but that will put a crimp in our operations."

"Just the two of us?"

"No, Anders and Claire are coming too. They'll hang back unless we need them."

"Okay, Dana." Sydney tied off her boot laces and stood. "Why me, though? Sounds like you are expecting a fight and that's not my bag."

"If it comes to that, that's what Anders and Claire are there for. You're there to put that smart mouth to use."

"Beg pardon?"

"You downplayed what you did in that jewelry shop but you talked a gnome with an itchy trigger finger out of killing you and I've seen how well you bullshit the merchants we deal with.

Marla wants to see if there is a way forward here without us having to break any heads. If we can go that route, it would be best."

Sydney licked her lips. "And if not?"

Dana shrugged.

"Great. No pressure, right?"

Dana's face remained neutral. "None."

"Swell."

Anders and Claire awaited them in the common room of the tavern. As it usually was at that morning hour, it was otherwise deserted. Based on what she'd seen Sydney didn't think it would start filling up until sometime after lunch.

Claire tendered Sydney a friendly smile. She was tall for a female faery, at just above six feet, and broad in the shoulders. She wore her light brown hair cut in a pageboy style.

Anders gave Sydney a brief nod. He was about her height and of average build, with dark hair and eyes, and somber face. Sydney found him a bit reserved.

The two were both from the Bramble Clan. Their scarlet wings, lined with orange streaks, were almost identical. Sydney sadly gazed at the two and flexed her own wings.

Never gonna find someone else with these, I'm afraid.

Dana tapped the hilt of one of her knives. "You two ready?"

"Yep." Claire hooked a sheathed axe onto her belt. "What are the odds Sturm is going to cause trouble?"

"Maybe fifty-fifty."

"Does he still have Urgon working for him?"

"Last time I knew."

Claire sighed and adjusted her axe. She looked at Sydney. "No weapon?"

"Uh, Dana just dragged me down here. I didn't get a chance to go to the armory."

Claire chortled and Sydney reddened, irritation tickling her stomach. She hated feeling like everyone was a step ahead of her.

Without a word, Anders offered her a belt, with attached scabbard. Sydney took it. "Thank you."

He nodded.

Sydney tied it around her waist. It was a short sword, like the ones she'd been training with. She'd gotten a little more proficient. A little. "Dana, is this something I should know about? Who's Urgon?"

"Urgon Thunderhand. Mercenary. He's a dwarf but he only works for Sturm because he's paid."

"Is he any good?"

"He might be the only one in Woodhollow who could stand toe-to-toe with Crol in a fight."

Sydney visualized the immense leader of the ogre Enforcers. "And you want to go up against someone who can do that?"

"That's where you come in, Sydney. If Urgon flips out, you'll have to talk him down." Dana grinned. "Like I said, no pressure."

"Fantastic."

*   *   *   *   *

As with every time she'd been out in Woodhollow, Sydney marveled at the mixture of different races that packed the streets. She'd seen a few dwarves come through Sylvan Valley as parts of trade delegations and she'd helped her Aunt Brigid at Fort Bloodwell, tending ogres wounded in their nonstop tribal wars. But she'd never seen so many different types working, trading, drinking, brawling, and screwing together.

A lizard wagon trundled past. The goblin driver glowered at them but said nothing.

Maybe they don't all get along that well.

"Dana," Anders said. His voice was low and he kept his eyes on the pavement. "To our left."

Something told Sydney to keep facing forward. She kept her head steady but shifted her gaze to the side.

A pair Cons lounged outside a butcher's shop. On spotting the faeries, their eyes narrowed and one whispered to the other.

They walked for another ten seconds before Dana said, "Are they following us?"

Claire motioned with her hands and pointed at something, then made an exaggerated glance over her shoulder. "Yep, they moved as soon as we went past. Looks like they are keeping about fifty feet back."

"What do we do?" Sydney said.

"Nothing, for now." Dana's face was a mask. "We have a job, let's concentrate on that."

She expected to smell the waterfront before they arrived but the cobblestone street gave way to wooden planks, almost without warning. The hollow echoes of their boots blended with those of the other pedestrians, reminding Sydney of nothing so much as a collection of irregular drumbeats.

She frowned. Even though they left the stone streets behind, she could not see the Woodrush. The taverns and shops packed as tightly together here as in the rest of the city. "Hey, Dana. Are we on the docks or not?"

"Not exactly. The Woodrush has a murky backwater here, kind of a shallow bay that's really little more than a swamp. It doesn't get more than eight feet deep until you get out into the middle of the bay. The Boardwalk is all built over that backwater, and over a hundred yards of the land that slopes down to it."

"Really?" She looked at the timber promenade. "There's water under there?"

"Yeah," Claire chuckled, "if you want to call it that."

"Meaning?"

Dana scoffed. "Meaning the runoff and waste from Woodhollow has been seeping into that backwater for two centuries. Slag from the goblin foundries, chemicals from candle and alchemical shops, blood and guts from the butcher shops. Even some magical byproducts. And that's on top of the results of thousands of people taking a shit every day. All of it ends up down there.

"That sounds nasty.'

"It is, Sydney, and it's not just the simple risks, like disease and parasites."

"I don't understand."

Dana hesitated. "There's...something...alive in that sludge. All that ruin and filth pouring into the bay made it the perfect breeding ground for some kind of monstrosity. People who linger around the edges of the Boardwalk at night have a habit of disappearing. Not very often, mind you. But enough. That's why all the work ceases on the docks right before sundown. Even the Rats, who love hanging out in the sewers, won't go under the Boardwalk."

Sydney laughed and looked at Claire. "This is where you tell the new girl you're teasing, that you're telling wild stories to pull a fast one on her."

Claire pursed her lips. "I wish I could."

Sydney glanced at the quiet member of their quartet. "Anders?"

He shook his head.

Sydney's smile faltered. "You're not kidding, are you?"

"No, Sydney." Dana's voice was flat. "Do yourself a favor and stay away from the fringes of the Boardwalk, especially after dark. And whatever you do, don't ever, ever go down there."

Sydney looked at the boards again, suddenly wishing they were much thicker.

They rounded a corner and came to the docks. Wide avenues of wooden gangplanks extended a good two hundred yards into the water. All manner of ships, from three-masted river cruisers to tiny rowboats to flat-bottomed scows, lined the piers. Beyond that, the sapphire current of the Woodrush River meandered past.

Sydney stepped to the edge and peered over. Even here, far out into the bay, tendrils of foul effluvia swirled from under the Boardwalk, mixing with the crystalline water of the river. Sydney shuddered.

The warehouse of Sunbolt Shipping was a massive three-story stone building. Sydney wondered how the wooden planks and support timbers of the Boardwalk could hold such weight. Then she realized the stone walls went through the boards and down beneath. She wondered if the building had been erected since the filth had been pouring into the bay, and had a mental image of construction workers slogging around in the mire while creatures lurked in the shadows nearby. The thought brought a surge of nausea.

Dana led them to the front of the warehouse. Sweating dwarves, trows and brownies hauled crates, barrels, and boxes to and fro. Dana stuck in her arm in front of one bare-chested porter to bring him to a halt. The dwarf set down the iron-banded crate and fixed her with a scowl. "What?"

"Looking for Sturm. Is he in?"

The dwarf motioned to the warehouse. "Last I saw, he was in his office. Do you mind? I got a quota to meet here."

He hefted his burden and resumed his march. Sydney and the others stepped aside to let him pass.

Dana dug in her vest pocket. "Crumble."

All four produced a mushroom packet and quickly ate it. Sydney had taken to keeping crumble packets in the pockets of each set of trousers she owned, so that no matter which one she grabbed when she dressed, she would always have it on hand. The familiar jolt of energy raced down her limbs, giving her a little emergency stash, just in case something went wrong.

And something always tries to go wrong.

Dana motioned to the side. "Claire, Anders. Hang out here. I'll try the standard signal if we get in trouble."

Claire gave her a thumbs up and a grin. "You got it, Dana."

Anders, as usual, said nothing,

Dana waved at Sydney to follow her inside. Sydney walked alongside the older faery. "What's the standard signal?"

"Screaming 'Help!' at the top of your lungs."

"I..." Sydney laughed. "Okay."

She wondered if they should have been a little more circumspect in their approach but Dana strode directly into the warehouse, almost daring someone to say something.

No one did. The workers glanced at her, shrugged, and returned to their tasks.

Dana angled towards a small door in the rear of the building. She knocked once, then opened the door without waiting for a response.

The office was not spacious, being perhaps twice the size of Marla's in The Log. As with Marla's the center of the floor was dominated by a thick-slabbed oaken desk. Behind it sat a dwarf with a braided black beard. He wore a patch over his left eye and his booted feet rested on the desk. The dwarf had laced his fingers behind his head and his eyes were closed.

Sydney cast her eyes over the remainder of the room. None of the lightstones were active, so the dim visibility was only provided by daylight filtering through the shuttered windows.

Her gaze settled on a hulking shadow in the corner. The dwarf sat but she guessed he would easily be six and a half feet tall. His arms were folded and he watched the two faeries with an impassive gaze. He was dressed casually in a leather vest and breeches but the heavy, notched axe at his side and his muscled forearms, as big around as Sydney's thighs, screamed *danger!*

The first dwarf's eyes flicked open as the faeries entered. "Dana. I was wondering when I would see you here. Well, you or Marla."

"Hello, Sturm."

He jerked his chin at Sydney. "Who's your friend?"

"Sydney. She's a new associate."

"She's cute." Sturm winked at Sydney, who fought to keep her expression neutral.

Dana paced to the front of the desk. "What's the deal, Sturm?"

"Nothing. My costs are up, so yours are too."

"Bullshit. The cost of getting ale downriver from Ascoria didn't double overnight. What's really going on?"

"Sacrist Allovian and the brewers are putting the squeeze on me. I'm passing that squeeze onto you. That's how it goes, Dana. Deal with it or find another supplier."

"There *are* no other suppliers of Ascorian ale in Woodhollow."

Sturm nodded. "Exactly. And if you elect not to buy it, someone else in Woodhollow will. I know at least two other taverns that would love to put it behind their bar."

Dana's mouth twitched. "We have a contract."

"Look again, Dana. The contract is only in place as long as I get paid."

"We've never missed a payment."

Sturm's smile did not reach his eyes. "That's true. So far."

Dana did not respond.

Sturm chuckled. "Exactly. Now, since we've covered the bounds of polite conversation, you can kindly get out of my office."

"Not without a few answers first."

"Urgon."

The dwarf in the corner stood. "Leave. Now."

Sydney shivered. It was the voice of a dead man.

Dana nodded. "Come on, Sydney. This isn't over, Sturm."

"Always nice of you to visit, Dana."

They left the office. When the door closed behind them, Sydney murmured, "Now what?"

"More than one way to skin a cat. Let's get the others."

They found Claire and Anders lounging outside the warehouse, sitting on a stack of crates. As Dana and Sydney approached, Claire hopped down. "Any luck?"

Dana shook her head. "None."

"Well, our shadows are still out there." Claire inclined her head to the left.

Sydney glanced that way and saw the Cons standing by the edge of a building a hundred feet away, in what looked like a failed attempt to appear unobtrusive. "They stick out down here on the dock, don't they?"

"I think that's the idea," Claire said.

Sydney frowned. "You think they wanted us to know they were following us? That defeats the point, doesn't it?"

"Not if they are trying to goad us into doing something stupid."

"Doesn't matter," Dana said. "We're not taking the bait."

Sydney peered into the warehouse. She thought she saw the door to Sturm's office slide shut but in the gloomy light, she couldn't be sure. "I wouldn't think Marla above rubbing out the competition."

"She's not," Dana replied, "but neither is she going to sanction two murders in broad daylight. There are far too many witnesses about. We'd all end up in a cell in the bowels of the Woodhollow Jail—or worse, in Lord Burnside's personal dungeons."

"That sounds like it would be bad."

"You'd be better off dying while resisting arrest."

They started their return trip to The Log. Sydney remained painfully aware of their tails and tried to force herself to stay calm. She reminded herself that she was with three experienced fighters, who would protect her.

Still, she knew leprechauns were one of the few races that could effect strong, destructive magic. Having the crumble charge in her system would help but Sydney had no illusions about her magical talent. If the very first bolt of fire or magical arrow was aimed at her....

But the return to The Log transpired without incident.

Marla awaited them in the workshop. The end of her ever-present cigar flared orange when the party entered. "Well?"

"No good," Dana said. "Sturm sicced Urgon on us before we could even take a seat."

Marla nodded. Her face was calm and her eyes distant. From her sister's expression, Sydney wondered if Marla had expected that exact outcome. She said, "What do you think?"

"For now, we pay." Marla's eyes hardened. "And we keep our ears to the ground. It's just a matter of time before Sturm gives us an opening. When he does, we'll be ready."

Chapter Six

Sydney rested her hands at her sides. She took a deep breath, exhaled half of it, and rolled her shoulders to loosen the tension. She tried very hard to banish thoughts of her audience.

"Now!" Marla yelled.

Sydney peeled the throwing knife from her bandolier and hurled it overhand at the target twenty feet away.

The diamond-shaped blade sunk into the center of the painted rings on the target board.

Sydney lowered her arm and smiled.

A smattering of applause broke out behind her. The gang members present in the workshop stopped what they had been doing to watch her throw. Knowing she had done well under their scrutiny caused her smile to widen.

Respect. Finally.

Marla grinned along with Sydney. With one hand, she grabbed her cigar and tapped ash from the tip. With the other, she slapped Sydney on the shoulder. "Good throw, Syd. You've become quite a natural with those."

"Thanks." Sydney fingered one of the blades lining the bandolier wrapped loosely around her chest. The five-inch steel knives were perfectly balanced for her grip.

"That was great," Lila said from her other side. "I wish I could throw that well." The look she gave Sydney was one of admiration—the first one she'd really seen from the young faery.

"Yeah, it was," a smiling Markus said.

Sydney grinned at him. "Well, your help and all. You practiced throwing with me every day for the last three weeks."

"That's good, Sydney, because you still can't swing a sword worth a damn."

"You said I was getting better."

Markus raised his eyebrows. "That means it takes me eight seconds to disarm you now, not five."

She allowed a mock pout to mar her face. "I'll get there. I just need more practice."

She touched the belt slung across her torso, from left shoulder to right hip. A half-dozen knives lined the soft leather strap, each with its own individual scabbard and stitched to the leather with a blue thread that matched the hue of her wings. A pouch at waist level, at the base of the bandolier, held another dozen replacement knives, in case she lost some or couldn't recover them. When she asked her sister where she'd gotten the bandolier, Marla had only smiled and changed the subject.

Did she have it made just for me?

Marla clapped her hands. "All right, people. Back to work."

The faeries dispersed to their tasks. Marla returned to her office without another word. Lila touched Sydney's arm, smiled, and followed her boss.

Markus lingered. "You might not be the very best knife-thrower I've ever seen, but like Marla said, you're a natural. Practice aside, you have the balance and light touch of a dancer."

"Thanks. Just how many have you seen?" she asked. "Knife-throwers, not dancers."

"A few in my years."

"And how many years are there, Markus?"

He chuckled. "It's impolite to ask a man his age."

"I thought it was impolite to ask a lady."

"Either."

Sydney walked to the wooden target and pulled her knife loose. It came free with a squeak. "Well, let's agree that I'm impolite and you answer it anyway."

"Since you put it that way, I am thirty-three."

"That's about the time most faeries start settling down. You know, getting married and having children...the works."

"Is that what your plan is?"

Sydney paused. "I haven't thought that far ahead. I'm only twenty-two, you know."

"I know." He gave her a direct look.

She stood in front of him and stared into his eyes. "You're bold."

"It saves time."

He took her hands in his gentle grasp, raised them to his face, and dragged his lips over her palm. "Sydney, you know I like you, don't you?"

She lowered her gaze. "I know. I like you too."

"Then why..."

"Being in Woodhollow has been a big adjustment for me, Markus. I've been trying to sort out my feelings about everything. I'm attracted to you but...I don't know if that's enough right now."

"I see." He released her hands. "I liked you the moment we met in the square, and I still do. Sydney, you know how I feel. If you change your mind, you know where to find me."

His gaze flicked over her shoulder. "You need me, Lila?"

"No, her."

"Okay. I should get back to things anyway." Markus spun on his heel and walked away.

Sydney glanced at a smirking Lila. "How long have you been standing there? What did you hear?"

"Enough. Marla wants you."

"Her sense of timing is impeccable."

When Sydney entered the office, Marla waved her to a seat. As soon as Lila shut the door, Marla said, "Are you screwing him yet?"

"Who?"

"Don't play dumb. Markus."

"Why ask? I thought you knew everything that was going on in this outfit."

"I only pay attention to things as they get important. Well?"

Sydney sighed. "No, we haven't slept together. Why do

you care, anyway?"

"Because of what kind of impact it might have on the gang. He's a leader and one of my lieutenants. I've seen how he looks at you."

"So? Maybe he just thinks I'm hot."

"I'm sure he does but it's more than that. Markus churns through a lot of women but when his eyes settle on you, they're almost tender. If you two start getting romantic, I can see you getting in hot water and him, feeling some degree of attachment, acting like he has to run in and save your dumb ass. That could get a bunch of other people killed if I didn't know and it caught me off guard. That's why I care."

"That makes sense." Sydney stared at Marla. "You ever....go there?"

Marla raised an eyebrow. "With Markus? Why, little sister? Would it bother you to know he's dipping his pen in both family inkwells?"

Irritation flared but Sydney kept herself calm. *She's just trying to rile you.* "I don't know and I wouldn't know until you told me."

Marla's mouth formed a half-smile, as if acknowledging Sydney's recognition of her taunt and rising past it. "Nah. He's good-looking and from what I hear, does well in bed. But for the same reasons I just mentioned, I don't play around with company assets. Too much potential trouble. I have a couple of friends outside the gang—a dark elf and a landy. I visit one of them now and again when I really feel antsy."

Sydney felt a sudden urge to needle her sister back. "Oh yeah? Either of 'em any good? Maybe I should give one a try."

Marla leveled her gaze at Sydney, appearing totally unperturbed. "Both of them are *very* good. If you're serious, I'll let them know."

Sydney sighed. "Never mind."

Damn it, does nothing ever get to her?

"Listen." Marla shuffled the stack of papers in front of her. "I have a report here from Ascoria."

"Ascoria? The wood elf realm?" Sydney blinked. "Wait, Ascorian ale. That's where our supply is coming from."

"Yep, straight from one of the big breweries right on the Woodrush. Sunbolt Shipping has an exclusive contract with that brewery to bring ale to Woodhollow. By contract, we're Sunbolt's sole customer. Ascorian ale is brewed by the elvish monks there and is pretty different from the other booze one finds in town. So, The Log has developed a reputation as a place to get a good drink."

Sydney nodded. "I had it once, when the tavern in Holly Grove got some. Expensive but different."

"Was that Old Abel's Taproom, in the center of town?"

"Used to be. It burned down about four years ago. Abel rebuilt it on the edge of Holly Grove."

"Too bad, the old place was nice." Marla tapped the report. "Anyway, it seems the elves are still charging Sturm the same price for his kegs of ale they always were."

"How did you get that?"

"I sent Will upriver to find out."

Sydney recalled the short, wiry faery from the Dandelion Clan, same as Lila. Lila said he was nice enough and he had always been pleasant to Sydney. "I was wondering why I hadn't seen him around the last few days. How'd he get a report here so fast?"

"Demon tube."

Sydney made a face. "What the hell is that?"

Marla sneered. "You really don't know anything, do you?"

"This isn't something they go over with every young faery, Marla. You know what we get taught: albino mushroom is for ceremony and war, and that's it. This is all new to me, so give it a rest."

"Yeah, sorry, that was bitchy." Marla sighed. "The stress is wearing me out."

"Apology accepted. Now, what is a demon tube?"

"An interdimensional transport, good for getting things quickly from one place to another."

"Like dimensional stepping?"

"No. Dimensional stepping is only good over a short distance—say, thirty or forty yards—and it has built-in safety protocols. You know the dimensional step will never let you land in some unsafe manner, right?"

"Yeah. From what I read, it will adjust you slightly or just not work. Is that right?"

"For the most part, yes. The demon tube is a lot more powerful. It can get stuff hundreds of miles in the blink of an eye. Takes a lot of practice, and a hefty amount of crumble to do it right, though. Will's one of our best at it, which is why I sent him on a barge upriver."

"Why didn't he just take this demon tube there and back himself?"

Marla shook her head. "Because things that go through the demon tube don't always make it through intact. Sometimes they come through charred and burned. On occasion, they don't make it through at all. And living creatures almost never appear at the other end. I've never heard exactly what that dimension really is, but whatever happens in there is pretty scary."

"Got it. Okay, the report."

Marla reclined her chair against the back wall. "Will wrote that Sacrist Allovian, the abbot of the brewery, says the prices for Sunbolt Shipping haven't changed in years. They have an ironclad contract with ironclad prices, as far as the wood elves are concerned."

"Any chance they were giving Will a line of crap?"

"I doubt it. You know any wood elves?"

Sydney shook her head.

"All elves have a strong sense of honor and wood elves more than most. They consider things like lying and being lied to as grave insults. You know they still have duels to the death in Ascoria?"

"What, really?"

"Yeah, usually with handbows. I guess about twenty years ago, an Ascorian governor tried to stop duels in his province and ordered the confiscation of all handbows. The elves rioted and strung up the governor from the walls of his own capitol."

"They sound like maniacs."

"You're not wrong," Marla said. "I'm getting a little off-topic. All that honor means they take the idea of a contract very seriously. From what I've seen, they'd rather set themselves on fire than knowingly violate one."

Sydney considered that. "And if someone else violated their contract?"

"The elves might set *that* person on fire. In fact, they started railing at Will the moment he arrived, telling him he wasn't going to ruin their business or besmirch their reputation."

"Why?"

"According to his report, the elves were warned that someone might try to show up and undercut Sunbolt Shipping and fracture the contract. Specifically, a faery."

"They couldn't have been happy to see Will, then."

"No, he said he had to do some fast talking but once he convinced them he wasn't there for anything shady, they relaxed." Marla chuckled a little. "In fact, they're pissed that Sturm is blaming them for his increase in costs to us. Not quite enough to break the contract but annoyed nonetheless."

Sydney crossed her legs. "Okay."

"Here's the kicker: when Will asked who had warned them, guess what Allovian said?"

Something clicked in Sydney's brain. "Cons?"

Marla nodded. "According to Will's report, Allovian's exact words were—" She glanced at the top sheet in her pile. "—'some feller with a red beard and big ole' green hat.' We already know that description only fits one group in these parts. You know, I was only annoyed with the Cons before, but after reading this, I'm actually pissed."

"Maybe that was the point, Marla. Maybe someone's just testing your patience."

"What do you mean?"

Sydney licked her lips. "Maybe someone is just trying to goad you into action against the Cons and setting them up to take the fall."

Marla stared at her.

Sydney shifted her weight, uncomfortable under her sister's unrelenting gaze. "What?"

"You really get off pissing in my pool, don't you?"

"What did I do?"

"I've been sitting here all morning, debating whether or not to go over to the Four-Leaf Club and rip McGee's balls off. Now, you made me second-guess myself. And you're right. There are other gangs in Woodhollow, that would love to set us off against the Cons. The Dryads, for instance."

"Sorry." Sydney uncrossed her legs and folded her arms. "But if me puncturing your angry reactions makes you think about this a little longer so we do the right thing, then so be it."

Marla slumped into her chair. She stared at the far wall, her brow furrowed.

"Marla?"

"What?"

"Let's just assume it was the Cons who planted the seeds of doubt against us at the brewery, and who are in cahoots with Sturm to put pressure on our front-facing business."

"*Our?* Since when have you considered yourself officially in the gang, Syd?"

"Never mind that," Sydney said. "Even if we know it was the Cons, how does that help us?"

"We can't put a stop to it unless we know who's doing it."

"I get that, but what's the immediate problem? What's choking us off?"

Marla slapped an open palm on her desk. "The price of the ale."

Sydney nodded. She'd seen the ledgers. While doubling the price of ale hadn't immediately crippled The Log or the Faery Gang itself, it virtually wiped out the tavern's profits and created a negative ripple effect on their other enterprises. For several weeks, Dana juggled funds back and forth but it had become clear to the entire gang that the tavern was becoming a drain on the gang treasury.

Markus had been in favor of shutting down The Log's tavern temporarily. Marla vetoed that immediately, saying the loss of face would be an admittance that the Faery Gang was losing its edge. Gordon had suggested giving up on Ascorian ale and moving to another source of booze but Marla had tabled that as well, for the same reason, saying they would only do that when they had no other choices left.

The members of the gang all looked to Marla for answers and for some reason, Marla had looked to Sydney. Now, as she sat and pondered the problem, Sydney thought she saw a way forward. A dangerous way, but maybe the only one.

"Are they still bringing it in?"

"What? Who?"

"Sunbolt Shipping," Sydney said. "Are they still bringing in the Ascorian ale or are they selling us stuff they had stockpiled?"

Marla scowled. "Oh yeah. One ship a week. I had Gordon and Caleb on the Boardwalk the other day, keeping an eye on Sturm's warehouse. Sturm's boys unloaded a bunch of kegs from the hold of a river cruiser, pointing and laughing the whole time. Like they know they have us over a barrel."

"They literally do have us over a barrel," Sydney said with a grin. "A barrel of ale."

Marla ground out the stub of her cigar. "Remind me not to put you on stage as a comedian."

"How magical are they?"

"Who?"

"Dwarves," Sydney said. "If I recall correctly, they aren't very attuned."

"Not at all. They have the magical sensitivity and intuition of a common rock. It's so bad that most of them can't even use simple magical devices. Those often fail as soon as dwarves pick them up." Marla paused. "But it does have a benefit for them. Dwarves have some degree of invulnerability to magic. Spells have been known to bounce off them."

"So they're unlikely to know when magic is being used around them?"

"Not bloody likely at all."

Sydney nodded, feeling more confident. A tremor of

excitement rippled through her as the outline of a plan coalesced in her mind. "Okay, good. Change of subject: how do you drop the price of a product? In this case, ale."

"What do you mean?"

"In economic terms. If demand is steady."

"If demand is steady, raise supply or lower the price of supply to lower the price of the product." Marla waved her hand. "But that's just it, Syd. We can't get any more and we can't get it cheaper."

"Maybe not from the brewery. But Sturm's ships are still coming down the river with ale on board. Lower the price of the supply? How much lower of a price do we get than 'zero?' "

"Wait a second." Marla leaned forward. "Are you proposing what I think you're proposing?"

"That depends on what you think I'm proposing."

"Syd, we're gangsters. We're not pirates."

Sydney laughed. "I didn't think you had that kind of conscience."

"I don't," Marla said. "But I'm practical. Sturm isn't dense; he mans his river cruisers with guards and mercenaries. Nobody here knows how to fight their way aboard a ship. It would be suicide to try."

"I agree, which is exactly why we're not going to do that."

Chapter Seven

Sydney squatted on the riverbank. Overhead, the crescent moon shone with a pale light that just barely kept the darkness from being total. The slow-moving waters of the Woodrush meandered past without a sound.

"This is insane."

Sydney glanced at Marla, who was nothing but a silhouette in the shadows. "Hey, you're the boss. It was just an idea. You didn't have to agree to it."

"I didn't have a better one."

"Any updates from Will?"

"Not since he confirmed the *Oakenhelm* left Ascoria. I told him to get the hell out of there. Whatever happens, he needs to get clear."

Sydney nodded, then remembered Marla couldn't see her. "Yeah."

She peered upriver again. The surface was unbroken and blissful.

Crazy, she told herself. *I must have been out of my damned mind to suggest this.*

Ten feet behind her and Marla, three more faeries huddled in the brush: Lila, Gordon, and a muscular bruiser from the Lilac Clan named Donovan. Claire perched on a tree branch twenty feet above. Her gaze was fixed upriver.

"I'm surprised you didn't want to bring Markus on this one," Sydney whispered. "You said he was your field leader."

"Exactly," Marla replied, her voice low. "No one would expect us to mount a major operation without him. I told him and Dana to grab some of the gang and move around in Woodhollow tonight. You know, show their faces and do stuff to draw attention. Maybe it will throw some suspicion off us."

"Even if the dwarves are magically inept, they can't help but suspect us if their casks of ale just vanish between the brewery and Woodhollow. Only so many races are magical."

"Yep. Us, the Cons, the Dryads, though we all have to access outside sources. Werevixens. And dark elves. *Vilas* and *landvaettir* have some minor magic."

"Right," Sydney said in agreement. "It's a short list of suspects. We'll be at the top of that list."

"We'll deal with that when it becomes an issue."

When she says things like that, I always wonder if I will live to see the sun come up.

"Hsst!" Claire's husky voice drifted through the leaves. "She's coming."

Sydney squinted her eyes. She could just make out the dark blot on the Woodrush as the river cruiser rounded the bend a couple hundred yards upriver. The low-hulled ship drifted with the current.

A harsh laugh rolled across the water. Sydney froze. A bobbing light danced along the rail of the ship, followed by another laugh. She realized it was a lantern. Two dwarves stood at the rail, chatting in their guttural voices. One of them moved off, followed a moment later by the other.

Marla touched Sydney's shoulder. "You ready to do this?"

She took a deep breath. "I hope so."

"You'll be fine, Syd. You did it twice at The Log, no problems."

That was practice, this is real! Sydney jerked her head up and down. "I'll be okay."

"Good. Crumble."

All of the faeries devoured their crumble packets. Sydney fought to control her breathing as the power surged through her. She hadn't had a chance to use the magical power before it faded on any other mission but tonight, she would for sure. She flexed her fingers like an eagle's talons and forced herself to wait.

The *Oakenhelm* crawled along the river. Just as it was parallel to their position, Sydney drew a dagger from her bandolier, took a deep breath, and concentrated on the lower half of the ship.

The world blurred. Color streaked past her head and her ears roared. Her vision came into focus and Sydney staggered under a swoon of dizziness. Her boots *clumped* softly on wooden planks. Despite her vertigo, she crouched, the blade in her hand.

She was in the ship's hold.

Sydney nodded. As with her practice runs, the dimensional step was disorienting but only momentarily. Within seconds, her equilibrium improved.

A brief flash of light lit the hold; Marla appeared. Sydney's sister blinked, shook her head and gave Sydney a thumbs up.

Gordon, Donovan, and Lila arrived one after another, each looking a little unsteady on their feet. Claire did not join them; the big woman remained on the river bank to create a diversion, if necessary.

The five faeries waited in silence for a moment. Nothing reached Sydney's ears save the creak of the ship's hull in the current and the occasional step of a boot on the deck above them.

Marla pointed to a nearby stack of kegs, strapped in place on wooden racks. Gordon nodded. He produced another crumble packet and ingested it. Gordon placed his hands on the nearest keg and closed his eyes.

The keg vanished in a puff of smoke. An acrid sulfuric odor invaded the cabin. Sydney wrinkled her nose.

Gordon fell to the side, gasping for breath. Marla touched his shoulder; Gordon nodded and gave her a thumbs up. She motioned to Lila. The young secretary ate a crumble packet, put her hands on the next keg, and sent it away. She placed a forearm on the rack and leaned into it, panting.

Marla pointed at Sydney. She replaced her blade in the bandolier and ate a dose of crumble. Under Marla's guidance,

Sydney had practiced using the demon tube a few times but nothing as large or as heavy as a keg of ale.

You can do this, Sydney.

She situated her hands on each side of a barrel and concentrated on one of the backrooms of The Log. She squeezed the barrel.

The keg vanished. A wisp of yellow smoke curled from the now-vacant cradle.

Sydney sagged. Her muscles felt like limp noodles, her head throbbed and she was struck by a sudden sense of being breathless. She limped out of the way and panted, trying to get some air in her lungs. The feeling was quick to fade, though. By the time Marla had sent her own keg tumbling through the demon tube, Sydney felt better.

They repeated the procedure for another cycle, and then again and again. By the time they had finished the seventh round, Sydney's head pounded. Nausea filled her gut and every breath brought prickles of pain in her chest. She gulped in the now-smelly air, trying to alleviate the ache.

A hard thump sounded outside the hold's door. The faeries froze. There was a second thump as though another door had been opened and closed.

"Another milk run," a voice said.

"Yeah but I'll be glad when it's over," said a second.

"Huh? Why?"

"Something about those wood elves. Allovian wasn't his normal polite self. He was distant and short with us. Maybe even a little hostile. So were his boys."

The first voice chuckled. "You're getting paranoid."

"No, I'm not," the second replied with a note of agitation. "He almost didn't take the payment, like he didn't want anything to do with us. He barely spoke to us. He's never been like that before." There was a pause. "You think those wingers got to him?"

Marla's nostrils flared. She took a step towards the door.

Sydney put a restraining hand on Marla's arm.

Marla glanced down and sloughed Sydney's hand away but did not move again.

The first voice laughed. "When would they have?"

"Rumor has it one of the faeries was in Ascoria just last week, hanging around the brewery. If they figure out what Sturm's up to—"

"You turning into a pussy on me?"

There was the sound of flesh striking flesh and a heavy thump. The second voice reverberated with rage. "Does that feel like a pussy to you, Brak?"

"N-no."

"No, what?"

"No, Captain."

"You're an idiot," the captain said. "Sturm isn't as safe as he thinks he is. If he didn't have Urgon glued to his side day and night, the faeries would have decorated Sturm's office with his entrails by now. The Cons will use him but they'll use him up. I know you're too dumb to know this but Sturm got turned down for membership in the Woodhollow Merchant League—again—so they won't help either. Sturm has no protection and he can't protect us. All he has going for them is that bitch who runs The Log wants the ale bad enough to pay for it. As soon as she figures out a way around that, Sturm is dogmeat, and so is anyone who stands by him."

There was a scuffle of boots and another heavy thump. "Get your ass up."

Sydney heard Brak scramble to his feet.

The captain spoke again, this time in a more controlled voice. "Get topside and tell the guards to keep an extra close watch. We're getting closer to Woodhollow and my gut tells me something ain't right. If any guard falls asleep for the rest of the way in, I will personally dig his eye out with a spoon. And if I so much as hear a single disrespectful word out of you, I will dump your body under the Boardwalk and find myself a new first mate. Is that clear?"

"Aye aye, Captain." Brak's voice was laden with fear.

"Go."

Brak hurried away. A moment later, a door closed and the corridor beyond fell silent.

Marla tapped Gordon and pointed at the next keg. A few minutes later, they were done.

Sydney felt wrung out. Her hands trembled and the pain in her head had only intensified.

"Let's get out of here," Marla whispered.

They took one last dose of crumble. Lila inhaled, took a step forward, and vanished in a rainbow streak. Gordon and Donovan followed.

Marla reached into her belt, withdrew something small and green, and dropped it on the deck. She winked at Sydney and motioned. Sydney nodded, took a deep breath, and stepped.

She ran headlong into the wall.

Sydney crumpled to the planks of the floor, landing on her knees. Her head swam and nose felt like it was on fire. She touched her face. Her hand came away with streaks of blood.

Marla tensed; her hand fell on the hilt of the dagger at her belt. They held their breath for a long, strained moment but heard nothing.

Marla grabbed Sydney under her arms and hoisted her to her feet. Her voice was scarcely more than a hiss. "Try again and don't fuck it up this time."

Sydney focused, imagining the darkened banks of the Woodrush. She took a step and nearly wept with relief when the familiar burst of colors streamed past her face. She collapsed to her hands and knees. The damp wet mud of the riverbank and the tickle of the reeds against her cheek were more welcome than she would have imagined.

A second later, Marla appeared beside her.

Shouts echoed from the ship. A cluster of focused lanterns appeared on the deck of the *Oakenhelm*. Beams of light stabbed the dark. To Sydney's eyes, too many of those shafts pointed to the riverbank.

Marla waved her hand. "Split."

Gordon, Lila, and Donovan vanished into the night. Sydney heard a flutter of wings as Claire leaped from her treetop perch and gave a few powerful flaps. She glided in front of the crescent moon and disappeared from view.

Marla helped Sydney to her feet again. "Come on, you clod."

"Marla, I'm sorry."

"Save it until we're safe back at The Log. Can you fly?"

"Fly?" Sydney hadn't thought about flying since she had first come to Woodhollow. The ever-present drakes soaring over the rooftops had been a powerful incentive for her to keep her feet on the ground, and they'd crept upriver on foot, to avoid being seen.

"Yeah." Marla pointed at the *Oakenhelm*. Dwarves scurried about the deck. Several pointed at the spot where Sydney and Marla stood. "We need to get away from the riverbank, and fast."

She saw Sydney's hesitation and snarled, "The drakes don't patrol out here. Burnside doesn't care about flying in the outlands. Go!"

Sydney's wings were folded, tucked inside one another and all but parallel to her back, much as a bird's wings lay against it's back when resting. She flexed, savoring the tendons releasing as her wings sprang to full stature. She took two steps and flapped. Her wings beat the air, bearing her into the night sky. She groaned in pleasure, enjoying the all-but-forgotten feeling of the wind streaming past her face, the stretch of her back muscles, and the ground speeding past a hundred feet beneath her. She wondered if the dwarves were armed with bows but rationed with the moon at but a sliver, they wouldn't see her. Before she could fully worry about being shot down, she and Marla left the Woodrush and the *Oakenhelm* behind.

Marla soared alongside her, the same dreamy contentment on her face.

In spite of her body's ache, Sydney could not help but feel elated. She smiled to herself.

We did it. We got away with it.

Her grin faded slightly. *Well, I guess the second part is still to be determined.*

She glanced at Marla and got a smile in return.

Something flickered in pale light beyond her sister. Sydney did a double-take but she could see nothing.

It almost looked like another faery, following us.

She shook her head. *Tired. Seeing things.*

They flew for about two hours before Marla called out to her. "We need to land."

Reluctance tore at her mind. *Here in the sky is where faeries belong.*

Another thought intruded. *How close do you want to get to Woodhollow with the drakes keeping watch?*

Sydney sighed and angled her wings. She spiraled to the ground in a lazy corkscrew. Her wings flared just as she reached the surface and she alit with the grace and dignity of a butterfly.

Marla slammed to the ground with a dull *thud*. The impact drove her to her hands and knees.

Sydney darted to Marla's side. "Are you all right?"

"Yes. I was never good at sticking the landing, remember?"

Sydney offered her sister a hand and helped her to her feet. "Yeah, but that was years ago. I figured you'd get better."

"I never did. Every landing still feels like running into a wall." Marla brushed the dirt from her knees. She pointed at the distant walls of the city, just visible in the pre-dawn light. The massive wood bulwark of the Sunset Gate stood open, ready for the day's business. "We're getting close, so let's walk from here."

Sydney snickered. "Worried some drake might get a little zealous?"

"Yes, Miss Smarty Pants, and you should be too. Have you seen what their flame breath does to someone?"

"Can't say that I have."

Marla's face was grim. "Well, I have. It's not pretty."

"I'll take your word for it."

The sun was over the horizon by the time they reached Bayberry Square. Sydney eyed the plaza and the entrances to the avenues leading away from it. "Looks clear."

"Of course it does. The ship is still a day upriver. Sturm can't know about this. It's not like any of his crew has access to magic, to get a message to him."

"Unless the Cons are helping him."

Marla frowned. "Yeah, true."

Sydney looked around Bayberry Square a second time but nothing about the citizens and wagons in the square struck her as out of place or threatening.

Just a matter of time before someone does show up over this, though. She said, "You know Sturm is going to blame us."

"He'll try. That's why I left them a little hint in another direction."

Sydney recalled the green object. "What?"

"A shamrock."

"Isn't that a little obvious?"

"I don't think so." Marla shoved past a gnome who glared at her and opened his mouth to protest. When he looked at her face, recognition dawned. He glowered and stomped away without a word. Marla continued as though the collision was of no matter. "I thought about one of their green hats but that *would* have been too much. This may throw them off just enough."

"It's not like all Cons carry shamrocks...or is it?"

"Of course they do. Cons think shamrocks are lucky. I'd call it their security blankie, for lack of a better term."

"Sturm has got to be smarter than that, Marla. He'll think, 'I'm working with the Cons, why would they raid my ship?' He won't fall for it."

Marla tilted her head. "He might. He's not as smart as you."

"We'll see."

"You're quite the pessimist, Syd."

Sydney shrugged. "Comes with the territory of being the baby sister to a know-it-all."

"You've called me worse."

"By the way, did you hear those two dwarves on the ship? One of them called us 'wingers.' I thought only the Cons did that."

Marla bit her lip. "Up to now, they were the only ones who have—at least, openly. If the employees of Sunbolt Shipping are adopting those expressions, maybe Sturm and his pack of merry assholes are deeper in bed with the Cons than we thought."

Dana awaited them at the front door. "Glad to see you made it back in one piece."

The tavern was empty. Robin toted a load of plates to the bar but the room was otherwise quiet.

Marla slumped at a table. Sydney followed suit. Dana flagged down Robin. "Can we get some coffee, please?"

"Sure, Dana." Robin vanished into the kitchen.

"The others make it back?" Marla asked.

"Claire showed up about a half-hour ago. The others haven't yet."

"They will," Marla said with confidence.

Robin returned with three mugs of coffee, placed them in front of Sydney, Marla, and Dana, and returned to the kitchen without a word.

Sydney watched her go. "We didn't run her off, did we?"

Dana took a sip. "No. Robin knows how things work. She's giving the gang leaders a chance to discuss things without interrupting."

"I'm not a leader."

Dana shrugged.

Marla toyed with the rim of her cup. "How'd we do, Dana? We sent thirty-two kegs."

"Thirty-one kegs made it through the demon tube. One broke apart when it landed and we weren't able to save any of it. The others are fine."

"Good. Make sure they get moved to the secured storage room."

"Already done."

Marla grinned. "And not a single copper paid for any of them."

Dana's mouth creased into a thin line. "We still might pay for it when Sturm finds out he's been robbed."

"Have you and Syd been collaborating on ways to ruin my mood? We'll cross that bridge when we get there. Let me enjoy the moment."

Dana smiled. "Sure, Marla."

They were still nursing their drinks an hour later when the exterior door opened. Lila, Gordon, and Donovan clomped into the room. All three were soaked and covered with dirt, scratches, and bits of leaves.

Robin emerged when they came in. She shook her head. "I'll get more coffee."

The three sat at the table. Deadpan, Marla asked, "Any trouble?"

Lila's lip curled. "Trouble? You mean like sneaking aboard a ship manned by foul-tempered dwarves to make off with their prize cargo and getting away, only to get lost in the dark and getting scraped to hell because we wandered into a dense thicket and then all three fell in a deep rain puddle? You mean like that?"

The secretary kicked off a filthy boot. Dirty water trickled out and pooled on the floor. "No, Marla. No trouble at all."

Chapter Eight

"Sydney, we need you out front."

Sydney raised her eyes from the mocked-up lock and gave Dana a slight glare. She felt a little more confident in her lockpicking skills but still needed the practice—and thus, she felt a swell of resentment at being dragged away. "What for?"

"No time for questions. Come out to the tavern."

"Why? What's wrong?" Sydney's heartbeat accelerated. It had been two days since their raid on the *Oakenhelm*. "Is it Sturm?"

"Worse." Without another word, Dana strode for the door.

Her belt of knives hung over the back of a nearby chair. She hesitated with the bandolier but then buckled it around her torso. Regardless of who was out front, she'd rather have it and not need it than the other way around.

She ran into Markus at the door to the tavern, as the latter clattered down the stairs. His face was unusually grim. "Markus?"

"Come on."

She followed him to the tavern, her apprehension growing with every step.

Marla sat at one of the tables. She kept her arms folded and she wore a scowl, though she locked her eyes on the table surface. The unlit cigar in her mouth shuffled back and forth in an angry dance.

Across from her sat one of the Cons. Although he slumped in a casual, relaxed manner, Sydney could tell immediately that their visitor was bigger than any other leprechaun she had seen in

Woodhollow. She estimated he stood six-foot-six and well on the high side of two-hundred-fifty pounds. He wore the same clothes as the rest of them, right down to the corncob pipe clenched between his teeth. An angry red scar spanned the Con's left cheek, from the corner of his mouth to his ear.

His brown eyes flicked at Sydney as she entered and she could not suppress a shiver. There was no mercy, no compassion in that gaze.

Sydney stood by Marla. Dana already waited to the other side. Markus took up position by the door to the back, his expression flinty.

A deep voice rumbled from the front door. "Well, well, if it isn't the would-be street brawler."

Crol, the head of the ogre Enforcers, stood in front of the exit, his arms crossed over his mail-clad chest. An iron-bound oak cudgel—in reality, Sydney noted, an entire thick, twisted tree branch—leaned against the wall. She guessed the weapon weighed as much as she did.

"You saw that. They started it, remember? I haven't been involved in any brawls."

"Maybe just a little light piracy, then?"

She'd been anticipating the question, so Sydney was able to keep a straight face. "No idea what you're talking about."

The ogre rolled his eyes. "Of course you don't."

The Con stood and faced her. Sydney made herself be still. He bowed low, keeping his eyes on hers. He took her hand and kissed the back of it. Though her skin crawled, Sydney fought from jerking it away. The Con's lips were cold as ice.

"Harlan McGee, at your service, darling."

She inclined her head. "Sydney."

"Ah, the wee sister. Very good." McGee returned to his seat. "Now we have all the players here. Crol?"

Crol straightened. The top of his head all but scraped the tavern ceiling. "Boss McGee leveled some serious charges against you, Marla."

"Oh? What kind of charges?" Venom dripped from every word Marla spoke.

"McGee says he and the Leprechaun Gang entered a new business contract with Sturm Sunbolt of Sunbolt Shipping, for delivery of Ascorian ale. That cut the legs out from under your business here at The Log. In retaliation, Marla, you and yours robbed the latest river cruiser bringing ale downriver."

Crol recited the words as if he'd repeated them in his head a dozen times. His tenor was one of boredom. But Sydney caught how his attention bounced between those in the room as if he was reading their reactions.

Marla's right; he's a lot smarter than he lets on. Sydney kept one eye on the ogre as the rest spoke.

"He claims?" Marla slapped her open palm on the table. "Is there any proof?"

"Only a shamrock found in the empty hold."

Dana tapped her finger on her chin. "That would indicate Con involvement, not ours."

"Yes, if you wingers could be trusted." McGee's grin made his scar wobble. "Anyone with a brain sees that was just a diversion you planted. I know it and you know it."

"There's no proof of that either," Dana replied, her voice calm. She looked at Crol. "Where was this piracy said to have taken place?"

"Upriver, about fifty miles."

"That's outside your jurisdiction, Crol."

"Dana, don't try to tell me where my jurisdiction is," the ogre growled. "To be honest, I could give a shit what goes on in the outlands, until it spills over into town. And if someone stirs up trouble out there and brings it to Woodhollow, that's going to put me in a bad mood. Is that hard for your pea brain to understand?"

Dana wisely kept her mouth shut.

Crol looked back to Marla. "Well?"

"We didn't have anything to do with it."

Sydney tensed as the Enforcer turned his gaze on her. Crol jerked his head at Sydney. "What about you, lady? You have anything to say?"

"No. We didn't do anything."

"There you have it, Crol," Marla snapped. "We didn't have anything to do with this. And if Sturm is going to accuse us of something, where the hell is he? Why is this idiot here in his place?"

Crol laughed. "You need to ease up on the outraged routine, Marla. You're overplaying it."

McGee folded his hands and placed them on the table. "Marla, I'm here because we have a vested interest in how the dwarf does his business. A monetary interest. We mean to see that he succeeds. No matter what. Do you understand me?"

Marla glowered. "I understand you're sitting in my establishment, threatening me, in front of the head of Lord Burnside's Enforcers."

"Not a threat, lass," McGee said with a smile but his narrowed eyes conveyed nothing to Sydney but anger. "Merely...a statement of the situation."

"You can take your statements and shove them up your ass."

"All right, that's enough." Crol glared at Marla and McGee. "I brought him here so you could hear his complaint but also to tell you morons something, so I don't have to go through this more than once. Lord Burnside wants Woodhollow to remain a peaceful city, so that's the way it's going to be. Stick to fleecing shopkeeps and running your drug rings. Anything more is going to get someone killed, and I don't mean me. You have a grievance? You come see me. There isn't going to be any open warfare."

He pointed at the Con leader. "McGee, go back to the Four-Leaf Club. Whatever you and Sturm Sunbolt are up to, keep it out of the streets. Keep it legal—or at least, out of my sight. You get me?"

McGee nodded.

Crol shifted his arm to aim at Marla. "Marla, I don't care what you do to get your ale but if it's gonna involve outright piracy, keep doing it well outside the city. If Sunbolt won't sell to you, figure something else out. None of your little raids better occur anywhere near Woodhollow. Is that clear?"

"Yeah."

"I think that's enough, then. McGee, time for you to go."

"I was planning on a drink before I left."

Crol barked a laugh. "Yeah, I'm gonna leave you here with all these faeries? I don't think so. Out."

McGee stood again. He touched the brim of his hat. "As always, was a pleasure, Marla."

The Con left without another word. Crol gave Marla a long dirty look, then ducked out the door and was gone.

Sydney exhaled, letting out a large gasp. It wasn't until then that she realized she'd been holding her breath.

"Well, now," Dana said. "That was interesting."

Sydney was impressed at the old faery's unruffled demeanor. Before she could comment on it, Marla stood and stretched. "Sure was."

Sydney frowned at her sister. "You seem decidedly less angry than you were thirty seconds ago. What was that all about?"

Marla shrugged. "I tried to act a little more upset than I was. I thought it might throw McGee off his game but Crol saw through it. I overdid it, I guess."

"I guess." Sydney collapsed in one of the chairs. "What do we do now?"

"We wait."

"Great, Marla, that really answered my friggin' question. You got anything better than that?"

"Nope." Marla sat next to her. Dana also took a seat. "McGee just came here to ruffle our feathers. He doesn't have anything on us."

"Then why was the Enforcer here?"

Dana drummed her fingers on the table. "He's acting on Lord Burnside's orders, and Burnside doesn't want chaos or bodies in the street. Beyond that, he doesn't care what we do. Crol wouldn't give a shit if we and the Cons murdered each other, as long as it didn't wreck the city."

Marla nodded. "I am sure McGee knows what happened to Sturm's ship but he doesn't have any evidence. Not enough to convince Crol that we're trying to start a gang war, anyway."

Sydney thought on that. "Why wasn't Sturm here, along with that big dwarf, Urgon?"

"Probably because McGee told him to stay away. Or Crol did."

"Are they going to? To stay away?"

"No," Marla said with a grin. "I am sure they hung back because Crol warned them off. But one thing I have learned from dealing with Sturm for years is this: he's predictable. Sturm will learn that Crol is dropping the issue and he's out the cash for the ale, Once he does, he'll lose his mind. I expect them to hit us in the next twenty-four hours."

Her grin became positively vicious. "And when they do, we'll be waiting."

Sydney hesitated. "And Urgon?"

"We'll see what happens."

*   *   *   *   *

Night blanketed Bayberry Square in silence. The last revelers left The Log two hours before. The lightstones arrayed about the edge of the square burned low; the Woodhollow Lamplighters Guild would not recharge them until the following evening. The eastern horizon glowed with the first thin hint of dawn.

Sydney yawned and shuffled her wings.

Whoever said that waiting was the hardest part didn't know the half of it.

She glanced towards The Log. A trio of carts rested before the Log. The cart-lizards sat unmoving, heads and bodies on the stones. Dana told her the lizards' metabolism slowed at night, until they were basically inert.

"Don't worry, Sydney," Dana had said. "They won't wake up and give anything away."

Sydney didn't care about the lizards. She was worried about reinforcements. In theory, Marla, Markus, and a dozen other faeries were secreted behind those carts, awaiting her signal.

In theory. The others were so silent and still that she wasn't sure any of them were still there. When she pointed out that the carts were too obvious a hiding place, Dana had said that tavern patrons often left carts and wagons overnight, only retrieving them by the time sunlight brought sobriety, so having them in front of the fallen tree was not unusual.

Sydney shook her head, hoping Sturm paid close enough attention to the comings and goings at The Log to actually know that little tidbit of knowledge.

She let her gaze wander around the Square. Nothing moved.

If Sturm and Urgon showed their faces, she hoped they wouldn't see her. During her trips with Brigid to Fort Bloodwell, Sydney overheard ogres talking about their scouts, often posted alone, far in front of the bulk of the unit. True, they provided good advanced warning of the enemy but their rate of casualties always horrified Sydney. Picket sentries, the ogres called those scouts.

She prayed that wasn't how her early morning vigil played out since she was now in the role of the picket.

One hand toyed with the ringed handle of one of her bandolier knives. Sydney had no illusions of her ability to stand against Urgon or another heavily-armored target. If the dwarves did come, as Marla and the others seemed to think they would, she hoped she'd have enough time to signal the others and fall back. The alternative was getting carved to pieces.

I guess then Aunt Brigid could say, 'I told you so.'

A collection of dark shapes crept from the shade of a building across from The Log and lumbered to the next one.

The hackles on the back of her neck stood up. Sydney hefted the shuttered lantern and aimed the signaling aperture at the front of the tavern. There was no answering response. She hoped Marla was paying attention. She signaled again to make sure, then slipped around the square in the opposite direction.

She was halfway to The Log when she was yanked backward against the storefront. Rough hands gripped her at the base of her wings and around her mouth. Her head slammed against the plate glass window fronting the building. For some odd reason, she remembered that it was a tailor's shop and recalled a fetching embroidered dress she'd seen in the front window.

She rocketed her elbow to her rear, making a solid connection. Her captor grunted but their grip never loosened. Hot breath touched her ears. "Knock it off or I'll break your neck."

Sydney stiffened. She'd heard that flat, gravelly voice once before.

It's him.

Urgon continued. "I don't want to kill you, so don't make me." He took the lamp from her unresisting fingers. "I guess you used this to signal your companions. Good plan. If I release you, are you going to scream?"

Sydney shook her head.

"If you do, I'll snap your wings off."

The hand moved off her face. Sydney took a deep breath, fighting to keep her voice low. "Call them off and they won't get killed."

Urgon chuckled. "That's Sturm's problem."

"You don't care if your boss dies?"

"Sturm couldn't pay me after his losses from the missing ale shipment, so my employment with him officially ended yesterday."

"Then why are you here?"

"Curiosity. Stay here, we can see how this plays out."

"I have to help my sister."

"That's too bad. You should have walked the other way around."

Sudden brilliance lit the square, revealing a band of six dwarves creeping towards The Log. Each carried a large, sealed ceramic jar.

Marla and the other faeries rushed forward, brandishing weapons. The leader of the gang pointed at a clearly-shocked Sturm. "Drop it, Sturm!"

The dwarf's face twisted. "You bitch!" He reared back, ceramic jar raised.

A crossbow bolt lanced across the distance, catching the dwarf shipping magnate in the chest. He staggered and toppled.

His compatriots stood staring at his twitching body. Like a tidal wave, Marla and the rest of the faeries fell on the remaining dwarves as the light faded and the returning darkness swallowed the square.

Sydney shut her eyes, trying to ignore what she had just seen. She could not block out the sounds of metal on metal, the screams of the injured, or the wet *whack* of blades carving flesh.

"It's never easy, kid." Urgon's voice was just a whisper. "But you'll get used to it."

She spun to face him but the mercenary was gone.

Sydney had no idea how long she stood there but it could not have been more than a few moments. Marla's voice, thick with concern, drifted out of the darkness. "Syd?"

"Over here."

Marla trotted to her, just another shadow in the dim pre-dawn light. She held a short sword. Blood dripped from the edge of the blade. "You okay? What's wrong?"

"He was here."

"Who?"

"Urgon." Sydney slumped, placing her hands on her knees. Her stomach churned.

I could be dead. I should be dead. Again.

Marla's eyes raked the area. "He's gone?"

"I think so. Sorry, Marla. I'm a bigger wimp than I thought. I was so scared I didn't even see him slip away."

"Did he say anything?"

Sydney fought to keep her churning stomach under control. "He said Sturm couldn't pay him anymore, so he walked. I guess he was being honest because he didn't kill me. The others. Are they..."

"Everyone is all right. At least, all of us are. Sturm and his boys aren't."

"The jars?"

"Firebombs." Marla wiped her bloody blade on a rag. "An old dwarven weapon. They must have planned to burn down The Log."

"Now what?"

"You go inside. Tell Dana what happened."

"What are you going to do?"

"We have to get the bodies under the Boardwalk before the sun comes up."

Too mentally drained to do anything else, Sydney said, "Okay.

Marla jogged away, gesturing and hissing commands to the gang members.

Sydney barely remembered staggering back to The Log. Lila and Dana met her at the door. The younger faery said, "How bad was it?"

"Bad." She related what had happened in the shadows and Marla's subsequent butchery of Sturm and the dwarves.

"That'll do for now." Dana jerked her head at the stairs. "Go get some rest."

Lila followed Sydney to their room. She watched Sydney kick her boots off. "You sure you're all right?"

"Yeah. I guess we stand by for the next retaliation."

Lila looked pensive. "That depends. If Sturm is dead, then I imagine his company will be in disarray for a few days. He has some relatives in town. I don't know which one will take over or what they will do. Sunbolt Shipping might even dissolve. If that happens, we can negotiate a contract with the wood elves for Ascorian ale ourselves, subcontract the shipping, and we'll be much better off. There are other merchants we can use to move the ale downriver."

"Nobody seems worried that Crol will figure out what happened here tonight."

"If the bodies go under the Boardwalk and aren't laying on the cobblestones, the ogres won't ask too many questions. Sure, they'll suspect us but guys like Sturm have plenty of enemies."

Sydney stared at her friend. "And Urgon? What about him?"

Lila looked away. "Wild card."

Sydney thought for a moment. "Lila, I have to ask you something."

"What?"

"Didn't this whole thing seem a bit...staged?"

Lila scrunched her brow. "You think someone put Sturm up to this?"

"Sort of."

"Why would Sturm go along with something that would get him killed? If they had successfully bombed The Log, they would have been dead dwarves walking."

"Marla always said Sturm was stubborn. He probably thought he could get away with it. I mean, they were working with the Cons." Lila tossed her brown hair. "It would be like them to use people."

"Maybe." Sydney shook her head. "Even if the Cons are trying to strong-arm us, doesn't this whole plot seem a bit advanced for a gang that, up til now, hasn't done anything more than some brawling and roughing up shopkeeps?"

She paused. "What if someone else is instigating this?"

"Like who?"

"I don't know. Maybe it's nothing."

It's not nothing, she thought as she climbed in bed. The thought pursued her to her sleep.

Chapter Nine

"That's the deal. You can take it or leave it."

The landy spread her hands. "Please. Can't I have just a little more time?"

Sydney chuckled, though she had to force it, resulting in more of a rasp than a laugh. "Vigdess, Marla already gave you two extensions and she didn't even increase your rate. You're getting off pretty easy if you ask me."

"But—"

"It's not our fault you can't stay away from Turtle Downs."

Vigdess sucked in a deep breath. "You know about that?"

"Of course we do." Sydney raised an eyebrow. "The question is, does your husband know you're pissing away the family fortune at the track?"

The woman glanced fearfully at the door but Sydney shook her head. "Relax. He isn't due to leave the sawmill for at least another hour."

Sydney looked at Gordon, who watched impassively, then back at the cringing woman. Vigdess cried silent tears and Sydney's stomach lurched.

She knew Marla had loaned Vigdess enough money, at an appalling rate of interest, to cover her gambling debts, and that the *landvaettir* had turned around and squandered the loan betting at the track. Marla was willing to cover both debts directly...but only for a price.

Sydney glanced around the modest home. Sturdy wooden furniture filled the crowded living space. A thick cabinet, loaded with dishes and woven wooden baskets, covered one wall. A large portrait of Vigdess and her husband, Kristof, hung on another It was the picture of domestic tranquility.

Cute place, she thought. *Too bad.*

"We don't have any money left," Vigdess said. She was tall, even for a landy, with a slender, willowy figure, milky skin, straw-colored hair, and bright blue eyes, though those same eyes were now full of dread. "I just need some time."

Gordon shook his head. "Vigdess, we're not a charity. We're not chumps either."

"I know but—"

"Consider yourself lucky. If we were the Cons, we would have already knocked you in the head and dragged you down to Belles, where you could work off your debt on your back."

Vigdess paled, going from fair-skinned to pasty.

Gordon gave what Sydney was sure an overly melodramatic shrug. "Fortunately for you, we're not the Cons. What we will do, however, is give you some extra incentive." He produced a document. "You see this?"

"What it is?"

Sydney resumed the attack. "It's the title to your house. We filed your breach of contract, along with a copy of the loan contract you signed. We now own this property. You have one week to repay your debt, with interest. If you don't, this house is ours."

"You can't!"

"We can, and we will." Gordon's thin smile was fierce. "And it's all legal. You can check it out with the housing office at city hall if you want but I don't see the point. We're not lying and you know it. One week, Vigdess."

The landy's face twisted in anger. For a moment, Sydney thought Vigdess was going to attack them. She rested her hand on one of her throwing knives. They stared at each other for a space of four heartbeats.

Vigdess slumped. Her eyes sought the floor. "Fine. You'll get your money."

Gordon nodded. He and Sydney headed for the door. He

paused and glanced back. "One week."

Vigdess didn't respond but continued to stare at the ground.

When the door closed, Sydney sighed. "How do you do that, day in and day out?"

"What?"

"Break people." Her gut continued to roil. "I don't think I have the stomach for this. Did you see her? She was about to break down completely."

Gordon chuckled. He strode away from the house. Sydney hurried to keep up.

"Don't let Vigdess fool you, Sydney. She might have looked like she was about to lose it but did you not see her face at the end? She was more angry than panicked because she's been in this position before. She was trying to play on your sympathies. I am sure her husband Kristof already knows all about her debts. He's as bad or worse than she is. Hell, I bet if we went to the sawmill, we'd find him deep in his own dice game right now. Why do you think Marla sent you out with me today?"

" 'Cause she's a bitch?"

"Yeah, she is. But she's a bitch with a motivation. She wanted you to see that our targets are usually not nice people either." Gordon gestured over his shoulder. "Vigdess and Kristof aren't just dirty, they're filthy. Scams, hustling, even a little light robbery. Both have been caught up in gambling rings for years, though never quite this deep. They'll scrape together enough money, somehow, even if they have to roll a few drunks to get it."

"You think?"

He nodded. "They always have before. Sydney, you've been with us—what, six weeks now?"

"About that."

"I know we're thugs and gangsters, but believe me: we pretty much only deal with other thugs and gangsters. None of the people we strong-arm are clean or virtuous. We tend to leave those people alone."

"How come? Not enough money?"

He smiled. "No, the clean ones go to the Enforcers when

you lean on them. We don't need that heat. Now, ready for the next one?"

She squared her shoulders. "As ready as I will ever be."

They walked for another ten minutes. Sydney felt a moment of tension when they passed a trio of Cons walking the other direction. Sydney kept a hand on one of her knives. All three Cons eyed her and Gordon but they kept walking.

Gordon leaned towards her. "Nervous?"

"I am just glad it wasn't the two who confronted me the first day. The one seemed to really want to have a go at me."

"Henry and Seamus, right? Henry's just a doofus. Seamus, though...yeah, I can believe it."

"Yeah," Sydney said. "He got a rep or something?"

"He's a sadist and a bully. He's beaten a few folks within an inch of their lives." Gordon's lip curled. "I've heard some other stuff about him that isn't so great either."

"What?"

"Rumor is he raped and murdered a dryad sometime back."

Sydney shuddered. "That's disgusting. I can't believe even the Cons are okay with that."

"I know," Gordon said. "Whether or not he's guilty of that doesn't much matter; Seamus is a bastard either way. But like the others, he's predictable and arrogant. If you end up having to fight him, try to get under his skin and throw him off-balance."

"I don't understand."

"Those guys—" Gordon gestured in the direction the Cons had gone. "—they act tough and they're bigger than us and strong. But they're brawlers, undisciplined, and in general, not very bright. If not for their magic, I doubt they'd be much threat at all. In a straight-up sword fight, someone skilled like Markus or Claire could probably take four of them at once. If you do get in a fight with one, try and bait them. Insult them. They can't handle it. They get mad and then sloppy, which you can exploit. Just don't get in a magic duel if you can help it."

"They're strong with magic?"

"Stronger than us. Not quite on par with the dryads but yeah, they're stout."

"Hmm, okay." She thought for a moment. "I admit, McGee seemed a lot more threatening than that."

Gordon grimaced. "He's something else altogether. McGee's a hell of a lot smarter than the rest and unlike the others, he's got a firm grip on his temper. He fights as well as any faery. Better than most of us, actually. He pretty much runs the Cons through sheer force of will and they all look at him with some kind of reverent fear. Sometimes I think the only thing holding them together is that they are all so terrified of McGee. Don't underestimate him."

Chilled by Gordon's words, Sydney could only nod.

Their next stop was another modest home. Sydney sized up the building's ramshackle appearance. "A little shabbier than the last one. Who's this?"

"Friedgar. Trow. Runs shrooms for us from time to time, but we haven't gotten any money since his last shipment. So here we are."

"Is he trouble?"

"He could be. Keep a knife handy."

Sydney nodded. She scanned the street, wondering if the Cons dared to double-back to harass them.

The hooded figure lurked four buildings down, hanging in the shadows. It was looking in their direction but froze when Sydney focused on it.

She elbowed Gordon. "Hey, look over there."

"Where?"

"Th—" Sydney pointed but the figure was gone.

"What?"

"There was someone over there, in a hood. I'm not sure, but I think he was watching us."

Gordon frowned. "You sure it was a he?"

"No. Just something about the way he or she carried their shoulders, made me think that."

"Con?"

"Not unless they have some that are about the same size as us."

"I don't know of any that small. They're all pretty bulky." Gordon returned his attention to the door. "Let's get this done."

Gordon knocked on the door, then pushed it open.

Unlike the previous house, Friedgar's home was filthy and poorly lit. Piles of trash heaped in random spots on the bare dirt floor. Sydney's nose crinkled as the stench of rotten food, stale beer, and unwashed bodies flooded past her.

A short form staggered off a stained cot in the corner. "What? Who's there?"

Sydney regarded the man. Like most trows, Friedgar stood about three feet tall, making him about the same height as the gnomes. Unlike gnomes, the dark-skinned trow had a great matted black beard that reached past his knees. His eyes—solid black orbs —squinted at the faery intruders.

Yeah, this one actually looks like a crook.

A vague sense of apprehension glided over her senses. Whereas interacting with the *landvaettir* had only induced pity and self-doubt, just being in the room with Friedgar screamed *danger!* Sydney tried to shake the feeling and placed a mild scowl on her face. She hoped it made her appear to be a mix of impatient and intimidating.

Friedgar's gaze focused on the two faeries. "Gordon. What the hell are you doing here?"

"You know why we're here, so don't act dense."

"I don't have it no more," Friedgar mumbled. He tugged on both sides of his beard.

Gordon shook his head. "You better have either the product or the cash, Fred, or this is going to end badly."

"If you can give me some time, I can get it back." His hands tugged even harder.

The trow's motion was too exaggerated for a nervous tic. Sydney's unease intensified.

"We're tired of hearing from people they need more time." Gordon cracked the knuckles on his left hand. The sound was ominous in the close quarters.

"Actually, I've made some new arrangements—and new partners." Friedgar's eyes flicked side to side.

Sydney followed his gaze. A pair of figures moved in the gloom.

I knew it.

She tore a knife from her bandolier. "Gordon, look out!"

Two hairy bodies hurled themselves at Gordon. He twisted, avoiding the first. The second tackled him and they both went to the ground.

The first jumped to its feet and whirled on Sydney. The attacker was about five feet tall and even more slender than the *landvaettir*. Coarse brown hair covered its body from head to toe. It wore nothing save for the blade-lined belt about its waist. Lips pulled away from jagged yellow teeth and quivering whiskers tipped the elongated nose. Pointed ears laid flat against its head. It held a long knife in its right paw.

"Squeeeeee!"

The rat lunged at Sydney with the knife held out in front of it like a spear.

Sydney lurched to the side and hurled her blade at her attacker. The throwing knife sank into the rat's shoulder with a meaty *thunk*.

The rat squealed again and fled towards the door on all fours. Sydney pulled another knife and flung it after her foe. The blade clattered against the door frame.

Damn, hurried the throw.

She heard a grunt of pain and wheeled to Gordon. The other rat crouched on top of her companion. Blood welled from the faery's side.

Sydney reached for another knife but Gordon leveraged the beast off his chest. The rat crashed into the wall and slid to the floor, dazed. Gordon scrambled to his feet. Without pause, he lashed out with his foot, just as the rat started to stand. The pointed tip of Gordon's iron-shod boot caught the rat in the chin.

The shattering grind of breaking bone filled Sydney's ears and the rat collapsed without a sound.

Sydney spun, eyes searching the shadows, but Friedgar had fled.

She ran to Gordon's side, who would have collapsed had his hand not found the wall. He stood askew, clutching his abdomen. His tunic glistened scarlet. "Gordon! How bad is it?"

"Just a scratch." He tried to straighten and nearly doubled over.

"Let me see it."

"Friedgar—"

"Screw him. This is serious."

She got him to lay on Friedgar's pallet. Gordon grunted. "This stinks."

"Yeah, getting stabbed sucks."

"No, his bed stinks."

"It's that or lay on the floor."

"Probably fewer fleas there."

Taking care to be gentle, Sydney inched his tunic up his torso. The wound was long but shallow. Sydney uncorked the flask at her side and tipped the container over the angry gash. A bit of clear liquid dribbled onto the injury.

Gordon yelled. "Damn it, that stings! What the hell is in there?"

"Red spirits."

"Why are you carrying around rubbing alcohol?"

"It's not quite rubbing alcohol." Sydney recorked the flask. "But I thought I might need some liquid courage to deal with this."

"With what?"

"Rousting deadbeats." She tore a strip from his tunic, bundled it up, and pressed the padded cloth against his wound. "Like I said before, I didn't think I had the stomach for this."

"Yet you reacted like a champ when that rat attacked you.' Gordon placed his hand over the wadded bandage and moved hers off.

"He got away and I think you killed the other one. Too bad; I would like to have questioned him."

In spite of his pain, Gordon's eyes sparkled with mirth. "Question him? Sydney, did you grow up reading bad mystery books?"

"No."

"Okay. That just sounded funny. I bet you've never interrogated someone before."

"No, I haven't."

"We'll talk about that later." Gordon coughed and his whole body spasmed. Sydney's heart leaped into her throat but Gordon relaxed and the spasms subsided. He continued. "In this case, it doesn't matter. When they are in rat-form, they can't really talk to us."

"Rat-form?"

"They look like us, minus the wings, before they switch over to that upright, half-rat appearance."

She arched her eyebrows. "Wererats?"

"Don't act so surprised." He inhaled and winced again.

Sydney looked at their prostrate opponent. As near as she could tell, he wasn't breathing. "Gordon, can you walk? We need to get out of here before someone calls in the ogres."

"Yeah, I can walk."

"You sure?"

He chuckled. "Yeah, the bleeding has mostly stopped and the pain's receding some. That, or I'm going into shock."

Sydney bit her lip. "Don't say that."

"I'll be fine. No choice, 'cause you're right: we can't stay here. And don't worry about that dipshit Friedgar. Marla will put out a hit on his ass."

"Kill him?"

He nodded. "What did you expect?"

"I...I guess I was expecting it to go like it went with that landy Vigdess; that there would be a less violent solution."

"Maybe before he brought a few rats in here to attack us. Since they tried to kill us first, all bets are off." With her help, Gordon got to his feet and took a few tentative steps. From what Sydney could tell, he seemed lucid and alert. "See? Told you I'd be fine."

"Get your shirt on."

While Gordon struggled into his tunic, Sydney checked on the fallen rat. The beast was not breathing. "He's dead."

"I figured as much."

"Gordon, why would the rats attack us? I mean they have their own gang, their own territory, don't they?"

"They do. We rub up against the other gangs once in a while. There's friction, an occasional skirmish or incident. It's rare but it happens. But we've been on basically good terms with the Rats for some time now."

"So why Friedgar?" She thought about it for a moment. "From what you said, Friedgar is a useless weasel, a low-level dealer. What would the rats want with him?"

Gordon's brows furrowed.

No matter how she twisted the attack around in her mind, Sydney kept coming back to the same conclusion. "I think they were here for us."

"Why?"

"Maybe they're allying themselves with the Cons." She then thought of the hooded figure she'd seen in the street.

Or maybe it's something worse.

She helped Gordon to the door. Even though a wounded rat and scared smelly trow had come bolting out of the building mere moments before, none of the passersby seemed to pay the faeries any mind. A few glanced at the darkening stain on Gordon's tunic but shrugged and moved on, as if such things were expected to happen between the criminals of Woodhollow.

Sydney kept a tight grip around Gordon's shoulder the entire way back to The Log. Half of her expected to be attacked by Rats or Cons right in the streets. The other half of her expected the ogres to show up to arrest them, flailing with clubs first and asking questions later.

They had no sooner entered Bayberry Square and The Log come into sight when Patrice hurried across the cobblestones to them. Sydney saw the blood drain from Patrice's face. "How bad?"

A grim smile lit his face. "I'll live."

Sydney's eyes raked the square but she didn't see Rats, Cons, or Enforcers. She also didn't see the mysterious cloaked figure. "Help me get him inside, Patrice."

Patrice slipped her arm around Gordon's waist. "Let me take him, Sydney."

Gordon tried to sluff her arm away. "I can walk, Patrice."

"Shut up." Patrice was a bit shorter than Gordon; she ducked her head under his arm and clenched her arm about his waist even more tightly. Gordon looked like he wanted to object but didn't. He stepped a little closer until they were practically glued at the hip. Patrice gazed at Gordon even as they walked.

Sydney smiled.

Chapter Ten

Patrons pounded on their tables, whistling and calling. Ale from mugs borne in careless hands slopped across the furniture and floors.

Sydney sighed. *How long is it going to take to clean up this time?*

On the other side of the entrance to the back rooms, Claire leaned against the wall, her arms folded. A drunken goblin staggered toward her. "Hello, pretty."

"Beat it, jerk." Claire's hand drifted to the axe hanging at her belt.

The goblin cringed and lurched back into the crowd, nearly colliding with Robin, who snarled and shoved him aside.

Claire frowned. "I wish Natasha would get out here and calm these idiots down."

"She'll be out soon enough," Sydney said. She shifted position. Her butt was sore from leaning against the wall. "They know it too; that's why they're so loud."

"I hope so."

"How's Gordon?"

"He'll be fine." Claire snickered. "Patrice will take good care of him."

"I bet she will."

"She's been in love with him for a long time."

Sydney nodded. "I got that impression. How's he feel about her?"

"He likes her but—" Claire shrugged. "—he's reluctant to commit."

"How come?"

"He's never said but I think it has something to do with life in the gang." Claire bent her left knee and placed the sole on the wall. "It's uncompromising and often doesn't end well."

"It's a hard way to live."

"Yeah, and any vulnerability, like a loved one, is one fast way to death. I don't agree with Gordon but it's his life."

Sydney's thoughts darkened. *Doesn't speak well about my future romantic prospects, does it?*

Just then, Natasha stepped onto the low stage. Her emerald dress sparkled and shimmered and, as usual, clung to her lush body like a second skin. She batted her eyes and waved to the audience, who responded with more cheers.

Her eyes met Sydney's. Natasha gave Sydney a slow, deliberate wink and puckered her lips in a kiss. Sydney blushed but the crowd roared in delight.

They probably all thought that was for them.

Natasha sang, quieting the assembled drunks. Her crystalline voice filled the tavern with a sweet, slow melody. Her wings fluttered in beat with the song. The tavern-goers wove back and forth in their chairs, as if in the grip of some magical lullaby. Sydney caught herself swaying along with the rest.

Claire edged across the door. "She's insanely good, isn't she?"

"Yeah, I never get tired of listening to her. Does she ever take a night off?"

"Only once in a while. She loves performing and she loves bringing the crowds in."

Sydney scratched her arm. "I can see that. Is that why she never goes on operations?"

"Jealous?"

Sydney shook her head. "No, just curious."

"Natasha can't really do fieldwork. Her face is far too well known in Woodhollow."

"Her face, and the rest of her."

Claire laughed. "Yes, there's also that."

"I'm surprised at how many women come to see her."

"Why?" Claire said with a smile. "Half the women in this city want her too."

Sydney blushed at the thought.

Claire continued. "Anyway, she pulls her weight for the gang, by packing the house almost every night. Well, her and the ale. Robin told me that since we got the ale situation squared away, the tavern room of The Log is in the black again."

"So I hear."

Having listened to Marla thinking aloud for the last month, Sydney already knew the tavern was out of financial peril. Profits were up. The need for retaliatory operations had fallen to almost nil, as though the underside of the city had gotten word not to get in the way of the Faery Gang's ascent. Even though they initially protested the events of the ale theft, the Cons had since gone quiet and were scarcely being seen on the streets at all. The Enforcers did not come to The Log over Sturm's disappearance. Sturm's nephew Scorin took over Sunbolt Shipping and by all appearances, seemed eager to honor his uncle's earlier deal with the faeries, and had even given them a discount to make up for the recent troubles. Urgon vanished; he had not been seen since the pre-dawn massacre of Sturm and his thugs. Even the confrontation with the Rats proved to be nothing; a stern word from Marla resulted in a hasty apology from Dominique, the leader of the Rat gang, and promises that the surviving ambusher would be disciplined.

All in all, the faeries' daring raid of the dwarven freighter had thus far produced nothing but benefits, and Sydney's concept and planning of that foray elevated her in the eyes of the gang. For the last five weeks, Gang business was going smoother than ever.

So why do I still have this nagging suspicion in the back of my brain?

Sydney rolled her shoulders, trying to loosen a kink.

She'd seen McGee's eyes. Though her experience in the world was limited compared to her compatriots, Sydney knew evil when she saw it. And when she had stared into the Con leader's face, Sydney saw an unremitting hatred and cruelty whose memory she could not banish, no matter how many times she washed her eyes.

Also, the presence of the Rats at Friedgar's place was troubling, as if they expected the faeries to arrive right at that time. *How could they have known? And why would they care?*

She'd derived several possible answers to those questions but none of them made Sydney feel better.

Natasha's song ended. As soon as the final note faded, the entire patronage jumped to their feet, hooting and clapping. Natasha curtsied demurely and blew kisses with both hands. A moment later, she launched into her next tune. As one, the crowd sat and stilled, enraptured anew.

Sydney shifted position again, ignoring the clink of coin in her pocket.

After the collection run in which Sydney had patched up Gordon, Marla insisted on formally indoctrinating her into the Fairy Gang, giving Sydney status as a member and entitling her to a weekly stipend. Sydney objected but Marla cut her off, saying that she couldn't have any share of the loot without being a formal member.

"Can't make exceptions," Marla said, "and you deserve it, Syd."

She'd agreed rather than continue to argue, though with her lodging and food covered, she hadn't found much on which to spend it.

Not much different than home, she mused.

Sydney's thoughts drifted to Sylvan Valley and Brigid's cottage in Holly Grove. If she were there now, she and Brigid would be cleaning up the last of the dinner dishes and settling down for a quiet evening before they got up to repeat their day in the apothecary shop.

Some nights, they would go to the local tavern on the edge of town, where Brigid would buy them a pint of ale and they would dance with the single men. Sydney never lacked for partners and many a night ended with her exhausted but happy, having danced until her feet hurt. More than one young man tried to coax Sydney into "going for a walk" in the dark woods behind the tavern but she had always demurred. Brigid herself still cut a striking figure and had her share of suitors. Sydney loved seeing her aunt whirling about the dance floor. It was one of the few times Brigid seemed to allow herself to relax and laugh and it did Sydney's heart good to see her aunt happy.

Sydney wondered how Brigid fared. She'd sent two letters —the first to let her aunt know that Sydney was okay, the second as a follow-up to reiterate that things were fine and hoping that Brigid was doing well.

Sydney's brow furrowed at the thought. Brigid had to have received the letters by now and she, like most good businesswomen, was normally punctual about answering correspondence.

Maybe she's been super-busy without me there. Maybe she's just mad at me. Even so.... Sydney shook her head. The tickle in her brain, the sensation that something was wrong, remained.

Claire's poke in the ribs jerked Sydney from her daydreaming. "What?"

"Over there, by the far wall. Faery. I don't know him."

Sydney followed Claire's gaze. The faery was of medium build and appeared older, perhaps fifty. His brown hair was streaked with gray and bound behind his head. He sat mostly in the shadows.

"Yeah, I see him. No idea who he is."

"Me either." Claire pursed her lips. "I know every faery in Woodhollow, in the gang and out, by sight if not name. He's new to town."

Sydney eyed the man. Like everyone else in the room, he watched Natasha, though his attention appeared to be of boredom rather than awe. "If he's new to town, maybe he just wandered in for a drink. Maybe someone told him where to catch a good stage show."

"Maybe. When we have a break, maybe we can go over and feel him out, you know? See what his intentions are?"

"Sure, I—"

The man shifted slightly, letting the light fall on him. Sydney's breath caught in her throat. She was vaguely aware of Claire's accompanying gasp.

The faery's wings were black, fading to a pale yellow on the fringes.

"What the fuck?" Claire said.

Sydney felt lightheaded. "It can't be. It's a trick."

"I'm not taking that chance." Claire's arm shot out, pointing at the man. "Garth! Garth, over there! Nightshade!"

The bartender followed her pointed arm. His eyes widened. Garth ducked under the bar and came up in a heartbeat with a loaded crossbow.

The strange faery locked eyes with Sydney. His face betrayed no emotion but something in depths of his gaze made her heart quail.

Then she blinked and he disappeared.

Natasha froze, her hand at her mouth and her eyes wide. Robin dropped her tray with a clatter and grabbed both knives tucked in her belt. The fear was plain on her face. Garth's mouth set in a grim line. Only his quivering wings conveyed his disbelief.

The patrons glanced about nervously, muttering among themselves.

Sydney ran on stage and took Natasha's hand. "Small delay in the show, folks. Just a minor glitch we need to work out. Natasha will be back in a few minutes. In the meantime, half-price on pints for the next hour."

Garth frowned at her announcement but nodded his compliance.

A light round of applause went up from the collected drinkers and the tension drained from the room. Sydney stepped off the platform, dragging a stunned Natasha behind her. They reached the storeroom as Claire emerged with the twins Lucas and Lucian in tow.

"They're going to watch the door for us," Claire said. "Come on. Marla needs to hear this."

*   *   *   *   *

"And then he disappeared. Claire ran back here to get the twins to cover the door." Sydney exhaled. "That's it."

Marla reclined until only two chair legs remained on the floor and the back of the chair rested against the wall, just beneath the magical window. Her eyes fixed on the ceiling. Wisps of smoke from her cigar formed a wreath around her head. Her face was unreadable.

Claire stood by the entry. She draped a comforting arm around Natasha's shoulder. The singer wore a look of worried fear. Her eyes flicked back and forth, as if she expected the black-winged faery to appear in Marla's office at any moment.

Lila sat to Sydney's left. She held a clipboard and notepad but the youngster appeared thunderstruck by their revelations. As far as Sydney could tell, the secretary hadn't taken a single note.

After a moment, Sydney said, "Marla, did you hear me?"

"I heard it all, Syd. I'm just trying to absorb it."

"You and me both. Natasha, you okay?"

"A little shaken." Natasha took a deep breath, causing her chest to heave.

Sydney averted her eyes, embarrassed to have noticed. "Uhm, do you think you can go back and finish your set?"

"I think so."

"Do, then. Let's keep things as normal as possible for our regulars. I'm not sure if anyone who's not a faery would understand the significance of what happened but let's replace those thoughts with some happier memories."

"You're right. I can do it. Good thinking, Sydney." She flashed Sydney a smile. "Thank you."

Sydney forced herself to smile back. "I try."

Claire hunched her shoulders and cracked her neck. "I'll head back out too. Doesn't hurt to have an extra set of eyes on the room."

"You do that," Marla said.

Claire and Natasha left. Marla jerked her head at the door. "Lila, give us a moment."

"Sure."

She exited and closed the door behind her.

Marla returned her seat to the floor. "So...."

"Yeah?"

"The Nightshade Clan."

Sydney nodded.

"They're only legends, Syd. Myths." Marla paused. "Nightmares."

"Marla, I can't tell you if this guy was an actual Nightshade or some kind of imposter. All I can say for sure is there was a faery with yellow-fringed black wings here in The Log. One who was able to vanish into the shadows—" Sydney snapped her fingers. "—just like that."

Her eyes widened. "Just like the guy Gordon and I saw on the streets last month. At least, I think it was a guy. He vanished as fast as I saw him."

Marla puffed on her cigar, took it from her mouth, and placed it in the ashtray. "You think someone is stalking us?"

"You tell me, Marla."

"Maybe he wasn't after just any random faery."

"What do you mean?" Sydney's heart skipped a beat. "Me? You think someone is stalking me?"

"Is there any reason why someone should?"

"Not that I know of. Why, what do you know?"

"About why someone would be after you? Not a damn thing." Marla bit her lip. "What the hell does it mean? Even if the Nightshade Clan is real, what would a member be doing here? In Woodhollow, and in The Log?"

"I don't have the foggiest frickin' idea. If it's not me, just what are you into here that would draw a member of a mythical clan of assassins to come take a look?"

"Nothing."

Sydney's lip curled. "You looked away when you answered. It doesn't have anything to do with the designs I brought, does it?"

Marla's eyes narrowed. "Leave it alone, Syd."

"Fine."

The sisters sat in silence for several long minutes, glaring at each other. At last, Marla broke eye contact. She picked up her cigar. "Why half-price?"

"Beg pardon?"

"Why'd you tell Garth to sell ale at half-price for an hour? You have any idea what that cost us?"

"Less than bad rumors and fear-mongering among our clientele."

"Not making the connection, Syd."

"I've been over the books with Dana ten times. Ever since you dumped Sturm under the Boardwalk, Scorin has been pissing himself in fear that he'll end up the same way. Profits from the tavern are way up—enough so that selling ale at cost for an hour isn't even going to nick our margin. After another hour of cheap drinking and staring at Natasha's ass, none of those idiots out there will remember anything odd about tonight. We're better off keeping things calm and happy than having some gnome running out and saying how the whole faery gang got spooked over a stranger's appearance."

Marla looked at her with amazement. "You thought through all that in the time it took to get Natasha off the stage?"

Sydney shrugged. "It seemed like a good moment for an executive decision."

"You're not an executive."

"None of you were there so someone had to fill in."

"I'll buy that." Marla took one last inhale before grinding out the stub of the cigar. She opened her desk drawer, produced a fresh one, and lit it with a flash of crumble-induced magic.

"You have a whole crate full of those things, or what?"

"Yeah." Marla slapped the drawer shut. "Come from Dylia. Green Elves grow good tobacco. And before you ask, I buy them with my personal cash, not gang funds."

Sydney placed her hands on her knees. "Since we were on the subject of executives, just what do you see as my role around here?"

"I haven't decided yet."

"Are you grooming me as your replacement?"

Marla scoffed. "Hardly. In any event, you'd have probably go wrestle with Markus for it."

"I'm sure he'd like that."

"You might too."

Sydney rolled her eyes. "You want me to be one of your lieutenants?"

"Let's just say that for now, you should remain in the role of 'special advisor' and let's leave it there. Now back to the matter at hand. Can you describe this other faery again? Aside from the black wings?"

"Maybe fifty-ish. Medium height and build. Brown hair, with some gray in it. I was too far away to see his eye color. Darker skin but not like a trow's. More like he'd spent a lot of time in the sun."

"Anything distinctive? Like a scar?"

"Not that I could tell in the low light."

Marla rubbed her chin. "Could have been some clown masquerading."

"I thought that too but Claire said she didn't know him. Marla, I admit I don't know a ton about the Nightshade mythology, other than the stuff parents fed to their kids to keep them in line." Sydney wiggled her fingers. " 'Eat your dinner or the Nightshades will get you and drag you away.' That kind of thing."

"I don't either. I know it will shock you but I never paid much attention to Brigid's history lessons."

"You know what? I'm not shocked at all."

A smile flitted over Marla's face. "We need to find out more about this before we make any decisions. I'm not saying the Nightshade Clan is real but if it is, I want to be ready."

"Nobody here strikes me as a scholar of faery history. Tell me I'm wrong."

"I wish I could," Marla said. "You know, Brigid is pretty smart on that stuff. She likes history and she was always tight with the Holly Clan Council. Especially whats-his-name."

"Elder Edmund?"

"Yeah, him. If he was sharing state secrets with anyone, it would have been Brigid."

"Speaking of Brigid, have you heard from her lately?"

Marla shook her head. "No. Why?"

Sydney tapped her foot. "I sent her two letters—one three weeks ago and one last week. I haven't heard back from her and that's not like Brigid."

"No, it isn't. Unless she's mad at you."

"I can't imagine Brigid is so mad she'd ignore me," Sydney said.

"You're probably right. But there's only one way to find out."

"Right, I'll go get a bag ready."

Marla gave her a curious look. "For?"

"For going back to Holly Grove."

"Who says I would send you?"

"Because the only ones who could ferret secrets about the Nightshade Clan out of Brigid are you and me. Because she's the only family we have left and we want to make sure she's safe." Sydney stood. "And because I'm going whether you tell me to or not."

"All good points." Marla paused to tap out some ash. "But not alone. Too dangerous."

"Marla—"

"Don't argue with me, Sydney. Gang business, gang leader decision."

"Not Markus." Sydney's eyes widened. "And not Natasha."

Marla chuckled. "No, Lila can go with you. Lila!"

The young secretary poked her head in the door. "Yeah?"

Sydney stretched her arms over her head. "Go upstairs and pack a bag, buddy. Time for a road trip."

Chapter Eleven

Sydney alit on the road. Her wings folded into their resting position, nestling around the brown leather pack strapped to her torso.

A second later, Lila landed beside her. She smirked at Sydney. "Getting tired?"

"Yeah, let's walk for a bit."

"You old people...."

"I'm all of three years older than you, Lila."

One corner of Lila's mouth turned up in a half-grin. "Older is older."

Sydney could not help but laugh. "At least you're a better flier than Marla."

"I've only seen her fly a few times," Lila said. "She seems to do all right."

"Right until she lands."

"Oh, yeah." Lila giggled. "She hits the ground like a sack of potatoes."

"She always did, even when we were younger. She used to get so mad at me because I would tease her. She's sensitive over it." Sydney paused. "You ever laugh at her landing?"

Lila glared at her. "Are you kidding? I like my heart on the inside, thank you very much."

Sydney gazed out over the verdant lands of Sylvan Valley. Lanes of white gravel ran past pastures and orchards bound by cobblestone walls and slat wooden fences. Groves of healthy green trees and neatly-furrowed fields dotted the rolling hills.

Pretty country, Sydney thought. *Peaceful too. I guess I always took it for granted.*

"How much further?"

"Hmm?"

Lila kicked off a boot and shook a pebble free. "How much further to Holly Grove?"

"We're in Holly Clan lands now, so maybe another hour if we stay on foot."

"That's fine."

Sydney took in the familiar land, feeling a swell of homecoming comfort. She recognized a farm here, a tree stump at an intersection over there. They passed a handful of faeries laboring in the fields and orchards. All had the characteristic pink and red wings of the Holly Clan members. Most of the workers waved to Sydney and Lila.

Lila returned a wave to an older woman tending a plump, contented-looking cow. "I guess I've been in Woodhollow too long. I'd forgotten how friendly most faeries are."

"Our work makes us cynical."

Lila smiled faintly. "I bet you were born cynical, Sydney."

"I was."

"Marla too, I take it."

"No. She was practical, for sure, but she was always the dreamer. She was always looking over the horizon for an adventure," Sydney said. "I'm sure she got that from our parents."

"Marla doesn't talk about them."

"She never did. I'm not sure who took it harder—her or me —when Mom and Dad died. Neither of us dealt with it very well."

"I can imagine."

"Are your parents alive, Lila?"

Lila shrugged. "I don't know. I haven't been back to the Dandelion Clan lands since I left. They weren't the best parents anyway."

"Sorry to hear that."

"Don't be, it's in the past. I guess you were pretty close to your folks?"

Sydney nodded. "Very. Both Marla and I were really attached to them, and they to us, but not as much as they were to each other. They were kindred spirits, which is funny considering their backgrounds were so different. Mom was a young noble, grew up in the Clan her whole life. She was being groomed for the Clan Council, perhaps more. I think I told you Dad was an unaffiliated wanderer, with no clan lineage."

"You did."

"Dad was twenty-one when he wandered into Holly Grove. He was from some other faery nation far to the east. Mom was a few days away from turning eighteen and her official coming-of-age ceremony."

Lila nodded. "Always a big deal in the Clans."

"Mom had been keeping time with a guy named Demetrius. From what Brigid told me, he was also a noble but with noble parents from two clans, so he was definitely connected and had been marked by both Clan Councils and the Clan Chief Council for bigger and better things."

"Which clans?"

"His father was in the Holly Clan." Sydney frowned. "I can't remember which one his mother was from. Brigid didn't like to talk about him. She didn't like him. Brigid tells me Mom tolerated Demetrius but wasn't all that keen on marrying him. But it was an arranged marriage and it was just supposed to happen. A big merger of noble families, you know? The ceremony was scheduled for the day after her coming-of-age.

"Then Dad showed up. He sauntered into Mom's cousin's candle shop, where Mom was working. It was love at first sight, for both of them."

"They run off or something?"

Sydney grinned, feeling a bit wistful. "Aunt Brigid said Mom never looked back. She didn't even go home and pack a bag. Mom and Dad disappeared into the wilderness. When they came back a year later, she was already pregnant with Marla."

A little girl with gossamer pink wings and leading a roped goat passed them. She smiled shyly and lifted her hand in greeting.

Sydney and Lila both returned her smile and wave. When the child was past, Lila said, "I bet that created quite a scandal."

"Are you kidding? Young noble faery turns up both totally in love with and knocked-up by a vagabond? Brigid tells me the entire Holly Clan was in an uproar. Half of them wanted to drag Dad out and string him up. The other half wanted them both exiled forever. Of course, in the end, they stumbled to a third solution." Sydney chuckled. "That's faeries for you."

"I take it they were allowed to stay."

"Yes. Mom's father found some archaic Clan law that said that blood members of the Clan could not be turned away when seeking asylum. I understand that set off an enormous debate. They even hauled Mom and Dad to Beechwood Hall and the Clan Chief Council read them the riot act. Mom and Dad were allowed to make a home here. But they had to give up a few things."

Lila tilted her head. "Like?"

"Mom had to renounce any claims to her titles and lands. She could no longer go by, 'Lady Jenna.' She was just 'Jenna' after that. Of course, she was so in love, she shrugged it off.

"That wasn't the worst part, though. When Mom learned she was pregnant, she used albino mushroom, obtained illegally, to cast the clan binding ritual. She wanted Marla to come out with the right color wings. When the clan chiefs learned that, it set off another debate. In the end, they decided to allow Marla to be born."

"What?" Lila's mouth fell open. "They would have—"

"I don't know if they would have actually tried to terminate Mom's pregnancy but it sure was talked about. In the end, they decided to let the baby be born with clan colors. Just that one. Any subsequent children would—" Sydney flared her nostrils. "—be born with whatever random colors fate decided."

"So that explains the difference between your wings and Marla's."

Sydney tried to keep the bitterness out of her voice. "Yeah. I got the wings nature intended."

"What about that guy your Mom was going to marry? Demetrius?"

"I guess he left Sylvan Valley and nobody has heard from him since. His father sits on the Holly Clan Council. He's been a dick to our family ever since but the other elders on the council keep him in line. He hasn't said a word to us since Mom and Dad died."

They walked in silence for a few moments. The road bisected a large, grass-covered embankment. Beyond, the road wound into a shallow valley dotted with homes and farmsteads. On the far side, just a few miles away, lay a square stone building with a shingled roof, nestled beneath an oak tree, that Sydney knew so well.

Lila said, "So they defied the odds, it seems. True love."

"For sure. They loved each other so much it was almost frightening. They loved Marla and me too. But they would leave us with Brigid a lot."

"Oh?"

"Yeah. Mom and Dad both had a bad case of wanderlust. They'd be gone for weeks or months at a time, only to pop back in without any announcement or warning. They'd stay for a few months but then we'd start seeing that far-away look in both their eyes and before long they'd be gone again, seeking adventure and fortune."

"Did they ever find anything valuable?"

"Oh, yeah. Ancient coins from long dead-races, carved gemstones, withered scrolls of forgotten knowledge. They loved the rewards but they loved the adventure more. They dug through ruins, explored lost tombs, and fought all kinds of beasts."

Sydney kicked a loose pebble. It bounced along the road and tumbled to the side. "I used to love it when they'd tell us stories. They would sit together, usually with Marla on Dad's knee, and me on Mom's. They tell us about their trips and show us the trinkets and treasures they brought back. They were good at it, too. They became fairly wealthy and fronted Brigid enough cash to start her shop. I think that's one reason Brigid took us in for good; she felt indebted to Mom and Dad after accepting their help.

"On one of their adventures, they found a schematic for an amulet that protected its wearer from poisons. Dad became obsessed with the idea. He tinkered around with it until he could build his own. He went so far as pester and bribe one of the clan smiths so that he could use the forge to pour the amulet's form again and again until he got it right and actually built the thing."

"Did it work?" Lila asked.

"It sure did. They draped their test amulet around a chicken's neck and fed it enough arsenic to kill a battalion of faeries. Nothing happened. They took the amulet off, fed it a few more drops and the poor thing keeled over. From then on, both of them were hooked."

"On making amulets?"

"On making anything. They would spend hours in the archives at Beechwood Hall, pouring over rumors, myths, and legends, trying to find designs for magical items. I'm surprised just how many they actually found. They cut back on their adventuring, only going out when they learned of a new design. They talked about opening their own little forge and making items for sale. They scouted out a plot of land just outside Holly Grove to buy, where they could set up shop. Dad even talked about hitting up a merchant route that ran to Woodhollow and taking the items there."

Lila took a swig from her canteen. "I can't imagine the Clan Chief Council was thrilled about any of that. I know how they feel about 'frivolous' abuses of magic."

"They weren't happy at all. Mom and Dad didn't care. They were already social outcasts and they weren't going anywhere near the sacred mushroom fields, so by clan law, there wasn't a lot the Council could do. I guess the Council could have shut them down but from what Brigid told me, there was a general consensus that Mom and Dad would end up destroying themselves. So rather than rock the boat, the Council left it alone.

"So Mom and Dad kept right on. They even experimented with designing and building a few of their own." Sydney laughed. "That was always fun. Marla and I would be out playing or tending the animals and hear this *Whoosh!* Smoke would billow out of the chimney and the windows. Mom and Dad would come out coughing, their faces covered with soot. Marla and I would always run to give them hugs. They'd tickle us and we'd all end up rolling around in the grass together. We were just glad they were okay."

Her laugh faded and she sighed. "Those were the days."

After a moment, Lila said, "So what happened?"

Sydney took a deep breath. "They went out on one of their trips and never came back. Months passed and we were all sick with worry. Brigid paid for an expedition to go find them. No faeries would go, so she had to hire a pack of ogres to get some answers."

"How did she know ogres?"

"She was a healer and a nurse before she ran her apothecary. Even after she opened the store, she kept her healer business open as a sideline. She goes to Fort Bloodwell a couple times a year when their tribal wars break out. She's good, she made a nice bit of money at it. She also made a lot of contacts with mercenaries and other unsavory types."

"I see."

"The ogres tracked my folks to the Cobalt Mountains, way up north." Sydney bit her lip.

Lila waited a moment. "Did the ogres find them?"

"They found Mom and Dad, all right." Sydney's voice cracked. Her eyes watered and she made an angry wipe at them.

Lila touched her shoulder. "Sydney, you can stop."

"No, it's fine. Believe it or not, it helps to talk about it." Sydney fought to control her quivering jaw. "The ogres said the worm had their bodies strung up in front of its lair, as a warning to other intruders. They went in and killed the beast, though half of them got shredded in the process. As the worm was dying, it confessed that it knew Mom and Dad were coming and had waited to ambush them. Someone had tipped it off."

"Who?"

"I wish I knew. Anyway, after that, we stayed with Brigid full time until Marla was nineteen. She and Marla used to argue a lot. I always thought it was because they were so much alike."

Lila chuckled. "Your aunt is a hardass?"

"She can be. I meant more that they are both confident,

stubborn, and even though they love their family, they hide it under a very hard shell."

"That makes sense. Sorry, go on."

"When Marla turned nineteen, she finally had enough and took off. I was only fifteen, so I stayed with Brigid and worked my ass off. She loves us but she's strict as hell. I knew Marla went to Woodhollow but I didn't hear from her at all until I got her message a few months back. I figured she was having a grand old time and had forgotten all about us."

"I don't think that was quite it, Sydney. Marla is pretty closed-off but I've known her since Markus took me into the gang, and I've been her secretary since she took over. Marla may enjoy running the gang in Woodhollow but that's about all she does: work. She doesn't smile or relax much. In fact, the only time I see her really happy is when she talks about you or your aunt."

"Hmm. Well, that's neither here nor there. She sent me the message regarding our parents' magical designs. She took nothing of Mom and Dad's when she left. I always felt a little guilty that she left everything to me. So even though I hadn't heard from her for years, I brought her what she asked for. You know the rest."

Sydney glanced at Lila. "So there's the whole story of my fucked-up life. Unaffiliated loser, abandoned by my parents and sister, who can barely cast a spell and can't swing a sword straight. Still care to be seen with me in public?"

Lila shrugged. "You have a few redeeming qualities."

"Yeah, like what?"

"Lots of guys think you're attractive."

"Great. A beautiful, useless ornament."

"Well," Lila said with a grin, "we all have to know our strengths."

The lane curved, ending in a neat grass-covered yard. A plain sign with painted red lettering hung at eye-level by the gate. It read, "Brigid's Apothecary." A stone path led to the front door of the building. Broad oak branches shaded land and building alike.

Sydney put her hand on the gate latch but hesitated.

Lila said, "What's wrong?"

"It's a pleasant day but the door and windows are closed. Brigid almost always has them open during business hours." Sydney reached into her belt pouch and withdrew a small packet. "Crumble might be a good idea."

She ate the packet, savoring the pulse of vitality that burst down her limbs. Lila mirrored her action.

They walked to the door. Sydney tried the handle. It was locked.

Lila glanced around. "Now what?"

Sydney bent and lifted a flower pot near the door, revealing a silvery key. "Now we go in."

The key clicked in the lock and the door swung open. Beyond, the room was dark. Sydney stepped inside and gasped.

The entire shop was in disarray. Smashed bottles littered the floor and mixed pools of oils and other liquids shimmered in a rainbow sheen. Papers and scrolls lay in crumpled heaps. Shelves had been pulled down from the wall. Even the curtains were torn and ripped.

"What the—"

Sydney darted behind the counter, fear clutching her heart. She half-expected to see Brigid's cold dead eyes staring up at her but the floor was empty.

"Lila, this is bad."

"No shit. Is your aunt here?"

"I hope not. I'll check the back room." She did. Even though the containers and barrels in the storage room were smashed and broken, there was no sign of Brigid.

Lila eyed her as she emerged. "Nothing?"

"No. She's not here, which is good, but there's no blood or anything else. Let's go to the cottage. Her house, I mean. It's right behind the shop."

They left the shop and walked around the stone building. Beyond lay a cozy-looking bungalow built into the trunk of the immense oak.

A flood of memories washed over Sydney. The small dwelling had been her home for years.

No. Find Brigid first. Time for memories later.

Sydney approached the house with trepidation. The door seemed closed but swung open as soon as Sydney touched it. She stepped inside. The scene inside the home—*her* home—was much the same as the apothecary shop. Furniture had been overturned and belongings thrown about.

She and Lila checked each of the rooms, all of which had been tossed. But there was no sign of Sydney's aunt.

Sydney paused in the room that had been hers. The footlocker that belonged to her mother was still there, though the lid was open. Like everything else, it was a complete mess. She knelt and absently picked through the belongings. They had been scattered carelessly, stepped on, smashed, or ruined. A jewelry box lay overturned and empty.

Sydney sorted through the footlocker with growing dismay. At the bottom of the locker, her fingers encountered a thin metal disk. She pulled it out, revealing a plain copper pendant on a brass chain. Sydney hoisted the pendant. It rotated slowly on its chain. Both sides of the pendant bore an engraving of a kite shield.

One of their trinkets. I wonder what this one does. Figure it out later. She pocketed the pendant and resumed searching.

Her hand fell on the tattered remains of a shawl. It had been her mother's. Jenna would sit in front of the fire, place Sydney in her lap, and wrap the shawl around the both of them. Sydney recalled many a night wrapped in both the shawl and her mom's arms. She had never felt as loved as that had made her feel.

She picked up the shredded garment and clutched it to her chest. Sydney closed her eyes but it was too late. Tears wound down her cheeks and she sobbed in silence.

"Sydney?"

She wiped her eyes. "What, Lila?"

"I checked the other rooms." Lila placed her hand on Sydney's shoulder. "No one's here. The good news is that there's no blood or any other sign that someone got hurt, just like in the shop. Maybe your aunt wasn't here when it happened."

Sydney took a deep breath, choking back her tears. The idea that Brigid had been gone when the buildings had been ransacked did make her feel better. "Okay. We still need to find her."

"That's fine but we need to get out of here."

"What? Why?"

Lila crouched next to Sydney. "Whoever did this may come back. Even if they don't, we don't want anyone else finding us here, especially the sheriff. They'll turn us over to the Clan Council, who will have too many questions we won't have the answers for."

"I...you're right. We can go."

They stood.

A dull pounding echoed from the hallway. A muffled voice reached their ears. "Open up, in the name of the Council!"

Lila grimaced. "Fucking hell. Too late."

Sydney nodded.

For us. Not too late for Brigid, I hope.

Chapter Twelve

Sydney fingered the packet in her pocket. The Councilguard had taken her knife bandolier and Lila's sword but hadn't bothered to search them further. Sydney could have had a blade under her tunic or strapped to her thigh and they never would have known.

She snorted. *Amateurs.*

The thought almost made her laugh. In just the short time she'd been in Woodhollow, Sydney felt as though both her powers of observation and her natural cynicism had grown exponentially. Working in Brigid's shop, Sydney had looked on bumbling, hapless customers as annoyances and pests—something to be endured as a matter of course. Now, she realized that she viewed incompetence as something that might get one killed. The last ten weeks had changed her perception of people and she didn't think it was for the better.

Of course, while you were off galivanting, something might have happened to Brigid.

She glanced at the guards flanking her and Lila as they trod the road towards the center of Holly Grove, to the Clan Council meeting hall. They were not the normal sheriff's deputies that patrolled the clan lands, dealing with minor crimes and were generally glorified babysitters. The Councilguard were the personal troops of each clan's elder council and generally dealt with the most serious crimes in Sylvan Valley. In terms of position and authority, they were only second to the Beechguard, who protected Beechwood Hall and the Clan Chief Council.

*A*nd *the Hearthglitter*, Sydney thought. *They protect that too, though if I could get my hands on that, I bet I could find out what happened to Brigid.*

Their ten-strong escort wore glimmering silvery mail, open-faced polished helms, and crimson capes tucked between their wings. They carried halberds in both hands and bore a look of measured determination. Though she recognized several, Sydney did not know any of them by name.

Sydney touched the packet again. She knew Lila had crumble on her too. They could probably get the magic-inducing mushroom in their mouths before the Councilguard could react. Magic use in the clans was restricted to ceremonies and war, meaning the soldiers would have no defense. She and Lila could bowl them over, take to the skies, fly away before their escort recovered.

Sydney sighed. If they did, she might never find out what happened to her aunt.

The Councilguard marched them into the center of Holly Grove. Faeries moved out of their path but watched the procession with curiosity. Sydney recognized a number of the townsfolk and tried to keep her face hidden before realizing what a futile gesture it would be. There was not another faery in Holly Grove with the gray and blue wings of an unaffiliated outsider. Cheeks aflame, she raised her head and ignored the stares, pointed arms, and whispers.

Their escort guided them to a large circular building in the center of town, nestled between the trunks of two giant elm trees. Sydney smiled a bit at the sight. In her mind, the blocky, functional buildings of Woodhollow—mostly trow and goblin-built—would never compare to curved, flowing lines of the faery structures, which were constructed to blend with the trees and landscape.

A middle-aged faery stood by the front doors. His wings flicked as they approached. "What do you have here, Lieutenant?"

"Intruders at a crime scene, Sir. *The* crime scene."

Sydney stared at the man in recognition. Her stomach sank.

The man glanced at Lila, then fixed his gaze on Sydney. "I know you. You're Brigid's niece. Sydney, right?"

"Yes, Elder."

"I thought so. We were wondering what happened to you."
He motioned to the Councilguard. "You can leave them with me."

The lieutenant looked startled. "Sir?"

"It'll be fine. They're no threat." He returned his attention
to Sydney. "Are you?"

"No, Elder."

"As I thought. I'll take their weapons."

The officer hesitated. The older faery's face hardened.
"Now."

The lieutenant handed over the knife belt and sword, and
motioned with his hand. As one, the Councilguard wheeled and
marched in the direction from which they'd come. The lieutenant
gave Sydney one last flinty look before joining his companions in
retreat.

The Elder regarded Lila. "Who's your Dandelion friend?"

"I'm Lila."

"Hello, Lila. I'm Edmund. Have either of you ladies been
before the Holly Clan Council before?"

Both Sydney and Lila shook their heads.

"Well, you're in for a spectacle, then. Come in, both of
you."

He opened the door to the Council Hall and motioned them
inside. Sydney took a deep breath and stepped through the door.
Lila followed.

Bright lightstones lit the circular chamber. Four faeries sat
at a curved table in the center of the room. All four looked up as
the trio entered. The man on the far right end stood. "Is this them?"

"Yes," Edmund said.

"Where the hell are the Councilguard?" The standing man
sneered. "Pretty arrogant and stupid to dismiss them, Eddie. These
two could be dangerous."

"My call, Philep." Edmund's nostrils flared. "And for the
last time, my name is Edmund. Call me 'Eddie' again and they'll
need a dustpan to clean you up."

"Gentlemen." The faery sat at the top of the arch—the apex
of the curved table. She didn't move a muscle or raise her voice

but both Sydney's escort and the outraged member of the council stilled immediately. She continued. "Philep, sit down."

For a moment, the angry faery looked like he wanted to argue. Then the head councilwoman flicked her eyes at him. Philep sat.

She returned her gaze to the three. "You too, Edmund."

The man gave Sydney a quick nod, then rounded the table and sat on the second seat to the left of the head, directly across from the antagonistic Philep.

The head said. "Young lady, do you know who I am?"

"Yes, Ma'am. You're Elder Rowena, head of the Holly Clan Council, Protector of Holly Grove, and member of the Clan Chief Council."

"Many honorifics. They make the job sound more glorious than it really is." Rowena lifted an eyebrow. "But I am sure you didn't come back from that stinking hole that is Woodhollow to talk about my titles, did you, Miss...."

"Sydney, and no, Elder, I didn't."

"And you, you're a long way from the lands of the Dandelion Clan. Is there someone over in Verdanton that I should notify about your status?"

Lila shook her head. "No, Elder. I left the Dandelion Clan on my own. I don't have a warrant out for my arrest or anything."

"Very well. Let's get to it, then."

Edmund cleared his throat. "Sydney, where is Brigid?"

"I don't know, Elder. Lila and I came to visit her and found her shop and her house torn apart. The Councilguard found us and delivered us here."

"Yes, you were spotted approaching Brigid's shop, which has been declared a crime scene. Your aunt has been missing for several days and her business and residence were discovered in the state they are in." He paused. "Why did you return from Woodhollow to Holly Grove?"

"I'd been away a while and wanted to visit. Lila is my friend and said she would come with me, for company and safety."

"That's it?"

Sydney nodded. "That's it."

Elder Philep pulled his lips back in a sneer. Sydney thought it might have been his default expression. "And we're supposed to just take your word for that? You were caught red-handed at a crime scene. You are a known criminal, keeping company with known criminals. In fact, your entire family has always been shady."

Sydney bit back a sharp retort.

Philep slapped a hand on the table. "Based on those facts alone, I think you ought to both be remanded to the Councilguard and held until we can decide what to do with you. Perhaps we could even call in the Beechguard and let them...encourage these two to tell us the truth."

"Overplaying your hand," Edmund said with a chuckle. "But subtlety was never your strong point, Philep. Give the histrionics a rest."

"You dare?"

"Damn right I do."

Philep snarled. "Edmund, I'm going to—"

"Shut up, Philep." Rowena said. "We don't jail our own without proof. Your personal issues with her family are immaterial. Do you understand? Now sit there and be quiet."

Philep glowered but said, "Yes, Elder." He slumped back in his chair, his face a thundercloud.

Sydney spread her arms. "Elder Rowena, I don't know what to tell you. I am in the dark. All I care about is finding Brigid."

"Very well. You are free to go, if for no other reason than Brigid went missing before you were spotted in Holly Grove. I expect that if we have further questions, or feel you can shed light on the matter, that you will make yourself available." Rowena frowned. "I don't think I need to tell you that you'll be watched the whole time you're here. We have, of course, heard rumors about the...the perversions of magic that your sister Marla practices in Woodhollow. I don't know if it or any of the other things we hear about your gang of thugs are true but we don't want any of that activity in Sylvan Valley. Is that absolutely clear?"

Sydney flushed. "Yes, Elder, very clear."

"We'll adjourn for now, then. Philep, stay for a moment, please. I require your assistance with a small matter."

Philep nodded, though his hate-filled eyes lingered on Sydney.

The council members stood. Philep and Rowena went through a door in the back. Two others moved to the side to converse in subdued voices.

Edmund approached. "Well, that wasn't so bad."

"Not so bad?" Lila's voice was a hiss and her fingers trembled. "What the hell was that guy's problem? It's like he wanted to kill us himself."

"Philep has certain problems with Sydney's family. He's a little outspoken about it."

"How does some fucking jerk like that get on a Clan Council?" Lila snapped. She did a double-take at Edmund and her face paled. "I'm sorry Elder, I didn't mean to offend."

Edmund raised his hand to stop her. "No, you were right. Philep is, and always has been, a complete piece of shit. But he's a piece of shit with family connections in this clan." He dropped his hand. "Let's take a walk before Rowena finishes stalling him."

They left the council chamber. The sun drifted towards the western horizon. "Do you two have a place to stay?"

"No, Elder," Sydney replied. "To be honest, I expected we would stay with Brigid."

"Please. When we're outside the chamber, it's just 'Edmund.' I have a room you two can share for a night or two."

"Okay, Edmund." Sydney hesitated as a pair of Holly faeries walked past them in the other direction. She recognized one as a long-time customer at Brigid's shop and returned the woman's nod of greeting. When they were past the two, she continued. "To be totally honest, I'm surprised you're so friendly with me. Given our history, I figured you'd want to burn me at the stake as much as Philep."

"Why? Because your aunt stood me up? Left me holding the bag, as it were, and chose not to marry me and instead went to take care of her sister's orphaned kids?"

"Yeah, that."

A knowing smile settled on his face. "I didn't agree with Brigid's reasons then and I still don't. I know that she suddenly went from being a free agent to being part of a package deal. I didn't care, you know. I would have been happy to have you all in my life. But Brigid wanted stability for you girls. Between the loss of your parents and adjusting to living with her, she thought adding a strange new man would be too much for you and Marla to take all at once. So she walked away. Because I love her, I didn't fight her. It hurt but I let her go because I wanted her to be happy with her choices."

"I'm sorry, Edmund. I didn't know all that. She only said you and she had a parting of ways. You must have really loved her."

"Still love, Sydney. I never stopped." His smile vanished. "Which is why I really want to know what happened to her."

"That's all I want but so far it's just been frustration," Sydney said. She chuckled humorlessly. "I even had this crazy notion of sneaking into Beechwood Hall, stealing the Hearthglitter, and using it to figure out where she is."

"That *is* crazy," Lila noted.

"You assume it would work for you," Edmund said with a smile.

"Legend says any faery can pick it up and use it," Sydney protested.

"But only if they are pure of heart and their intent is pure of heart. Are you that pure, Sydney?"

"Don't answer that," Lila said.

"Why not?"

"I don't want to get hit by the lightning that strikes you when you lie and say yes."

Edmund laughed.

Sydney grumbled.

They walked in silence until they reached Edmund's spacious cottage. His home was built into the side of a hill. Curving stonework walls blended with the flow of the land and a sloped tiled roof of red slate completed the ensemble.

"It's not much," Edmund said, "but it's home."

"Very nice, Edmund. Brigid always said we should stay away from your home because we'd remind you of what you lost.

He nodded. "Sure. Besides, I only think about her every day, so I doubt that would have made it any worse. I'm sure she didn't want me working on you or Marla, to change her mind. I suspect she wouldn't want me talking to you even now."

Sydney elbowed Lila. "You're gawking."

"Sorry. I grew up in a house half this size and shared a room with three siblings. The only time I've ever had my own room was in The Log before you came."

"You want me to move out?"

"Nah." Lila giggled. "Even with your snoring, you're fun to have around."

Sydney frowned. "I don't snore."

"Yeah, okay."

They followed Edmund inside. The front room contained carved wooden furniture, including several comfortable-looking padded chairs and a thick woven rug.

"Kick off your boots and sit for a moment, ladies." He hooked their weapon belts on a coat-rack peg near the door. "Can I get you anything?"

"No, I'm fine," Sydney said as she sat.

"No, thank you," Lila echoed. She plopped down in a soft chair with a sigh.

Sydney rubbed her knees. "Edmund, is Philep going to cause any trouble for us?"

"Not as long as you stay with me. He blusters a lot but he knows what will happen if he starts something with me."

"And he knows this how?"

"Experience," Edmund said with a grin. "He tried to get a little physical some few years ago. That was a mistake on his part and he sported the bruises to prove it. He knows how I feel about Brigid and he hates anyone associated with your family. Philep still hasn't gotten over your mother jilting his son."

Lila sat up straight. "His son was that Demetrius guy you

told me about?"

"Yeah. I told you he's had it out for my family ever since."

"That he has." Edmund lit a small fire in the fireplace. When he had it crackling to a nice steady warmth, he sat across from them. "So, why did you really come back to Sylvan Valley?"

"I came to see Brigid."

"I believe that but there's something else, isn't there?"

"I don't know what you mean."

Edmund sighed. "Sydney, we can do this dance if you want but as far as I'm concerned, it's a waste of time. Brigid came to me with a problem just before she vanished."

"What kind of problem?"

"What do you know about the Nightshade Clan?"

Sydney's skin went cold. "That's just a myth."

"You don't believe that."

She glanced at Lila, who had gone deadly pale. Sydney took a deep breath. "Okay, let's assume that's true. What does it have to do with Brigid?"

"She had a visitor at her shop a few weeks back. A faery but hooded and cloaked. Even though she never got a look at his face, Brigid thought he was familiar. Before she could figure it out, he backed into the shadows right before her eyes and vanished."

"There has to be more to it than that, Edmund."

"Of course there is." His eyes bore into hers. "The stranger was asking about you. He wanted to know where you were."

"Why?"

"Who knows? But believe me, his questions about you scared Brigid quite a bit. That's why she came to me."

Lila leaned forward. "I don't understand. Why did she come to you? What do you know?"

"She came to me because she can trust me, even with everything that's happened between us."

Sydney nodded. "Like you said to me, though, there's something more. Right?"

Edmund shifted his gaze to the fire. For a few moments, he said nothing. Just as Sydney opened her mouth to speak, Edmund said, "Because I was one of them. I was a Nightshade."

Sydney gasped. "Bullshit."

"Not exactly."

Edmund stood and moved behind his chair. He stared into Sydney's eyes. He was still staring into her eyes as he discorporated. Fragments of his body wisped away, like shreds of fog before a morning breeze. A heartbeat later he was gone.

Sydney's mouth went dry. "What the f—"

"Behind you."

The voice whispered just a millimeter away from her ear. Sydney catapulted from her chair and almost fell into the fireplace. She grabbed for her knives before realizing they weren't around her torso.

Edmund stood behind her seat, his face somber. His red and pink wings had darkened, replaced with the yellow-tinged black ones she knew from legend. "Don't feel too bad. Seeing the shadowdance up close unnerves a lot of people." He felt the chair where Sydney had been sitting. "I'll give you credit, though. You didn't pee yourself."

Edmund closed his eyes and gritted his teeth. His fingers trembled. The black color flowed from the wing membranes, seeping away as though draining from a punctured waterskin. A moment later, his wings glowed with their previous red and pink hues.

He opened his eyes and exhaled. "Every time I use those old skills, it gets just a little bit harder to force the transformation back. And more painful."

"Damn," Lila whispered. Her wide eyes stared at Edmund.

Sydney found her voice. "How?"

"Like I said. Nightshade. At least, I was. Still have some of the skills, if not the taint in my soul." Edmund sighed and took a seat. "Now, let's talk."

*   *   *   *   *

Sydney landed on the road, a good mile or more outside Woodhollow. A second later, Lila landed next to her. "I don't want to get any closer in the air."

"Good thinking." Lila pointed to a pair of drakes circling over the nearest gate. "Getting charbroiled would be a hell of a homecoming."

"Yeah. Besides, the walk will give me a few extra minutes to sort some shit out in my head."

"Like telling Marla that your aunt is missing? Or that the man that was almost your uncle is a member of a sect of spies and assassins, that we've always thought were just a legend?"

"Yeah, all that. Jeez, Lila. Belabor it a little more, why don't you?"

"Just keeping you on your toes, buddy."

Sydney swung her arms to loosen her shoulder muscles. "What did you think about all that stuff Edmund told us?"

Lila shrugged. "I don't know Edmund, so I don't know."

"Well, I believe him when he says he doesn't know what happened to Brigid."

"Okay." Lila hesitated. "What *are* you going to tell Marla?"

"The truth—at least, what little I know of it."

They passed under the arched entry of the Pine Gate. Sydney tried to keep her face passive as they strode past the ogre guards, but the bored-looking sentries didn't so much as glance at them.

The Log's tavern had a moderate crowd but no one paid attention as they entered. The faeries by the back door—Anders and a talkative lady named Vivian—nodded to Sydney as she and Lila went past.

Dana met them as soon as they entered the workshop. Her demeanor was calm as ever. "Glad to see you made it back."

"You sound like you're surprised we did."

"Relieved is more like it. Come back to Marla's office."

Marla was not alone. As usual, Sydney's sister sat behind her desk. She faced the magical screen on the back wall and stared at the relative tranquility of Bayberry Square.

Beside the desk was a somewhat older faery. Her short brown hair hung straight to her collar, and her eyes were a piercing blue. She stood with a somber face and folded arms. Her red and pink wings marked her as one of the Holly Clan.

Sydney stood dumbstruck for a moment. Her voice fell to a whisper. "Brigid?"

"Hello, Baby Girl."

Sydney launched herself at her aunt and flung her arms about her. "Brigid, you're okay!"

"Of course I am."

"What happened?"

Brigid sighed. "It's a long story."

"And not a pretty one," Marla said. "I'm glad you two made it back. I wasn't sure you would."

Sydney gave Brigid one more squeeze before releasing her. She placed both palms on Marla's desk and leaned forward. "And why is that?"

Marla swiveled her chair to face the others. She ground out her cigar. "Someone in the Nightshade Clan wants us dead. And that's not the worst of it."

"What?" Lila burst out. "How much worse can it get than that?"

"They may be working with the Cons."

ACT TWO

COMPLICATIONS

Chapter Thirteen

Sydney's head whirled. *The Cons? And the Nightshade Clan?*

Marla said, "Lila, you look beat. Why don't you get some rest?"

"Uh, sure." Lila glanced at Sydney and left the room. Dana followed, closing the door behind her.

Fatigue gipped Sydney. She slumped into a chair. "Brigid, we thought something happened to you."

"Just because I wasn't home?"

"No, because someone tossed your shop. And your house."

Brigid sighed. "That's unfortunate but I guess I'm not surprised. How bad was it?"

"Pretty bad." Sydney faced her sister. "Marla, whoever it was also trashed Mom and Dad's stuff. The footlocker was a mess."

Tears clouded her eyes. "They destroyed everything. They even tore up Mom's shawl."

Marla stared at the surface of her desk, her face morose. "Was there anything you could save?"

"Not really. It's gone." Sydney choked back a sob. "It's all gone."

"Okay, enough of that," Brigid declared.

"Brigid—"

"Don't 'Brigid' me, Sydney. I know what you're thinking but at the end of the day, those things are just that: things. We all still have the memories of your parents and the wonderful people they were. Whoever did this can't take that away. I know Jenna and Max would not want you sitting around moping because some objects got ruined."

Sydney felt a surge of anger and was half out of the chair before she caught the look on Brigid's face. Her aunt's cheeks were still and her mouth relaxed...but there was a tightness around her eyes that spoke of anguish and loss. In a flash, Sydney's ire vanished.

She feels it, too, and it's not the first time. How often? How often did she push down her own grief and despair over her little sister's death, because Marla and I needed her?

Sydney completed her motion and embraced Brigid in a bear hug. Brigid's arms encircled Sydney's shoulders, pulling her close. Her pain receded, replaced by overwhelming love. She was only vaguely aware of Marla joining their embrace. Brigid held the three of them close and they stood together for several long minutes.

As Marla pressed into her, the copper disk Sydney rescued from her parents' footlocker jabbed Sydney in her thigh. In the rush of events, she had forgotten about it. Before she could say something, Brigid took a step back and gave voice to a throaty chuckle

"You girls are too big to maul me like that. You just about squeezed the breath out of me."

Sydney smiled and returned to her seat, as did Marla. Brigid took her own seat.

Sydney ran her hands over her trousers, fingering the pendant. *Later.* "Brigid, what's this about the Nightshade Clan? I always thought they were a myth, and even given recent events, it still seems far-fetched as hell."

"No," Brigid said. "They are quite real. Unfortunately."

"Why do they want us dead?"

"I have no idea. I was in my shop a few weeks ago when I had a visitor."

"I know all that. Elder Edmund told me."

Brigid narrowed her eyes. "Why were you talking to Edmund?"

"The Councilguard found Lila and me at the house and took us in, on suspicion of having something to do with your disappearance. Philep wanted to lock us up and throw away the key. Fortunately, Rowena and Edmund put a stop to that."

"He always was a jerk, even before what happened between Jenna and Demetrius."

"Edmund bailed us out of there and took us to his place. He told us you'd had a visitor—a Nightshade-type-of-visitor—and that you had come to him."

"I see. Is that all he told you?"

"No. He told me you and he were lovers once and even though he wanted to marry you, you left him to take care of Marla and me."

Marla sucked in a sharp breath.

Brigid nodded, though she refused to look in Sydney's eyes. "True, though it was a bit more complex than that."

"I know why you went to him, Brigid. He's a Nightshade—or, ex-Nightshade, as he tells it."

"He told you that?"

"He did more than tell me. He faded into the shadows and popped up behind me before I could react. If he wanted to kill me, he could have done it without a problem."

Marla's eyes widened. "I bet that scared the crap out of you."

"Of course it did, but I must be a veteran hooligan now. I didn't faint or anything. His wings changed to black when he did it but he was able to force them to change back to Clan colors, though it looked painful. I guess without those, no one would suspect him."

"Yes," Brigid said. "He said their wings turn black during the rituals that corrupt their hearts and convert them into emotionless killing machines, though I understand they can mask the colors for short time with magic."

Brigid's voice cracked. "I guess Edmund had to work hard to get both his wings and his soul back."

"No kidding." Marla dug in her desk drawer, hefted a fresh cigar, and lit it.

"You shouldn't be smoking, Marla."

"I do a lot of things I shouldn't do, Brigid." Marla blew out a smoke ring. "Don't change the subject. A Nightshade on the Clan Council? That would be quite a scandal. You think Rowena knows about it?"

"I am sure she does," Brigid said. "She's pretty smart and she has spies all over Sylvan Valley, not just in the Holly Clan lands. I wouldn't be surprised if she knows who all the Nightshades are."

Sydney took a deep breath. "Put aside Edmund for a second. What is this about the Cons and the Nightshades working together?"

Brigid cleared her throat. "Edmund told you a stranger visited me, right?"

"Yes."

"It was a few weeks ago. He came in at the end of the day and even though it was fairly warm that day, he wore a cloak and a hood."

"What color were his wings?"

"The cloak covered his back, so I couldn't tell. Anyway, he came in and stood in front of the counter without speaking. I greeted him and asked if I could help. He said nothing and I admit, it made me nervous. While he stood there and I watched him, getting a little more anxious each moment, something about him felt familiar. I couldn't place it. Before I could, he asked me about you, Sydney."

The hair on the back of her neck stood up. "What about me?"

"He wanted to know where you were. No pretense, no introduction. He just said, 'Where's Sydney?' That set me back a little. I told him you weren't there and asked him what he wanted with you. He didn't answer me. I started to lose my nerve a little. I opened my mouth to tell him to get lost before I called the sheriff. Before I could get a single word out, he stepped back into a shadow and—" Brigid grimaced. "—melted away."

"Melted?"

"That's the best word I could use to describe it."

Sydney nodded, remembering Edmund's demonstration. "Then you went to Edmund?"

"Darn right I did."

"Because he used to be a Nightshade?"

Brigid blushed. "Yes. Because he knows them, knows their ways. Most faeries think they're just ghost stories or that it's some underground conspiracy. But I know they're real. I've always known."

Marla placed her cigar in the ashtray. "So you went to him knowing he would help you because he's still enthralled with you. You went to play on his love, right? Kind of low of you, Brigid."

"I suppose I deserved that. And yes, I was scared for me and for the two of you. I...I've always known how Edmund felt, so I yes, I went there counting on him to protect me. Don't think too bad of me, girls. I do love Edmund but the times just didn't work in our favor."

Sydney shook her head. "If you say so. What did he tell you? He was pretty close-lipped with Lila and me, other than explaining to us some basics about what happened. You skipped out on him, again, and he had no idea where you went."

"I came to Woodhollow to warn you and Marla. It was only after I got here that I realized that you had gone back to Holly Grove to look for me. I am sorry I wasn't there for you."

She leaned over and took Sydney's hand in her own. "Baby Girl, had I known you were coming, I would have waited, no matter how scared I was."

"That's fine, Brigid. I'm just glad you're all right." Sydney squeezed her aunt's hand and released it. "Now what is this about the Nightshades and the Cons?"

"Well," Marla said, "when you and Lila left, I heard that you were being tailed by a couple of Cons. A pure thug named Bartley, and Seamus."

Sydney suppressed a shiver. "Oh, yeah. *That* asshole."

"The two of them shadowed you and Lila all the way to Sylvan Valley."

Sydney frowned. "How do you know that?"

"They followed you, I had Will follow them. I gave him a huge wad of crumble. He kept me informed via the demon tube."

"Thanks, Marla, that's great. Maybe next time, just dangle me at the end of a fishing pole as bait. "

"I was looking out for you, dumbass. Will had so much mushroom he could have leveled an entire pack of Cons and, as far as I know, they can't access their caches in Sylvan Valley, so they were cut off from their magic. You were as protected as I could make you, so don't get your underpants in a bunch, if you even bothered to wear any."

"Now, now, girls," Brigid murmured.

Sydney fought back her irritation. "Okay, Will was following the guys following us."

Marla rolled the cigar from one side of her mouth to the other. "He lost them about the time they reached Holly Grove so I had him come back. I could have had him go to the sheriff but like a lot of the gang, Will has warrants out for his arrest in Sylvan Valley. I had to trust you and Lila could take care of yourselves. I didn't think two Cons would want to stir up the entire clan and the deputies are relatively competent, if naive, so I had to hope for the best."

"All right, Marla. That makes sense, even if I don't agree with it."

"The day after Will came back, Brigid showed up here at The Log, with her disturbing news about the Nightshades. So we just sat tight." Her face softened. "Believe me, Syd, I was very glad to see you two walk back in that door. I'd miss you if something happened to you."

A small smile lit Sydney's face. "I bet it hurt to say that."

Marla snorted. "I'm pretty sure the Cons were the ones that thrashed Brigid's shop."

"I agree," Brigid said. "From what Edmund told me, the Nightshades are much more subtle."

"Or they just let us think that and framed the Cons." Sydney crossed her legs. "What were they looking for?"

"Information on us, I'm sure," Marla said.

"But what could they find that a Nightshade couldn't?"

Brigid stirred. "Sydney, Marla and I have been talking."

"Obviously."

"Don't be a smart-alec, Baby Girl. Even if these Cons and Nightshades are working together, they may not be sharing information. Everything Edmund told me is that the Nightshades aren't above using people to do their dirty work or even just muddying up the water to keep the focus off them. That may be all this is."

Brigid made a face. "Marla admits you all are making drugs and the Cons are trying to horn in on it. If that's true, they may be working together for mutual benefit."

"But why?" Sydney spread her hands. "Why do they have such an interest in us anyway?"

Brigid hesitated. Sydney spotted her aunt's facial expression. "Spit it out, Brigid."

"I think it has something to do with the designs your parents collected."

"Why now? Those laid dormant for years."

"Until you brought them to Marla."

Sydney slowly turned her head towards her sister. "Marla?"

"I may have built a few things that drew their attention."

"What kinds of things?"

"Weapons, Syd. The kind of weapons I'm trying to build threaten them."

Brigid gripped the arms of her chair with tense fingers. "I told you not to screw around with those things. I *told* you."

Sydney ignored the older woman. "Who else knows about this?"

"Just Dana."

"You weren't going to tell me?"

"I knew you wouldn't approve," Marla said, looking away.

"Of course I don't approve! Why would you do this?"

"Because we need them!" Marla slammed a fist on her desk. She exhaled and leaned back in her chair. Her expression relaxed. "Syd, I know you've only been here for a few months or so and things have been going well. They haven't always. Every time we start to get a leg up, we get smacked down again. The

Cons, the Hobs, the Dryads...they've all taken their potshots at us. The faery gang was the laughing stock of Woodhollow's underworld for years. The only reason we held onto The Log as long as we did was because of Natasha packing the tavern."

Marla took a deep breath. "Now, since I took over, I've had more success than failure but it's been on a razor's edge. I always feel like we're just inches away from the next disaster. Frankly, that's one of the reasons I've been so eager to listen to you, Syd. Your mind is so damn quick and you always seem to come up with winning answers, without even trying hard."

"Okay. If I go along with that, then hiding information about weapons you're building from your smartest advisor is a dumb thing to do. How can I advise you if I don't know what the hell you're doing?"

Marla glared at the table for a moment. "Fair point."

Sydney tilted her head. "How close are you?"

"I'm not. A minor success or two but none of them are anywhere near ready. I've had to keep it all off the books and that's slowed me down."

"Why the secrecy?"

"Partly to keep you from riding my ass about it but mostly because I'm breaking my own rules. I'm using gang funds for the research—funds that should be dispersed to the members." Marla sighed. "If you want to be really strict about it, I'm embezzling from the company. Some in the gang would understand but a lot would be pissed over it, with good reason."

"You really can be a titanic bitch."

"If I can make this work, I'll wear that title with pride."

Sydney fought to control her temper. "So what exactly are you doing? And why is it a threat to the Nightshades?"

"Because the rings I am trying to develop would allow us to not only use magic without mushroom crumble, they would also allow us to detect magical use instantly. It would keep the Cons from ever being able to get the drop on any one of us." Marla's eyes were intent. "We'd never have a repeat of the Bell Street Massacre again."

Brigid nodded. "I am sure that's what the Nightshades fear.

If you can get the rings working, I doubt they would be able to use their shadowdance skill to ever ambush a wearer. They see that as a major threat. I suspect they are just using the Cons as muscle."

Sydney's brow furrowed. "If that's the case, why haven't they simply showed up and slaughtered us all before you *do* get them to work. They could slip in here and kill everyone in the gang in a matter of moments, then destroy the plans."

"I don't know," Brigid admitted.

"There's something we're missing," Sydney said, scratching her chin.

"Like what?"

"I don't know. It'll come to me eventually." She looked at her aunt. "Brigid, how well do you know Edmund?"

"Well enough, I've loved him for years. Wait, Sydney, you don't suspect Edmund, do you?"

"It occurred to me."

"Well, un-occur it. I trust him. He hasn't been part of the Nightshades for two decades."

"So he says."

Brigid scowled and started to reply but Marla spoke first. "We'll have to figure that out later. Sydney, I am sure you're tired."

"What?"

"I think you need to relax. Take the rest of the day off."

"You just want me out of the way so you and Brigid and can continue to shut me out."

Marla nodded. "Basically, yes. So would you give us a few minutes, please?"

A sudden wave of exhaustion rolled over Sydney. Not physical fatigue but mental and emotional. She was tired of the sneaking, the fighting, the secrets being kept between kin. Just as she thought she had found her footing in Woodhollow, she realized she still didn't know Marla at all—and worse didn't have her sister's trust.

She says she wants me around. Does she want me? Or just my ideas? The notion hurt worse than she thought it might. *And Brigid...how am I going to believe any of them again?*

"Fine. I'll go entertain myself. Whatever secrets you two want to trade while I'm gone, just try not to let them get me killed."

She ignored Marla's frown and Brigid's stricken face and left the room.

Dana hovered near the outer office door. "Sydney, what—"

"Marla will be in there with Brigid for a bit longer."

"Do you know how long she'll be?"

Sydney stared at the older faery. By Dana's expression, Sydney never would have guessed the woman was keeping anything from her. "Dana, you will have to ask her that yourself."

She brushed past Dana and went to her room. She dreaded Lila's inevitable questions but fortunately, her friend wasn't there.

Sydney kicked off her boots and slung her knife bandolier on a wooden wall peg. She laid on the bed, laced her fingers behind her head, and stared at the ceiling.

Chapter Fourteen

"Hey, Vivian."

The faery looked up from her workbench. A pile of uncut gems lay in front of her. "Hey, Sydney. How you doing? Been well?"

"Good." Sydney glanced about. The workroom was otherwise empty. "I need to go out for a bit and since Marla said no one goes out alone, would you mind going with me?"

"Go out? Well, I suppose I could. I mean, I should finish sorting these gems so Dana can run them to the fence. But I guess that could wait if you wanted to go out now. Where do you need to go? What's up?" Vivian's crimson-streaked pale green wings trembled as she spoke.

Sydney sighed. Vivian's wings marked her as one of the Ivy Clan, which was on the far side of Sylvan Valley from Holly Clan lands. Sydney didn't know any of the clan, save Gordon and Vivian. While Gordon was calm and placid, the mid-twenties-ish Vivian was talkative, nervous, and constantly in motion—and her high-pitched voice bordered on being squeaky.

Unfortunately, she was also the only unoccupied faery currently in The Log that Sydney didn't know well, meaning she was the only one in whose company she felt comfortable.

She'd avoided Marla since the day before. She hadn't seen Brigid. Dana and Markus were out on gang business. Lila had tried to talk to her a bit. Wondering how much Lila knew of Marla's secret projects, Sydney had answered in monosyllabic statements. Lila had given up but Sydney had seen the hurt on the face of the faery she now considered her best friend.

She wanted to get out. She considered just walking out and defying Marla's dictates. But Sydney couldn't do that.

Well, it's not that I can't, she thought. *It wouldn't be very bright.*

Regardless of her differences with Marla, the danger in Woodhollow was still very real. It would be foolish to go out and about without some kind of backup, especially with Nightshades lurking about.

Nightshades. Sydney suppressed a shudder at the thought. The notion that one of the black-winged faeries could suddenly appear behind her and cut her throat before she knew the enemy was there wasn't just disturbing, it was terrifying.

She frowned at the thought. If a mythical guild of assassins wanted them all dead, they would be dead. Something about the whole affair still bothered her.

Sydney blinked and noted Vivian staring at her. She wrenched her mind back to the present and forced a slight smile to her face. "Yeah, just a little day trip. There's a wine store over by the Acorn Gate that I would like to check out. I've heard a few tavern patrons say the vintages are very good."

"All right." Vivian beamed. She tucked her loose blonde hair behind her ears. "Let me go get my knife belt and I'll meet you in the tavern. I'll ask Garth if we can take some dried meat with us so we can have something with our wine. Some beef? Maybe some pork? Okay? That sound good?"

"Uh, sure."

Vivian scampered out. Sydney gathered up the neglected gems, swept them into a work bin, and tucked the bin under the bench, to wait for Vivian to return and finish sorting.

She meandered to the tavern room. It was still before noon and as usual, the tavern was devoid of patrons. Garth stood behind the counter, wiping it down with a rag. He looked at her as she approached. "Sydney."

"Garth."

"What's up?"

"Vivian and I are going to head out for a bit."

"Girls' day out?"

"Something like that."

He paused his wiping. "Well, be careful out there. Be a shame if something happened to that tight ass of yours."

Sydney looked at him, startled. But Garth only grinned at her. She relaxed. "You pervert, you're old enough to be my father."

"I'm not your father," he said with a leer. "But I could be your daddy."

Sydney laughed, in spite of herself. "Maybe another time."

"Ah," he said, with a touch of mock regret, "us old guys are always left out of the fun."

"I'm sure Dana would be happy to entertain you. She's about your speed."

"She's married to her job."

"So are you."

He smiled again. "True enough."

Robin set a tray full of clean mugs on the counter. "Good grief, Garth, stop flirting with this child. You're such a dirty old bastard."

"Robin, you're just mad no one wants your tired, wrinkled old ass."

She smirked at him. "I can get all the action I want, smart guy."

"So can any slut."

She huffed and walked away.

Sydney watched her slam open the door to the kitchen. "You guys have an...interesting relationship."

"Trust me, Sydney, it's just how we show our affection. We've been insulting each other since we were kids. Not so different than you and Marla. Just a little more vicious."

Sydney nodded, not trusting herself to answer. Thoughts of Marla's secrecy were still sharply painful.

Vivian came boiling into the tavern. "Garth, can I get some — Oh, hi Sydney, you're already here. Did you get something to take with us? I brought a knapsack, in case we buy something. We can put food in it too. Oh, I brought some cash, in case we find a good wine. I like wine, you know. Do you have enough money? Do you—"

"Vivian, Vivian. Slow down, okay?"

"Oh, okay."

"Garth, can we get something to eat we can take with us?"

"Sure." He pointed at the kitchen. "Help yourself."

A few minutes later, Sydney slipped a paper-wrapped pack of dried pork and apples into Vivian's pack and the two of them strode out the door.

Vivian maintained a steady stream of chatter. Sydney nodded and answered as needed, though her attention was only partly on the conversation. She kept the bulk of her attention on their surroundings.

They didn't encounter any Cons, so her mind cycled to the secondary threats. She especially eyed the dwarves, wondering if any of Scorin Sunbolt's underlings were about, nursing a grudge over Sturm and looking for a stray faery to pick off. None of the dwarves paid her any mind. She spotted a pair of wererats but the rats only glanced and nodded to her before moving off in the other direction.

"It doesn't have to be them, you know."

Sydney blinked. "What?"

Vivian jerked her chin at the retreating rats. "It doesn't have to be them. Or the dwarves. They could just as easily hire someone to come after you as do it themselves. There are all kinds of mercs in this city, so you shouldn't be looking at just our enemies or the ones mad at us. You need to keep your eyes on everything."

Sydney arched her brow. "I was that obvious, eh?"

"Yep, if one knows what to look for. I noticed you tensed up every time a rat or a dwarf walked past. I know all about the incidents with Sturm Sunbolt and the dwarf freighter and what happened with you and Gordon and the rats while you two were collecting. It's not like any of that was uncommon knowledge in the gang, you know." Vivian pushed a strand of frizzy hair behind her left ear.

She does that a lot. Nervous habit, I guess.

Vivian went on. "I'm not stupid, you know. Everyone in the gang thinks I'm dumb."

"Vivian, I never thought you were dumb."

"Just airheaded, right? It's okay, everyone does. I know I talk a lot. I always have, ever since I was a kid. Between that and the fact that I am always playing with my hair and waving my hands and saying, 'you know' all the time, and I sound like I'm ten years old, I admit I come off as a stereotypical dumb blonde. But just because I like the sound of my own voice doesn't mean I'm stupid and it doesn't mean I don't see and observe things."

Vivian looked at Sydney. "Just like I can tell there is some stress between you and Marla. Again, obvious if you look, you know? Does it have something to do with that woman who showed up the other day? Brigid, is that her name? Or was it something to do with your trip to Sylvan Valley? Do you want to talk about it?"

Sydney chuckled. "No, not just yet. But you're right, Vivian. I guess I thought you were a little more scatterbrained than you are. Sorry about that."

"Oh, you know, it's all right, I'm used to it. It's good cover. Well, if you don't want to talk about that, do you want to tell me about Markus? He seems to like you."

Sydney hesitated. "Is that common knowledge too?"

"Not as much. He doesn't brag or anything and I don't hear anyone else talking about it. But I see how he looks at you, at how he watches you when you walk across the room. He likes you a lot."

"Yeah, so I've heard."

"So what about you? Do you like him too? He's handsome and strong, you know. A lot of girls have swooned over him. He's been quite a heartbreaker to a lot of girls."

"Including you?"

Vivian smiled. "Nah. He showed me some attention when I joined the gang but I played dumb. I know, hard to imagine. Markus lost interest and moved on. He always does with girls, usually after he scores."

"A real 'love-em and leave-em' type, huh?"

"Kinda. But as far as I know, he doesn't lie and he's never

committed to anyone. He doesn't tell stories to get them in bed. I do know he hasn't been with anyone since you came to Woodhollow, so I guess you made quite an impression." She paused. "Same with Natasha, She likes you a lot, too."

Sydney stepped around a pair of arguing dark elves. "I get that, but I don't swing that way."

She left aside that thoughts of Natasha were more confusing than anything.

"Even if you did, I don't judge," Vivian said with a shrug. "Speaking of judging, what do you think...."

Vivian launched into a long diatribe about two faeries—one in the gang, one out—who were supposedly involved in a very torrid, very on-again, off-again romance. Though the love story Vivian laid out was probably exaggerated and more dramatic than the reality, Sydney relaxed and listened to her companion's rhythmic and upbeat voice with growing contentment.

Pretty easy lady to listen to. Acts like she doesn't have a care in the world.

Vivian spotted a shop selling candies and sweetmeats. She squealed in delight and dragged Sydney by the hand into the place. An elderly and somewhat portly *vila* with a wide smile and booming laugh tended their needs. He offered them samples and poked gentle fun at the faeries, saying they needed fattening up. Vivian purchased a variety pack of truffles and frosted candies. "So I can try a whole bunch of different stuff," she said, "and see which ones I like, which will be all of them because I love sweets."

Sydney laughed at that. Vivian's good mood was infectious.

The shopkeep gave them each a long hug; not a lecherous hug, Sydney felt, but the act of a happy-go-lucky old man who loved dealing with his customers.

"They're all like that," Vivian said when Sydney voiced the thought. "*Vilas*, I mean. They're house spirits, so they're all good cooks. Men or women, old or young, they're always happy and mostly fat, since they eat so well. I like dealing with them. Never a mean one in the bunch." She popped a chocolate in her mouth. "Mmmm, good stuff."

"He was right about one thing. All that sugar is going to stretch out your hips."

"Nah, I work it all off when I talk and wave my hands. Come on, let's go find this wine shop of yours."

They found the Dancing Bear Wine Shop about one city block inside the Acorn Plaza, by the gate of the same name. A battered wooden sign hung over the street, bearing a painted depiction of the store's namesake. Sydney pushed open the door and went in.

She paused in the doorway, trying to adjust her eyes to the gloom. Vivian crowded behind her and shut the door.

As she did, a tall, slender dryad in a sleeveless white gown emerged from the shadows in the corner. Her pale green skin contrasted with her lustrous chestnut brown hair. Large emerald eyes peered at the two faeries.

The dryad inclined her head. "Welcome to the Dancing Bear. I am Choy-na-Sal. What is your pleasure?"

Sydney's cheeks turned pink. The dryad's sultry voice was more suitable to a boudoir than a wine shop. "Nothing specific, thanks," she stammered. "We're just looking."

"Please," Choy said, with a sensual smile, "make yourselves at home. Try some samples and let me know if I can help you with anything."

She moved towards the back of the shop. Sydney elbowed Vivian. "I think I know why this place was rated so well."

"Good wine?"

"Sexy-voiced owner."

"That makes sense." Vivian pointed to a set of bottles on a small circular table, with corks already loosened. "Let's try some samples. I like red wines. I mean, there's nothing quite like Ascorian ale but we can get all of that we want, right? Still, I want to try a few of these. Look, here are a couple of glasses. They look clean enough."

Sydney poured two fingers of the deep red liquid into each of their glasses and handed one to her companion. "Mud in your eye, Vivian."

"You too, Sydney." They clinked glasses.

"Sydney?" Choy returned from the rear of the shop. "You are Marla's sister?"

"Yes."

"Does she know you're here?"

Choy's tone was even but there was an unmistakable menace buried inside the question. Sydney flicked her eyes at Vivian, whose brow scrunched in concern. Sydney drained her wine glass, replaced it on the table, and let her hand rest on one of her throwing knives.

Damn it. Should have made us both eat crumble before we left The Log. Stupid, Sydney.

"Of course she knows. She always knows where her people are."

Choy narrowed her eyes. Sydney returned the dryad's stare.

The shopkeep nodded. "I see. Well, ladies, I regret to tell you that I must close for an unscheduled inventory. You'll need to leave now, I'm afraid."

"Sorry to hear that. We'll be going." Sydney backed towards the door, herding Vivian behind her.

Choy stayed in the center of the floor. Her luminous eyes never left Sydney's.

They left the shop. The moment the door shut, Sydney all but collapsed. Vivian grabbed her. "Sydney, you okay?"

"Yeah, I'm fine. Lemme go, Vivian."

"Sorry." Vivian released her. "I thought you were going to keel over there. What happened? Why did she throw us out? Dryads usually aren't like that. In fact, I have never seen one be so rude. Maybe a little snotty but—"

"I don't know but she has some problem with either Marla or the gang in general. Did you see her demeanor go south when she heard my name?"

"I sure did. Her attitude changed in a flash. And that means something too, Sydney, that she knew your name. For better or

worse, you're getting known here in town." Vivian grinned. "You
should be happy. Building a reputation usually takes a long time,
you know?"

She's right. Shit.

"Let's just get back to The Log." Sydney lowered her
voice. "Did you bring any crumble?"

"Of course, I have some packs right in my pocket. Do you
need some? Do you think we need to eat it now?"

"Yes, pass me a pack and take one of your own, just in
case."

They ate the packets and started back to The Log. A troop
of ogres stomped past. One leered at Sydney but they never broke
stride.

Marla and Markus were in the tavern having an early-
afternoon ale when Sydney and Vivian entered The Log. Garth
busied himself behind the bar. Marla glanced at them. "Where'd
you go?"

"Out."

"Vivian, Dana was looking for you."

"I have some gems to sort for her. Sydney, this was a lot of
fun, even getting thrown out of the wine shop."

Sydney winced at Marla's raised eyebrow but Vivian
rambled on. She patted Sydney on the shoulder. "We'll do it again
sometime. Maybe next time we'll go to the Boardwalk. There's a
place down there where we can get some very tasty smoked fish
and fried potatoes. It's run by *vilas* too, so you know it'll be good.
Know what I mean? That sounds like a great time, doesn't it?"

Sydney gave her a weak smile. "Sounds good."

Vivian laughed and hurried out.

"You managed to get thrown out of a wine shop?" Marla
ran a finger around the rim of her ale mug. Her slight smile
conveyed her amusement.

Sydney watched Markus take a swig of his mug. His eyes
never left Sydney.

She shrugged her shoulders. "Yeah, the owner tossed us as
soon as she knew I was your sister. I guess the name 'Marla' is
poison at the Dancing Bear."

Markus coughed and spit his ale across the table.

Marla jumped to her feet so fast that on instinct, Sydney's hand fell on her closest throwing knife.

"Syd, are you insane? Dancing Bear is run by Choy-na-Sal. She's the head of the Dryad Gang! She would love to get her hands on one of my inner circle, especially my very dumb sister. You being ransomed might be the least of the bad things that could have happened."

"You never told me the Dryads were our enemies."

Marla gave her a pained look. "Sydney, they're *all* our enemies. Don't you get that?"

"Even if that's true, did you ever bother to tell me to avoid that store? Or anywhere else in particular? You just let me stumble around until I get in trouble and then tear my head off. Vivian has been here much longer and she obviously didn't know. How the hell was I supposed to? It's just one more time you kept me in the dark."

Marla glared at Sydney for a moment. She glanced at Markus. "Before either of you leave this room, make sure she knows every danger zone in Woodhollow forward and backward. If I have to listen to her mouth much longer, I'm going to lose my shit."

She spun and stomped to the back.

Markus shook his head, ignoring Garth's laughter. "Come here and sit down, Sydney."

"You know what? I'm tempted to tell you to fuck off just so I can jam my thumb in that bitch's eye. Where does she get off?"

"She's worried about you, Sydney. You scared her, is all."

"Well, she has a funny way of showing it."

Markus motioned to the seat again, so Sydney took it. He said, "Look, it's pretty simple. There really aren't that many places you need to avoid. This won't take too long."

"What about Vivian? Shouldn't she know this too?"

"Nah. She wouldn't remember it anyway."

Vivian's words, back in the street, flashed through her head. Sydney chuckled. "Sure, she wouldn't. Okay, go ahead."

Chapter Fifteen

Sydney entered Marla's office and suppressed a grumble. The inner door was closed, meaning someone was already in there.

Lila glanced up from her paperwork. "Sydney, she'll be just a moment."

"Whatever."

She folded her arms and stared into space. Lila gazed at her a second, as though she wanted to say something. Instead, she sighed and returned to her ledger.

The door opened and Dana emerged. Behind her came a broad-shouldered man dressed all in brown leather. He stood about four feet tall, though his presence made him seem much larger. His skin and hair were both a deep woody tone. His forked beard tucked into his jerkin. Only the pale green of his stocking cap and his bright blue eyes gave him any color at all. The deep lines on his craggy face told Sydney that the man's scowl was his default expression.

Brownie, Sydney thought. *What's Marla into now?*

The man followed Dana out. He walked past Sydney without looking at her.

"Syd?" Marla's voice drifted from the inner office. "Come on back."

Sydney entered the room, shut the door and flopped into the chair across from Marla's desk. She didn't speak.

Marla eyed her for a moment. "Well?"

"Well, what?"

"Syd, you need to quit being a bitch to everyone."

"I don't know what you're talking about."

Marla glared at her. Then her face softened. "Look, I'm sorry about what happened last week. I apologize for keeping secret my research on Mom and Dad's designs. And I apologize for blowing up over your trip to the Dancing Bear. Anything could have happened to you and believe it or not, I got scared. I reacted poorly and again, I'm sorry."

Then Marla's eyes narrowed and her conciliatory tone vanished. "But you have got to drop the attitude. The others are starting to notice, and not just Markus and Dana. You're impeding my authority and right now, we can afford that less than ever. If you keep it up, you're going to have to leave."

"That's right, just flush me away like last night's refuse."

Marla continued as if Sydney hadn't spoken. "I love you, Syd, and I am glad we've reconnected over the last three months. I never realized how much I missed you until you were here. But the Faery Gang is my life now. It's where I belong. If you insist on trying to upset our stability, then sister or not, I'll have to send you away, even if I have to kick your ass to do it. I don't want to do that, so please don't put me in that position. Do you understand?"

Sydney bit her lip. "Yeah, I get it."

"You're angry at me and I probably deserve it. I should have brought you in on the rings sooner because I do trust you." Marla lit her cigar. "Be mad all you want but quit taking it out on everyone else in the gang, and stop sassing me in public. You're undermining me and I won't tolerate it anymore. When we're in private, you can blister my ears to your heart's content. If you want to fight it out, we'll go somewhere and do that."

Marla smiled and Sydney thought it was free of deceit. "I'll even let you throw the first punch. Deal?"

"Yeah, Marla. Deal."

Guilt tickled Sydney's mind. She *had* been acting out, snarking at everyone that came close and performing her tasks in sullen silence. The other faeries started avoiding her, even Lila and Vivian. Sydney realized that Marla was not only dead-on in her assessment of the situation but she probably allowed Sydney more leeway than she deserved.

Sydney sighed. *I am going to need to have my head examined before all this is said and done.*

She took a deep breath. "Now that we got it settled that I've been a jerk, you wanted to see me about something?"

"Yeah. How did collections go this morning?"

"Fine. Why?"

"No issues?"

"No." Sydney frowned. "Should I have been expecting some?"

"Not really. I was just curious." Marla gave Sydney a pointed look. "And no, I didn't set you up with some piece of crap that's been giving us trouble, to see how you'd handle it. This one should have been a milk run."

"It was—and you don't need to show me any special favors."

"I didn't, it just worked out that way."

Sydney jerked her head at the door. "Who was the brownie?"

"Wulf, son of Warth. He's the head of the Brown Gang."

"Making new associations?"

Marla cracked another smile. "Yes. I heard a good idea somewhere and decided to put it into play."

"Which was?"

"To find some gangs that weren't too antagonistic to us and subcontract them to sell Shroom in their own territories. The one who came up with that plan thought that we could expand our reach without much work. We give a cut of the profit to the other gang and get a bunch of coin back without having to fight over territory or seek out buyers. All we have to do is grow the Shroom we're already growing, process and deliver it, and sit back while the money rolls in. The profit-to-effort ratio would be lovely. Even better, the person who thought of this said we should pick a non-magical gang, who wouldn't have the capability or even any idea how to manufacture their own Shroom, meaning they wouldn't be able to reverse-engineer some Shroom, discover the formula and run us out of business."

She exhaled a smoke ring. The wispy circle wafted towards the ceiling. "It's a great idea. I should probably thank the person that came up with it. A real genius, that one."

Sydney listened as a steady flush enveloped her cheeks. She'd pitched the idea to Dana a few weeks back. In reality, Sydney had been brainstorming and had free-formed the whole concept on the fly. She had no idea Dana was paying so close attention. "And Wulf?"

"I brought him here to discuss it and he's on board. He's going to take a few hours to get his folks organized and then they come back for their first shipment later today."

"Do you trust him?"

Marla laughed. "Of course not, he's a crook. But Wulf knows this will make him a ton of coin so he'll go along for now. We'll see how it works out. Thanks for the idea, Syd."

"I was just thinking out loud, really."

"That's why I keep you around."

"It is why, isn't it?" Sydney couldn't keep the downcast look from her face. "Not because I'm your sister. Right?"

Marla's smile faded. "No. Your big brain just a bonus. I really am glad you're here and I hope you believe that. Even if you couldn't do squat, I enjoy having you around."

"As long as I don't undercut you."

Marla shrugged. "We all have our limits."

Sydney changed subjects. "Did Brigid make it home?"

"Yes, I got a demon-tube-message from Donovan this morning. He and Claire will keep a good eye on her."

"I hope she's not still angry with me."

"You know, she said the exact same thing about you just before she left."

"I'm not. Do you think she'll be all right?"

Marla flicked some ashes in the ashtray. "Donovan said the first thing she did was go to see Edmund."

"I thought Donovan was wanted for crimes in Sylvan Valley."

"I thought so too. I was going to have him turn back once they were safe but Edmund said Donovan would have a temporary stay as long as he remained in Holly Grove. I guess his warrant is only out in Hedge, in Lilac Clan lands, and only for minor stealing" She grinned. "It seems he played up the extent of his crimes when he joined."

"He lied."

"I would say he bragged."

Sydney digested that. "Brigid and Edmund?"

"Edmund dragged her before the Council. I guess Philep started blustering and asking Brigid about wasting Council time on an investigation when Rowena told him to shut up again."

"Yeah, that guy. I knew he hated us but it's gotten downright vile. I don't know what changed."

"I don't either." Marla ground out her half-finished cigar and placed it in the desk drawer. "I told Claire to keep her eyes on him. We can't rule out that he's tied into all this somehow."

"You're overly suspicious, Marla."

"I believe I live longer that way."

Sydney nodded. "Okay, it's something we have to revisit if we hear anything from Claire or Donovan."

"Agreed. In the meantime, I know you were out all morning so take the rest of the day off and get some rest. We have an operation tonight and I'd like you to go."

"Another shop raid?"

"Of a sort." Marla stood and stretched.

"Who's on this one?"

"Besides you, it'll be Markus, Patrice, Vivian, Will, Kent, and Trish. And me."

Sydney blinked. "You're going?"

"I think I need to."

"It must be important."

"It is. We might have someone trying to grow their own albino mushrooms. If so, we need to shut it down."

"But not the Browns?"

"I don't think so. We'll find out tonight." Marla paused. "You think you'll be rested up enough by midnight?"

Sydney nodded. "I should be. I'm going to get some sleep, then."

"Me too, as soon as I get Wulf's conversation transcribed."

"What do you mean?"

"I use a little crumble to record all my dealings." She noted Sydney's look. "With outsiders, Syd. I can replay the conversation and write down everything. Helps me keep track of who says what."

"Probably not a bad idea."

"Not at all. It was something Tripp used to do." She snorted. "About the only good idea that old bastard had. On your way out, tell Lila she's dismissed. She'll be manning the back door tonight with Dana."

Sydney found the young secretary with her head down on the desk. Alarmed, Sydney shook her shoulder. "Lila?"

"What?" Lila sat up sharply, her wide-open eyes darting around. "Oh. Sydney."

"You okay?"

"Exhausted. I didn't sleep well."

"Something bothering you?"

Lila nodded. "Yeah, but I don't want to talk about it. You finished with Marla?"

"Yeah. She says you're done for the day. She has an op planned for tonight and wants me to go."

"I know. Give me a moment and I will walk up with you. If we sleep at the same time, we don't have to worry about waking each other up."

"I'm going to shower first."

"Good idea."

They trod up the stairs, ignoring the cheers coming from the common room. Lila snickered. "The sun isn't even down and those idiots are getting drunk."

"Drunk fools pay the bills. Besides, as we move into summer, the days will just get longer." She smiled. "No sense in waiting later and later to let them get their jollies."

"I suppose."

"Hey, Lila...." Sydney put her hand on her friend's shoulder, bringing them both to a halt. "Sorry, I've been such a jackass lately. I let things get to me and I took it out on the wrong people."

Lila smiled and patted Sydney's hand. "No problem. It happens."

"Still friends?"

"We never stopped being friends, Sydney. I just had to wait for you to pull your head out of your butt."

Sydney laughed as they resumed climbing. "I'm slow like that sometimes."

"I noticed."

After a day in the increasingly-warmer city collecting from foul-tempered debtors, Sydney felt grimy. She grabbed a towel and headed to the showers. Lila did the same.

Sydney stepped into the stall and popped a crumble packet. Warmth and power coursed down her limbs. She summoned with the storm cloud with a negligent flick of her wrist and smiled at the thought. She'd been using her magic so much that routine uses no longer required much effort.

She and Lila finished about the same time. She was just about to step out when Anders and Markus came in. Markus was in the middle of a statement but trailed off when he saw Sydney's head over the stall walls. "Uh, hi, Sydney."

She blushed. "Hi."

He hurried into his own shower stall. Sydney toweled off, trying very hard not to look at him. She suddenly wished she had a robe or something other than the towel to wrap around herself.

Markus kept his eyes on the walls as she left.

Lila elbowed her as they walked. "You want to go back and join him?"

"Uhm, no."

"Push-pull with you two, isn't it?"

"Yeah. I like him but I don't know if it's enough."

They entered their room. Lila sat on her bed. "Why isn't it enough?"

"I'm not sure he's in it for anything other than a piece of ass." Sydney shed her towel and put on a dry tunic. "Plus, you remember I told you about my folks? About how much in love they were?"

"Yeah."

"I want that, Lila. I don't have anything against people having casual flings—" She shivered as she thought of her last time with Jacob. "—but that's not what I'm looking for. I want a soulmate."

"You might be waiting a while, Sydney."

"I know. I'm willing."

"Then I understand why you're so reticent around Markus."

"Maybe I just like quiet guys like Anders."

Lila shook her head. "Sydney, Anders likes quiet guys like Anders. Notice how he didn't even glance at you in the showers."

"I thought he was just shy."

"Nope, he's got a boyfriend and everything."

"Okay. He never mentioned it."

"No," Lila said. "He's very private about his love life. You of all people should understand that."

"I do." Sydney paused. "Along those lines, here's a random thought: those unisex races like the Cons. I guess they all have to hook up with other races, right?"

"Exactly. The Cons, for example, really like dryads for some reason and they aren't shy talking about it."

"How do dryads feel about that?"

"Honestly? I think they hate it. I don't blame them." Lila shuddered, disgust etched on her face. "Why do you ask?"

"Just curious. I hadn't had a lot of dealings with other races before I came to Woodhollow. Some would stop at Brigid's shop on their way through Sylvan Valley. Dwarves and gnomes, mostly, but there were a few others. But those were brief business transactions. We didn't mix socially."

Lila nodded. "I see. I know it was frowned on in Sylvan Valley but no one in Woodhollow cares about cross-race hook-ups. You see that, right?"

"I've noticed."

"It goes to the point that the girls—and the guys, for that matter—who work down at Belles have to agree to take on all customers, regardless of race, unless it is a matter of physical danger because of, uhm—" Lila blushed. "—size difference. I mean, not everyone can take on an ogre."

Sydney snorted. "A whorehouse with a 'no-racism' clause. I've seen everything now."

"Makes good business sense, doesn't it?"

"Yeah, I admit it does."

"Zota's not quite in Marla's league with business savvy but she's pretty quick."

"Zota." Sydney arched her brows. "She runs Belles, I presume."

"Yeah. Goblin, in her sixties. Used to be a working girl herself. Pretty ugly." Lila shuddered. "But she's efficient and not a little ruthless. She's also avoided being under the thumbs of the gangs, too."

"Surprised no one has made the effort. Every time I walk past the place, it looks like the lines are around the corner. It's gotta be lucrative."

"Oh, some have tried. The Hobs, most recently. Four got killed and another dozen needed sutures and casts." Lila smiled viciously. "It's hard to put pressure on someone who can see to it that the Enforcers all get entertained for free."

Sydney frowned. "I didn't see Crol as that type."

"He's not, but his boys are." Lila yawned. "I'm gonna hit the sheets."

"Me too."

Lila doused the room's lightstone. Sydney laid her head on the pillows and pulled the sheets to her chin.

Sydney tossed and turned for an hour. She flopped on her back and stared into the darkness.

Lila's gentle snores drifted across the room. Sydney rose from her bed on silent feet, trying not to wake her friend. She donned her tunic and pants and slipped out the door.

Anders and Allie manned the tavern door. Both nodded and smiled as Sydney entered the tavern. Patrons careened back and forth with mugs in hand. Chatter and laughter filled the room.

Garth placed a goblet of raspberry wine on the bar as Sydney approached. She hefted it. "Thanks. How'd you know what I wanted?"

"Good bartenders always know," he said with a grin. "Besides, you ask for that about three of five times so I gambled."

"You did well."

Sydney had only taken a single sip when she sensed a presence at her shoulder. She glanced at the hooded figure. Her eyes widened for a split-second before she realized the figure was the wrong size.

Not nearly as big as that Nightshade.

The figure turned and winked from the depth of her hood.

Sydney gawked. "Natasha?"

"Shhh!" The singer raised a finger to her lips. "It's the only way I can walk through the tavern without being mobbed by these guys."

Garth polished a mug. "Successful trip?"

"As always."

Natasha gazed at Sydney with her sparkling eyes until Sydney blushed and looked away. The singer's laugh was throaty and rich. "Not making you nervous, am I?"

"You always do."

"Good." She touched Sydney's forearm. "I don't bite, I promise. Well, maybe I nibble a little."

"Natasha—"

"Don't worry, Sydney, I understand. Just let a girl have her dreams, okay?"

Unable to speak, Sydney nodded.

Natasha faced Garth. "I'll be back in thirty."

He glanced at the clock. "Right on time for the show, then."

Natasha wove her way through the crowd, careful to keep her head down and face hidden. Anders and Allie admitted her without a second glance.

"She's going to give me a heart attack," Sydney muttered.

"I doubt it," Garth said. "She flirts like mad but she's harmless."

"What were these trips she was making?"

"She gets her hair styled every other week, just for her shows."

"I figured she had a hot date with a girlfriend or something."

"Nope. She hasn't been with anyone for a long time—since before you arrived." Garth's pensive eyes regarded Sydney. "In fact, when she talks, its almost as if she's holding out for someone special."

Sydney drained her wine glass.

Oh boy.

Chapter Sixteen

Marla looked around the room. "Everyone got it?"

Sydney gave a quick nod. Markus, Patrice, Will, Kent, and Trish all did the same. Vivian's head bobbled up and down like a jack-in-the-box.

"Good," Marla said. "Take the back way out."

They filed to the far end of the long hallway. Dana and Lila waited by the back door. "Square is clear. Go by twos. Markus and Patrice, Trish and Kent, Will and Vivian, Marla and Sydney."

Dana darkened the lightstones, cracked the door, and peered out. "First team, go."

Markus and Patrice slithered out. Dana shut the door and silently counted.

Sydney took a deep breath. She ran her hands across her black cloth trousers. Her long-sleeved and hooded jacket, of a similar black cloth, was tucked into her pants. A pair of slits let the garment fit over her wings, though she and Marla had to help each other get their jackets on. They'd taken turns rubbing ashes on their faces and their wing surfaces until they were dull and blackened. When Sydney asked why they went with the jackets instead of the usual cloaks over their wings, Marla said, "Because the cloaks are too restricting and I'm expecting action tonight."

Sydney grunted. Her sister's answer hadn't made her feel any better. She gestured at her darkened wings. "Going to take forever to get this crap off."

"Take some extra crumble and stay in the shower a bit longer," Marla said. She left her cigars behind and Sydney realized she wasn't used to seeing Marla without one.

Marla went on. "An extra long shower will give Markus more of a chance to check out your skinny ass."

Trish and Kent openly laughed. Vivian emitted a high-pitched giggle and Will grunted. Dana only smiled.

"If you say so." After almost three months in Woodhollow, Sydney had come to realize her sister's way of coping with stress was to make incisive comments, so she let it go.

She pushed aside memories of Markus in the shower, and visions of his strong, muscular back and arms. True, he was on the operation with them but this was business, not pleasure, and in Sydney's mind, she'd become adept at separating the two. They'd both be professional.

She fingered her bandolier. All six throwing knives sat secured in place. The replacement blade satchel hung from her belt. She had hooked her long knife to the belt and strapped the scabbard to her right thigh. She'd tucked her lockpicks in her left pocket, a half-dozen packets of mushroom crumble in her right. She spent the hour before their muster oiling her boots until they barely made a sound.

Dana cracked the door. "Second team, go."

Trish slipped out. The bound bun of her dark hair swayed as she walked. She was Holly Clan; though Sydney could not recall ever having met her before coming to Woodhollow, they'd talked a bit and knew some of the same folks. She was friendly and competent. Sydney liked her.

She tried to avoid her lip curling as Kent followed Trish outside. He was from the Bramble Clan and Sydney thought him a bit of a loud-mouthed braggart. But he was strong and fast and loyal to the gang, so she kept her mouth shut.

Dana closed the door and started her count anew.

Vivian gave Sydney a mock punch to the shoulder. "Ready for some fun, Sydney?"

"Fun?"

"Of course! All these missions are great. It's so much fun to sneak through alleys, just like when I was a kid back in Shaleburg. Got into all kinds of trouble but it was always worth the whippings. Did I ever tell you—"

"Sheesh, Vivian," Sydney said. "When do you even catch your breath?"

"When I sleep."

Lila sighed and shook her head.

They waited in silence for a moment before Dana said, "Will, Vivian. Go."

Will ambled out, followed by a fleet-footed Vivian. She winked at Sydney as she exited. Dana closed the door yet again.

"Just us sisters now, Marla."

"Yep."

"Hey," Lila said. "What am I? Chopped liver?"

Sydney smiled. "A different kind of sister. A sister in a life of crime."

"And me?" Dana asked.

"Spinster aunt," Marla supplied.

"Hmpf."

Sydney's smile faded. "Marla, you sure about this?"

"Never one-hundred percent sure, Syd, but about as sure as we can be."

A baker's shop run by a goblin named Gort—at least, on the surface. The shop itself was a front. That in and of itself was nothing unusual, since half the businesses in Woodhollow were fronts for some kind of illegal activity, even if it was just a standing dice game among friends.

Marla's information stated this was a little different. Rather than something innocuous, this bakery hid a laboratory and grow field for albino mushrooms. Someone was trying to recreate Shroom.

Sydney didn't ask how Marla came by this information. She knew her sister had contacts with a lot of informants in Woodhollow, and not a few movers and shakers.

Considering their fresh deal for distribution, Lila suggested the Browns had already gotten overly greedy over it but Marla had shot that down immediately, saying that production of Shroom required a race with magical ability to detoxify it, which the Browns didn't have. Sydney agreed.

That didn't leave a lot of suspects. The Cons were magical, though she'd been told they had to be able to reach out and touch their caches, which they could only do during the day. Dryads could perform brutally strong magic if they could commune with their trees and there were plenty of them in Woodhollow too.

Sydney pursed her lips. There were a few others. *Landvaettir* and *vilas* had very minor magical skills but nothing so focused or powerful as to be able to create Shroom on a large scale. Werevixens had an innate magical talent but the foxwomen tended to be standoffish loners, not given to working together.

There were the dark elves but their magic was much more primal and raw than that of the other races. Sydney recalled from the old stories that they'd been cursed among elves and that their magic was an offshoot of that curse. It involved taking power from their own futures, which had an impact on their lifespans. She'd heard one dark elf call it, "stealing from tomorrow to save today." Most of the dark elves she'd met came across as very reluctant to use their magic for anything trivial.

That's pretty much everyone I know about. It's a short list, she thought. A stray notion bolted through her mind. *Unless—*

"Last team, go."

Marla hustled out the door, dragging a distracted Sydney behind her. The gang leader's voice was a hiss. "Syd, get your mind on business."

"What? Oh, right, sorry."

They stole across the darkened plaza. Only the lamps from a few shop windows provided any illumination in Bayberry Square. The two faeries skirted those pools of light and darted through the shadows.

Sydney trailed a few steps behind Marla. Her mind lingered on their target. When they reached an intersection, she whispered, "Marla."

Her sister glanced up both streets. "What?"

"This supposed Shroom field. What if it's none of the other gangs? What if it's the Nightshade?"

Marla nodded in the gloom. "I thought of that. It's possible."

"Then doesn't it feel like we're running headlong into a trap?"

"I don't think so. My source on this is reliable."

They skirted around a busy compound. Even at the late hour, bright lamps bathed the courtyard and outer walls in a near-daylight brilliance. Sentries patrolled the wall tops. As they passed the double gates, Sydney got a glance of an orange glow within. "Forge?"

"Yeah. Salmonika. Dwarf-owned, like every other big conglomerate in Woodhollow, though goblins do the most of the actual forging."

"Really? I thought dwarves did the best metalwork."

"Dwarves can't forge for shit, Syd. That's just a rumor they spread so they could sell their crappy products. Goblins do the best smithing I know of. I think it's because they can stand so close to the forges without torching themselves. Dwarves, and just about everyone else, would get immolated at that distance."

"Learn something new every day." Sydney gazed through the open gates. Gangs of goblins, gnomes, and trow swarmed all over, carting weapons and armor or dragging carts of ore and refuse. "They look busy."

"They are. They have an exclusive contract to supply the Enforcers and half the armies in Dylia and Ascoria. Those elves like to fight, so Salmonika runs day and night."

"I don't think I have ever been down this street, so I never noticed."

"You need to get out more." Marla pointed. "Salmonika makes some really neat shit, Syd. I even saw a goblin there do a demo with an electrified sling stone. Lots of crackles and a huge spark show when it landed."

"How's that possible? Magic?"

"I'm not an engineer. How the hell do I know?" Marla pointed. "Make a right up there."

They turned the corner, leaving the glow and ruckus of the forge behind.

They found the other six members of their party waiting in an alley down the street from the bakery. Marla huddled the gang members together. "Crumble."

Each faery popped a packet in their mouth. As always, Sydney luxuriated in the cool burst of energy firing down her limbs.

Marla shivered, evidently experiencing the same. "All is good, no change in plan. Same order."

"Gotcha," Markus said with a nod. "C'mon, Patrice."

Sydney grabbed his arm. "Markus, wait."

"What?"

"You said you watched this shop every night for the last few days, right?

"Yeah?" His voice was heavy with impatience.

"Does Gort have a habit of leaving a lightstone lit or something?"

Markus frowned. "He never has before. He's always put out his lights and been in bed by ten."

"Well, then, maybe he's having a late night." She pointed at the storefront. The faint glow within was unmistakable. The light bobbed, as if the source was moving, then settled. A moment later, it moved again.

Sydney touched her sister on the shoulder. "Marla, something isn't right here."

"Don't get all paranoid on me, Syd. It's a coincidence."

"No." A deep sense of unease settled into her gut. "This is too convenient. I think we're being set up. We have to wave off."

"No, we can—"

"Is it worth the risk? Can't we check it out further first and come back another night?"

Marla gazed at Gort's shop. "Syd, if they are making Shroom, we need to put a stop to it as soon as possible."

"Another night or two won't matter if it gives us a chance to learn more."

Markus nodded. "I agree."

"Me too, boss," Patrice said.

Will and Trish also nodded.

Marla frowned but said, "Okay. Split."

The other six faeries melted into the darkness. Markus met Sydney's eyes for a brief moment before he disappeared.

Marla rose from her crouch. "Let's go."

"Yeah."

"Use that clever brain and start thinking about how we can re-approach this, Syd." Marla flashed her a sneer. "You can't get by on your looks forever."

Sydney opened to her mouth to retort but before she could, a new sound reached her ears. She put her arm out to block Marla's path. "Wait. Do you hear that?"

"Yes." Marla's eyes narrowed. "Someone coming."

The sisters huddled in the shadows. The footsteps grew closer and two men stepped into view at the intersection.

Sydney could not suppress a shudder. It was McGee and another Con she didn't know.

The two stumbled along the street, McGee supporting the other one. The second Con slurred, "Where we headed, boss?"

"Just taking in some night sights, lad. Steady, now."

"I feel a little ill, boss." The Con staggered and would have fallen had McGee not supported him. "I didn't think I had that much beer."

McGee chuckled. "You didn't, Chauncey. I made sure you had something extra in your pint."

"Why?"

"Because I wanted to show you something."

McGee leaned Chauncey against a nearby building. He reached into a pocket and withdrew a small silver ball not much bigger than an acorn. McGee tossed the sphere into the air. The ball burst in a soft explosion of light and mist. Droplets sparkled in the brilliance. A rainbow prism of lights bathed the two Cons.

Chauncey gaped. "Ancestors be praised. That's amazing, boss. Where'd you get that?"

"Just something I had some goblin friends of mine whip up. Gives access to my cache, even in the middle of the night."

A brown clay pot topped with shimmering golden coins

materialized at McGee's feet. The Con scooped both hands into the pot and closed his eyes. "Ah, yes, just what I needed."

He dropped the coins into the pot, which vanished a second later. The light faded and the mist settled to the ground.

Chauncey levered himself off the mortar wall. His drunken eyes were wide. "That was incredible."

"Aye."

"Can I get some of those marbles?"

McGee smiled. He plucked a second orb from his pocket, flipped it in the air, and caught it in his other hand. "Now why would I want to give you one of these? Especially when I found out about your debt."

The awe fell off Chauncey's face, replaced by nervousness. "I don't know what you mean."

"Oh, sure you do." McGee stepped towards Chauncey. "The debt you earned when you took gold from the gang coffers and hid it in your own cache. That debt."

"Boss, I—"

"Shush, Chauncey." McGee put his arm around the drunk Con's shoulders. "I know you felt you deserved it, just like you felt a wee bit slighted when I passed you over to make Seamus my second in command. I understand, I really do."

McGee paused. The smile slid off his face. "But understanding and forgiveness...well, those are two different things, my lad."

A glittering dagger appeared in McGee's hand. He pivoted and rammed it in under Chauncey's ribs. The meaty thunk echoed in Sydney's ears. She winced.

Chauncey's eyes widened. He gripped McGee's shoulders. His mouth opened but no sound emerged.

McGee lowered him to the cobblestones. Chauncey gurgled something unintelligible.

"Chauncey, I'd be lying if I said this upsets me. You've been a pain in my arse ever since you arrived in Woodhollow, with the non-stop complaining and shirking your duty. That wasn't enough to punch your ticket. But stealing from the gang—your *family*, Chauncey—that's over the line."

McGee straightened. He wiped his blade on Chauncey's jacket. "But look at the bright side, lad. You have a chance to repay your debt to the gang. How? Because your death will be laid at the feet of those wingers, that's how."

Chauncey wheezed. He strained to sit upright, then slumped limply to the street. His vacant eyes stared at nothing.

Sydney opened her mouth to whisper something when she felt *it*. The sensation crawled over her skin like a spider and in spite of herself, her whole body spasmed.

Marla shuddered as well. "Shit, he found us."

McGee whipped his head towards their hiding place. "Ah, there you are. I knew you were here somewhere." He laughed. "That mushroom field we were supposed to be growing? Pure bollocks. But I'm happy to note you're as predictable as ever, Marla."

Marla stood and emerged from the alley. "Cut the crap, McGee. You just killed one of your own in the middle of the street. No way we'll take the blame for this. Crol will never buy it."

"I'll risk it, especially since I plan to add a winger corpse to make it look good."

She didn't see the attack as much as feel it. Sydney hurled herself to the ground as flame crackled overhead. The dry heat of the scorching air contrasted with the cold damp of the cobblestones and dull amusement invaded her mind, that she would even notice such a thing in the moment.

Graceful and agile as an acrobat, Marla dove away from the attack. She rolled to her feet with her sword in her hand and lunged at McGee, murder in her eyes.

The Con leader backpedaled, dodging her stab. He thrust his hand towards her, palm out. The air rippled and a gale burst from his hand. Marla staggered under the blast but raised her sword and hacked at McGee again.

Sydney hopped to her feet. She yanked a throwing knife from her bandolier and gauged her throw.

Marla spun away from another gout of fire. McGee followed, exposing his back to Sydney.

She hurled the blade at the spot between his shoulder blades.

Just as she thought it would sink into his skin, McGee whirled, shot out his hand, and plucked the blade from the air as if it were standing still.

McGee grinned at Sydney and backhanded a charging Marla without looking back. "Nice try, darling, but you're not that fast."

Sydney forced her shaking fingers to draw another blade. "Don't worry, asshole. This one has your name on it."

"As much as I'd love to keep this up," McGee said with mock sincerity, "it's time to move this along."

With that, McGee raised Sydney's knife and plunged it into his own shoulder.

Sydney's mouth fell open. "What the—"

"Help! Help!" McGee yelled. He hunched over and clutched at the blade lodged in his arm. "The faeries are attacking me, right on the street!"

"No, you attacked us, we—"

Marla darted to the alley. Blood covered her lips. "Forget it, Syd. Run, just run!"

Galvanized by Marla's words, Sydney sprinted away from the wounded Con. She was aware of the boot slap of leather behind her. She hoped it was Marla. Sydney ignored stealth, she ignored the possibility of encountering a patrol. She simply fled, leaving the Con shrieking behind them.

She wasn't sure how long she'd been running when a pair of hands grabbed her and pulled her to a stop. She made to fight them off but Marla's voice cut across her resistance. "Syd! Knock it off."

"Let go of me."

"Quiet!"

The fight went out of Sydney. She let Marla manhandle her into an alley, where the older faery shoved her into a pile of garbage. Stench invaded her nose and Sydney gagged.

Marla's voice was a hiss. "Syd, if you don't shut up, I'm going to cut your tongue out myself."

A dark shape glided between her and the night stars, followed by another. Sydney took a deep breath and lowered her voice to a whisper. "Drakes?"

"What else? Why do you think I wanted you to be quiet?"

Sydney inhaled again and it was only then she realized she was panting. She tried to slow down her breathing and shot an accusing glare at Marla. "You aren't even breathing hard."

"Crumble," Marla said. She never took her gaze from the sky.

"Why didn't—" Sydney shut her mouth and concentrated. Soft waves of energy rippled through her body as the magic of the crumble burned away her fatigue. A moment later, she felt as rested as ever, though she noted, with some sadness, that her magical energy had vanished. She climbed to her feet. "I should have thought of that."

"Yes, you should have."

"Why didn't you use yours in the fight?"

Even in the low light, she could not miss Marla's grimace. "And that's what *I* should thought of. I was too mad to think right and it almost cost us."

She wiped the blood away from her mouth. "I think that fucker dislodged a tooth." She felt around with her tongue. "Yep, it's loose."

Sydney said, "You going to be all right?"

"Not the first time. No matter. Get a little crumble in Garth and he's an excellent healer. I'll live with it until I have some time with him."

"What do we do?"

"We need to get back to The Log as fast as we can. This shit is about to get a lot deeper."

Chapter Seventeen

Sydney nodded. "Let's go."

"Wait."

Sydney froze. Another pair of silhouettes flashed across the starlit sky. "What the hell are they doing? I've never seen this many drakes out at night."

"Yeah, they normally only have two or three up at night, if they fly at all. I've already seen a dozen." Marla eyed the darkness overhead. "Someone called them out after McGee's stunt back there."

"Think they're looking for us?"

"Probably."

"Will they arrest us? Or barbecue us?"

Marla raised her hand to a horizontal position and tipped it to either side. "They aren't ogres. If Lord Burnside ordered them out, he'd be pissed if they didn't bring us back but angry drakes tend to flame first and ask questions later."

"That assumes the drakes are angry."

"I would be if I got rousted from bed and sent out to look for reprobates in the middle of the night."

Sydney thought for a moment. "If Burnside is mad enough to have the drakes out in force, then we're liable to be arrested even if we're at The Log."

"True, but that'll be ogres, not the drakes. They won't kill us if we don't resist." Marla paused. "I hope."

"You're not much of an optimist."

"Family trait, Syd."

They darted from shadow to shadow. After a few moments, Marla said, "Hang on, Syd. I got a stupid rock in my boot. Step in that alley."

Marla flopped to the ground and pulled her footwear off. Her braid was loose and her black hair shrouded her face, drowning her in the murk of the narrow space.

She's just another shadow in the night, Sydney thought. Aloud, she said, "What happened back there? Is McGee that strong? He was faster than anything I've ever seen."

"No, he got into his cache. That's their trigger, like crumble for us. It's harder for them to get access. They need a rainbow. But when they do, their magic is much stronger than ours. That's why they're so damn dangerous."

"So that's what it means."

"What?"

"All this time, you guys talked about the Cons getting into their cache. I always thought that was a euphemism for drug use or something. I never knew it was a literal pot of gold at the end of the rainbow." Sydney chuckled. "It sounds pretty silly."

"No more silly than eating dried mushroom," Marla's lips pressed together in a thin line. "And it looks like the Cons found a way to get at their cache at will during the night, which was always their biggest weakness. Before, they always had to set it up in advance, with focused lightstones and mists of water. They couldn't do it on the fly. Now they're even more dangerous."

"Someone made those silver marbles for him. Some goblin, by the sound of it. You suspect someone?"

"Not at all. Cons are racist bastards. Normally they wouldn't associate with goblins." Marla shook her head. "Doesn't matter, we'll have to figure that out later."

Marla pulled her boot back on and climbed to her feet. She produced a thin piece of twine and bound back her loose hair. "It looks clear. Come on."

They scuttled along the street, pausing several times to catch their breath and listen for pursuit. After a few moments, they reached the end of the avenue, which opened into a wide-open space. Oakbark Square was older and more run-down than

Bayberry Square. A large fountain of alabaster mortar, depicting a great tree, dominated the center of the plaza. A raucous tavern occupied the west side of the square; even from the distance, the drunken singing and carousing were clear enough for Sydney to hear every word.

Marla motioned to the left, away from the pub. She crept along the edge of the storefronts, sticking to the shadows.

Sydney tailed her, hoping they would not be surprised by a sudden appearance of the drake patrols since there was nowhere to hide.

Marla stopped, causing Sydney to almost run into her. "Marla? What is it?"

"Someone is standing over there, just to the side of that wagon. They aren't moving."

"For us?"

"How the hell do I know?"

Sydney squinted in the gloom. She couldn't see anyone where Marla indicated. She dug into her pockets and found one packet of crumble. Just one.

The others must have come out while I was running. Shit.

She ate the packet and concentrated on her vision.

The darkness of the plaza vanished. A gradient of red and green shades sprang up in its place. She instantly spotted the hulking form not a hundred feet away. "Oh, crap."

"What?"

"I think it's Urgon."

"How can you tell?"

"Because I've been practicing a night-vision spell and he's the only one I know with that build." Sydney eyed the dwarven mercenary. He leaned against a building, arms folded. He did not look in their direction but stared at the front of the tavern across the way. "He's not doing anything, just standing there."

"Do you think he spotted us?"

"I don't think so but we can't go that way. We'll have to backtrack."

Marla growled. "We don't know if he's here for us."

"We don't know that he *isn't*. I don't really want to test it."

"Syd, if we go back, with Cons and maybe drakes and ogres behind us, there's only one way to get to The Log."

"I know. We'll have to use the Boardwalk. At night." Visions of the sinister presence lurking beneath the piers filled her head. She quailed at the notion but she forced herself to remain calm. "I don't see where we have a choice."

"Me either."

They hurried back the way they'd come. Sydney glanced over her shoulder at regular intervals. The last time she did, she was certain Urgon's head turned their way. A shiver crept down her spine but he didn't move. She blinked away her night vision and let her eyes adjust to the returned darkness.

"Syd, look."

A gang of Cons carrying lightstone lamps and torches stomped into the far side of Oakbark Square. Sydney picked out Henry, one of the two that had accosted her the first day in town. He pointed and the Cons dispersed, fanning out towards the fountain.

Sydney and Marla stole away from Oakbark Square and turned down a side street. They hadn't gone more than two hundred yards before the tang of the harbor reached Sydney's nostrils. Moments later, they hit the wooden planks of the Boardwalk.

"Take some crumble," Marla said.

"I'm out."

Marla snorted. "Amateur."

She hefted two packets and tossed one to Sydney. "Concentrate on your feet; you should be able to make them light enough to not make any noise."

Sydney devoured her packet. The now-familiar surge coursed down her limbs. At the same time, she felt the telltale pinpricks in her forehead and temples. They abated after a few seconds.

Using too much of this stuff, just like back when we stole the ale on the boat.

Sydney concentrated on her feet and took a step. She heard no *clump* of boot heel on wood.

Marla nodded in approval.

The Boardwalk was still. Sydney and Marla clustered in the shadows several times as drakes glided overhead, and once for a passing ogre patrol. Their sound-dampening spell seemed to be holding. She wondered if it would last long enough for them to get off the far side of the Boardwalk.

They edged past the Sunbolt Shipping warehouse. Sydney half-expected the place to be jumping, like the Salmonika forges but the building was quiet.

Sydney frowned. She had just met Scorin Sunbolt the one time, after his uncle Sturm's untimely demise. The little bastard had acted all contrite and cooperative with the faeries—at least, outwardly. Something about his demeanor left Sydney doubtful. She wondered if he was as involved with the Cons as his uncle, and if so, whether it was safe to be near his place, even at this late hour.

Marla halted. She stuck out her arm to block Sydney's progress. Her voice was a mere breath of air. "You hear that?"

"No. What?"

"Sounded like someone whispering."

They waited in silence. Sydney found herself holding her breath.

Marla relaxed. "I guess it was nothing."

A brilliant shower of light erupted to their left. Through squinted eyes, Sydney spotted a trio of Cons. Two wielded heavy clubs in their calloused hands. Rainbow-flecked water droplets filled the air around them.

The third knelt with his hands in a pot full of gold coins. A stout cudgel lay on the ground next to him. The Con raised a handful of coins and let them *clink* back into the pot. His gaze met Sydney's and he grinned. "Hello, girlie."

She pulled a throwing knife from its sheath. "Seamus."

"Now, Sydney, we'll have that talk I wanted to have the first day I saw you."

"I'm terribly sorry that Crol and his boys interrupted your chance to beat me up."

Seamus hefted his club and stood. His cache flickered and vanished. "No ogres here this time, lass."

"How lucky for me."

"Besides, after I've worked you over a little, maybe I can make you scream in another way."

Sydney supposed his implications should have terrified her but any fear she might have felt was shoved aside by a sudden, searing anger. "Bring it."

Seamus pointed at Marla. "Kill that winger bitch. Leave her friend to me."

"Syd, catch!"

Sydney caught the crumble packet with a backhanded grab. She had just enough time to get it under her tongue before the Cons fell on them. The light from the Con's rainbow ball faded, returning them to starlit darkness.

Seamus lunged with his club, a mere blot in the shadow of the Sunbolt warehouse. Sydney twisted to the side, avoiding the blow. Faster than she would have thought possible, he pivoted and shot out his booted foot. She couldn't avoid it altogether; the hobnail grazed the outside of her thigh. Pain radiated up her hip.

She made an exaggerated gesture and launched a knife at his head. As she hoped, Seamus ducked to avoid it. Sydney kicked, aiming for his lowered chin. He caught her foot in his free hand, spun, and slammed her whole body into the building wall.

Sydney's head crashed into the stone and the breath left her lungs in a whoosh. She crumpled to the ground. Her mind swam and her eyes couldn't focus.

Get up, Sydney, or you're going to die right here.

Shroom-power flushed the wooziness from her brain and muscles. Sydney scrambled to her feet.

Seamus blinked. "You got a little magic yourself, I see. Will it be enough?"

Gordon's words echoed through her mind: *bait them, they can't take it.* "Try me and find out. Or are you too much of a wuss?"

"I think I'll try you in every way, Sydney, in every hole you got." He advanced. "Don't worry, you'll enjoy it."

"Hurry up, limp-dick. I haven't got all night."

Seamus bellowed and raised his club in both hands.

Sydney tensed.

I better time this right.

Just as Seamus reached her and started his swing, Sydney grabbed the Con by the lapels of his green jacket. She rolled backward with his momentum, curled her knees into her chest, and pulled him atop her. For a split second, she found herself face to face with her snarling attacker. The overpowering stench of cabbage and beer beat against her face. As her back hit the ground and the momentum of the roll elevated her hips, Sydney channeled her remaining crumble power down her legs. She thrust her feet into his gut and shoved with all her might.

Seamus's expression changed from rage to stupefaction as Sydney's magic-powered kick jetted him twenty-five feet into the air. The leprechaun arced in a lazy broad fall, disappearing over the side of the dock, with a muffled shout and a dull splash.

Sydney kicked herself to her feet. The joint of her left wing throbbed; she'd landed on it wrong. She grabbed a knife from her belt. "Marla?"

"Over here, Syd."

Marla crouched on one knee, a silhouette in the gloom. The point of her sword rested on the boards and she leaned on it with both hands. Her wings and shoulders heaved as she panted.

Sydney knelt beside her and placed her hand on her sister's arm. Marla's skin was slick. "You're bleeding? How bad?"

"Just scraped, nothing serious. I'm okay." She pointed at the two Cons, who lay inert nearby. "They're not. Seamus?"

"He went swimming. Come on, let's go."

A heavy thump sounded behind them. Sydney whirled.

Seamus stood on the edge of the dock. Water streamed from his clothes. He'd lost his hat and his eyes glittered with anger.

"You winger bitches, you killed my mates. Now I'm gonna —"

As dark as it was, for years afterward Sydney wished it had been even darker.

A tentacle, gray in the murky light and lined with pulsing suckers, snaked from beneath the dock. It slithered about the Con's leg and yanked.

Seamus landed on the boards with a *thud*. His gaze darted to his attacker and he screamed. His hands hammered at the tentacle, to no avail. The coiled appendage pulled, dragging Seamus backward. His legs disappeared over the edge. The harsh scrape of fingernails on wood rent the night.

The Con's terror-filled eyes met Sydney's. "No! Sydney, I'm sorry. Help me, please! Don't—"

Seamus jerked over the side. His cry was cut short by another splash.

Quiet descended over the dock, broken only by the ragged breathing of two frightened faeries.

For a long moment, Marla and Sydney sat huddled with their backs against the warehouse. Sydney stared at the edge of the dock. Even in the pale light, the gouges in the wooden planks were painfully visible.

It just as easily could have been Marla. Or me.

Marla whispered, "Do you think it's gone?"

"I don't know. I don't want to stay here and see if it comes back."

"Agreed. Syd?"

"Yeah?"

Marla's hand found hers. "Stay away from the edge."

The two faeries crept off the Boardwalk in silence. Sydney tried to blot her would-be rapist's cry and terror-filled words from her brain. Had the situation been reversed, she knew the vicious Con would have shown her no mercy. That notion did little to dispell the horror in her mind.

The worst was the look on his face. He knew what was happening—and he was absolutely powerless to stop it.

She closed her eyes. *I am not sure I will ever stop seeing it.*

Bayberry Square was still when they arrived, though Sydney didn't know how long that would last. They hadn't seen any more of the Enforcers but she was certain Lord Burnside's underlings hadn't given up.

Marla guided them to the back door. It opened before they even reached it.

"Marla, Sydney, thank the Gods!" Lila grabbed them both and pulled them inside.

"Did the others make it back? Is everyone okay?"

Sydney stared at her sister, feeling a growing pride and admiration. Even in the wake of their own terror-filled flight, Marla's first thought was of her people and their safety.

No wonder they follow her so devotedly.

Dana appeared from down the hall. "Yes, some time ago. When Crol arrived, we feared the worst."

"Wait, Crol was here? When?"

"Twenty minutes ago." Dana's voice was calm but her eyes held a fair amount of tension. "Marla, did you kill a Con and dump his body in front of Gort's shop?"

Marla shook her head. "No. McGee set us up."

"Okay. Crol said he'd be back and that you'd stay here until he got back if you knew what was good for you. Want to fill me in?"

"It'll take a few moments to explain. Lila, please go round up Markus and Gordon."

Lila jerked her head up and down. "I'll get them and bring them to your office." She scampered off.

Dana eyed the sisters. "Something else happened, didn't it?"

"Yeah," Marla said. "I only want to go through it once. Dana, we'll join you and the others in a second."

"Sure, Marla." Dana retreated.

Sydney stretched her wings. The left one still hurt., "What are you going to tell them?"

"The truth."

"Including what happened on the Boardwalk?"

"Yes, though they won't believe it. I was there and I barely believe it." Marla hesitated. "We better have our stories straight for Crol."

"Yeah," Sydney said. "And quickly, since I bet he won't be long."

A dull booming echoed the length of The Log.

Sydney slumped. It was the sound of a massive fist hammering the front door of the tavern. "Like I said, not long at all."

Chapter Eighteen

Sydney took a deep breath.

Here goes nothing.

She turned the doorknob and stepped into The Log's tavern, with Marla right behind her.

The room was devoid of patrons, though that seemed a recent development; chairs were overturned and flagons of ale lay untouched on almost every table.

Like they got told to leave, and did, in a hurry.

Dana and Markus were there, as were Lila, Gordon, Garth, and Robin. The six of them sat at two tables. All of them rested their hands flat on the tabletop. Markus scowled and Dana projected her normal sense of calm. The others all wore looks of nervous fear.

Ogres crowded the room. Half wielded heavy double-bladed swords. The other half carried crossbows.

One crossbow-bearing Enforcer stood behind each of the seated faeries, their weapons pointed at the gang members' heads.

The guards parted and Crol stepped through. The ogre looked pissed. "Marla. Sydney. Come with us. Now."

Marla glanced around the room. "You arresting us?"

"Yes. If you resist, every faery in this room dies. I'm not kidding, Marla."

Sydney swallowed. The Enforcer's tone left no room for argument.

Fortunately, Marla appeared to reach the same conclusion. She raised her hands. "All right, Crol. We'll come. No need to hurt anyone."

He pointed at a table. "Put your sword there. If you have any other weapons, toss them too."

Marla removed her sword and laid it on the indicated surface.

Crol jerked his head at Sydney. "You too. Lose the knife belt and everything in your pockets."

Sydney nodded, not trusting herself to say anything. Taking care not to move too quickly, lest she provoke a reaction from a trigger-happy ogre, she undid the buckle of her bandolier and shucked it over her shoulders. Her injured wing protested the motion.

I might be lucky if that's the only thing that still hurts in a few hours.

She laid the bandolier and her pouch of extra blades on the table next to Marla's sword, then unbuckled her long knife from her leg.

Beside her, Marla divested herself of a handful of knives from various places in her clothing.

Crol said, "Crumble too."

Marla sucked in a breath as if to protest.

"Marla," Sydney murmured.

Marla slumped. She tossed a handful of packets on the table.

The head Enforcer glared at Sydney. "You?"

"I'm out."

"We'll see. Hands above your head."

Sydney and Marla raised their hands. Crol patted down each of them. Sydney reddened when the ogre's big hands brushed under her breasts and creased the inside of her thighs. But Crol's expression never changed and his hands didn't linger, so she didn't say anything.

"All right, you two, out the door. I'm not going to handcuff you but try anything funny—" He shot Marla a particular glare.

"—and my boys will riddle you with bolts. Got me?"

"Yeah." Marla's voice was sullen.

Sydney just nodded again.

"Okay, out. The rest of you stay put until we're gone. I'm leaving an armed detachment out front for an hour. They have orders to fire if they so much as see a faery wingtip. I wouldn't even go near the windows. Are we clear?"

"We got it," Markus said.

"Good." He motioned to Sydney and Marla.

They left The Log. A stiff breeze sprang up as they stepped outside. Sydney hoped that wasn't an omen.

Ogres formed ranks two-deep around them. Crol walked to the side of the group.

"Hey Crol," Marla said, "you really needed this many of your boys to arrest two little faeries? Are you that scared of us?"

"There's an old ogre saying, Marla: 'Why take a hundred ogres and beat the enemy when you can take two hundred and crush them?' And if I were in your rather tenuous shoes, I wouldn't be mouthing off."

The group tromped towards the center of town. Marla pointed. "You know the Woodhollow Jail is west of here, right?"

"We're not taking you to jail."

Sydney's heart skipped a beat. She said, "Where are you taking us?"

"Lord Burnside would like a word with you."

Sydney came to a halt so suddenly that the ogre walking behind collided with her, knocking her to the ground. In an instant, four crossbows swung in her direction.

Marla grabbed her arm. "Get up, Syd."

"Come on, come on," Crol said, his voice irritated.

Sydney let Marla haul her to her feet. She straightened her back and glared at the Chief Enforcer.

He spat at her feet. "Don't snarl at me because you tripped over your own footsteps, little girl. Keep moving."

Marla's lip curled. "Isn't this where you say something trite like, 'We can't keep the Lord waiting.' ?"

Crol's free hand curled into a fist. "You're testing my patience, Marla. Lose the attitude."

"Or else what?"

"Lord Burnside ordered me to bring you two to him. He didn't say what kind of shape you had to be in. Keep it up and I'll knock that sneer right off your face."

Marla lowered her eyes and nodded.

"That's what I thought," Crol said. "Get going."

*   *   *   *   *

Lord Burnside's manor occupied the center of Woodhollow. Broad avenues surrounded the walled compound, separating it from the rest of the city by over a hundred yards in each direction. The walls stood a good twenty feet tall.

Sydney passed the plaza before but had never gotten close. As they approached, she began to appreciate how massive the manor house itself was.

Crol steered them away from a tall iron-bound gate manned by a handful of nervous-looking ogres. They skirted the manor wall.

"Why didn't we go in there?"

"That leads into the gardens," Crol said, as if such a reason were self-explanatory. "The front gate is on the far side."

Sydney waited a moment for further explanation but when none seemed forthcoming, she said, "And we can't go through gardens because?"

"You might be interested in dying, Sydney, but none of us are."

She glanced at Marla, who said, "Burnside lets it run loose in the garden every night."

"What?"

"The mauler."

"And what is that?"

"A big animal of some kind. I don't know what exactly, I've never seen it. They say it's Burnside's pet and loyal to him alone. No one who goes in there ever comes out."

"True enough," Crol said. "The Lord told us Enforcers to never go in there after dark, no matter what. During the day, it sleeps in an underground pen but wakes up when the sun goes down. I've tried to spot it but the darkness beneath the trees masks exactly what it is. All I know is, it's big—a lot bigger than me. Sometimes, the Lord tells us to toss his enemies in there. They always scream but only for a few minutes."

"Wait a second, back up." Sydney pointed in the direction of the gates. "Burnside has people thrown in there to get killed?"

"He has them thrown in to get eaten," Crol replied. "Saves on the price of tossing a pig or cow in every other night."

"The mauler? Some monster under the Boardwalk?" Sydney fought down a mounting sense of panic. "Marla, how the hell do you all live here? Seriously!"

"Easy, Syd. Because there's money to be made."

She glanced at her sister. Marla only smiled.

She's nervous too. Being flippant is how she copes. Okay, Syd, get it together. She took a deep breath.

Crol laughed. "A little tense, Sydney? You need to lighten up."

"Bite me."

"Another time, perhaps."

They reached a set of arched double gates even more impressive than the garden gates. Sentries patrolled the walls and another two ogres stood guard at the gate. They came to attention as the party approached and saluted Crol. After he returned the gesture, one of the guards motioned to the wall top.

The door opened on silent hinges.

Sydney nodded. "Impressive."

"The Lord likes his silence in the evening," Crol said.

"So why drag a couple of blabbermouths like us in?"

"I don't think he is expecting silence from you, Sydney. Maybe some screaming."

She didn't know what to say to that.

They walked under the gatehouse and into the courtyard beyond, which was perhaps fifty yards wide. Several buildings lay around the perimeter of the courtyard. Crol steered them towards the largest one, directly across from the gate

Sydney noted the front doors of the manor as they approached, which were at least fifteen feet tall.

Marla made the same observation. "Big doors, Syd. Kind of ostentatious."

"Yeah."

"You know what they say about men who have to have everything around them oversized."

"Marla," Crol said, "shut up."

She started to retort, evidently thought better of it, and closed her mouth.

Sydney was mildly surprised when they entered. The center of the building was one grand round room. Lamplight reflected from gold and silver inlaid murals adorning each wall. Overhead the stars winked beyond a crystalline dome Pillars of ivory etched with intricate patterns of polished wood and beaten brass flanked the perimeter of the hall.

Marla gasped.

A sea of treasure filled the hall. Hundreds of neatly-stacked gold ingots lined one wall. Uncut gemstones and beautiful goblin-crafted jewelry lay in careless piles, amid mounds of enameled armors and elf-forged weapons. Oil paintings adorned every wall. A tremendous crystal chandelier, lined with concentric circles of glowing lightstones, hung over the center of the hall.

Lying under the chandelier, on a small mountain of gold and silver coins, reposed a wingless worm.

A cold shiver bounced down Sydney's spine.

The worm's snaky body lay half-buried in the piles of loot. Its shimmering white scales winked and glittered with the reflected brilliance of its hoard. Sydney guessed it was at least seventy feet long and almost a dozen feet across in its shoulders.

The worm shifted as they entered, setting off sparkling cascades of coins and jewels. Its whiskered head rested on an enormous velvet pillow. Propped before its head was a wide glass prism. On the other side of the prism stood a podium, upon which lay an open book. The worm stared intently into the prism, its eyes scanning back and forth.

Sydney suppressed a sudden urge to burst out laughing. The worm's lips moved as it read.

"Lord Burnside,' Crol said, "I have here the faeries you sent for."

Burnside looked away from the reading glass. "Ah yes," it rumbled. "Crol, please stay. The rest of you are dismissed."

The other ogres hurried out without looking back.

Not that I blame them, Sydney thought.

Burnside fixed his gaze on Sydney. She felt transfixed by the worm's golden eyes and blinked to shake free of the sensation.

"You would be Sydney."

She responded with a jerky nod.

His eyes switched to Marla. "And Marla. Leader of the Faery Gang."

Marla cleared her throat. "Lord Burnside." Her voice held steady. Only the tightness around her eyes conveyed to Sydney that Marla was on the very edge of controlling her fear.

"Lord Worthington Burnside the Alabaster." The worm inclined its head. "Not my real name, of course, but what passes for a name in this region."

"Uhm, Lord Burnside," Sydney said, "may I ask why you wanted to see us?"

The lord's chuckle reverberated through the hall. A tiny wisp of smoke drifted up from his nostrils. "I thought you were supposed to be the brains in your operation, Sydney."

"I don't know about that."

"You're more intelligent than most of the creatures in this town. You must have guessed as to why I called for you."

"I really don't know."

Burnside sighed. "So tedious." He stretched his legs and dug his sword-like talons into the mounds of coins. He glanced at Marla. "You?"

"We haven't broken any laws, if that's what you mean."

"You haven't?" Burnside's mouth turned up in a reptilian grin. "You've done nothing but break my laws since you've been in Woodhollow—the most recent infraction being your dispatching a few of the Leprechaun Gang earlier this evening."

"That wasn't our fault," Marla said. "They attacked us first."

"I see. Crol?"

The ogre straightened. "Yes, Sir?"

"Have the bodies on the Boardwalk been policed up?"

"Yes, Sir, and returned to the Four-Leaf Club, per your instructions. We let them know what happened."

"What?" Marla took a step forward. "They'll want to take revenge on us for sure!"

The worm shrugged. "Perhaps. But they won't."

"Why not?"

"Do you know why I insist that Woodhollow remains a peaceful town?"

Marla shook her head.

Sydney couldn't resist. She said, "Peaceful towns pay more taxes."

Burnside nodded. "Yes, that's it."

"I was kidding."

Burnside seemed amused at her comment. "Why joke? Trade in Woodhollow has expanded by a factor of ten in the last three decades. People know it's a relatively safe place to do business. There are, certainly, those of your ilk that might pick their pockets—figuratively or literally—but that pales when compared to the open warfare between merchant houses in Kroven or the constant tribal battles in ogre lands, or even the runs on the banks so common in the elven republics. Woodhollow is a secure town for those who come to make a profit. Profits lead to taxes, taxes lead to the growth of my hoard you see here. Strife, war, violence in the streets...these things lead to people caching and guarding their wealth."

He shook his head. "That's very bad business."

"I don't understand," Sydney said. "You could just go out there and take it all, couldn't you?"

"Of course I could. I could destroy Woodhollow and everyone in it without breaking so much as a scale."

Burnside's eyes shone with an intense fire. Sydney's heartbeat quickened but before she could even take a step back, the glow in the worm's eyes faded.

Burnside continued. "But why should I do that, when I can sit back and encourage the growth of Woodhollow's prosperity? My hoard grows while I immerse myself in study and pursuit of knowledge, which, truth be told, is something I prefer to killing and plundering. Much easier on the claws and much more satisfying. A case in point: this treatise I am reading, on the engineering of hydraulic cranes, is fascinating and quite inspirational. The ideas in this tome could revolutionize our basic understanding of construction and—"

Burnside halted. Sydney thought the worm must have noted the confusion on her face, as the Lord said, "But I digress."

Sydney pursed her lips. "I apologize, Lord Burnside. I hadn't expected such a measured response from a...uhm...."

"From a dragon?"

"Well, yes."

"We can't all be bloodthirsty beasts—such as, for example, the worm who killed your parents."

Marla's eyes widened. Sydney heard nothing, save a rushing in her ears. She was vaguely aware of her fingernails digging into her palms again. This time, she felt the warm trickle of blood.

Burnside nodded his great head. "Yes, of course I am aware of what happened to your family. Faeries and Leprechauns don't have an exclusive hold on magic. An hour of arcane scrying told me all I needed to know."

"Why?" It seemed inadequate but it was the only word Sydney could muster.

"When you became of interest to me, I made it my business to find out as much information as I could about you, which was considerable." Ringlets of steam rose from his jaws. "I knew Lady Charlene Windsor the Azure. She was a snotty little hatchling right from the time she cracked her egg five hundred years ago. I never liked her; she had distasteful notions regarding killing lesser creatures as a matter of sport rather than when necessary. So uncivilized. And arrogant. Despite being a mere whelp of a dragon, she thought she was invincible. Did she spend several thousand years growing and learning before embarking on a life of plunder? No, she hurried into it, to her ruin. A compatriot of mine, Lord Dane Rothschild the Vermillion, told me centuries ago that he was sure she would, in her hubris, die at the hands of vermin. He was, as he usually is, correct."

Sydney flashed a glance at Crol to see if he was upset at ogres being referred to as "vermin" but the Enforcer's face remained unperturbed.

Burnside shifted his bulk, setting off another avalanche of coins. "While I cannot condone that intent of Max and Jenna of the Holly Clan to steal from one of my kind, I do not mourn that their actions led to Charlene's death. You are in no danger from me on that count."

"No?" Marla said through clenched teeth.

"No. Vengeance is an emotion for lesser creatures."

Marla put her hands on her hips. "You still have not explained why you had us dragged here like a couple of potato sacks. Are you going to stop wasting our time at some point?"

Crol's eyes narrowed. "Marla, show some respect before I have to slap the crap out of you."

"Marla, it's very simple. Woodhollow will remain peaceful." Burnside spoke as if Marla's disrespect was of no matter. Sydney supposed it *was* of no matter to the worm.

I mean, would I be upset if I was disrespected by a beetle?

"That may not be up to us," Marla said.

"A protracted war between you and the Leprechauns will damage what I have spent a century building and I have no intention of letting that happen."

"Then you probably ought to drag McGee down here and give him this speech, not us."

"What makes you think I haven't?"

"Uhm...." Marla finally shrugged. "I don't know. Have you?"

"Yes, just before Crol fetched you for me. In the interests of full disclosure, I will tell you this: McGee has asked for special permission to declare a limited war between the Leprechaun Gang and the Faery Gang. There is precedent in Woodhollow history. From a more savage time than my reign, I assure you, but precedent nonetheless."

Sydney's gorge rose. *War?* "What...what kind of war?"

"A battle, to decide the fate of the Woodhollow's underworld. It would be limited to one day and one place...a 'winner-take-all' event, as I believe you might call it. Naturally, the winners would be responsible for any damage inflicted on the town."

Marla folded her arms. "And?"

Burnside gave them a slight shrug. "I haven't decided yet, though I admit the idea has merit."

Sydney paled. "You'd let them destroy us?"

"One gang in control of all the criminal activity leads to stability. That's what Woodhollow needs."

"Could we talk you out of it? Is there something else you want?"

Burnside chuckled. The dry, raspy sound reverberated through the hall. "What could you possibly offer me?"

Sydney spread her hands. "Well—"

"I suppose—" Burnside flexed his talons again. "—you could offer me the Hearthglitter from Sylvan Valley. That jewel is unlike any other to my knowledge and having it in my hoard would provide me great esteem with my brothers and sisters."

Sydney felt faint. *He can't be serious.*

Burnside wasn't. "Though I can't see you stealing and handing to a dragon the most powerful and sacred object in faerydom just to prevent something that might not happen anyway." He paused. "Then again, vermin are not always known for acting with their heads. And the jewel does intrigue me."

Burnside flicked his eyes at his reading prism and sighed again. "In any event, I am mulling McGee's request. While I do, there shall be no further fighting between gangs and no further retaliation. McGee and the Leprechaun Gang are aware of my dictates on this issue and will act accordingly, as will you."

"Or what?" The words were out of her mouth before Sydney could stop herself. She saw Crol frown and lean forward. She braced for the blow.

It never came. Burnside eyed her. "Or any violators will answer to Chief Crol. And to me. And if my direct orders are broken, I believe I will actually be vexed."

"I guess we all get tossed to the mauler or something."

Burnside smiled. "Or something. I request that you stand down any retaliatory operations you have planned against the Cons, or against the other gangs in Woodhollow, for that matter."

Marla snorted. "Request?"

"Requests are more civilized. Don't you agree?"

Marla shook her head.

"Such bad manners. I believe I have made myself clear. As such, there is no need for further discussion. Chief Crol, please escort the young ladies out. I would like to get back to my reading."

"Yes, Sir." He motioned towards the exit.

Sydney and Marla followed him to the edge of the hall. Just as they were about to the turn the corner, Burnside said, "Sydney?"

She faced him. "Yes...yes, Lord Burnside?"

"What do you know about the Nightshade Clan?"

Ice formed in her stomach. She forced her voice to stay even. "The Nightshade Clan is just a myth; something faery mothers tell their children to get them to behave."

"Ah."

She could not tell if Burnside was disappointed that she had nothing to tell him or that he knew she was lying. She thought to ask but he had returned his attention to his reading prism.

The other ogres waited outside Burnside's hall. They formed up around the two faeries. One looked at Crol. "Jail or gallows?"

"Neither. Walk them to the front gate and turn them loose."

If the ogre was surprised he didn't show it. He and the others herded Sydney and Marla towards the exit.

Crol walked behind the band in silence. When they reached the compound gates, he said, "Marla, can I offer you a little friendly advice?"

"I can't stop you."

"If I were you, I would toss away any plans you had to go after McGee or the Cons. If Lord Burnside finds out you did, he'll have no choice but to order us Enforcers to exterminate the whole lot of you, and I'll do it without hesitation. After all the hard work you did rebuilding your gang after the Bell Street Massacre, it would be a shame to throw it all away."

Marla's lip curled. "Is that all?"

Crol scowled. "Yeah, that's all. Go on, beat it."

She stomped through the gate. Crol leveled his gaze at Sydney. "You seem a bit more level-headed than your sister. See if you can talk some sense into her, for both your sakes."

"I'll try."

"Do that. I hope I don't see you any time soon. Now go on."

Sydney caught up to Marla when she was halfway across the avenue. "Well, that was enlightening."

"I don't see what you're in such a damn good mood about." Marla spat on the cobblestone pavement. "We just had our hands tied."

"How? Burnside didn't tell us not to loanshark. He didn't tell us not to run Shroom. He just said to lay off the Cons."

"Yeah, right until he decides to grant the Cons permission to go to war. If he does, we're screwed." Marla shot Sydney a guilty look. "Syd, I hate to admit this to you. I would hate to admit this to anyone."

"What?"

"If it comes to a big battle, they're going to smoke us. There are more Cons than faeries in our gangs."

"How many more?"

"It could be more than twice as many. I've never gotten a full headcount on them." While Sydney absorbed that, Marla continued. "It's not even the numbers but their magic. When we catch them off guard, that's one thing, but if it's planned ahead of time, they will have time to prepare. Every one of them will dig into their caches in advance, like they did before Bell Street.

Individually, a Con charged with magic from his cache is as stout as two faeries sky-high on crumble. The only other advantage we'd have—to fly and pelt them with crossbow bolts from above —would be neutralized by the drake patrols. Even in the event of a formalized battle, I doubt they'd allow us free reign of the sky. Too easy to torch the rest of the city. And at the speed this is going, I am not going to get the magic rings perfected, or even in decent working order."

Her face was glum. "If something doesn't change, we're going to have to flee or we're going to get wiped out."

Sydney chewed her lip while she digested everything Marla said. They turned east towards The Log. The first rays of morning had just lightened the eastern horizon. And with the light came a flash of insight.

"Okay, Marla, let's assume everything you said is correct. As I see it, we just need to recruit."

"Syd, there is no way we can get more faeries into Woodhollow or into the gang as trained, trusted members. Not in time to do any good, anyway."

"No. We need allies. And I think I know how to get them."

Chapter Nineteen

Markus stared at the exterior of the plain brick building. "You sure about this?"

"Sure?" Sydney barked a short laugh. "Hell, no. For all I know, they're going to kill us without even hearing us out. Brownies are lunatics."

She studied the store. By all appearances, it was a simple pottery shop. An enameled sign over the door bore the silhouette of an eared vase and the title, "Wulf's Pottery."

In truth, it was the front for the Brown Gang.

Sydney shifted her weight from one foot to the other. She was stalling and she knew it.

Her debate with Marla was fiery. Marla wanted to be the one to extend the offer of alliance, stating that it should come between leaders and equals. Sydney replied that if she went, as an unofficial envoy, that should the offer be rejected, she could always be said to be acting without the blessing of the gang leaders and thus avoid a loss of face for all of them.

She also wanted to target the Browns. Contracting the Browns for the sale of Shroom had already started paying dividends after just a few days, and to Sydney, it seemed a logical extension of their arrangement. Marla countered that she didn't trust the brownie gang and that they should not place all their faith, business, and allegiance in one source. Sydney countered *that* by saying that Marla didn't trust *any* of the other gangs and that the faeries were simply in the position of having to take a chance.

They had gone round and round, for almost a week, without reaching a conclusion.

When they brought in the rest of the leaders for the decision, Gordon withheld his opinion, saying he'd go along with whatever the others decided. Markus supported Sydney, which Marla angrily dismissed—in her charming way—as his dick doing his thinking for him. That had set leader and lieutenant to yelling at each other, which was only broken up when Dana threw her weight behind Sydney as well.

Dana's decision took the wind out of Marla's sails. She agreed rather curtly, told Markus to keep an eye on Sydney so she didn't get herself killed, and ordered Sydney not to make a mess of things before dropping the matter.

Now, standing before the store, Sydney wondered if she'd outsmarted herself.

She didn't know much about the Browns, save that they all wore green stocking caps and chestnut-colored tunics and pants that matched their skin and hair. Even though most were only four to four and a half feet tall, they were all quite a bit stronger than a faery and every single one of them had a violent streak.

"Yeah, that's just the regular ones," Markus said.

"Huh?"

"You said brownies are lunatics. I agreed, saying those are just the regular ones."

"What do you mean?"

"They all have a temper but some slip over the edge and go outright homicidal. When that happens, they stop wearing long green hats and start wearing crimson ones. Other brownies call them redcaps."

"I've heard of them. Are they as bad as their reputation?"

"Probably worse. It's not quite so bad that they attack people on sight but they all have a hair-trigger and they turn into berserkers at the slightest provocation. When that happens, they become utterly unafraid of anything. I've heard of redcaps that keep on fighting with an insane look on their face, while their guts are slashed open and their entrails dragging behind them."

"I guess it wouldn't be a good idea to insult one, then."

He shrugged. "It would be an easy clean-up afterward."

"How so?"

"There wouldn't be much left of you."

'Swell." She squared her shoulders. "Well, let's get this done."

She pushed open the door to the shop. A bell hanging in the path of the door gave voice to a dull ring. A moment later, an aged brownie pushed aside a curtain and entered from a back room. He wore a pair of wire-rimmed glasses over a hooked nose and a green stocking cap. He nodded to the two faeries. "Good morning. Something in particular I can help you find?"

"Good morning, sir. We're here to see Wulf."

The old brownie peered over the top of his glasses at them. "I take it you're not here for a vase or a couple of plates."

"No, we're not."

"Wychia!"

The curtain parted again and a young woman emerged. Sydney thought the new arrival was about her age. Like other brownies, she stood around four-feet tall and her skin was a nutty brown, as were her tunic and pants. A mop of dark curls hung halfway down her back and a scowl etched her face. Most significantly, the woman wore a crimson stocking cap.

She sneered at the old man. "What do you want?"

"Take these faeries back to your father."

"Why?"

The old man snarled. "Because I told you to."

"So?"

"Do I need to thrash you to make the point?"

"I'd like to see you try."

She folded her arms and waited. The old man glared at her. Her returning gaze was just as flinty. The man's hand twitched.

Wychia grunted and looked away. "Fine. You two, come with me." She turned and flounced through the curtain without waiting to see if Sydney and Markus were following.

The old man sat and flipped open a ledger, grumbling to himself.

Sydney motioned to Markus and pushed the curtain aside, just in time to see the receding form of the young brownie at the end of the hallway. She let one hand rest on the hilt of a knife and followed.

They passed several open rooms. Various brownies shuffled around spinning pottery tables, slopped half-formed clay on the floor, loaded formed dishes, mugs, and pots into roaring kilns, or applied glaze to finished pieces. Here and there, shouting and shoving matches erupted. Brownies got nose to nose, screaming in each other's faces for a few seconds before returning to their tasks. One man and woman came to blows, rolling around on the floor before their comrades separated them. The two glared at each other before returning to work.

A light sheen of sweat broke out on Sydney's forehead. "They're all crazy."

"If I remember correctly, those two are married to each other."

"We're gonna die."

Markus chuckled. "You'll do fine."

Wychia reached the far end of the hallway and glanced at them. A fresh frown creased her face when she saw how far back the faeries were. She said, "Come on, hurry up."

"Sorry, miss."

"It's Wychia, lass of Wulf, not 'miss.' "

"Okay, Wychia." Markus donned his most charming smile as they hurried to catch her. "We'll keep up. That's the least we can do to see if we can't get in your good graces."

Her gray eyes hardened. "With that leer, I think you're more interested in getting into my pants than my good graces."

Markus eyed her. "Would that help our deal?"

Sydney frowned.

Wychia gave an unimpressed snort. "It might help your pecker relocate to Briar Street while the rest of you is on Tower Street."

"Well, it was worth a try," Markus said with a laugh.

"A feeble try. Save your charm for the old man." She opened the door. "In there."

They stepped inside. Sydney recognized Wulf. The brownie hunched over a set of ceramic bowls. The nearest bowl sat on a slowly turning disc. Sydney saw Wulf's knee rise and fall and realized the disc was connected to a foot pedal. Wulf gave the pedal regular, gentle taps, causing the disc to rotate.

Wulf's brows were furrowed in concentration. He held a three-pronged brush in one hand, which he guided around the bowl. His instrument left a series of narrow lines on the exterior.

Wychia slammed the door. "Pop!"

Wulf did not flinch or look away from his bowl. "Wychia, how many times have I told you not to try to screw up my designs?"

"Straight lines aren't designs. You have visitors."

With his free hand, Wulf pointed at a bench. He never took his eyes from the bowl. "Have a seat, faeries. Wychia, don't you have something else you should be doing?"

"No."

"I don't care. Get out."

Wychia snorted and left, slamming the door again.

"Damn kid." Wulf placed the brush in a shallow tray and looked at Sydney. "What do you want?"

"I'm Sydney. This is Markus."

"Marla's flunkies?"

"Lieutenants," she replied.

"Marla already getting tired of our arrangement?" He glowered. "Or is she angling for a bigger cut? If so, scoot your asses out the door right now."

"No, this has nothing to do with the Shroom trade. Marla is happy with the way things are going so far. Aren't you?"

"Yeah, it's fine." Wulf leaned against the back of his chair, clearly nonplussed. "So what do you want?"

"We have a proposition for you."

"I figured."

Markus said, "You're aware of our difficulties with the Cons?"

"Of course," Wulf said with a smirk. "It's all over the underside of Woodhollow that Lord Burnside might be about to let you duke it out....which means all you faeries will end up in traction or dead."

"And where do you think that will leave you Browns?" Sydney asked.

"We'll be fine. Yeah, we might lose the Shroom trade, or we might be able to replicate it. I know a couple of Scales in the swamps to the south; they might be able to handle albino mushrooms without poisoning themselves until we can get the mixture right."

Sydney thought of the lumbering lizard-men, who were reputed to be immune to poisons, and made a mental note to bring it up with Marla. She said, "That might be true but that's not what I meant. What happens when the Cons decide they want your territory too?"

Wulf's smirk faded. "That's not going to happen."

"One domino falls, leading to the next."

"One what?"

"Dominoes. It's a faery game played with tiles. I'm sorry, I've never seen it played outside Sylvan Valley."

"Then why the hell would you bring it up?"

Sydney clenched her fists, fighting down her own irritation. "The point is that once the Cons knock us out, they are going to start looking at the rest of the gangs. You, the Dryads, the Rats, the Hobs... The Cons are already the single strongest gang in Woodhollow. If we go and they absorb our business and our territory, they'll be even stronger."

Wulf stared at the wall, a pensive look on his face. "Okay. How would we avoid that?"

"Join us."

Wulf blinked. "Do what now?"

"Join us. Ally with us. Declare that the Browns stand with the faeries against the Cons."

"What was your name again? Sibby?"

She ground her teeth. "Sydney."

"Sydney, I'm sure people tell you you're pretty because you are. But you're also pretty stupid. If we do that, the Browns might as well be drawing targets on our backs. The Cons have always left us alone as long we kept to our own territory. As soon as we allied with you, the Cons would fuck us up. And unlike you, we don't have any magic to defend ourselves. Why would I want to sign us up for that misery?"

Here we go. "Because we would agree to sell you Shroom, at cost."

Wulf's eyes narrowed. "What's the catch?"

"No catch. The faery Gang would provide as much Shroom as you could sell, for the cost of production. Marla is willing to sign documents to the effect and file them with city hall, keeping the contract in place as long as the faeries and Browns remain allies."

"That's...that's a lot of coin you would be giving up. You know that, don't you?"

"Can you put a price on security?"

"No, I don't suppose you can." Wulf nodded. "I'll have to give this some thought and bounce it off a few of my people. In the meantime, get lost. I have bowls to finish painting."

"Wulf, we'd really like an answer now."

The brownie's walnut face turned an even darker shade of brown. "Do I need to go redcap on your asses? I said I'd think about it. Now get out!"

Markus grabbed Sydney's elbow and stood, dragging her up with him. "We'll come back in a few days, Wulf. The Browns are Marla's first choice for an alliance but there are others. We'll wait but we can't afford to wait forever. Think about it."

"I'll let you know."

They left the workroom. Wychia stood waiting, her arms folded and her face a thundercloud. "You done bamboozling my father yet?"

Sydney opened her mouth but Markus stepped on her foot. "Yep, all done."

"I don't know what you faeries are up to but it better not cause us any trouble."

Markus smiled and held up his hand in a mock salute. "No trouble, I swear. Mind walking us out?"

"Keep your hands to yourself or I'll gut you."

"I wouldn't have it any other way."

Wychia led them to the front room. Sydney kept her eyes ahead and her back straight.

The redcap ignored the grunt of acknowledgment from the old man in the front room. She opened the door and gave the faeries a pointed look.

Markus treated her to a slight bow. "My lady, I hope we'll be seeing more of each other. As allies, of course, not socially, though I wouldn't be ashamed to do that either."

"How long did it take you to think up that line?"

"Only a few hours. May I?"

Markus moved his hand slowly and took hers. Wychia tensed but otherwise didn't react. He bent his head and raised her hand to his lips, giving her a brief kiss on the back of her hand. He grinned at her. "Until next time, my lady."

Wychia's eyes softened a little. She jerked her head at the exit. "Go on."

Sydney and Markus stepped outside. The door behind them slammed so hard Sydney was surprised the wind didn't ruffle her hair.

"Well, now what?" She glanced at Markus but his eyes were stuck on the shop door. "Markus!"

He blinked. "What? Oh, sorry. My mind was elsewhere."

"Between Wychia's legs, I'm sure."

"What?"

Sydney slapped him in the shoulder. "Pay attention. I said, what now?"

"We move on to the next one and float Marla's offer."

"All right. The Hobs?"

"Yeah," Markus said. He gave Wulf's shop one last look.

They set off in silence. Sydney's eyes roamed over the crowd. There were not any Cons in view but she recalled Vivian's words from before.

She was right: anyone can be a threat.

She scanned a trow here, a *vila* over there, and a gnome even further.

"I wasn't flirting with her."

Sydney didn't stop her view of the passersby. "Of course you were."

"I was just trying to work us a better deal and—"

"Save it, Markus."

He nodded but did not respond.

Sydney refused to look at him. She shouldn't have been annoyed; she knew of Markus's interest and though she had not spurned him, she had not pursued it or allowed him to pursue her. She knew she had no reason to feel slighted.

But she *did* feel slighted. The logical part of her brain knew she was being childish. It still hurt.

It's just disappointment, that he was looking at someone else. Face it, Sydney, you were taking his attention for granted.

Lost in their own thoughts, the two faeries trod down the street.

Chapter Twenty

Sydney slouched into the office and flopped into a chair.

Marla dropped the inventory report she'd been reading. "Okay, give it to me."

"The Browns are considering it. Wulf seemed receptive but wanted to mull it over. His daughter is a psycho."

"Wychia? She's a redcap. They're *all* psychos."

Sydney hesitated. "Markus kept flirting with her."

"That annoyed you."

"Yeah." She didn't bother to lie. "I don't have any claim on him, so it shouldn't have. But it did."

"So it's just jealousy?"

"Yeah, probably."

Marla hefted her cigar from the ashtray and inhaled. The tip glowed orange. "I'm sure he just wants to fuck her, Syd."

"I'm sure. At first, I thought that was all he wanted out of me too. I was just starting to think otherwise. Now, I have no idea."

"My point is: he'll probably come back sniffing around you once he does."

"Is that supposed to make me feel better?"

"Hey, I am just laying it out there."

"Not what I want, Marla."

"What *do* you want?"

Sydney placed her hands on the arms of her chair. "I don't want to be used and tossed away. I know, I get it, it's not being used if we both go into it with the same mindset. But Marla, I'm not interested in a casual fling."

"You want what Mom and Dad had." When Sydney nodded, Marla put her cigar down again. "You know the odds of that, of finding a 'soulmate,' are pretty long. You could go your whole life without ever meeting that person."

"I know," Sydney said. "But I'd rather wait for someone who won't even look at another woman than hop into bed now just to get my rocks off."

Marla chuckled. Sydney said, "What?"

"You always said I was the dreamer, the idealist, and you were the cynical, pragmatic one. Don't look now, Syd, but I think we've switched places."

"Could be."

"What happened with the Hobs?"

"Shut us down cold. Wouldn't even let us in the door."

"Hmmm." Marla frowned. "Not what I expected but all right."

"So two tries and two misses." Sydney grimaced. "I suppose this is where you say, 'I told you so,' isn't it? That it wouldn't work?"

"No, rubbing it in faces is your schtick, not mine. Besides, the Browns may still come around."

"And the Hobs?"

Marla shrugged. "Half a loaf is better than no loaf at all. I know Grak-salk, the leader of the Hobs. I'm surprised he wouldn't even see you. He's headstrong but usually logical."

Sydney thought for a moment. "Maybe they are already in bed with the Cons."

"Why do you say that?"

"Wulf knew about the Cons' war request. Said it was all over the underworld. Maybe the Cons are a step ahead of us and are recruiting allies."

"That's a terribly depressing thought. If you had to make a call, which way do you think the Browns will fall?"

"I think they'll join us," Sydney said. "You should have seen Wulf's face when I told them they could keep all the money from the Shroom sales. His greed was so strong I could smell it."

"Well, good." Marla's voice was slightly pained. "It went against all my instincts as a criminal to extend that offer."

"We can make more money. We can't do anything if we're dead."

"That's true enough."

There was a knock at the door and Lila stuck her head in. "Marla, Dana is here with a visitor."

Sydney shot Marla a triumphant look. "Is it Wulf, son of Warth?"

"Nope. It's a dryad. She says her name is Drith-an-Bidi."

Marla ground out her cigar. "Okay, give us a minute and send them in."

Lila nodded and shut the door.

Marla opened a desk drawer and withdrew two crumble packets. She skidded one across the desk. "Take that."

"You know this dryad?"

"Vaguely know who she is but never met her, so this concerns me. You met the leader of the dryad gang, Choy-na-Sal. She's no friend of ours, so just be ready for anything."

Lila returned with a dryad in tow. Drith-an-Bidi was nearly six feet tall and very slender. Like other dryads Sydney had seen, Drith's skin was a pale green and her jet black hair hung in a long braid. She wore a sleeveless leather vest, cotton trousers, and pointed boots. A pair of long knives dangled from her belt. The jade orbs of her eyes fixed on Marla. Drith sat next to Sydney without pretense.

Dana followed Drith into the office and stood by the back wall. Lila left and closed the door.

"Come in. Sit down. Make yourself at home." Marla's tone carried a hint of irritation.

"Thank you." The dryad's voice was throaty and soft.

"What do you want, Dryad?"

Drith frowned. "The name is Drith-an-Bidi and I came here to offer you something. If you want to flip me attitude, I'll leave."

Sydney recalled Markus's flirtation with redcap Wychia, lass of Wulf, and how at the end, Wychia's demeanor softened. She didn't like it but had to admit, the diminutive brownie berserker became a smidgeon less hostile.

More flies with honey, and all that.

She swiveled her chair towards Drith and donned what she hoped was a disarming smile. "Let's start over. I'm Sydney." She offered her hand.

Drith looked at Sydney, took her hand, and gave it a ginger shake. "Drith-an-Bidi."

"Okay, Drith, what can we do for you?"

"I want to ally the Dryads to you."

Sydney shot Marla a glance but her sister maintained a neutral expression. Dana rubbed her chin, her face contemplative. Sydney said, "Okay, I'm listening."

Drith flicked her eyes at Marla. "Who's in charge here? You or her?"

Sydney placed her palm on her own chest. "Just pretend it's me for the moment."

"Very well." Drith settled into her chair. "I'll be very blunt. I know the Cons are moving to run you out of business."

"Yeah," Marla said, "we heard that too."

"If they do, they'll assume complete control of the underworld of Woodhollow. Every other gang in town will be forced to work for the Cons, including ours."

Sydney nodded. "That seems the most likely result."

"I don't want to see the Dryads crushed by the Cons. We might survive as an independent gang but best case, we'd be subordinates. Worst case, we'd be their go-to whores." Drith made a face. "Cons prefer us for some reason and if they get us under their thumb, they won't be happy with the few dryads working at Belles."

"Your concern makes sense," Sydney said.

Drith leaned forward and jabbed her finger on Marla's desk. "I want us to maintain some independence. Marla, I know your reputation for being ruthless. You also have a reputation for being fair. If I swear to put the Dryad Gang behind you, I want your promise that we'll be allowed to run our territory as we see fit. We'll even sell crumble for you, the way you're doing with the Browns. In return, we'll support your operations and if it comes time for a war, we'll stand with you there too. We'll bring our magic to the table and frankly, if you go against the Cons, I think you're going to need it."

Marla reclined her chair until it was against the wall. "What does Choy-na-Sal say about this?"

Drith grinned, though it didn't reach her eyes. "Choy won't be in a position to do anything about it."

"You're going to kill her?"

"Don't worry about the particulars. Plenty of Dryads are ready to shuck her leadership."

Sydney studied Drith. Something about the dryad's demeanor sparked a specific thought. "Drith? What did Choy do to you? Or was it the Cons?"

"Nothing. Not to me."

Sydney waited.

Drith's shoulders drooped. "My sister. Our acorns came from the same tree and her birth oak sprouted right next to mine, fifty years later. She wanted to join me in Woodhollow. I didn't want her here. I worried about her safety. I suppose you know what that's like, Marla."

"I do."

"Linni-da-Myn was a beautiful girl. She was so gentle, so sweet. She never harmed a soul."

Tears filled Drith's eyes. "I found her body in an alley. The Cons.... That bastard Seamus used to brag about it." She stared at Sydney. "I understand you were the one who removed that piece of shit from the living world. Thank you for that."

Sydney nodded, not trusting herself to speak. Seamus's fate still haunted her dreams.

Drith continued. "McGee wasn't there but he ordered it. He still laughs about it whenever he sees me. They didn't even let her live. When they were done, they cut her throat."

She growled and wiped her eyes. "And why? Because they were pissed at something Choy did. Some infringement on their territory. They took it out on Linni because of Choy's decisions. 'Make an example of a Dryad,' the Cons said. Choy refused to strike back. And when I pushed for revenge, Choy beat me and broke a handful of ribs. I still have trouble breathing when it's cold and damp. So I want to see Choy dead and cut up in as many pieces as possible."

"Pretty risky telling us all this, Drith." Sydney crossed her legs. "Aren't you worried we're going to go running to Choy with this, to get her on our side?"

"No. Choy-na-Sal hates you all. She'd never side with you faeries, no matter what."

"Why is that?" Sydney asked.

"Jealousy. She's jealous of your power, your reach. Marla, you took over this gang just a few years ago, when it had bottomed out and was the worst pitiful band in Woodhollow. In that time, you totally turned it around. The Faery Gang is getting more powerful all the time. Only the Cons are stronger at the moment.

"On the other hand, the Dryad Gang has done nothing but struggle. We're basically where we were five years ago. It doesn't have to be rational but Choy blames you for that. She thinks the Dryads should have taken the faery territory while you were weak. She didn't make a move then and now she's mad about it."

"Hardly our fault," Marla protested.

Drith smiled faintly. "Immaterial. But then, she's twisted, just like her maple." She paused. "So what do you think?"

Sydney chewed her lip. "Drith, I suspect you know we've already entered negotiations with...with other gangs, for an alliance."

"The Browns, I assume. Or the Hobs, since you visited both earlier."

Sydney suppressed a twinge of irritation. "You were following us?"

"Of course I was. I wanted to see how you all made out before I approached you."

"You're good. I never saw you. I guess Markus didn't either."

"He kept staring off into space. I guess he was concentrating on your negotiations."

Or thinking about Wychia! Sydney shook her head to clear the thought.

Marla brought her chair back to the floor with a *thump.* "We're getting far afield here. What my sister is trying to say in her own clumsy way is that we may be entering an alliance with another gang. How are you going to feel about that? You Dryads have been at odds with pretty much every gang in Woodhollow."

"We have our moments, for sure."

Marla snorted. "You're stuck-up bitches, is what you are."

Drith nodded. "Yes, we are. But even bitches can get along with people when they need to." Her eyes narrowed. "I am not crazy about some of the other gangs. Most of you are so beneath us that believe me, it galls me to abase myself this way.

She plucked at her vest. "Just as it does to wear these rags, though I needed them to move about the streets less obtrusively. I will be so much happier to switch back to one of my beautiful gowns."

Sydney's lip curled. "So sorry you're having to lower yourself just to save your skin. Very tragic."

"Your sarcasm is cutting, Sydney." Drith smiled again. "And accurate, of course. When push comes to shove, we will ally ourselves for our survival, to anyone. Except the Cons. I have over half the dryads behind me already. By the time you need us, I will have control of the Dryad Gang."

Her eyes hardened. "Now, do we have a deal?"

Marla glanced at Dana, who raised her eyebrows and shrugged. The faery leader switched her gaze to Sydney, who said, "Your call."

"Great."

Marla pondered her desk for a moment, then stood. "Provisional allies, Drith. Take care of Choy and assume control first. Do that, and promise to stand with us against the Cons when the time comes." She leaned across her desk and extended a hand. "Deal?"

Drith stood. She spat in her hand and stared at Marla.

Marla grunted, spat in her own hand, and extended it a second time.

Drith took it. "Deal."

Sydney exhaled. The die was cast.

No going back now.

Chapter Twenty-One

Sydney hurled the throwing knife with her right hand. The blade sank into the center of the painted rings. She twisted and tossed the second one with her left, in a snapping backhand motion. The blade tumbled in flight, bounced off the wooden target, and fell to the floor with a *clang*.

"Hmpf. I can't quite seem to get that right."

"What's that?" Lila asked.

"I can't get it right with the left."

Lila blinked. "Right with the left? What?"

"Sorry," Sydney said. "I meant, I can't seem to get the correct motion down with the left hand, at least when I throw backhanded. Overhand with both hands is fine. Backhand with the right hand is okay. But when I throw backhand with the left, the knife always tumbles."

Lila bent, picked up the knife, and handed it back to Sydney, handle first. "Well, keep practicing. You'll get there. Shit, you're still better than anyone here with throwing knives."

"I was considering some crumble, to maybe see if it would steady my throw."

"It might. Or maybe a stiff drink. Or grab a couple of guys for a stiff something else."

The thought elicited a genuine laugh from Sydney. She enjoyed the feeling and realized she hadn't had a good laugh in a long time. Lila's irreverent—and filthy—sense of humor always seemed to pop up just when Sydney needed a dose of it. "That's not a bad plan—the former, anyway. Maybe we could take the day off and get drunk."

"Tempting." Lila grinned. "But we're supposed to make the payment run to Sunbolt Shipping today."

"Yeah, I was trying to forget."

Lila tilted her head. "You're still thinking about what happened that night?"

"Guilty as charged."

The memory of her last trip to the Boardwalk was never far from Sydney's mind. She still awoke more nights than not, bolting upright in her bed, sweat pouring off her body, from the nightmare of seeing Seamus yanked beneath the docks by...whatever it was.

Still, it's the middle of the day. And no one has ever been reported missing when the sun is up. And I have to take my turn.

"Sydney, our folks made three trips to Sunbolt Shipping in broad daylight since then and nothing has happened."

"I know." She took a deep breath. "Who's going with us anyway?"

The corners of Lila's mouth turned down. "Vivian. Unfortunately."

"You don't like Vivian?"

"She talks too much. She's brainless."

"Maybe she's smarter than you give her credit for."

"Not likely." Lila sighed. "But with Gordon still laid up, Donovan and Claire in Sylvan Valley, Natasha getting over her sore throat, and Will locked up for peeing in that fountain, we're the only ones left that haven't gone lately."

"There are other members."

"Yeah but no one else Marla trusts with a money purse."

Sydney nodded. "Speaking of Will—"

"Dana and Anders are on their way to bail him out. I don't know what the hell he was thinking."

"When it comes to Will, I don't believe he *was* thinking. He's great with the demon tube but beyond that, he's not very bright."

"He just doesn't think. He tears off without considering what he's doing." Lila giggled. "An uncle of mine described faeries who fly the way Will acts as 'all flap and no direction.' "

"Hah, I like that. Well, no point in putting this off. Let's go get Scorin's payment for the week."

"Already done." Lila jingled a coin purse, then tucked it in her tunic.

"Okay, then. Let me go round up Vivian."

Sydney found Vivian in the common room, chattering in Garth's ear about something or the other. The look on the older faery's face was neutral but his wings quivered with tension. Robin moved through the early afternoon patrons, her standard scowl firmly in place.

Vivian looked up as Sydney entered. "Oh, hey Sydney. Is it time for us to go to the Boardwalk? It's you, me, and Lila, right? Just us girls? Are we ready?"

"Yeah, Vivian. Unless Garth wants you to stay here and keep him company."

Robin glared at Sydney, her eyes full of murder.

Garth slowly shook his head. "No, Vivian, I couldn't deny you from having a nice day out with Sydney and Lila. You ladies go on and enjoy yourselves."

"You sure, Garth?" Vivian's wide eyes stared at him. "You don't want me to hang out here and talk? I mean, we have so much in common. You're a lot like my father, you know? He was a good listener too."

Robin slammed her serving tray on the bar surface. "He would have to have been, Vivian, because you never shut up."

"Really, you don't mind, Garth? Thanks, you're the best." Vivian stood and hugged the bartender, pressing his head into her chest. She gave him a hard squeeze and let him go. "Come on, Sydney. Let's do this!"

She skipped out the door.

*   *   *   *   *

"So, anyway, these same two hobs kept circling back through the crowd and trying to give me drinks—like, every five minutes, you know?" Vivian waved her hands as she walked.

"They were trying to get me drunk. I think they wanted to make a hob sandwich with a faery in the middle."

She gave Sydney a direct look. "You know what I mean?"

Sydney chuckled, ignoring Lila's disgruntled huff. "Yeah, Vivian, I know what you mean."

Vivian continued to describe the party in detail. Sydney listened with one ear; most of her attention remained focused on their surroundings and the citizens in the street.

She spotted a pair of Cons traveling in the opposite direction, coming right towards them. "Vivian, hold that thought. Look over there."

"I see them," Lila said.

Sydney flexed her fingers. They had all taken a dose of crumble before leaving The Log. She eyed the Cons, mentally preparing herself.

One of the Cons spotted them. His eyes locked with Sydney's. She tensed. The Con made an obscene gesture with his tongue between his forefinger and middle finger. Sydney flushed and tried to keep her face neutral. The Cons both laughed and strode past them.

The tension fled her frame and it was all Sydney could do not to stagger.

Damn, I will never get used to that.

Lila glared at the retreating Cons. "Bastards."

"Oh, don't let them get to you, Lila." Vivian grinned. "They're just trying to get under your skin, you know? That whole tongue thing. Wishful thinking on their part. Just ignore it, or better yet, flip them some attitude back, you know? Works wonders, they don't know how to handle it."

Lila blinked then slowly nodded. "Yeah, I guess you're right.

Sydney kept her eyes on the crowd. She noticed that many of the citizens eyed the faery trio more than usual. Their looks were curious and interested, not hostile.

I guess they feel it coming too. Gang war.

The notion sent a chill down her spine. Sydney didn't really want to think about it too much but it was a near certainty now. Only Lord Burnside's edicts kept it from breaking out immediately. If he relented and allowed the Cons to pursue a formal battle before the faeries could find allies....

Sydney shook her head to clear the thought.

One thing at a time.

She just happened to glance behind them. It was something she did intermittently on the streets of Woodhollow. She tried to do it at uneven, non-predictable intervals, lest any potential stalker or spy figure out what she was up to.

The hooded figure lingered almost a hundred yards behind them, just at the intersection of Elm and Well Streets. He leaned against the unlit lightstone post, arms folded.

Sydney's heartbeat accelerated.

She glanced back a second time but the figure was gone.

This shit is going to give me a heart attack.

"You okay, Sydney?" Lila said. "You look a little pale."

"I think our shadow is back. The hooded faery."

Vivian's eyes widened. "The Nightshade?"

"Yeah." She thought for a moment. "Maybe you two want to head back to The Log, and let me do this alone."

Lila's eyes narrowed. "Why?"

"Aunt Brigid told me this guy is after me and Marla specifically. If he does make a move against me, I'm probably dead. I don't want anyone else getting hurt."

"But—"

"No 'buts,' Lila. It would be safer for you two to—"

"Oh, that's bullshit, Sydney!" Vivian exclaimed. She stopped dead in the street, ignoring the inquisitive looks from pedestrians. "You're our friend, you know? We're not going to just run away and leave you to get hurt. That's not what friends do to each other. You wouldn't do that to us. Right, Lila?"

"Uhm, right." Lila nodded, though the look on her face suggested amazement at Vivian's outburst.

With one hand, Vivian pushed her frizzy blonde hair behind her ear. With the other, she waved her finger under Sydney's nose. "I know we're not sisters like you and Marla but we're just like family and family doesn't abandon one another. So knock off that crap right now. We're with you so you better get used to it. You get me? You hearing me, Sydney?"

"Yes, I hear you, Vivian. So does everyone else."

"Oh." Vivian dropped her finger and smiled a bit ruefully. "I guess I got a little carried away. I do that sometimes."

"No kidding."

"Let's go, I want to go see Scorin. Maybe he'll have some other wines he brought in with the Ascorian ale. He does sometimes, you know? He's given me samples before. Come on." Vivian resumed walking.

"Wow," Lila murmured. "I'm...impressed."

"Yeah." Sydney could not help grinning. "Hey, Vivian? What was all that with Garth?"

"He hit on me the first day I joined the gang. Not just a little, either, but a full come-on that ended with an invite to his bed. I turned him down but he came back at me the next day. I found a way to deal with it. I just talk until his eyes glaze over. Shoving his head in my breasts was just a little extra torment." Vivian's high-pitched laugh tickled Sydney, improving her mood even more.

"So you never...."

"Nah, he's too old for me. But I love teasing him, you know? Don't worry, he can take it. Drives Robin crazy too, 'cause she knows exactly what I'm doing."

Lila found her voice. "You're more devious than I thought, Vivian."

Vivian beamed. "I choose to take that as a compliment."

A few moments later, the three young faeries passed onto the Boardwalk. The *clump* of their booted heels blended with dozens of others.

Sydney's eyes drifted to the Boardwalk. Somewhere beneath those thick oaken boards lurked the monster. The thought was almost enough to arrest her progress. She steadied her courage.

Sunbolt Shipping in daytime was just as she remembered it. Work gangs rushed about, lading cargo aboard a trio of river cruisers tied to the pier, or walking shipments from the ships' holds to the warehouse.

A pair of armed dwarf guards eyed them as they entered the warehouse but didn't say anything. Sydney led Lila and Vivian directly to the office and knocked twice.

"Come," said a muffled voice.

She turned the handle and opened the door.

A stumpy dwarf sat behind the desk, frowning at the contract in his hands. Scorin was a young dwarf, probably only fifty or so. He kept his red-tinted beard combed and braided and though his face was rough and craggy like his uncle's, it was not twisted with the cynicism and experience Sturm's had borne.

Scorin glanced at his visitors and quickly stood. "Sydney! What can I do for you?"

"It's that time again, Scorin."

Relief flooded the dwarf's face. "Oh, I see. I wondered if I had missed a shipment or something else had happened."

"As far as I know, everything is good. Ale has been on time and the count has always been correct."

"Good. Good." Scorin slumped in his seat.

Sydney nodded to Lila, who withdrew the money pouch and set it on the desk. Sydney stared at Scorin for a moment. "Aren't you going to count it?"

"No, I trust you."

"Why?"

"Do I have a choice?"

"Of course you do. You could have gone your uncle's route. Honestly, I am somewhat surprised you haven't. I figured a little revenge might be in the works but it never came. Why not?"

"Shut the door, would you?"

Vivian closed it.

Scorin regarded them. "I never agreed with the way Sturm handled things with you. I told him to stay out of the gang business, to not pick sides, but he did it anyway, and look what happened to him."

"Yeah, Scorin, I am sorry about that."

"I am as greedy as the next dwarf, Sydney, but I am also

fond of being alive. When Sturm involved himself between you and the Cons, there was no way this would have ended up any different. All the money in the world doesn't do you any good if you're dead. I have an agreement with you and I will keep selling to you. Same as the Cons."

She blinked. "You're selling to the Cons?"

"Yes."

"Selling what?"

"I'm not going to violate the contract by speaking too much on it. I've probably said too much as it is." He sighed. "Don't take it personally. I have already spoken to Crol and to Gorim Brightforge, the head of the Merchant League. Both assure me that as long as I deal with all comers fairly, they will back me up if some hotheaded gang member decides to come after me."

Lila cleared her throat. "Aren't you worried the Cons will come after you for ratting them out?"

"No, because I flat-out told them I wouldn't lie about it. And I told them the same thing I just told you: I am neutral, so don't try to involve me in gang disputes. As long as someone offers me the coin we agree on, it's just business."

Sydney bit her lip but nodded. "All right, Scorin. I guess we have to accept that."

"I'm sorry, Sydney. You're nice and I like you, but I have kin, a business, and a reputation to uphold."

"Fair enough."

She concentrated. Her mind located the power of the crumble coursing in her veins. Sydney focused and released the power.

A nimbus of energy, visible only to her, surrounded Scorin. A glow emanated deep from within his body. In an instant, his pulsing heart and network of arteries and veins shone under the power of her enhanced vision. The *thrum* of his heartbeat reverberated in her ears.

"One last question, Scorin."

"Shoot."

"Why did you set you spies on us?"

He frowned. "Spies? What spies?"

"The hooded figure I keep seeing following us and the Rats that attacked us."

"I don't know anything about that." His heartbeat did not change. "I don't know why you suspect me when you have so many other enemies and I've dealt with you fairly."

She blinked and the glow from his veins faded. A second later, her vision and hearing returned to normal. "Okay, I had to ask. Thanks, Scorin, we'll get out of your hair now."

"Good luck, Sydney. And I mean that."

She herded Lila and Vivian out the door and unobtrusively popped a fresh crumble packet in her mouth to replace what she's spent.

Her comrades were cagey enough to not say anything until they had left the warehouse. When they were fifty feet away, Lila said, "What do you think he's selling?"

"Could be nothing," Sydney said. "But if I had to bet, I'd say it's more of those marbles that allow them to access their caches at night. Marla never did figure out where the Cons were getting them from."

Lila creased her brow in thought. "I thought you said McGee said he got them from a goblin."

"Might have said that for our benefit, just to throw us off the track. I wouldn't be surprised if they were having them made somewhere outside of Woodhollow—by the dwarves in Kroven, maybe—and shipped into town. I could be wrong, Sturm could be selling them something else entirely."

"Okay," Lila said. "And then you brought up our shadow. Was that smart?"

"It was a gamble. I wanted to see what he'd say."

"Do you believe him?"

"Yes. I read somewhere that one's heartbeat speeds up when they tell a lie. His never wavered."

Vivian raised an eyebrow. "How do you know his heartbeat never sped up? How could you tell? You—oh, wow, you used the crumble, didn't you? You did, didn't you?"

"Yes."

Lila whistled. "Neat trick. How'd you figure that out?"

Sydney shrugged. "I just tried it and it seemed to work. Since then, I spent some time refining it. Seems pretty accurate."

"Have you caught me in a lie?"

Sydney smiled. "I'll never tell."

Lila laughed, though it sounded forced. "Well, guess we better get back and tell Marla things went well."

"She won't be back for a while." Sydney kicked a pebble. "She went to see Wulf, to finalize the arrangement."

"Might be good to have some allies," Vivian said. "We'll probably need them, you know? I heard from someone that Dominique was seen going into the Four-Leaf Club and stayed there for some hours."

"Dominique, leader of the Rat Gang?"

"Yep." Vivian's hands started moving. "See, I was out at the market on Bell Street. I was looking for some new boots because the ones I have were worn out on the inside edge. I walk on the insides of my feet, you know? Anyway, my boots were pretty shot, so—"

"Vivian, Vivian." Sydney stopped and put her hand on the gregarious faery's shoulder. "Just this once, cut to the chase. What did you hear?"

"Oh, just that Dominique went into the Four-Leaf Club and stayed there for a few hours before coming out. Since then, I guess the Cons and the Rats have been mingling together and sharing some resources."

Sydney felt poleaxed. "Why didn't you tell anyone this?"

Vivian shrugged. "I tried telling Markus and Dana yesterday but I got the feeling they weren't listening, so I gave up. You know how when you talk to people and they—"

"Okay, Vivian, we'll come back to that." Sydney faced Lila. "You think they're on the same side now?"

"Wouldn't surprise me. I know McGee and Dominique had an on-again, off-again relationship for a while. Friends-with-benefits kind-of-thing, but they hadn't been seen together for months. I guess that's changed."

"Wonderful, I—"

A distant rumbling echoed through the city. The ground

quivered. Windows rattled and specks of mortar drifted down from nearby brick buildings. The citizens of Woodhollows quieted and looked around, fear plain on their faces.

Sydney gazed skyward. A column of smoke furled up from the far side of the city.

The drake patrols, who had been making lazy circles overhead, immediately wheeled and flapped towards the source of the smoke and noise.

Vivian put her hand over her mouth. "That was near Wulf's Pottery. You don't think...."

"I don't know but I'm sure we'll find out soon enough," Sydney said. "We better get back to The Log."

Chapter Twenty-Two

Dana jumped up as they entered the tavern. "Sydney! Where the hell have you been?"

"At Sunbolt Shipping, making the payment run. What's going on?"

"I don't know exactly. I just know that someone or something blew a hole in Wulf's Pottery and leveled half the place. Marla, Markus, and the twins aren't back and I don't know what happened to them."

"Who else is missing?"

"Now that you three are back, no one." Dana collapsed in her chair. "Just Marla and her group. The rest of the gang is all here.

Sydney peered around the tavern. Save her, Lila, Vivian, and Dana, the room was deserted. Even Garth was gone. "Where is everyone?"

"I closed The Log the moment we heard." Dana passed a hand over her weary face. "I felt I had to do *something* but...."

Sydney looked at her companions. Lila's eyes filled with tears. Vivian stood with her mouth agape. Dana's demeanor was calm but the expression on her face indicated that she didn't know what to do.

I guess it's up to me.

Sydney took a deep breath. "Dana, there's nothing we can do about Marla and company for the moment. If everyone is here except them, then we have thirty-six faeries under this roof and we need to protect them. Enforcers may show up here, looking for answers. Hell, for all I know, we've already been blamed."

"Why would we be blamed?" Lila protested. Her voice cracked, on the verge of panic. "We're teaming up with the Browns. Why would we blow up our own allies? Why—"

"Do the ogres know that? I don't know what they've been told or what they believe. Maybe the Cons did this and they're marching to attack us even now—hit us while we're off-guard. Maybe Burnside gave his approval for the battle and we didn't get word. We can't assume anything; we have to prepare for the worst."

Sydney motioned at the back room. "Dana, every faery in the building should get juiced up on crumble, with more on their persons, and keep their weapons on them at all times. Set some faeries on the roof to keep watch, others at the windows. Make sure all the approaches to Bayberry Square are under constant surveillance."

Dana shook her head. "If the Enforcers come for us, anyone on the roof will be vulnerable to drake attack."

"It's a gamble but I don't see any other options. If the drakes and ogres come, we may be better off going down with the ship rather than risking capture and the mercies of the Woodhollow Jail. That's just a call we'll have to make at that time."

Vivian's voice was subdued. "What else can we do?"

"That's all I can think of at the moment. Do me a favor, Vivian, and go find Will. I don't care if he's eating, asleep, on the can, or getting laid. I need him here right now."

"Why?"

"Marla says he's the best with the demon tube."

Vivian looked confused. "I don't understand. Do you need to send a message? To whom?"

"I need him to recall Claire and Donovan from Sylvan Valley."

"What?" Dana sat up straight. "What about your Aunt Brigid's safety?"

"When he sends the message to Claire and Donovan, Will can have them tell her to go to Elder Edmund's house. Brigid may not like having her movements restricted but Edmund can protect her. Claire and Donovan are two of our best fighters and we are going to need all hands on deck before this is over."

"Marla ordered Claire and Donovan to Sylvan Valley," Dana said.

"Marla's not here!" Sydney fought down her own panic. "Look, she might come back and thrash me for contradicting her. But something has to be done. If we sit here scratching our butts and wait for Marla to come traipsing home, we might all be dead by the time she does. So we're going to batten down the hatches and ride out the storm."

"Uh, Sydney?" Lila looked at her askance.

"What?"

"What's with all the nautical slang?"

"That's like the last question I expected, Lila. I was just thinking about the ships we saw at Sunbolt Shipping and it seemed appropriate."

Sydney tapped the hilt of one of her daggers. "Let's move, people."

Dana all but fled the room, Vivian on her heels.

Lila stared at Sydney, who found her gaze unsettling. "What?"

"It's just.... You sounded so in charge."

"Well, don't get used it. Marla will be back soon and I'll fade back into the woodwork and keep my mouth shut."

"Do you really think she will?" Lila's eyes swelled with hope.

Sydney put her arm around Lila's shoulders and forced some optimism into her voice. "Yeah, I'm sure. She'll come back."

"I hope so. We need her."

"I know we do."

Vivian returned a few minutes later, half-dragging Will. As soon as he walked in, he shrugged loose of Vivian's grip and glared at Sydney. "Syd. I'm hungover. What do you want?"

"I need you to send a demon tube message."

"Nah." He yawned and stretched. "I'm too tired and that's too much work."

"I'm not asking you, I'm telling you. Message Claire and Donovan and have them come home as quickly as possible. If they expend their crumble for extra flight energy and haul ass the whole way, they can be back here in two days."

"Did Marla order that?"

"No, I'm ordering it."

"Screw off, Syd. You don't have any authority."

Sydney drew one of her throwing knives. "Listen to me very closely, asshole. One, Marla and Markus aren't here. Gordon is still healing and Dana is following my lead, so that puts me in charge. Two, if you don't do it, I am going to stab you. Three, I only allow Marla to call me 'Syd.' Do it again and I'll stab you whether you use the demon tube or not."

An ugly sneer twisted his face. "You're boring me. I'm going back to bed."

He turned and reached for the door.

Sydney hurled her knife. The blade clanged off the brass handle.

Will whirled, his eyes wide. His green and amber wings trembled.

Sydney palmed another knife and raised it, as if to make another throw. "You're going to send that message right fucking now. You got it?"

"Okay." His voice was a whisper.

"Tell Claire and Donovan to get back as fast as possible. They are to tell Brigid to go to Elder Edmund for protection. Repeat that back to me."

He did.

"Get to it. Vivian, make sure he sends the message and gets it right. If he screws up, come tell me immediately."

"Sure, Sydney, sure." She bobbled her head. "Come on, Will. Let's go send your message."

They left.

Lila touched Sydney's shoulder. "Would you really have stabbed him?"

"I guess we'll never know."

"Nice throw, by the way."

Sydney sheathed her knife. "Well, in the interest of full disclosure, I was aiming for his hand. I guess this was more dramatic."

Lila laughed. "Yeah."

"Sunlight's burning, Lila. Let's get to work."

* * * * *

Sydney rested her palms on the ledge wall of the roof. Nothing moved in Bayberry Square. The storefronts—usually so vibrant and crowded with traders and customers—were still. Shortly after Sydney posted sentries on the roof, Thom reported that a detachment of the Enforcers marched through the Square, bellowing for everyone to return to their homes. The citizens present hurried away, leaving Bayberry Square empty.

She heard the creak of the roof trapdoor, followed by a pained grunt. Without turning, she said, "Gordon, I thought I told you to stay in bed."

"I'm not good at following orders. Not even the ones Marla gives." He leaned against the waist-high wall and let out a sigh. Bandages swathed his torso.

Sydney eyed him. "How's the ribcage?"

"Hurts."

"You should have healed from that Rat's knife by now; at least, better than you have."

"Yeah, I know. I don't know if it was poisoned or what. It's just been very slow." Gordon took a deep breath, winced, and exhaled quickly. "If nothing else, I guess I can sit on the roof here and snipe if we're attacked."

"And if the Drakes come?"

Gordon smiled. "Well, then I won't have to worry about my ribs anymore."

Sydney chuckled.

His smile faded. "Sydney, what's really going on?"

"You know as much as the rest of us."

"Do I?"

Sydney looked out over the Square. "Of course."

"Okay. Well, unless you need me to stay out here, I'm gonna go in."

"Since you're up here already, why don't you take the rest of my shift and keep watch? Give yourself a chance to rest before you have to climb down again. Robin should be up in an hour to relieve you."

"I can do that."

She looked at him for a moment. "You going to be all right?"

"Yeah, I haven't broken my stitches in a week. This is the first set of bandages I haven't bled through within a few days. If you can, have Patrice bring me something to eat so I don't have to go all the way down to the kitchen."

"I'll ask her." Sydney paused. "Gordon, this is serious business. Don't ask me to send Patrice up here so you can get a blowjob and get distracted and miss something important."

"Sydney, I'm not that kind of guy," he replied, though Sydney noted he could not keep a broad grin off his face.

"You totally *are* that kind of guy. Look, I know how Patrice feels about you and I think you at least like her. I don't care if you two screw 'til the cows come home—when you're off duty. I'm serious, okay? Pay attention to what's going on. If you can't, head downstairs and I'll stay up here."

"I get you, Sydney. We'll behave. This...this could be it for all of us, couldn't it?"

"I hope not."

She flipped open the trapdoor and shimmied down the ladder. A soft *whuft* sounded as Gordon closed the door behind her.

Sydney conveyed Gordon's dinner request to Patrice, then made her way to the workroom, where she found Dana. The older faery sat on a high stool, hunched over the lab table. Dana held a test tube in her hand. She swished around the contents and frowned.

"Hey. Working on a new mix?"

"Sydney. Oh, hello." Dana sounded flustered. "Yes, I just needed something to keep my mind busy. The twins were trying to isolate some of the hallucinogenic qualities of the albino mushrooms, to make the Shroom a little more potent, without making it more dangerous. I figured I'd work on it while they're gone."

Sydney noted the test tube shaking. "You sure you're all right?"

"Yes...I...."

Dana placed the test tube in the rack and lowered her face to her hands. A moment later, a convulsing sob tore through her.

Alarmed, Sydney put her hand on Dana's shoulder. She forced her own voice to be steady. "Dana, it's going to be fine."

"I'm trying to be strong." She raised her hands, revealing a tear-streaked face. "Sydney, I know I come off as unflappable and sometimes cold. I'm the oldest faery in the gang, by fifteen years at least. I've been here a long time and I have seen a lot of faeries come and go. More than one died in my arms. With each one, it's almost like losing one of my children. I basically had to hold Tripp's arm to keep him from ramming a knife into his own throat after Bell Street, when all I wanted to do was the same thing. I've always managed to maintain a stoic face. But it's never been easy and I've kept it buried inside a long time."

Dana sniffed and let out a choking cry. "I just don't know if I can go through it again. If we lose Marla...I don't know what we'll do. I don't know what *I* will do."

"Dana, trust me." Sydney squeezed her shoulder. "Marla is the toughest faery I know. If there's a way out of this, she'll find it. This gang is her life and her family. She won't give it up."

Dana wiped her eyes. "Sydney, I owe you an apology."

"What for?"

"When everything happened, I stood there gaping. I could barely respond. All I could think is that it was Bell Street, all over again. I am supposed to be Marla's lieutenant. I've been doing this for decades. I should be ready for such bad news. Instead, I froze.

"You, on the other hand, have only been here a few months and you stepped in right away."

"Dana, I don't have any idea if I did the right thing here."

Dana shook her head. "Doesn't matter. You acted, decisively. You gave everyone something to do and kept their minds off whatever disaster is coming." She sniffled. "If Marla makes it back, she's going to owe you, big time."

"When Marla makes it back, I guarantee you she's going to be mad enough to chew steel. I'll wait to bring up any debt she has."

"Maybe that's smart."

"Okay, Dana. Think you're going to be all right?"

The older faery smiled and wiped away her remaining tears. "Sure. This old broad will pull herself together."

Sydney smiled back. Relief flooded her mind. *Last thing we need is one of our oldest and wisest coming apart at the seams.* "I'm going to make a circuit and see how everyone is doing."

"Okay." Dana stood and the two embraced.

Sydney walked to the common room. A dozen faeries sat about. Most clutched ale mugs and wore expressions of grim anticipation.

Garth waved her over. "Sydney."

"Hey, Garth." She kept her voice low. "How are they holding up?"

"They're hanging in there. Most of them are worried, of course. Several are pretty mad. I'm feeding them some ale."

"Not too much. We may need them in fighting shape."

"Gotcha."

The door to the living quarters opened and Patrice tore into the common room, panting. Her eyes darted about until she spotted Sydney. Patrice dashed to the bar. "Sydney! Outside, it's—"

The outer door slammed open and Marla stomped inside, her face twisted in a scowl. Mortar and dust rendered her normally-black hair white. Sweat and blood streaked her skin. Behind her came an equally-dirty and weary-looking Markus, and the twins, one of whom limped and leaned on the other.

Sydney ran to her sister. "Marla! What the hell happened to you? Where have you been?"

"We got blown up, that's what. And we're been sitting in jail, that's where. Now, do you want to get out of my way? I need a shower."

"Wait. Are we in trouble? Are the Enforcers coming for

us?"

"No. Why would they?"

Sydney slumped. A wave of dizziness washed over her and her apprehension drained away.

We're...we're going to be all right. This time, at least.

She realized Marla was staring at her. Sydney said, "Okay, everyone, you heard her. Back to normal. Patrice, pass the word to the sentries and drag Gordon off the roof."

She nodded. "Can do, Sydney."

A babble of relieved conversation broke out in the common room.

Sydney grew aware of Marla's narrow-eyed gaze. "What?"

"Syd, what have you been doing here?"

"Let me grab a chair and I'll tell you about it while you shower."

*   *   *   *   *

"So that's it." Sydney unfolded one leg and crossed the other. "We just tried to sit tight and see what happened. We didn't know if the ogres were going to come arrest us or what. Then you and the others walked in."

Marla spit out a stream of water. She scrubbed her scalp with bent fingers and ran them through her shoulder-length hair. It was not as long as Sydney had originally thought and she realized that since she'd been in Woodhollow, she had only ever seen Marla wear a tight braid.

"Why do you always braid that?"

"Huh?"

"Your hair. It's the first time I've seen it down."

Marla twisted her hair in her fingers, wringing the bulk of the water from it. "Too easy for an enemy to grab loose hair."

"Okay. Now, Marla, I've told you what we were doing. Would you kindly tell me what happened at Wulf's?"

She shrugged. "Gnome."

"Gnome what?"

"Wulf robbed a prominent gnome named Balsi some time ago. Not 'robbed,' as in lifted his wallet. 'Robbed' as in ruined his glass-blowing business, torched his warehouse, and turned him out into the street."

"Damn."

"Well, Balsi hit rock bottom apparently. His wife left him and his sons disowned him. From what Crol told us, Balsi spent the last of his coin convincing some goblin to build an explosive device. Balsi strapped it to himself, walked in the front door of Wulf's Pottery, and set it off, while we were in the back. Blew himself and the whole front half of the building straight to hell."

Sydney's heartbeat accelerated. "How bad was it?"

"Decently bad. Before we got yanked out of there, I saw at least six Browns that were dead."

"Wulf? Wychia?"

"They're fine." Marla extinguished the raincloud over her stall and reached for her towel. "Well, they're pissed but physically fine."

"Is this going to affect our alliance?"

"Nope. In fact, Wulf isn't convinced the Cons didn't have something to do with this. Crol told him and Wychia both he wasn't letting them go until he was sure they were calmed down. Last I saw, Wychia was throwing herself at her cell bars over and over. Crol yelled at her to stop but she'd gone berserk. He had to sedate her." Marla laughed. "It took three ogres to hold Wychia down long enough to get a needle in her arm and she cursed a blue streak the whole time."

"What did the Enforcers have to do with this?"

"They and the drakes showed up after the explosion. They arrested us, thinking we were attacking the place."

"I'm surprised you let them."

Marla snorted as she dried herself. "We didn't have a choice. We were all barely conscious. I didn't really get my hearing back for a full hour or so. Anyway, we've been rotting in the Woodhollow Jail while Crol put together the pieces. Once he did, he turned us loose."

"Gods, Marla. You really had us worried, you know."

"Yeah, sorry about that. But it sounds like you did all right."

Sydney shook her head. "I was just winging it. I was scared shitless."

"Syd, sometimes bravery just means taking action in spite of your fear. I saw the way the others were looking at you in the common room. They respect you...and I'm proud of you."

A warm sensation glided through her soul. "So, big sister, you're glad I came to stay with you?"

Marla gave her a hug. "You bet your ass I am."

ACT THREE

THE
RUMBLE

Chapter Twenty-Three

Lila stuck her head in the bedroom. "Sydney? Marla wants you."

Sydney blinked her eyes open and groaned. "What time is it?"

"A little past nine." Her friend's eyes danced with mirth. "You really tied one on last night."

"Tell me about it." Sydney sat up and swung her feet to the floor. Her stomach shrieked in protest, followed by a loud hammering in the front of her head. "It was a celebration and I was celebrating."

"Celebrating the safe return of our delegation by almost drinking yourself into an early grave?" Lila leaned against a wall and folded her arms. "You Holly Clan women have weird ideas."

"Must you be so chipper?"

"I must. I only had one ale, so I got a good night's sleep."

"Why only one?"

Lila's face took on a look of chagrin. "A year ago, I had too much at once and almost ended up in bed with a goblin I didn't know. Ugly one, too. Since then, I never drink more than one an evening."

"Bed?" A fragment of a memory slithered into place and a sinking sense of horror filled her mind. "Lila, did I kiss Markus last night?"

"Sweetie, you kissed *everybody*. You were so happy and babbling about Marla making it back that you just let the spirit take you. Markus, Lucius, Lucian, Gordon, Garth, Donovan, Noah, Anders. It might be easier to list the people you didn't kiss."

"I thought Anders was gay."

"He is but that didn't stop you. You even kissed Natasha and everyone got a kick out of that."

Sydney held her head in her hands. "Awesome, now I'm the gang slut."

"Don't beat yourself up. They know it was the ale." Lila paused. "At least, I think they do."

"Fabulous."

Lila helped Sydney to her feet. "That will all have to wait. Like I said, Marla wants to see you. She says it's important."

"She always says it important." After a few steps, Sydney's balance returned but her brain barked at her, letting her know that such a privilege could be revoked at any moment. "Please tell me she's hungover too."

"A little but not as bad as you. I'll help you downstairs."

They traversed the staircase. They nearly bumped into Anders on the way. His eyes widened when he saw Sydney and he refused to meet her gaze. Her skin burned with embarrassment.

Marla sat behind her desk, her customary cigar in her mouth. She grimaced when Lila opened the door and banged it into the wall. "Do you have to slam that so hard?"

"Probably not, boss. But I have to find my fun somewhere. Here's the baggage you asked for." She dumped Sydney in the chair in front of the desk. Bereft of Lila's support, Sydney collapsed into the seat. She wanted to yell at Lila but didn't have the energy.

"Thanks, Lila. I'll call you if we need you."

The secretary left.

Marla eyed Sydney. "You got plastered something fierce last night. One of the best ones I've ever seen."

"Don't remind me."

Marla chortled. "You were a regular kissing machine."

"Don't remind me of that either."

"Spoilsport."

"Is there any way I can use crumble to get rid of this?" Sydney squeezed her temples. The ache receded a fraction but made a roaring return the second she let go.

"Funny thing about albino mushroom crumble." Marla exhaled a perfect smoke ring. "It doesn't seem to have any interaction, for good or bad, with alcohol or alcohol poisoning, or any side-effect thereof, including hangovers. Maybe because it's an intoxicant itself. Nope, Syd, you're going to have to ride this one out on your own."

"That figures. What did you want?"

"I need you to go out on the Shroom delivery for the north route. It was supposed to be Patrice, Anders, and Will, but Will left early this morning and hasn't come back and the only people not already on a job are in worse condition than you this morning."

"Worse? Impossible." Sydney frowned. The dull thud behind her eyes clouded her thoughts and she had to fight through the haze. "What do you mean Will left? Alone? You said people were only supposed to go out in groups."

"He did have someone with him. Charley went with him. He said Will wanted to go down to the Love Market in front of Belles. Charley said he started looking at some gloves and when he looked up, Will was gone."

Sydney visualized Charley. Hulking, broad-shouldered, the faery was nice enough...but dumb as a box of rocks. Losing a partner would be about normal for him.

The Ivy Clan should have asked for their money back on that guy.

"You think someone grabbed Will?"

"Anything's possible, though I don't think so. Both Lila and Patrice said he was acting all moody last night."

Sydney dribbled some sarcasm into her voice. "Probably still mad that I tried to stab him."

Unfortunately, it flew right past Marla. "I know. He should be over that by now."

"So you believe he ran off. Why?"

"If we're lucky, just to sulk."

"And if we're not?"

"He might have left the gang. I don't know why, just a gut feeling and I've learned to trust those. As soon as I feel up to it, I am going to poke around here and see if anything is missing. If he did leave, I wouldn't be surprised if he stuffed his bags full of gang loot first."

"You want some help with that?"

"No, you already have a job." Marla motioned to the door. "Patrice and Anders are waiting."

"So you're back to being the head-bitch-in-charge and I am back to being a go-fer." Sydney snapped her fingers. "Just like that?"

"You have a remarkable grasp of the situation, little sister. Besides, you've done well. I trust you to get things done."

"No good deed goes unpunished."

"Pretty much," Marla replied with a smirk.

"I am going to assume you are just fighting off a headache and it's making you crabby." Sydney stood. "Instead of assuming you're being a harpy on purpose."

"A safe assumption."

"If it hurts so much, why do you keep smoking those cigars? They can't help."

Marla shrugged. "Takes my mind off it. Let me know how the delivery goes."

Sydney stopped by her room to grab her knife bandolier and meandered to the tavern.

Patrice reclined in a chair, one booted foot up on a nearby seat. Her hand rested on the pommel of a slowly-rotating dagger with its tip stuck in the table. She looked as hungover as Sydney felt.

Anders stood against the wall, his arms folded. He nodded at Sydney as she entered but did not meet her eyes. On the nearest table to him waited three bulging satchels, each with a long leather strap.

"Anders?"

"What?"

"Sorry about last night."

He sighed. "Yeah, okay."

"I mean it."

"I know you do, Sydney, Just...let it go, okay?"

"Okay.

Patrice stopped spinning her dagger. "Don't I get an apology too?"

"Did I do something to you, Patrice?"

"No." She stood, holding the knife in her hand. "But you did lock lips with my man."

Sydney's face burned. "Oh. Sorry about that."

Patrice glared at her. "Sorry isn't going to cut it this time."

Beads of sweat broke out on Sydney's forehead.

Suddenly Patrice smiled. She lowered her weapon. "Just fucking with you, Sydney."

Sydney slumped. "Gods, Patrice, you just about gave me a heart attack."

"Yeah, well, you deserved it a little," she said with a grin. She patted Sydney on the shoulder.

"You're not upset?"

"Nah. By the time he and I got to bed, I made sure he forgot all about it."

Anders sighed and shook his head. "Can we go do this? It should be an easy one."

Patrice made a face. "They're always easy until something goes wrong."

"Ain't that the truth." Sydney slung one of the three satchels over her shoulder, taking care to not get the strap tangled in her wing. "You're right, Anders. Let's get this done."

*   *   *   *   *

Sydney upended her satchel, dumping dozens of corked vials of Shroom on the rickety table.

"Oh, yes," Kristjan said. "Very, very nice."

Sydney suppressed her annoyance and kept her voice level. "Kristjan...you haven't been in the Shroom yourself, have you?"

The landy raised his bloodshot eyes from the bounty. "What? Uh, no of course not."

"Because we want our sellers to be on top of things. Like how much money they owe us for each shipment."

Kristjan scratched his tangle of filthy blond hair. "Well, uh...uh...."

"Sydney."

"Yeah, right. Sydney, I'm sorry, I am, uh, a little light this time."

"That's unfortunate, Kristjan. I guess this has to come back with us." She opened the flap on the satchel and made to sweep the vials inside.

Kristjan grabbed her wrist. "No!"

Sydney looked at his grip, then into his eyes. She didn't say anything but simply glared at him.

After a moment, the landy released her hand. "Sorry," he muttered.

"Kristjan, I don't think I have to tell you that if you touch me again, Patrice and Anders are going to rip your heart out through your nose."

Kristjan's pale skin grew even lighter.

"And if you don't have the money you owe us, Marla is going to do worse than that. I'll give you three days. In the meantime, no Shroom for you."

"What?" The landy's face was stricken. "You can't. I need it...I mean, my customers need it. I have commitments. You can't take it back."

"Watch us."

"I'll go to the ogres!"

"And tell them what? That we wouldn't give you any illegal drugs?" Sydney laughed. "Go ahead. They'll likely run you out of town. I bet they even tell you they are doing it to save your skin before we decide to give you a little late-night dagger party. In fact, if you plan on running, you better start now."

Patrice flicked her wings. "Faeries fly fast. And you won't want to be caught."

Sydney swept the vials into her satchel. "Three days. And no more product until then."

They left the landy staring at the table, his hands just starting to twitch with the telltale sign of Shroom withdrawal.

Sydney glanced about as they stepped into the street but didn't see anything suspicious. She tapped the small magical reserve remaining from the crumble she'd eaten an hour before and focused.

A thin glimmering outline of light, visible only to her eyes, sprang up around each of the milling citizens of Woodhollow. Sydney nodded to herself; she had tried the spell a few times and felt like she was getting closer to it working the way she wanted.

She inspected the aura of each person that passed them. Most were warm colors—reds and oranges—indicating a being that was neutral or well-disposed towards either to Sydney in particular or the faeries in general. A handful were medium colors —yellows and greens—which told her that those beings might be disinclined to like faeries or were already just generally annoyed about something. She did not see any blue aurae, which would have indicated an active hatred towards either her or faeries.

And what will I do if I see a violet aura? Run, most likely.

She couldn't remember when the idea of translating a being's anger and hostility level to an aura she could read had first occurred. Like all of the other times Sydney had used the crumble for something unusual, she just decided to eat a bunch of mushroom, wing it, and hope for the best.

She huffed at the thought. She would have loved to be able to ask someone to help her figure out the best way to focus her mind on what she wanted. The problem was that most often Sydney didn't fully understand it herself. The one time she had tried to explain it to Lila, her young friend looked so confused, Sydney gave up.

It's not really magic, she thought. *Not in the witches-casting-a-spell sense, because we don't have to recite words or make specific gestures or anything. It's more like we're tapping some mysterious force through the crumble. With enough power and concentration, we can do almost anything.*

A side thought occurred. *I wonder if the Cons and Dryads are using the same force, just through different methods?*

She shook her head. *You should have been a philosopher, Sydney.*

"You'd make Gordon proud, Sydney," Patrice said, jerking Sydney from her introspection.

"Huh? Why?"

"He said that on the day he was stabbed, you were very reluctant and tentative when dealing with the marks." Patrice smiled. "You're a pro now."

"School of hard knocks, I guess. Any more?"

Anders shook his head. "That was the last one."

"Good, let's head back."

It was mid-afternoon when they returned to The Log. Sydney kept an eye out for trouble but drunks wandered in and out the double doors without concern, so she figured things were under control.

Garth waved her over as soon as they entered. Sydney handed her satchel to Anders. "You guys go on, I'll see what he wants."

"Hey, Sydney," he said as she approached. "Marla wants to see you right away."

"I'm really starting to feel like her damn servant. She's constantly calling me back and forth, back and forth."

"Don't feel too bad. She does it to all of us. She just thinks you're more competent than most. That's why she relies on you so much."

Sydney blinked. "You think so?"

Garth nodded.

"Okay." Sydney paused. "Garth, sorry about last night."

He chuckled. "If you think I am going to object when a pretty girl kisses me, you're nuts."

Sydney stammered, "Yeah, well...."

"Hey, don't worry about it. Everyone was happy last night. It happens."

"Bet you wish it had been Vivian."

"Vivian? No, why would I?" He tried to look innocent but that faded to a sheepish grin. "Okay, maybe a little. You go on back."

She turned and nearly collided with Robin, who threw up both hands. "Don't kiss me, Sydney, I'm not in the mood."

"I'm never going to live this down, am I?"

Robin's answering smile was downright vicious. "Not while I'm above ground, you won't."

Sydney grumbled and pushed past the waitress.

She found Marla in the workroom, which was otherwise deserted. Sydney's sister hunched over a worktable, reading an unfurled parchment. Her brows creased and the corners of her mouth turned down. A pair of leather-bound tomes lay on the table.

"You bellowed for me, Your Highness?"

Marla didn't look up. "You're not as funny as you think you are, Syd."

"Where is everyone?"

"I told them I needed some time to work on a secret project and that I needed the space in here." She put down the parchment. "Everyone not on a run has the rest of the day off."

"Wow, you actually told them all the truth."

"I do, most of the time."

Sydney tried to keep the bitterness from her voice. "Which is more than you do for me."

Marla frowned but Sydney continued before her sister could respond. "Are you making any progress on Mom and Dad's designs?"

"Some, but I hit a dead end. That's why I wanted to see you." She tapped the parchment. "I think I have just about got this design modified enough to make it work. I did a few small experiments and it looks promising."

"But?"

"But I can't get the object to retain the magical charge long enough." Marla flashed her hand to Sydney, revealing a thin band of beaten copper on her index finger. "The ring will absorb a dose of crumble power—a strong dose now—without blowing up."

"Has that happened?"

"A few times."

Sydney laughed. "I wondered what happened to your face."

"Har de har har. Anyway, I can, in turn, extract and use, just as if I had eaten the crumble directly. And it's faster than the packets, much faster."

"How much faster?"

"Instantaneous."

"Okay, what's the hitch?"

Marla sighed. "The ring won't retain power. I can charge it and then draw on its energy, but once the ring is powered, it starts to fade, just like when we eat the crumble. After an hour or so, the charge is completely gone."

"Okay."

"I kept digging through Mom and Dad's designs, looking for a solution. There is one, a small battery for light, that acts like a lamp. To make it work, when you melt down the metal for the frame, you have to powder and toss in a lightstone."

"So toss in some crumble in this one."

Marla shook her head. "I tried. But crumble is temporary, so it didn't work. With the lamp, it uses lightstone, which has a permanent glow. I thought if I built a few trinkets and melted them down with this one, it might work, but no dice. I made one of those anti-poison amulets Dad tested on the chicken. The ring held the charge a little longer but it still faded. I have to come up with another permanent source of magic but one that's stronger."

Marla stared at Sydney with intensity, to the point where her skin started to crawl. "Such as?"

"I've been doing some reading. Some books recommend magical creatures as a source for such components."

"Marla, if you reach for a knife to saw off my finger, I am out of here."

"Sheesh, Syd, that's not what I was thinking at all. Besides, faeries have to access albino mushrooms to perform magic, so our magic isn't permanent enough."

"So you're saying the reason you aren't mutilating me right this second is only because it wouldn't work, not because you'd have to dismember a sister?"

"Don't twist my words," Marla snapped. "Anyway, that's not quite what I was thinking. We have to eat the mushrooms. Cons have to touch their cache at the end of the rainbow. Dryads have to commune with their trees. Beings like werevixens, *landvaettir*, and *vilas* have their magic at all times, but it's too weak, and dark elves just don't have the same type of magic as ours. Theirs is less like magic and more like a loan against their lifespan, right?"

"As I understand it, yes."

"There are some creatures who have inherent magical talent," Marla said. She drummed her fingers on one of the books. "They're born with it and can tap magic at will, much more strongly than we can, and don't rely on an external power source. The magic penetrates every fiber of their being, making them all very potent as sources of components."

"What kind of creatures are we talking about here?"

"Rare and powerful beings, and very old ones. As you might expect, there aren't many creatures in Woodhollow that meet that criteria but there is at least one."

"What?"

"Wingless worms."

"Wingless...." Sydney's eyes widened. "Lord Burnside?"

"Well—"

Sydney threw up her hands. She didn't even try to keep the irritation from her voice, which climbed in pitch. "Marla, seriously? Burnside could kill us all with a single flick of his tail. I have zero desire to end up like Mom and Dad."

"Oh Gods, no, Sydney." Marla looked taken aback. "I wasn't suggesting we fight him. I was thinking something along the lines of a trade. Worms shed their scales. I noticed several laying around his lair. Maybe we could bribe him in exchange for a few."

Sydney tried to keep her temper under control, with little success. "What could we possibly give a worm who's already sitting on a hoard we could never match?"

Marla hesitated. "Uhm, he expressed interest in the Hearthglitter."

Sydney's eyes widened. Every muscle in her body clenched and her voice rose to a scream. "You want to trade the most valuable object in Sylvan Valley and the lifeblood of our entire race for a handful of worm scales? Are you out of your fucking mind?"

"Sort of."

"Sort of out of your mind or you sort of want to make a trade?"

Marla held up two fingers.

Sydney's eyes narrowed. She spoke through clenched teeth. "Define 'sort of' and define 'trade.'"

"You know the old stories, Syd. They say the Hearthglitter is tied to the land, that it will always return to Beechwood Hall, no matter how far away it's taken."

"That's a legend, Marla."

"With some basis in fact," Marla fired back. "When Flagar the Cruel and his goblin horde raided Sylvan Valley a thousand years ago, they took the Hearthglitter away with them, and a few months later, it returned. It just showed back up in its cradle in the ruins of Beechwood Hall without any fanfare."

"Yes, and Sylvan Valley suffered three months of plague and famine while it was gone. If you want to believe the legends, Marla, believe them all. The Hearthglitter protects Sylvan Valley from massive amounts of harm. Even Flagar's invasion of our homeland barely killed anyone, at a time when he was razing entire nations. But the Hearthglitter went missing and POOF! More faeries died in those three months than any other time in our history. The Daisy Clan died out altogether. You want to risk visiting that fate on our people? I can't go along with that."

"Syd—"

"No, Marla. This obsession of yours has got to stop. You are out of control."

"Syd, just shut up for two seconds and listen to me. I am not proposing endangering our people. I have a plan."

"Every time someone says that to me, the hair on the back of my neck stands up."

"Just listen to my idea."

Sydney listened. When Marla was done, she said, "See any flaws?"

"Tons, Marla. It's risky. Super risky. We can't do this. No way."

"We don't have a choice. I understand McGee was at Burnside's manor again yesterday, with a second request. From what the folks at City Hall told me, he again filed for limited war and it sounds more and more like Burnside might grant the request. So we are going to have to gamble. The alternative is to flee the city and give up or surrender and basically become slaves to the Cons in all but name. I don't think you want that."

"I don't. But I don't want to endanger our home either."

"Syd, I swear to all that is holy that we can do this."

"You don't believe in anything holy."

"You know what I mean."

Sydney hesitated. "I think you should put it to the gang. They have to know what kind of danger we're risking to them and to the Valley."

"You know we can't. Easier to get forgiveness than permission."

"What if Burnside sees through your lies?"

Marla bit her lip. "I think I can fool him."

Sydney closed her eyes and pinched the bridge of her nose between her thumb and forefinger. "Marla, I...."

"Syd, if you have a better idea, I would love to hear it."

"I don't." Sydney took a deep breath, praying she wasn't making a colossal mistake. "Okay. Okay, Marla. I am going to trust you. I hope I don't regret it."

"Me too, Syd."

Chapter Twenty-Four

Marla froze. Her reaction was so sudden that Sydney almost ran into her in the near-dark. As it was, she just managed to avoid a noisy collision. "What?"

"This isn't going to work."

Sydney struggled to keep her voice to a whisper. "This was your plan!"

"I know. I'm reconsidering."

"Next time, my flakey sister, you let me make the plan and do the thinking, all right? You stick to busting heads."

"Deal."

The crunch of boots on gravel reached her ears. Sydney grabbed Marla's arm. Both faeries quieted.

A pair of grim-faced Beechguards strode past their hiding place. Unlike the halberds carried by the Councilguard, each of the Beechguard toted a pair of wide, double-bladed swords that shone in the moonlight. Legend said the swords bore the power of the Hearthglitter itself. They were reputed to be virtually weightless and capable of cutting through stone. The Beechguard wielded one in each hand in battle.

And yet I don't think a single one of them has ever drawn a sword outside of ceremony and training...at least not in the memory of anyone still alive. Sydney grimaced. *I hope we're not about to break that streak.*

Sydney and Marla waited motionless until the patrol passed. Marla snorted. "Sloppy."

"Hey, I'm glad about that. I'd just as soon we not get found here."

"You got that right. Come on."

They crept towards the front doors of Beechwood Hall. Sydney swiveled her head from side to side but from what she could tell, the Beechguard weren't so much incompetent as they were complacent. When she murmured as much to Marla, her sister replied, "Maybe they're more vigilant when the Clan Chief Council is in session."

Sydney shook her head. *No, it's because they'd never expect someone to try something like this. And only because anyone who did would be insane. Like us.*

Marla pulled the left door handle. Sydney expected a horrible creak but the door opened on oiled hinges. Marla slipped inside and, holding her breath, Sydney followed.

Two rows of carved wooden columns covered in intricate weaves of leafed branches stretched to the ceiling. Hooded lightstone lamps hung from every other column, casting long shadows across the middle of the hall.

In the center of the hall, the rows of columns curved outwards, forming a rough circle, before resuming their parallel course on the far side. A great oaken table occupied the center of that rough circle. A massive crystal chandelier, lined with faintly-lit lightstones, hung over the table. Ten high-backed chairs circled the table at even intervals, one for each of the clan, including the extinct Daisy Clan.

Sydney eyed the tenth seat as a sense of discomfort enveloped her. The perpetually empty chair was a reminder of the last time the Hearthglitter had been removed from Sylvan Valley.

At the far end of the hall, beneath a converging network of light beams, sat an altar of obsidian and white quartz on a raised dais. A brass cradle of interwoven metal strands squatted on the altar on six stout legs. Amid the weave lay an amber-colored gemstone about the size of Sydney's fist. The stone glowed with its own dancing inner light.

Marla elbowed her. "Come on, stop gawking."

"Yeah." Sydney squared her shoulders.

They stole up the side of the hall, behind one of the rows of the columns. Sydney's heartbeat accelerated.

It had taken the two of them four days to reach Sylvan Valley and work their way to the center of the faery lands without being seen. They perched outside Beechwood Hall for another day and a half, learning the patterns of the guards and finding gaps they could exploit. Even with the predictability of the Beechguard's patrol patterns, it had taken them hours—and every trick they had learned skulking the streets of Woodhollow—to even approach Beechwood Hall.

Now they were here, inside the most ancient and sacred building in the faery nation.

Marla's plan was simple. They would seize the stone. Marla had acquired a collection of recall motes—ancient, magical homing crystals, used to summon an object remotely. Marla would attach a recall mote to the gem and place another in the gem's cradle. They would return to Woodhollow with the Hearthglitter, present it to Lord Burnside in exchange for some of his scales. Marla expected the dragon would be delighted to add such a unique jewel to his horde and would readily agree to the exchange.

Sydney wasn't so sure. Burnside wasn't a mindless beast. The dragon was highly intelligent, perceptive, and, she suspected, knew a lot more than he let on. She thought he would see through the ruse. He might even sense the presence of the recall motes.

If Burnside accepted the trade, once they were securely away, Marla would trigger the recall mote in the cradle, which would yank the Hearthglitter across the intervening distance and return it to the hall. If Burnside found or disabled the mote, the Hearthglitter would return on its own accord before long.

Sydney ground her teeth. She wasn't in favor of the plan at all. She wavered back and forth between following Marla's lead and telling her sister that they should just flee Woodhollow. But they were here and committed now. She'd have to punch out Marla to dissuade her at this point and Sydney knew she'd never win such a fight. All she could do was hope for the best and try to keep a disaster from unfolding.

The Hearthglitter pulsed as they approached as if acknowledging their presence. The gem's inner light flickered.

She'd never been so close to the Hearthglitter. Sydney stared into the jewel's radiance. A great sense of peace settled over her.

"Hey, you still with me?"

Sydney shook her head. "Sorry. It's entrancing. I feel like I could just sit here in its presence and let the sense of contentment lull me to sleep."

"I know, Syd. It's...it's amazing. I almost want to give up this mission." Marla paused. "Almost."

"Marla, can't we just...."

"Syd." Marla touched Sydney's arm. "We need this."

"They say any virtuous faery can pick it up. You think either of us is pure enough?"

"Pure? I think 'virtuous' means benevolent, not virginal."

"Good, because otherwise you'd be burned to a crisp just standing this close."

Marla glared at her.

Sydney said, "Seriously. Do you think we can do this?"

Marla shrugged. "We'll find out in a second."

Sydney sighed. "Get the motes out."

Marla dug in her belt pouch. She withdrew a thick glass tube containing several tiny crystals, each no bigger than the eye of a needle. "You sure these will work?"

"No, I am not sure about any of this," Sydney hissed. "But if we're going to go through with this hair-brained scheme, we're going to get the Hearthglitter back here as fast as we can. I don't care if we have to crawl it back on our hands and knees."

"All right, settle down before your crying pulls the guards in." Marla pulled the cork stopper on the tube and tapped out two of the crystals. She stepped onto the dais and reached for the Hearthglitter.

"You should stop right there."

A faery materialized from the shadow behind the altar.

Marla recoiled from the Hearthglitter and ripped her sword from its scabbard. Sydney drew a knife from her bandolier.

The newcomer stepped into the light. Sydney's mouth went dry.

The faery's wings were black and yellow.

His eyes fixed on her. "Hello, Sydney. We meet at last."

She raised her knife. "Stay back."

"I must admit, I was hoping to speak to you much sooner than this but I have had to settle for following you about Woodhollow these last few months." His eyes flicked to Marla. "You would be the sister."

"What do you want, assassin?" Marla spit the last word. Her eyes narrowed and her lips pulled back in a feral snarl.

"Nothing from you, Marla."

"Then you can fuck right off."

The Nightshade shook his head. "As much as it pains me, I can't just yet. I need to speak to Sydney. Alone, if you don't mind."

"In hell!"

Marla stabbed with both hands on her weapon. The Nightshade pivoted so fast all Sydney saw was a blur. Marla tumbled to the side of the dais. Her head slapped against the tiles and she went limp. Her weapon fell with a noisy *clang*.

Sydney hurled her knife but the Nightshade had vanished.

"Now, now, Sydney," came the calm voice behind her.

She spun. The Nightshade stood less than a foot away.

On instinct, Sydney shot her knee up, trying to catch him in the groin. The intruder simply thrust his forearm down and knocked her knee aside.

She aimed a quick jab at his face but hit empty air. The lack of contact threw her off balance. Sydney spun in a half-circle and found herself face-to-face with him yet again.

"There's really no need for this, Sydney." The Nightshade spread his hands. "I didn't come here to hurt you."

"Then why did you come here?"

"To meet you. To speak to you."

"Why?"

He chuckled. "We have a greater destiny together—one that will pull you away from the squalor and misery of

Woodhollow and elevate us both where we truly belong. I'd like to say it's a happy coincidence that I ran into you here but the truth is, I have been waiting, trying to figure out a way to approach you and this seemed a good time."

Sydney glanced at the gemstone.

"Yes, we'll be taking the Hearthglitter with us. I would have taken it before but I was never quite ready with a convincing cover-up. Since we're here, I might as well get it now. Your sister can take the blame for its theft. With it in our hands, Sylvan Valley will bend to our will. But I think I should hold on to it until I am convinced you are..." He paused. "...thinking the correct way."

"You can't take it. I won't let you."

He smiled. "It's adorable that you think you have a choice."

He turned his back on her and ascended the dais. Sydney drew her long dagger with one hand and a throwing knife with the other. She jetted the throwing knife at his unprotected back and slashed with her dagger.

The man twisted to his right. The thrown knife passed harmlessly over his shoulder, between his neck and his wing. The move was minimal and an analytical corner of Sydney's mind suspected he had moved just enough to avoid the weapon.

He whirled and blocked Sydney's clumsy melee thrust. She tried to make a second strike but something struck her head. The world spun end over end and she found herself on her back. Her vision swam and a great ringing sprang up in her ears. Over the din, she heard him say, "I didn't want to do that. Please do us both a favor and stay down."

Sydney pulled herself to her feet as the man stuck out his hand to take the Hearthglitter. She wanted to cry out but her senses felt soupy and uneven and her mouth refused to cooperate. She took one staggering step towards him.

The man's hand closed on the gemstone.

A burst of light and clap of thunder filled the hall. The Nightshade screamed and stumbled back from the cradle, clutching his blackened and bloodied hand. Wisps of steam rose from his fingers and the smell of charred meat invaded Sydney's nose.

"Well," she said in a slurred voice, "that's one way to cook dinner."

His rage-filled eyes focused on her. "Bitch! Just like your mother!"

Mother? "What are you—"

But the man was gone.

Sydney half-walked, half-stumbled to Marla. She collapsed beside her sister and grabbed her shoulder. "Marla, come on, we have to get out of here."

"Huh?" Marla's unfocused eyes blinked.

"Marla, come on. The Beechguard will be here any second."

"Okay." Marla tried to stand but collapsed in a heap. She looked at Sydney. "Leave me."

"What? No!"

"Too woozy...can't focus...go, before we're both caught."

Dimensional stepping. But—

Panic pressed in from all sides. Sydney had practiced the dimensional step since that first shaky night when they stole the kegs from the *Oakenhelm* until she could do it in her sleep. Trouble was, she didn't know the grounds outside Beechwood Hall and couldn't see. It was impossible for her to materialize inside a solid object but she might accidentally try to land inside of a tree and bounce off the outside of it, knocking herself cold.

She looked at Marla, fighting back tears. *I don't even know if I carry us both.*

She heard a muffled shout from outside. *But we have no choice now.* She fumbled in her pocket for a crumble packet.

A man hunched over Marla. He hadn't been there a heartbeat before. It wasn't the Nightshade. He grabbed Marla in both hands, leaned back into the shadows and vanished. So did Marla.

Sydney gave a strangled gasp.

The doors at the front of the hall flew open. Shouts of outrage echoed the length of the hall and booted footfalls slapped against the hardwood floor. Sydney raised the packet to her mouth.

Strong hands closed over her shoulders. She opened her mouth to scream but a voice muttered, "Relax, Sydney."

Realization dawned. "Edmund?"

Her field of vision filled with a blackness broken only by narrow streaks of light and she knew no more.

*   *   *   *   *

A gray light filled her eyes. Voices twittered in her ears like tiny birds. Sydney concentrated. Slowly, her eyesight resolved and her hearing focused. She blinked away the fog.

Two blurry faces hovered over her. One coalesced into a male face in his fifties. The man's face was grim, if not angry. The other was a female face she knew so well. Sydney's voice rumbled deep in her throat. "Brigid?"

"You idiot!" Brigid's voice was taut and her eyes wild. "What's gotten into you?"

Sydney groaned and winced. Brigid's voice set her temples pounding. "Something stupid, like always."

"No shit! You nearly got yourself killed!"

Sydney flinched. Brigid rarely cursed. *She must be furious.* "Marla?"

Edmund jerked his head to the side. "She's over there, on the other couch. She's fine, but still unconscious. Shadowdancing is hard on those who aren't used to it and whatever happened in there is going to leave her with a nasty black eye."

Sydney sat upright. Stars popped in front of her vision but after a moment she regained her equilibrium. She spotted Marla across the room. Her chest rose and fell with regular breathing but Sydney could already see the ugly bruise forming on her sister's upper cheek.

She looked at Edmund, who stood over her, his arms folded. An implacable, dour expression marred his otherwise handsome face. She said, "You pulled us out of there."

"Yes, against my better judgment. If it had been up to me, I would have left you to the Beechguard, who probably would have killed you on the spot."

Sydney's cheeks reddened and guilt stained her mind. "I guess I owe you, Brigid."

Brigid's nostrils flared as she visibly struggled to control her temper. "What in the world were you thinking? Are you crazy? Strung out on drugs? Do you know what could have happened to all of us if you had removed the crystal from the Hall? Don't you care about us at all?" Her eyes filled with tears. "I thought I raised you two better than that."

Sydney lowered her gaze, unable to look her aunt in the eyes. "Brigid, you're right. We were stupid. And desperate."

She laid it out for Brigid and Edmund, including everything happening in Woodhollow, their audience with Lord Burnside, Marla's quest for a perfected ring, and the imminent confrontation with the Cons.

"And that's how we ended up in Beechwood Hall, in need of rescue."

Brigid collapsed in a chair. To Sydney's perception, the emotional numbness in her aunt's voice was only exceeded by the hollow sadness in her eyes. Tears wound down her cheeks. "I don't even know where to begin. I knew you and Marla were up to trouble in Woodhollow. But this? Planning a fight to the death that you can't win? Gambling your lives on the whims of dragons? Tempting fate with some aquatic monster? Sydney, I...." Brigid's voice dissolved into sobs. She slumped forward and placed her face in her hands. After just a few seconds she rose and fled the room. A door slammed.

Edmund stood to Sydney's side. His right arm folded across his chest, holding his left elbow. His left hand held his chin. His concerned eyes tracked Brigid as she left, then returned his attention to Sydney.

Sydney stared at her lap.

At last, Edmund spoke. "Who was this other man that confronted you in Beechwood Hall?"

"I have no idea. He's the one that's been stalking me around town."

"Describe him."

"I guess he was in his fifties. Brown hair with streaks of gray. Every time I've seen him, he's had it bound back from his face. Dark eyes; brown, I think. Medium height and build. Normal voice, not high or low-pitched. All-in-all, pretty average. No distinguishing marks or scars that I could see."

"Hmm."

"You were in the Nightshades. Does that sound like anyone you knew?"

He shrugged. "Could be any one of a dozen men I knew. Or none of them. I've been out for two decades and they doubtless pulled in new members."

Sydney sat up as a memory returned. "He did say something specific. He said I was just like my mother."

Edmund frowned. "I don't like the sound of that."

"I didn't either. That means he knew my family. That makes it personal and means we're all in a lot of danger."

"Not directly, or he would have killed you both right away. He wants something else."

Sydney nodded. Edmund's thought made sense.

"You're sure this is the same man who's been tailing you in Woodhollow?"

"Yes. I recognized him from the first night he came into the tavern of The Log. I've also seen him on the streets but he's never spoken to us or made a move until now."

"And you said he wanted the Hearthglitter."

"Yes, that's what he said. If the Nightshades wanted the Hearthglitter, why hasn't one of them just shadowdanced in there and taken it already?"

"The Hearthglitter can only be used with the purest of intentions. Anyone with evil in their hearts....well, you saw what happened. Every one of the Nightshades has a pall over their soul." Edmund hesitated. "Even now, after putting the Nightshades behind me and doing my best to atone for things I've done, I wouldn't try to pick it up."

Sydney nodded again. "Okay, that seems reasonable. Wouldn't he have known that?"

"I would have thought so. For some reason, he seemed to think he could touch it. But then, this faery's actions don't seem consistent with anything the Nightshades practiced in my day."

"How so?"

"The Nightshades were never interested in direct confrontation. They prefer to work behind the scenes, via subtlety and plotting. They are interested in power, yes, but as a means, not an end."

"That doesn't make any sense," Sydney complained.

"Try not to think of the Nightshades as a cabal. They are more of a death cult, Sydney, and their concerns are not earthly." He grimaced. "I shouldn't say any more than that."

Her blood chilled by Edmund's words, Sydney didn't argue the point

He went on. "I still have some contacts in the clan. I'll poke around and see what I can find out."

"When?"

His answering smile held no warmth. "When I get around to it. See to Marla. I'm going to check on Brigid."

He left the room without another word.

Sydney leaned over the couch and touched Marla's shoulder. "Wake up, sis."

Marla groaned and stirred.

"Hey, come on back to us."

"What? Syd?" Marla's eyes blinked open. "What happened?"

"We got our asses kicked."

"Hearthglitter?"

"Still in Beechwood Hall."

Marla sighed. "So we blew it."

"Pretty much. We're in Elder Edmund's house. He pulled us out just before the Beechguard busted in to tear our heads off."

"Edmund?" Marla's gaze finally settled on Sydney. "Is he going to turn us in?"

"I doubt it, or else I think he would have left us there. He's in the other room consoling Aunt Brigid. She's having a hard evening." Sydney's lips pressed into a thin line. "Apparently, we're incredible disappointments as nieces and faeries."

"Well, she's not wrong. Help me up, would you?"

Sydney did.

Marla took a few wobbly steps to a table where a ceramic pitcher and several crystal goblets waited. She poured herself a glass and downed it. "Ugh."

"The wine gone bad?"

"No, it's water."

Sydney chuckled. "It won't kill you."

"Says you." Marla poured and drained a second glass.

"You're going to have one hell of a shiner. That guy nailed you good."

Marla shrugged. "Hazards of the trade. You aren't looking so hot yourself."

Sydney spotted a mirror across the room. A quick glance revealed a spreading blotch on her forehead. As if viewing the image had triggered it, her head began to ache.

"Great. Well, smartass, what do we do now?"

"I don't know." Marla raised an eyebrow. "Do you? You're supposed to be the genius here."

"I don't know either. If we can get out of this without Brigid disowning and hating us, I'll call it a win."

"What are the odds of that?"

Sydney took a deep breath. "Based on what was said, we had a better chance to steal the Hearthglitter."

Marla didn't respond, just nodded glumly.

The sisters sat on the couch in silence. Sydney rose to get her own goblet of water. Marla nursed hers. She stared at the wall and appeared to be deep in thought.

Sydney's mind circled back to their problems. Somewhere out there was a faery with the powers of the Nightshade, whether in the clan or not, who had a personal interest in Sydney and her family, for some reason. She had an enemy and one who could appear and disappear at will, and who was clearly capable of defeating Sydney and Marla together without even trying.

Sydney licked her lips. If her head didn't hurt so much, the idea would have been outright terrifying.

Their problems with the Cons had not vanished. If anything, they were rapidly approaching a moment when they would have to make a decision on their future in Woodhollow—a decision that would probably result in their living or dying.

And no matter what, Sydney felt the need to mend her fence with Brigid, the only mother she had known for over a decade.

Edmund returned. His eyes settled on Marla. "You're up. Good."

"I suppose I have you to thank for hauling our asses out of the fire." Marla's voice was tart.

If Edmund was offended at Marla's tone, Sydney couldn't tell. He said, "No, you have your Aunt to thank for that. She had me keeping an eye on you for a while. When you came to Sylvan Valley and I realized you weren't coming to Holly Grove, I watched. I was curious. I'm not sure I was more angry or concerned when I realized what you were doing."

Sydney and Marla glanced at each other. Marla said, "So much for us being discreet."

Edmund poured himself a goblet and sat across from them. He folded one leg across the other.

Sydney said, "How's Brigid?"

"She cried herself to sleep. She's worried sick about you two, though given the way you both act, I have no idea why. You're a menace to yourselves and everyone around you."

Marla and Sydney stared at the floor.

"But for whatever reason she has, she does love you both, so that's enough for me."

Marla drained her water goblet. "So if you aren't going to turn us in, what are you going to do?"

"Nothing. I am going to turn you loose."

Sydney stared at him. "Really? Because of Brigid, right?"

"What do you think? Of course because of Brigid. Like I said, left up to me, I would have let you rot. By the way, either of you know a faery named Will? Little nervous guy from the Dandelion Clan?"

Sydney groaned. "Yeah, he's one of ours. What did he do?"

"He was seen in Holly Grove about the same time as the two leprechauns who we suspect wrecked Brigid's shop and house."

"No worries there," Marla said. "We had him tailing the Cons, to keep an eye on them."

"Oh?" Edmund's brow creased. "From the reports I've gotten, he was walking, talking, and working with the leprechauns."

Chapter Twenty-Five

"Marla, if you don't stop carrying on, I am going to leave you behind."

"You wouldn't dare."

Sydney glanced over her shoulder. The wind streamed hair across her face. She glared at her sister.

Marla scowled but said, "Fine," and lapsed into sullen silence.

They flew for another hour before Sydney saw the familiar walls of Woodhollow on the horizon. She motioned to Marla and they both descended, angling their wings to glide towards the ground. Sydney flared her wings at the last moment and alit with the grace of a butterfly. A second later, Marla landed with a heavy *thud* and tumbled to her hands and knees.

Her lip curled. "Not a damn word."

"Wouldn't dream of it."

Marla stood and set off a fast walk. Sydney arched her back and folded her wings, then followed her sister.

After a moment, Sydney said, "You over it yet?"

"What do you think?"

"I think you plan on roasting Will over a slow fire."

Mala sneered. "Maybe after I pull his testicles off with a pair of pliers."

"Graphic."

"Don't give me any lip, Syd. He betrayed us. He helped the Cons. He put Brigid's life in danger, for Gods' sake! He's been playing us all for chumps. I am going to make him pay."

Sydney nodded. "Well, at least we know now why he's been avoiding us lately. Who knew we were going to Sylvan Valley besides Markus, Dana, and Lila?"

"No one."

"Then maybe he doesn't know that we know, and—" Sydney clamped her mouth shut.

Marla looked at her. "What?"

"How well do you know Lila?"

"Very well. Hell, you know her as well as I do. Why?"

"Well, she's Dandelion Clan too."

Marla halted and thrust her arm into Sydney's path. "Stop right there. How can you think that about Lila? She's your best friend, Syd, and she has been loyal to the gang forever. Do you really suspect her? Seriously?"

A pang of guilt echoed in her head. "I guess not. It's just all the deception and betrayal we've been through lately."

Marla's lips pressed into a thin line. "I suppose that includes what I did."

"Yeah. With everything that's going on, I'm having a hard time trusting anyone right now. I must be going crazy."

"Do you trust me now?"

"I do. Now."

"Then trust me when I say this: Lila won't betray us. Not now, not ever. She and Will might be from the same clan but her loyalties are with us. I'd stake my life on it."

"I hope you're right."

"I'm always right." Marla tossed her braid over her shoulder. "Haven't you figured that out yet?"

"Like when you thought stealing the Hearthglitter was a great idea?"

"Well, maybe ninety-nine percent right."

Sydney burst out laughing and started shaking so hard she had to stop and brace her hands on her knees to stay upright. The sensation cleansed her mind and her stress evaporated even as her legs trembled and shook.

Marla halted. "Sheesh, it wasn't *that* funny."

"I know." Sydney wiped tears from her eyes. "I think I just needed to get that out my system."

"Well, are you done now?"

"Yeah." Sydney straightened and they continued.

Her mind rushed back to Edmund's revelations. If the Clan Elder was right, then Will had not only betrayed them but had probably been colluding with the Cons for some time. Marla had recalled at that point that Will was supposed to be in the group that had been attacked on Bell Street but had excused himself at the last moment, citing illness.

Was he working against us even back then? Sydney wondered.

She wanted a reasoned approach. Her anger burned as hot as Marla's but she knew she'd have to keep a lid on her temper until she got some answers. Then she looked at Marla. Her sibling's face had been twisted in a snarl since they left Edmund's house.

Sydney shook her head. If they got back to The Log and Marla saw Will, she was going to rip him limb from limb. While Sydney understood her fiery sibling's emotions, she wanted to get ahold of Will first.

Otherwise, we aren't going to learn what's really going on.

They passed under the arch of the Pine Gate. Sydney was sure the ogre Enforcers guarding the gate recognized her and Marla but they didn't say or do anything as the faeries entered the city. Her eyes raked over the crowd but she didn't see anything abnormal. No one paid them much attention.

Well, at least nothing major happened.

By the time they reached Bayberry Square, The Log was bathed in the orange glow of the setting sun. Patrons streamed in the double doors, which Sydney also took as a good sign. She and Marla joined the throng and entered.

Sydney spotted Natasha on stage, just as she finished her current song. As the last note faded away, the patrons erupted in applause, cheers, and catcalls.

Natasha's eyes widened at the sight of them. Sydney expected Natasha to wave or blow her a kiss but the beautiful faery did neither. In fact, her stricken face belied the cheery melody she'd just finished.

Sydney's stomach tightened.

Natasha donned a forced-looking smile and launched into the next piece of her set. Her luminous tear-filled eyes never left Sydney.

Claire and Thom stood by the door to the back. Sydney thought they were so tense that she could almost taste the stress coming off them.

Claire exhaled and her shoulders slumped as they approached. "You're back."

"Yeah." Sydney hollered to make herself heard over the cheering mob. "What's the hell's going on?"

Thom shook his head. His face was grim. "You need to hear it from Dana."

Marla frowned. "Where is she?"

"Back there. Your office."

They stepped into the back hallway. Thom shut the door behind them, muting the tavern noise. Sydney said, "Something's wrong. Something's badly wrong."

"Yep." Marla's tone was even.

"You're not very panicked."

"Can't afford to be right now. Whatever it is, I'll have time to flip out later."

They entered the workroom and nearly collided with an exiting Lila.

Lila's face lit with recognition. The secretary shrieked. "Marla! Sydney! Thank the Gods!"

The breath left Sydney's lungs as Lila hurled herself into Sydney's arms. "Hey, Lila."

"I'm so glad you're both back." Lila's eyes shone with sincerity and Sydney felt another bolt of guilt.

How did I ever suspect her?

Marla shot Sydney a knowing look. "Okay, Lila. Where is everyone?"

"Dana's in your office. Garth, Robin, Claire, and Thom are out front with Natasha. Vivian's upstairs. Everyone else is out. Even Gordon said he felt good enough to go out and look."

"Look for what? Or who?"

"Will."

A sense of dread crept into Sydney's soul. "Lila, why are they looking for Will?"

Tears filled Lila's eyes. "He killed Donovan!"

An image of the hulking, muscular faery from the Lilac Clan flashed through Sydney's mind. They hadn't spoken much and she couldn't claim to know him very well but Donovan had always been respectful to her and to Marla and by all appearances, had loved the Faery Gang.

And now he's gone.

Marla's scowl deepened. "When?"

"Yesterday. Will was—" Lila's lips trembled and she fanned her face with her hand. "I better take you to Dana."

They tromped to Marla's office and went in. Dana sat sideways at Marla's desk. She had one eye on the stack of paperwork in front of her, the other on the magical screen showing the view of Bayberry Square. She sagged as the sisters entered. "Marla. You have no idea how glad I am to see you. I see by the look on your face you already heard."

"Lila told me. How ugly was it?"

"He stabbed Donovan in the heart. It was almost instant. Then, on the way out, he ran into Vivian. She tried to stop him and caught a knife in her chest."

Sydney's heart skipped a beat.

"Fortunately, it seemed to miss everything vital. She's bandaged and resting in her room." Dana smiled thinly. "She must be going to make it because she still hasn't shut up. From what she said, they traded a few punches before he knifed her. Speaking of punches, you both look like you took a few of your own."

"Never mind that. I'll tell you about it later."

"Marla, Will got the plans."

"Which plans?"

"Your plans. The magical implement designs."

Marla's hands curled to fists. "No!"

"Yeah. Donovan caught him in the act of pilfering the office, which is when he got stabbed."

"That motherfucker!"

Dana nodded. "Yes, that's been the sentiment around here for the last twenty-four hours too."

Marla tensed and let out a deep breath. "Dana, we have got to find him. We need those plans back."

"Don't you think I know that? Markus has had teams out combing the city for him all night and day. We're turning over all his usual haunts. We've even got the Browns looking for him."

"That's not going to do any good," Sydney said.

"And why not?"

"Because he didn't just turn on us yesterday. He's been working with the Cons all along."

Dana gasped. "How do you know that?"

"Found out while were in Sylvan Valley. If it's true, and I think it is, then there's only one place he would have gone."

Lila's mouth fell open. "The Four Leaf Club?"

Sydney nodded. "That would be my guess."

Dana slumped in her chair. "We're screwed then."

"Not necessarily," Marla said. "There are options."

Sydney stared at Marla, feeling the chagrin creep over her face. "Marla, you aren't thinking...."

"You're damn skippy I am."

Lila looked confused. "Thinking what?"

"Our dear leader is considering breaking into the Four Leaf Club at knifepoint," Dana said with a grin, "and forcibly extracting our turncoat and finding our missing plans."

Sydney snorted. "That sounds like a great idea, Marla."

"Thanks, Syd."

"Except that is exactly what the Cons will be expecting. I bet they are practically drooling at the notion. One outcome is they ambush us and wipe us out again. They'd love that and besides, I thought you wanted to avoid a repeat of Bell Street."

Marla scowled at her.

Sydney went on. "Two, it gives them the perfect excuse to pitch their war idea to Lord Burnside. He's already teetering on the idea of having one gang in control of Woodhollow's underside. Showing that we are ready to wage open war in the streets—and let's face it, that's what an attack on the Four Leaf Club would be seen as—might push him over the edge to let the Cons fight it out with us before any civilians get caught in the crossfire.

"Or Burnside might decide we've overstepped our bounds and just send the ogres and drakes directly after us. Marla, I know you're dying to run Will over a rusty razor but attacking the Four Leaf Club is asking for trouble, no matter how it plays out."

"I suppose you have a better idea."

"An idea, yes. Better? Well, we'll have to see."

Chapter Twenty-Six

Sydney watched the dryad careen up the poorly-lit street. The girl wore a skin-tight silken dress a shade darker than her own pale green skin. She wove towards the front door of the Four-Leaf Club on unsteady feet.

Marla crouched beside Sydney in the darkness of the rooftop. She muttered, "This had better work or else we're falling back to my plan."

"Marla, walking in the front door and yelling, 'Give me the designs,' before you start stabbing everyone isn't a plan. It's desperation."

"Besides," Sydney added, with more confidence than she felt, "it'll work. Trust me."

"I hate when someone says that."

"You say it all the time."

"Yeah but that's different. That's me."

Sydney peered along the street in both directions but the lane was still in the late hour. She and Marla had watched the Four-Leaf Club all afternoon and evening from their rooftop hiding place. Once a curious drake patrol swooped overhead but since the two faeries hadn't been doing anything but sitting there, the big lizard left them unmolested.

Marla cracked a knuckle. "You better hope your hooker out there doesn't put two and two together and decide she can make more money by ratting us out than she can by doing her job. How much did you pay her, anyway?"

"A thousand."

"A thousand!"

"Marla, keep it down!"

Marla glared at her. "Syd, we could have gotten a half the floor at Belles for that!"

"Yeah and that wouldn't have been suspicious or anything, having a whole battalion of whores marching down the street. As it is, it's just one girl looking to get her kink on. And as to her ratting us out, what does she know?"

Sydney eyed the dryad, who neared the front doors of the Club. The two Cons out front—neither of whom Sydney recognized—spotted the dryad and watched her approach with interest.

"She knows some faery she didn't know paid her to come to their door. Sure, she could tell them that but I swear, she saw the gold and her eyes lit up like lightstones and then got even brighter when I told her that if everything went well, we might be repeat customers. She won't say shit. And as for the Cons, I'm guessing those two will be more interested in getting off than asking a lot of questions."

Marla shook her head. "I think you're underestimating them."

"Overestimating your enemy is as bad as the other way around. Everyone tells me the Cons think with their dongs and because of that, I don't think they'll turn down a free hummer."

"Jeez, Syd, you would think you were an expert on the male sex drive. You've been with exactly one guy."

Sydney bit back an angry retort. "Well, in the next five minutes, one of us will get to be right. Maybe you'll be able to say you told me so."

"Like I said before, rubbing it in faces is your thing, not mine."

The dryad didn't say a word. Instead, she offered the Cons a coy smile. Her beckoning finger was unmistakable. The Cons looked at each other, then at the door, then back to the hooker. One left his post and followed the dryad into a nearby alley. The other leaned against the door and waited.

"Only one left," Marla said.

"Not a problem. Just wait."

A moment later, the Dyrad emerged from the alley, more unsteady than before. Her honeyed voice drifted to the faeries' position. "Your friend could use a little help."

"What's wrong with him?"

She donned a most winsome leer. "Nothing, I could just use the two of you...together."

The Con nodded. Lust painted his features. He followed her into the alley.

Marla grunted. "Okay, you were right."

Sydney smirked. "Give it a few minutes and all three of them should be out cold."

"What was that stuff you gave her?"

"Extra-strong Shroom mixed with something the twins said was a quick-acting sleeping agent. When the dryad asked, I said it would make her charms irresistible, so of course, she downed half the bottle at once. I mean, did you see how she was walking? She could barely stand up. As soon as she touches the Cons, she'll pass it on to them and knock them out too."

"All right, let's get down there."

They stole from the rooftop and hurried towards the door of the Four-Leaf Club. Sydney had no idea how long the door guards would be out but she wanted to be in and out in less than five minutes. She glanced in the mouth of the alley. The dryad and the two Cons lay tangled in a heap. One of them let loose with a soft snore.

"Crumble, Marla."

"On it."

Each of them placed a packet under their tongue. Sydney focused her thoughts on her body, willing it to fade, to vanish. She glanced at Marla.

Her sister was gone.

"Marla?"

"Right here," Marla whispered.

"Can you see me?"

"No."

"Okay," Sydney said. "How long do you think this is good for?"

"A few minutes at most, so let's not screw around."

"Right. Just remember that this just makes us invisible, not inaudible."

"What? Speak straight, damn it."

"They can still hear us, Marla, or feel us if they run into us so stay out of their way."

"Let's go, Syd."

Sydney cracked the door of the Club, half-expecting a dozen angry Cons to come boiling out. But since nothing happened, she took a deep breath and slipped inside, with Marla right on her heels.

Dim lamplight filled the space beyond the door, which appeared to be a cloakroom of some kind. Overcoats hung on numbered hooks and a few pairs of muddy boots lined the baseboard. Odd music and snatches of muffled conversation drifted from the next room.

Sydney kept her voice at a whisper. "As we discussed."

"Yeah."

She cracked open the far door.

The room beyond was vast. Rectangular tiers bounded the room, dropping in height towards the center of the chamber, which was occupied by a great bonfire. Tables and chairs lined the tiers. Carousing Cons filled the entire room. Most carried a mug in their hand, or in both hands. Not a few engaged in drunken song, grasping each other around the shoulders and swaying to their own melodies. At the far end of the room, a quartet of Cons with wooden instruments played a jolly tune. A handful of the green-clad men danced to the beat.

Working girls moved through the throng. Each wore a seductive smile and not much else. One of them moved in front of a lamp and for just a moment, her profile was backlit. Sydney had a glimmer of recognition but the woman vanished behind the inebriated Cons before she could make a positive identification.

Sydney scanned the room for exits, noting several. One seemed to be a kitchen of some sort; Cons went through the door and returned moments later with fresh ale or hunks of meat still on the bone.

Marla whispered in her ear. "Let's try the door on the other side."

Sydney nodded, then remembered Marla couldn't see her. "Right."

They stepped into the room and edged around the perimeter. At one point, a wobbling Con—Declan, she thought his name was—stopped abruptly, not three feet in front of her. He leaned against the wall and folded his arms. His lids sagged over bloodshot eyes and his body reeked of whiskey.

Sydney froze. Due to the tight space, she could not brush past the Con without him feeling her. He was so close she was feared any movement would reveal her. A mounting terror crawled over her mind: that the crumble was about to wear off, leaving her and Marla exposed and at the mercy of three dozen of their worst enemies. Her stomach wrenched.

Just as her anxiety reached an intolerable fever pitch, Declan leveraged himself from the wall and half-stepped, half-stumbled down the tier to another group of sitting Cons, who welcomed him with slaps on the back.

Sydney scuttled through the tables and darted in the open door. She ducked inside a tiny closet. Not three seconds later, Marla appeared before her. "That was close."

Sydney looked at her shaking hands.

Too close.

"We need to take another dose."

"Yeah, but—" Sydney hesitated. "How sensitive are the Cons to magic use?"

Marla shrugged. "About the same as we are. They can feel it around them if they're paying attention but most of these guys are drunk and on their last legs for the evening. I bet this goes on every night."

A smile lit her face but did not reach her eyes. "Which is something for me to remember in the future. If we're going to hit them, better when they're all pixelated and can't fight back."

Sydney said. "What if one of them nearby isn't drunk?"

"Then we're probably dead. But we're already in here, right? No going back now."

"Yeah." Sydney took a deep breath. "Okay."

They looked at each other, devoured another packet each, and cast their spell. Sydney tensed but she heard nothing that indicated a reaction from the Club's residents.

Maybe Marla was right about charging down the door. This sneaking business is fraying my last faery nerve.

"Okay," Marla said from nearby. "Let's keep going."

The sisters crept up a flight of stairs. Marla reappeared and ate another crumble packet, and vanished again. Sydney knew what her sister was doing: casting out her mind, looking for the device plans. Since they were magical and Marla was familiar with their aura, she might be able to detect them. It made her burn through her invisibility spell quicker but Marla judged it worth the risk.

Considering that repeated spell casting was eventually going to draw some Con's attention, Sydney hadn't agreed and preferred to minimize their exposure. She'd said as much.

But Marla's going to do what Marla wants to do. No sense in fighting it. She smiled to herself. *Like any other force of nature.*

Marla whispered, "Not feeling them."

They slunk down a long hallway. Loud Con voices and the good-natured shrieks of females of some race or the other mingled with the merriment from below. At one point, they had to wait when a door flew open and a naked landy ran giggling into the room across the hall, pursued by an equally naked and clearly-aroused Con.

Sydney's lip curled. *Gods, they really are all led around by their peckers.*

"Sydney!" Marla's soft voice held a hint of triumph. "I think I have them. Down the hall, here."

They slid to the door at the end of the hall. Marla said, "I don't hear anything inside, do you?"

"No." Sydney tested the knob. "Locked."

"Well, pick it."

"Marla, I suck at picking locks."

"So do I."

Sydney sighed. "Fine."

She withdrew her set of lockpicks from her belt pouch. She only carried the slender brass needles out of habit, since she was nearly as inept as when she had first started her training. It galled her that something so simple to everyone else in the gang—even Natasha, who didn't do fieldwork—was so hard for her. She took a few deep breaths to calm her shaking nerves and inserted the thin rods into the keyhole. She applied pressure and twisted.

The tumblers clicked and fell into place.

Sydney grunted in surprise. "Huh. Piece of cake."

"Stop congratulating yourself and get inside. The crumble's going to wear off any second."

Sydney opened the door. It was an office, not dissimilar to Marla's back in The Log. A lightstone lamp, set to a low glow, filled the room with hazy light. She slipped inside and felt a brush of air as Marla did the same. No sooner had Sydney shut the door when Marla appeared.

Marla raised an eyebrow. "That's two close calls."

"Yeah. We won't get lucky a third time." Sydney turned the lock bolt. "Find those designs so we can get the hell out of here."

Marla rifled the desk for a moment before uttering a low growl of delight. She withdrew a bound sheaf of pages.

Sydney reached for another packet but Marla shook her head. "Not yet. I want to make sure they're all here first."

"Marla—"

"It'll just take a second." She untied the strip of cloth around the pages, unrolled the bundle, and started flipping through.

Sydney's anxiety mounted as seconds ticked off the clock. With each passing moment, her certainty that they were going to be caught increased. How long would the dryad and the guards stay unconscious? How many more times could they use the crumble without the Cons detecting it? What if there was a group in the hallway having a conversation and they couldn't slip past?

"All here," Marla said. "Let's go."

Sydney had just eaten a packet when she heard the muffled

voices in the hallway outside. "Marla, quick."

The sisters dissolved from sight right as the lock clicked and the door opened.

McGee stepped inside. He was every bit as big as Sydney remembered. His face, which had been so amiable when he came to The Log, was hard and cold as a winter wind. It took Sydney a moment to remember where she had seen such malevolence before the memory struck her. His face reminded her of a painting of a demon she had seen in a book years before. The recollection made her shiver.

Behind McGee came Will. Sydney's fear vanished, replaced by a wave of smoldering anger.

The turncoat wore a brown hooded cloak over his tunic and trousers. Despite being inside, Will kept the hood pulled over his head, as if he thought that even in the heart of Four-Leaf Club, he needed to conceal himself from the wrath of his former colleagues.

McGee moved around his desk, passing not four feet from Marla. He paused and his brow furrowed. His eyes raked over the corner in which Marla crouched.

Sydney hurled a silent prayer to the Gods that Marla would remain calm.

McGee blinked and shook his head. He sat at the desk and gestured Will to sit across from him. Will did. He doffed his hood. Sydney noted with satisfaction that Will sported several purple bruises on his face and neck.

I guess Vivian landed a couple of good ones.

Sydney's eyes bored into his. Will was haunted, tired. She wondered how much regret he felt at that moment.

McGee placed his feet up on the desk. "So, what are your plans now?"

"Leaving town." Will's voice held no warmth, no life...only fatigue.

"And going where?"

"North, probably."

"I'm asking a specific question, lad. Where?"

Will shrugged. "I don't know yet."

"Then you're not leaving town."

"What? Why not?"

McGee smiled. "We might need you once we've settled accounts with your old friends."

"Why would you need me?"

"Legitimacy. You might need to assume control of whatever shreds are left of the Faery Gang."

"I want out. This is my chance for a new life."

McGee's laugh was ugly. "Will, you know the old saw: once you're in, you're in for life. Until death."

Sydney thought, *Is that true? Am I in this to the death now?* Her attention wrenched back to the conversation.

"My patron might have something to say about that."

"Your patron has already given me free rein to use you as I see fit." McGee flexed his fingers. "We clear?"

Will sighed. "Fine. Give me my money."

"You know the drill. Half now, half after." McGee's eyes narrowed. "And don't even think about running."

"I won't."

They sat in silence for a moment. Beads of sweat dotted Will's forehead as he squirmed under McGee's gaze. "Are we done here?"

"Not quite. I need to kill a few more moments before I have to go downstairs and deal with that stupid bitch again. She's getting on my nerves."

"Why did you invite her here, if you don't want to deal with her?"

"Don't be stupid. It's for an alliance, plain and simple." McGee grimaced. "I'll probably have to fuck her a few times but it is what it is."

"That sounds terrible," Will said, his voice sarcastic.

"It's a necessity. Women are just a distraction, lad. Don't get me wrong; I enjoy a piece of ass as much as the next leprechaun but in the greater scheme of things, I have a hundred other things I'd rather be doing."

"What would Dominique say?"

"Nothing. Why would she care?"

"I thought you and her—"

McGee made a flipping dismissive motion with his hand. "We're not attached at the hip. It's a relationship of convenience. Besides, Dominique and the Rats would betray us in a heartbeat if they thought they could get away with it. So she won't care in the slightest. Hell, maybe I can convince her to join in. Maybe the bitch swings both ways and her and Dominique can go off and do their own thing. Get them both out of my hair so I can concentrate on business."

There was a knock at the door. McGee said, "Come!"

A pair of Cons hurried in. "Boss, we have a wee problem. Aidan and Quinn abandoned the front door. We found 'em across the way, out cold. They were tangled up with one of the dryads from Belles. When we shook her awake, she mumbled something about having been paid by faeries!"

McGee jumped from his seat. "Seal the front doors. Start a room-by-room search of the whole Club."

"You got it, Boss."

He leveled a finger at Will. "Get your arse back to your room. Don't fucking move from there until I say so. Go!"

Will scampered out.

McGee went to the door. He opened it but paused. The Con peered back into the room with narrowed eyes, shook his head, then left, slamming it behind him.

"Marla?"

"Syd, we have to get out of here right now."

"No shit."

"We need to crumble again, we can't have more than a few seconds left.'

"No, Marla, they're all alert now. They'll feel it for sure."

Marla's voice dripped with tension. "We'll never make it to the front door."

Sydney's mind raced. "We passed another set of stairs in the hallway. Let's head to the roof."

"We'll be pinned up there."

"Maybe we can shimmy down the outside of the building or something. We're out of choices. Come on."

They opened the door just a sliver and darted into the hall.

Angry voices and the thump of boots on the wooden floors echoed from below. Sydney started up the stairs as a group of Cons arrived from the first floor.

"Fan out!" one yelled. "Check every last corner!"

Marla appeared in front of her. Sydney hissed, "Move!"

The staircase ended in a landing. A short ladder led to a trapdoor, much as in The Log. Sydney motioned Marla up. Marla ascended the rungs and unhooked the trapdoor.

A pair of Cons hurried past in the hallway below. Sydney reached for a throwing knife. Fortunately, neither of the Cons looked up the stairs.

"Come on, Syd."

She hurried up the ladder and scrambled onto the wood plank rooftop. Marla made to close the trapdoor but it slipped out of her grasp and slammed shut with a *blam*.

The blood froze in Sydney's veins. "Oh, shit."

"We don't have any choice, Syd. We have to fly out of here."

Sydney glanced at the night sky. There was nothing in sight but stars and cloud. For the moment. "But—"

"It's that or stay here."

Sydney unfurled her wings. "Then let's do it."

She took a step and leaped off the roof. Her wings slapped the air, thrusting her higher. Despite the danger, the joy of flight and freedom flooded her soul.

Marla beat her wings alongside Sydney. Her face held the same dreamy contentment.

Sydney glanced behind. A group of Cons milled about on the rooftop. None of them looked up. The sisters rapidly left the Four-Leaf Club behind.

We did it, Sydney thought. Her heart exulted. *We got the plans and escaped, with no one the wiser. Now we just need to get down before—*

"Excuse me, Miss. What do you think you're doing?"

A bulky form pulled alongside her, gliding as effortlessly through the dark as any faery.

"Uhm—"

"You and your friend better set it down."

Another drake took up position behind Marla.

"All right," Sydney said. "I'll land. Marla?"

"Yep, me too," Marla called, though her voice was curt.

Sydney changed the slant of her wings and glided towards the ground. She alit as gently as ever. Marla thudded the ground, just as always.

The two drakes landed, one in front, one behind. Though their motion was graceful and sinuous, the windows of nearby buildings rattled at the impact.

The front drake held up a lightstone. A golden badge hung from a chain about his neck and a blue peaked cap perched on his head at a jaunty angle. An irritated scowl adorned his scaly face. "Let's see your permits."

"Permits?"

"Flying permits, you mooks."

Sydney shuffled her feet. "We don't have permits."

"Of course you don't." The drake snorted. A puff of steam belched from his nostrils. "You faeries....give it to 'em, Lou."

Sydney whirled, her hands up. "No need to—"

The rear drake craned out his paw. He clutched a tiny slip of paper in his talons. When Sydney didn't react, he thrust it at her, "Take it, it won't bite."

She did.

The drake handed Marla a similar slip. As soon as she did, he took to the air. The wind from his launch blew Sydney's hair from her face.

The Drake that had first spoken gave them a withering look. "Stay on the ground." He flapped and joined his companion.

Sydney's apprehension faded, replaced by confusion. She said, "Marla? What just happened?"

Marla looked at the sheet, scowled, and spat on the ground. "Read it and weep."

"Why, what is it?"

"A flying ticket."

Chapter Twenty-Seven

"That's some tale, Sydney." Lila poured Ascorian ale into Sydney's glass. "So did you at least get everything?"

"Yeah. Marla flipped through the plans and said they were all there. That bastard Will was there too but we didn't get a chance to even things up with him."

"Too bad."

"This isn't the end." Sydney took a swig of her drink. The thick liquid trickled down her throat. "Don't worry. I'll make sure he tells us what he knows and after that, we'll take turns peeling the skin off his hide."

"You're turning as bloodthirsty as Marla."

"Yeah, I know."

Lila laughed and shook her head. "She had a fit when she went to pay the flying tickets at city hall and earned herself another ticket for creating a nuisance. Then as soon as she got here, she got a message and had to turn right around and head right back over. Probably some paperwork snafu."

"She'll live," Sydney said. "On a more positive note, Vivian seems to be getting better."

"Yeah, she's recovering faster than Gordon, in fact."

"I don't understand that." Sydney took another gulp. "Gordon was stabbed weeks ago. He should be well on the road to mending."

"The twins and Garth are all stumped. They've been checking Gordon's wounds about every other day and they can't figure it out.

Sydney grimaced. "I wish I had thought to grab the blade that Rat was using. Maybe it was poisoned or something. They could have analyzed it."

"Don't beat yourself up. He *is* getting better, just slowly."

"Yeah, I guess."

Lila drained her own cup. "Sydney, what's eating you? You've got something on your mind."

Sydney put her cup on the floor. She kicked off her boots and lay back on the bed with her fingers laced behind her head. "Do you believe in intuition, Lila? Precognition?"

"You mean like being able to predict the future?"

"Yes."

"I never really thought about it. Why?"

"Maybe it's not really being able to see the future but maybe it is a combination of instinct, our inherent magical talent, and our subconscious recognizing signs our waking brain doesn't."

Lila chuckled. "That's some deep shit right there."

"Sorry, I didn't mean for it to be." Sydney propped herself on one elbow. "But I do have a feeling we're getting close to the end of all this."

"What do you mean?" Lila sat on her bed, facing Sydney.

"We're coming down to the final moves. Between us and the Cons."

"Why do you think that?" Lila asked. "Things could go on like they have been for the last few years. I mean, Lord Burnside may never agree to a war declaration and the Cons wouldn't dare attack us without that. The ogres would wipe them out."

"Maybe, maybe not."

"I don't understand."

"You weren't there, Lila. I looked into Burnside's eyes. I think he's going to grant the Cons their war—for his own personal amusement if nothing else. Burnside would watch us and the Cons fight to the death the way we might watch two ants fight over a crumb of bread." Sydney shifted and rolled her neck to loosen the muscles. "And he was right about one thing. One gang running the whole underside of the city would be more peaceful and more profitable for Woodhollow than the competition we have going on now."

"Yeah but none of that is new information, Sydney. What's changed?"

"That Nightshade. He's been at the center of everything that's been happening. I wouldn't be surprised to find out he's been whispering in McGee's ear since I came to Woodhollow. Maybe even Burnside's. He wants something from me."

"You? Why?"

"He knows me, Lila, or knows of me. Remember what I told you about him showing up in Beechwood Hall?"

"What, the secret mission you and Marla went on without telling anyone what you were really doing?" Lila said. Her nostrils flared and irritation trickled into her voice. "Yeah, I remember."

"Don't be like that."

"Honestly, Sydney, I don't know if I was more angry or hurt. Angry that you two endangered our ancestral home with that stunt, or hurt that you didn't trust me enough to let me in on your plans."

Sydney opened her mouth to protest.

Isn't that exactly how I felt when I found out Marla was making magical devices?

"You're right, Lila. We should have let you and all the trusted members of the gang in on it."

Lila slumped her shoulders. "It's because of Will, isn't it? Because we're the same clan? You're worried that I might turn on you too."

Guilt burned a hole in her heart. "No, Lila. I mean yes, the thought crossed my mind, but when I honestly think about it, I know I can trust you."

"You sure about that?"

"Lila, you're my best friend. I did have a fleeting moment of doubt. Marla straightened me out. I'm ashamed I ever thought it. I trust you with my life. You know that, don't you?"

Lila looked skeptical but nodded.

"I hope you do because it's true." Sydney sighed. "Anyway, I'm just waiting for the next shoe to drop. Something about the Nightshade. He flattened Marla without hesitating but with me, he was almost conversational. So maybe this is all my fault. Everything that's happened here in Woodhollow may just be because I came here."

"That's awfully fatalistic, Sydney—not to mention self-pitying."

Sydney laughed. "Yeah, I know. Still, I wonder if I should leave. Maybe the gang would be safer without me here."

"If what you say is true, then all that would mean is that you wouldn't be here when the war finally starts. Nightshade or not, it sounds like we'll be fighting them sooner or later and I think we'll really need that big brain of yours when the time comes."

"Maybe. I don't want to leave, Lila. I just want everyone to be as safe as possible."

Lila donned a gentle smile. "Then stick around and make sure we are."

"Okay." Sydney grinned. "Thanks, buddy."

"Anytime. In any event, we need to get down to the workroom. Marla called a meeting for the gang."

"About?"

"I don't know. Right after she got back from City Hall, she dragged Dana in the back. When she came out, she told everyone to be ready to meet by mid-morning."

Sydney nodded. "Well, let's go see what's up."

*   *   *   *   *

With the entire gang in attendance, the workroom was crowded. Sydney wormed in between Claire and Lucas. She scanned the room. Save for Garth, Robin, Gerry, and Anders—all of whom were out front in the main tavern room—and Vivian, who was still laid up, the entire gang was present.

Well, everyone except Donovan and Will, she thought.

The moment Sydney and Lila settled into place, Marla emerged from her office, her face grim. Right behind her came Dana, who seemed just as serious.

Well, this can't be good.

"I'm not going to beat around the bush, people." Marla put her hands on her hips. "I just came from city hall. McGee signed his declaration of war. Lord Burnside has approved a limited conflict."

Even though she had been expecting it, the announcement was like a physical blow. Sydney's stomach twisted and her vision dimmed.

Marla raised her hands. The murmurs which broke out around the room quieted instantly. She went on. "Lord Burnside declared the conflict limited to Bayberry Square, right here in front of The Log. No war engines, no magic that exceeds the bounds of the Square. Any conflict goes outside the Square will be subdued by the Enforcers, who will be standing by."

Markus cleared his throat. "When?"

"The day after tomorrow, the gangs go to war."

"Two days? We're screwed," someone moaned.

Marla shook her head. "Look, I know this isn't going to be pretty. Fighting never is. We are risking everything, including our lives. But I, for one, would rather die than roll over and give the Cons everything we've worked so hard to build."

"But Marla," Patrice said, "there's no way we can win. The Cons outnumber us and if they get into their magic, they will just run over us."

"I have some ideas on that, Patrice. And we won't be alone. The Browns and all of their members will stand with us, including their Redcaps."

"Well, that's something," Lila muttered.

"Unfortunately," Dana broke in, "we also heard, unofficially, that the Rats are going to stand with the Cons."

Marla glared at Dana, who returned the look without fear. "Marla, they deserve to know everything."

"We don't know if the Rats are going to stand with them for sure."

"Come on, Marla," Markus said. "Their territories don't overlap and they trade nonstop. You know McGee and Dominique are still fucking about once a week. Of course the Rats are going to side with them."

Marla nodded reluctantly. "There are still the Dryads."

"We've heard nothing from Drith-an-Bidi. As far as we know, Choy-na-Sal is still in charge over there and she won't side with us. And...." Dana hesitated.

Sydney caught her expression. "You've already laid most of it out, Dana. You may as well tell us the rest."

Dana glanced at Marla, who took a deep breath. The faery leader said, "The declaration also said the Hobs will march with the Cons."

"Well, that's it, then," Claire said. "We're done."

The room fell silent. Disheartened faeries glanced at each other. Marla scowled at the floor. Dana looked ill. Markus held his chin in his palm. Patrice and Gordon held each other, their faces tight. Lila's eyes were full of tears.

Sydney stepped forward, to the center of the room. A nervous tremor rippled through her as she realized every eye was now on her.

"I know I'm a relative newcomer here. I haven't been in the gang as long as many of you. I also know I'm probably the single worst fighter and thief here."

There were some scattered chuckles.

She rotated as she spoke, making sure she made eye contact with every faery in the room. "But I also know this: Woodhollow and The Log are my home. And you are my family. I can't just walk away from this place, or any of you.

"The Cons threaten to crush us. If we run away now, what's the threshold to run away next time? Someone looks at us wrong? No. There's a line and it's been drawn."

"But Sydney...." Natasha's eyes were downcast and her voice timid. "Fight the Cons, Rats, and Hobs all at once? You're asking us to do the impossible."

"No. I know it seems like that but I have some ideas on how we can win this. I know everyone here has liked some of my ideas in the past."

A murmur of agreement rippled through the gang.

She paused. "The important thing is this: no one can make you stay. No one can make you fight. The Rats are cowards, who turn on each other at a single moment of weakness. The Dryad ranks are breaking over a personal squabble. McGee bullies the Cons to get them in line and kills them when they won't. We're not like that. I was told a long time ago—" She pointed at Dana. "—the one thing that made this gang unique and special was that everyone is here of our own free will. Everyone contributes. We work as a team because we want to. And that gives us a strength no other gang can match.

"So if you stay, it's because you choose to stay. If you fight, it's because you choose to fight. And if we win, it's going to be because we choose that too.

"This gang—all of you—are my family now. I won't give up on my family without a fight. I won't lie; it's going to be bloody. Some of us probably won't live through this. But I promise you this: I am not going to let those bastards beat us. Not while I have breath in my body. If you put your trust in me—if you believe in me—I *will* find a way to win, and those of us who survive are going to dance on McGee's grave. I swear it."

Sydney stopped, her words exhausted.

Silence descended over the room. None of the faeries would meet her gaze. Not even Marla.

Sydney was assailed by a sudden sense of emotional fatigue. Her shoulders slumped and her knees went weak. She lowered her head, fighting back tears.

I guess this is it, then.

A hand touched her shoulder. Sydney raised her head.

Lila stood before her. "I'm with you, lady."

Natasha hovered at Lila's side. "You can count on me too."

"Really?"

The singer's eyes shone with adoration. "After that speech, you have to ask?"

Markus nodded. "Let's do it."

Lucas and Lucian stepped forward. In unison, they said, "We're in."

One by one, the faeries spoke up. Despite the differences in spoken words, all of them were in agreement: no matter what happened, they backed Sydney's position. The room erupted in excited chatter. The faeries crowded together around Sydney. All of them tried to touch her.

Sydney wiped a tear from her eye.

"All right," Markus said, shouting over the hubbub. Immediately, the gang stopped chattering with each other and focused on him. He motioned to Dana.

Dana nodded. "We have two days, so you all know the drill. Get all your blades sharpened and oiled. Stock up on crumble and make sure you have it on you day and night. As of today, the tavern is shut down until this is over. All personnel are excused from normal duties except for cooking and cleaning. We'll set a watch schedule. And nobody leaves The Log." She pointed to the tavern. "Go eat and drink up. We'll need to be sharp in two days. That means no booze tomorrow, so get your fill this afternoon and tonight."

Dana smiled. "Go relax, while you have time."

The faeries tromped out. Lila gave Sydney a squeeze on the shoulder. Natasha turned as if to go, whirled back to Sydney, and planted a soft kiss on her cheek. Natasha flashed Sydney a shy smile, then left to join the others.

Markus gave Sydney a lingering look before he exited the room.

Moments later, only Sydney and Marla remained. Marla stood with her feet slightly apart and her arms folded. She stared at Sydney, who returned the gaze with more confidence than she felt.

"Well," Marla said at last, "that was some speech. Did you mean it? Everything you said?"

"Most of it."

Marla shrugged. "Doesn't matter now. We're committed. In two days, the Faery Gang goes to war."

Sydney's self-doubt grew. "Do you think I just signed all our death warrants?"

"Ask me again in three days."

Chapter Twenty-Eight

Sydney stood on the roof of The Log, holding a half-filled mug of ale in one hand. Even the cool evening breeze and majesty of the setting sun did not distract her from the business at hand.

Marla spat over the edge, then drank from her own mug. "Why did you drag me up here? I have tons of stuff to do."

"Surveying the lay of the land, my dear sister. Since Burnside dictated that our fight was going to take place here, there's a lot we can do to prepare for it."

"Such as?"

"Booby traps. Tripwires, maybe. Caltrops. We could soak the cobblestones in oil and set it ablaze. We can't use ballistas or anything like that but there's plenty else we could do. We can rig a bunch of crossbows to fire all at once and saturate a kill box." Sydney frowned. "Unfortunately, Burnside didn't set the Square off-limits to anyone, so all those idiots are still out there shopping and clogging the streets with their errands. We're not going to have much time to do whatever it is we want to do—pretty much just after sundown tomorrow, until the morning. We'll have to prioritize whatever will be the greatest force multiplier."

A curious expression lit Marla's face. "Where did you learn all that?"

"That faery Jacob, from the Poppy Clan. He studied military history and battle tactics and talked about it all the time. He's the one I used to...uhm..." Her cheeks reddened.

"Hook up with?" Marla supplied.

"Yeah. Anyway, he aroused my curiosity on the subject, so I read up on it a bit. The library in Holly Grove contains a surprising number of books on war strategy and tactics."

Marla placed her forearms on the short wall surrounding the roof and leaned on it. "Speaking of hooking up, if you plan on going out with a blast, you have a few candidates here."

"Yeah, I know but— Wait, what do you mean going out with a blast? Do you expect us to lose?"

"Seems the most likely scenario. I've heard most of the bookies already have us as three to one underdogs."

"That's sobering."

"It sure is." Marla's face was grim. "Syd, if we do go down, I plan on dying on my feet rather than living on my knees."

Sydney blanched. "Why would you say that?"

"Hear me out, Syd. If the Cons win, I doubt they'll just murder us all. One, it's a lot of trouble to chase down whoever survives. Two, if some of us manage to escape, Burnside will be pissed if they run around town killing whoever's left. And three, subdued peons are more productive than dead bodies. Whoever survives the fight will become Con errand boys and go-fers. They might even leave the gang territory intact, so long as the Faery Gang was obedient and forked over most of their earnings."

Marla snorted. "You heard McGee the other night. He said he would put Will in charge, and you know when Cons said, 'Jump,' that ass-licker's only response would be 'How high?' They'd probably force a few down to Belles as 'independent' contractors from whom they could extract more coin. Natasha, for example, would be a huge draw."

An image filled Sydney's mind, of the lush-bodied singer in her stage outfit, surrounded by leering Cons. She shivered and shied away from the thought.

Marla continued. "Even though they won't kill everyone, doesn't mean there won't be some messy object lessons. Because I have been such a pain in McGee's ass, there's no way he'd let me live. If they catch me, I can pretty much expect to be drawn and quartered." She shook her head. "Nope. If things go pear-shaped, this girl is going down swinging."

"Marla, why are you telling me this?"

"Because if all is lost, you have to live. You have to get back to Aunt Brigid and let her know what happened."

"Marla—"

Some of Marla's grimness faded, replaced by concern. "No arguing, Syd."

"I may not be able to get away either." Sydney put her hands on the wall. "McGee blames me for Seamus getting eaten that night on the Boardwalk.

"Says who? I was there."

"I hear things out in town, same as you. If this whole idea goes horribly wrong, I'll be following right behind you to that sweet by-and-by."

"No. If you have the chance to escape, please take it. Promise me, Sydney." Marla raised one hand and put it on Sydney's shoulder.

She wanted to object but when she looked into Marla's eyes, Sydney saw past the bluster, the constant irritation. Her gaze penetrated Marla's icy exterior and for the first time since before Marla left Sylvan Valley, Sydney saw her sister's soul laid bare.

Marla was terrified.

Not of death, Sydney thought, *but that something is going to happen to me.*

At that moment, Sydney surrendered. Overwhelming love and devotion filled her heart and all the resentments she'd held against Marla evaporated as wisps of fog before the rising sun.

Sydney put her hand over Marla's and smiled. Even though she knew it was a bald-faced lie, she felt no guilt as she said the words. "Okay, Marla, I promise."

Marla studied Sydney for a moment before facing the Square again. "You said something interesting a moment ago."

"What was that?"

"Something about soaking the cobblestones with oil. Setting a few of those fuckers on fire would make facing my death a whole lot more satisfying."

Sydney smiled and for once, the happy feeling radiated down to her toes. She leaned against her sister. "The idea is for us not to die."

"Yeah, well, good luck with that. You think they'll have more of those marbles that let them recharge their magic?"

"I expect them to," Sydney said. "And I suspect they'll already be juiced up before they even show their faces."

"How do we work around that?"

"I have an idea or two. By the way...do you remember that night we were out creeping past the forge. What did you call it again?"

"Salmonika?"

"Yeah. You said something about electrified sling stones. What do you think about...."

They discussed their strategy for a few more moments before Marla excused herself. She climbed through the trapdoor and vanished.

Sydney watched as the sun slid below the horizon. The remaining light cast a crimson glow across the clouds.

Wonder if that's a bad omen.

From below, she heard the sounds of singing and merry-making from the tavern. The gang was really whooping it up.

A pair of goblins and a gnome approached the front doors. One rattled the handle and frowned. He spotted Sydney. "Hey, up there. What gives?"

"We're closed."

"Closed?" The goblin sputtered in outrage. "What the hell for? The Log is open every night. It sounds like there's a great party going on in there. We want in."

"Haven't you heard?" Sydney said. She let a little sarcasm enter her voice. "We have a few emergencies to deal with before you guys can come swill our ale."

The gnome's voice carried a note of genuine perplexion. "But...we came to see Natasha."

"She'll be on again in a few nights. Come back then."

The trio grumbled but departed.

Sydney chuckled. *She is such an asset for this gang. She's incredible.*

Natasha.

Sydney's chuckle faded.

She thought of the beautiful lounge singer and built an image of the faery in her thoughts: long, lustrous black hair. Dark eyes, which contrasted beautifully with her alabaster skin. White-toothed smile. A body to die for.

She thought of Natasha's husky, sensual laugh, her sudden switches between aggressive wanton and demure sweetheart. When Sydney had gently rebuffed Natasha's advances, she had expected the woman to move on to another conquest. After all, that was the image of a sexually free spirit that Natasha herself always projected. Instead, Sydney never saw Natasha with anyone, and the singer's eyes always settled on Sydney.

Sydney nodded to herself. Natasha was beautiful, charming, and had a very loving, gentle soul. If she wanted to be with any girl, she'd be a fool to turn that away—and, Sydney had to finally admit to herself, she was open to at least testing the idea. But she couldn't do it, especially now.

If I took advantage of her feelings to satisfy my own curiosity and by some miracle we live through this, then I reject her...Gods, what a worthless sack of shit I'd be to use her like that.

Her thoughts shifted to Markus. The look he had given her in the workroom had been direct, and clear.

He was handsome, for sure. Tall, with a chiseled, square-jawed face. Bright green eyes. Straight dark hair that curled at his neck. Muscular arms and shoulders, a v-shaped torso, narrow waist, and strong legs.

Markus was a leader, an inspiration. He could play the warrior, thief, and diplomat with equal skill and daring. He was decisive, confident, and sure of himself and his upbeat nature was infectious, uplifting his comrades when needed. Other faeries followed his lead and spoke well of him. He was strong. Yet his touch when his skin met Sydney's was gentle and even though he was direct about conducting the business of the gang, he had never spoken a truly harsh word to her, even when she was screwing up.

Yep, Sydney thought, *a lot of women would trade their left wing for a guy like that.*

She knew he liked her, at least some.

So how do I feel?

She paused. *About the same, I guess. Markus has good intentions but I can't shake the feeling I'd be just another notch on his belt. He had absolutely no problem flirting with Wychia and I know he's been back over to Wulf's on "business." He likes me and I know he'd love to spend more time with me but there's nothing long-term there. He's just in it for the score. On the other hand, Natasha is half in love with me. I'd crush her if I used her. Either way, I can't do it. These are my friends. It wouldn't be right or fair to them.*

And even though I like them both, I know I don't love either.

She took a drink from her mug.

And that's the rub of it, stupid. Like Marla said, you're holding on to that impossible hope of meeting a soul mate so you can be like Mom and Dad. It's something that may never happen. And now, you're probably out of time. So maybe just make a decision and seek a few hours of happiness while you can.

She sighed. *Why do I wrap my head around this stuff?*

The trapdoor opened. Sydney expected to see Marla. Instead, a pile of frizzy blonde hair atop a smiling face popped through. "Heya, Sydney! Marla said you were up here."

"Vivian, you shouldn't be up. You should be resting and healing."

Vivian scoffed. "Seriously? That's a bunch of crap."

She winced as she pulled herself onto the roof. Sydney reached out to help but Vivian waved her away. "I'm okay. I'd have been up earlier if Lucas and Lucian hadn't tied me to the bed."

"You're exaggerating."

"Nope, they did. I finally managed to get the knots loose." She stood next to Sydney and followed her gaze. "See anything good out there?"

"Not really. Just thinking."

"About the war? About all of us dying? That kinda thing?"

"Yeah, pretty much."

"That's all anyone is talking about, you know?" Vivian leaned her hips against the wall and folded her arms. A flicker of pain crossed her face.

"Vivian, go back downstairs and get in bed before you open up your stitches. You're going to have to sit this out anyway."

"Oh, like hell I am. What do you think the Cons will do to me if they find me helpless in bed? I'd much rather die on my feet than face that nightmare, you know?"

"I know." It was too close to Sydney's own thoughts for her to deny it.

"Besides, you are going need every hand you can get down there. I'm healing just fine and I can cast a mean flame spell. I hear the Browns are with us but that's it, right? The Dryads haven't committed? Why not?"

"I don't know. I wish I did."

"Well, it is the talk of the gang. I heard about your speech. Pretty cool stuff."

"I just spoke from the heart and said what needed to be said."

Vivian's face broke into a wide grin. "That's what leaders do, you know?"

"I'm not a leader. That's Marla's job."

"Different types of leaders, Sydney. Marla's willing to wade into battle at the head of our group and kick some ass—show us how it's done, you know? You're the talker. You put into words what we're feeling. You inspire us. And then there's the fact that everyone here knows how stinking smart you are, and how much trouble you've saved the gang. Most of them are in awe of how fast you think on your feet. Trust me, they look up to you every bit as much as your sis."

Sydney stood gape-mouthed for a moment. "Vivian...I don't know what to say to that."

"Don't say anything. I fill in the silence pretty well. Anyway, the gang was all abuzz about your words and whatnot. Now that they've had a chance to think everything through, it's kind of dawning on them all that this isn't going to be a walk in the park. Know what I mean? The reality is setting in and almost everyone is downstairs getting drunk, convinced they are all going to die the day after tomorrow."

Sydney sighed again. "I didn't want them to do that."

Vivian made a flipping, dismissive motion with her hand. "Eh, don't worry yourself. They'll get over it. It's kinda funny if you think about it, you know? They're all scared. Even Markus and Dana. Hell, maybe even Marla. But every one of them is too proud to back down. They all think that if they flee, they'll be branded as traitors and cowards forever and worse, be shunned in the eyes of their comrades. That scares them all more than death. See what I'm saying? Does that make sense?"

"Damn, Vivian, you never cease to amaze me."

"It's a gift."

"If we make it through this, I promise I will try to get the gang to realize what a genius is hiding behind that ditzy facade."

"Nah, don't bother. I like it this way, you know? Less pressure." Vivian waited until Sydney had raised her mug to her lips. "So, are you going to sleep with Natasha?"

Sydney gagged and sprayed ale over the side of the roof.

*   *   *   *   *

Sydney tossed and turned. Despite her fatigue, sleep would not arrive. Her jumbled mind kept revisiting her words, the reaction of her friends, and their subsequent moments of emotional sobriety, followed by physical drunkenness. She wondered yet again if she had done the right thing.

Soft snores drifted from across the darkened room. In spite of her glum thoughts, Sydney snickered. She'd had to practically drag Lila up the stairs from the common room. For all her talk of never drinking more than one an evening, the gang secretary had developed such a roaring drunk that when dared, she mooned the entire room and in the process of pulling up her trousers, fell face-down on the floor. She muttered incoherent jibberish the entire time Sydney steered her up the stairs and into her bed. Sydney had time to get Lila's boots off before the latter passed out completely.

She laughed again. Because Lila wasn't a heavy drinker, she'd likely be a hurting soul on the morrow.

But slowly, grim reality shouldered its way into her thoughts, shoving the happier ones aside.

Her stomach growled. Sydney sighed and flung the blankets off her legs. She shucked her nightshirt and donned her normal tunic and trousers. She opened the door as quietly as she could, slipped into the hallway, and closed it.

There was little sign of life in the tavern. Garth and Robin circled through the tables, hoisting empty mugs and wiping spills with hand towels. A handful of faeries lay passed out at in their seats. More than one was facedown in a pool of ale or wine. Claire lay on her belly on the floor. Loud snores erupted from her throat. In a far corner, Patrice and Gordon slumped together, arms twined around each other.

Sydney did a double-take at the couple. Patrice wore a thin band of gold around her finger.

"Never thought I would see that happen," Garth said as he edged past Sydney.

"What, a ring?"

"Yeah, Gordon isn't the committing type," Robin said. She loaded a tray with half-filled mugs. "But Patrice is a good woman and she's perfect for him. He knows it too. I just hope he doesn't do something stupid like survive the battle and then try to back out of it. I'll kick his ass if he does."

"If he does, Robin, I'll help you."

Garth nudged Sydney. "You want something to eat?"

"How'd you know?"

He laughed. "Because you're not drunk and you didn't come in asking for liquor. I figured you were hungry, lonely, nervous, or just wandering. I took a guess."

"All four are right," Sydney said. "I haven't eaten since this morning."

"I have a roast pork haunch out. I'll bring some from the kitchen."

"I'll give you a hand."

Sydney helped Garth cart the dirty dishes back to the kitchen. "Should be we wash them too?"

Robin shook her head. "Hell, no. We can deal with all this tomorrow."

"We could let a couple of days of dishes pile up, until after the battle," Sydney said. "It'd be the Cons' problem if they won."

"No," Robin grumbled, "with our luck, we'd win and then have to deal with it after. I think I'd rather die fighting than scrub three days worth of dishes."

It took about a half-hour but they had the common room cleaned and the dishes soaking in the deep-basined sinks in the kitchen. A few taps and a kick or two sent what drunks were still capable of moving staggering to their rooms. Garth let Claire, Gordon, and Patrice sleep.

Robin wadded up her apron and tossed it behind the bar. "I'm going to bed." She patted her brother on the shoulder and left.

Garth told Sydney to sit, went back to the kitchen one last time, and returned with two plates of steaming pork, carrots, and greens.

Sydney raised an eyebrow. "You had all this standing by for dinner?"

"No, but I figured why waste it when we all might be dead in two days."

"Good point. How'd you get it hot so fast?"

"Crumble, how else?"

Sydney laughed. "I always scorch it when I do that. Maybe when this is all over you can show me how to do it right."

"Sure, no problem."

She took a bite of the pork. The meaty flavor, mingled with garlic and paprika, rolled across her tongue. She even detected a hint of apple. "Good stuff, Garth."

"I wanted to be a gourmet chef when I was younger. Guess I still have some lingering aspirations."

"Maybe you should chase that dream. Get out of the gang, go somewhere such talent will be appreciated."

"And give up all this luxury?" He gestured around the tavern.

"Well, yes, that would be tough," Sydney said with another laugh.

"Seriously, remember what you said about family?"

"Garth, you weren't even in the room when I gave that speech."

"So what? Anders, Gerry, Robin, and me used crumble to listen. It was important to hear the discussion, and you."

Sydney recalled Vivian's comments and said nothing.

Garth went on. "You were right about family. Well, this gang has been my family for a decade. I can't just cut and run."

"I know you and Robin never go on missions because you run the kitchen and bar. Can you guys fight?"

A lopsided smile sprang to his face. "Better than you, anyway.'

"Well, that wouldn't be hard." She raised her ale mug. Garth clinked it with his own water. Sydney said, "Cheers. Here's to the Faery Gang."

"To the Faery Gang," he repeated. "May it live forever."

"Gods willing," she muttered. She took a deep drink. "So what's with your obsession with Vivian?"

Garth's eyes widened. "I'm not obsessed. Okay, maybe a little."

"You come on a little strong at first?"

"Yeah, probably. You may not know it but I was once quite a ladies' man. Maybe not in Markus's league but I did all right."

"I believe that."

"I don't know, there's just something about Vivian. Yes, she's cute but not really beautiful. Yes, she talks too much and can be an annoying pain in the ass. She teases me outrageously and I'm not sure she even knows she's doing it. All the same...." Garth rubbed his chin. "There's something to her. I can't quite put my finger on it, though."

Sydney raised her fork to her mouth, hoping the act of chewing would keep the smirk off her face.

They had only taken a few bites when the outer door opened and Marla entered. She was dressed in black, wore a dark cloak over her wings, and had soot smeared on her face.

Sydney glared at her. "I thought no one was supposed to leave The Log."

"They're not."

"You're setting a piss-poor example as a leader, Marla. 'Do as I say and not as I do,' isn't going to cut it."

"When did you become an expert on leadership, Syd? Get off my back." Marla shucked her cloak and stretched her wings. "Ah, much better. Besides, this was super-important."

"It always is."

"One, shut up. Two, listen to me."

Sydney flipped her the bird.

"As long as you're quiet, you can make any motion you want. Looks good, Garth." She scooted a chair up to the table, reached into Garth's plate, and snatched up a piece of pork with her fingers.

Garth stared at her. Sydney rolled her eyes.

"What?" Marla said.

"I'll go get you a full plate. Or myself a new one, maybe." Garth stood and departed for the kitchen.

Marla grabbed another piece of meat. Sydney resisted the urge to smack her hand. "Okay, Garth had to good grace to give us a moment of privacy."

"He always was a smart one."

"Where have you been?"

"Reconnoitering."

Sydney ground her teeth in frustration. "And?"

Marla gave up the pretense, pulled Garth's plate in front of her, and dug in. "I found out a few things."

"Marla, am I going to have to wait until I am old and gray to get answers?"

Marla drained Garth's mug. "I found the Dryad grove."

Sydney blinked. "The what?"

"Their sacred grove of trees. All dryads are connected to trees. That's the source of their lifespan and of their magic."

"Do they die if their tree dies, as the legends say?"

"Nothing so dramatic, but they can't use any magic and are kind of lost and emotional until they establish a new link. Most of the dryads in the Dryad gang severed their connection with their old trees when they came to Woodhollow and made a connection with a new one. If they have seeds from their birth trees, they can encourage a new one to grow to full size in a matter of months. Anyway, I found their grove."

"How did you manage that?"

Marla grinned. "Drith-an-Bidi. I tracked her down to a fleabag inn on the far south side of town, right on the edge of the Boardwalk. She about pissed herself when I opened the door to her room."

"Why, did she think you were there to kill her?"

"Seems so. She was worried I thought she had betrayed us."

"Uh, she does know Dryad magic is much stronger than ours or the Cons, doesn't she? Did she think she couldn't defend herself?"

"Maybe not," Marla said. "Dryads don't react very well when they're surprised. Besides, Syd, we've got a rep as vicious killers and I am sure that was in her head."

"An exaggerated rep, if you ask me."

"Some, yes. Anyway, after I got her calmed down, I pulled the whole story out of her."

Sydney bit her lip. "I guess her coup attempt failed?"

"Oh yeah, it was tits-up from the beginning. Choy had a double-agent inside the rebels and as soon as they made their move, Choy rounded them all up, drained their power, and flung them in a cage just inside the grove. Without being able to touch their trees, they can't recharge." Marla paused. "Sucks to be them. Their trees are all within sight but those dryads can't reach out and touch the bark or commune with them. Kind of like us seeing the blue sky above and not being able to fly, but amplified."

"Harsh punishment," Sydney murmured. "Probably damn effective at breaking their resistance, too."

"That's what Drith thinks Choy is doing, trying to get the rebels to fold, by dangling the connection with their trees right in front of them. Anyway, Drith managed to avoid the sweep and she's been hiding out ever since. She doesn't know if anyone else got away."

"Damn." Sydney slapped her hand on the table. "I was really hoping we'd have the Dryads. This is going to be a lot harder without them."

"Well, we might yet. In the course of spilling everything, Drith told me where the Grove is."

"And?"

"And we're going to spring the rebels."

Sydney wanted to throw up her hands. "Marla, we're already up to our armpits in things that need to be done. Not only that, Choy will surely be expecting that move."

"Not as much as you might think. Apparently, she's been spending a lot of time at the Four-Leaf Club."

The memory clicked into place. "That was her—the one I saw by silhouette the night we stole back the plans. I couldn't place her in the dim light but that fits. She was working the room with a bunch of the whores from Belles. What's her deal?"

"I suspect she was 'the bitch' McGee was talking about."

Sydney frowned. "Why would McGee even bother? He didn't sound like he really wanted anything to do with Choy and the Cons's coalition is already stronger than ours."

"Divide and conquer. If the Dryads side with them, they can't side with us, and their magic is a lot stronger than the Cons."

"Okay," Sydney said. "That makes sense."

Marla tilted her head. "Maybe she's trying to screw her way into an alliance, or maybe she was just enjoying herself. Could be any number of things. Drith said Choy is an enormous slut but I thought she was being catty. Maybe Drith was just telling it like it is. Doesn't really matter. I tailed Choy a little bit ago. She's over at the Four-Leaf Club now, so if we're going to move, it needs to be soon."

"What exactly are you proposing? Where is this grove of trees?"

"In an underground cavern beneath Choy's wine shop." Marla smiled, though it didn't reach her eyes. "As for what I am proposing, I say you and I and Drith go down there, kill the guards, and burn down the tree of every dryad that isn't on our side."

"If we do that, every Dryad that stayed loyal to Choy-na-Sal is going to lose their combat effectiveness. We really need them all, Marla."

"A bird in the hand, Syd. Having half the Dryads with us is better than having none, or possibly having them side with the Cons."

"And what if something goes wrong?"

"We're behind in this race. We have to take a few chances. And if we botch it...well, we won't be around to see what else goes wrong."

"Great." Sydney sighed. "Where is Drith?"

"Hiding in a wagon around the corner. Cons are watching The Log, so I didn't want to show my hand."

"They'll probably try to tail us when we leave."

"I'm counting on it, Syd. It'll be two fewer Cons to do the fighting. Well?"

"Well, what?"

"Don't be stupid. You ready to come with me? Spring us some dryads?"

"Gods, Marla, you sound like you're enjoying this."

"It beats acting all morose and pessimistic. Positive thinking, Syd."

"All right, Marla, I'm in." Sydney hesitated. "Try not to get us killed, please."

"I'll do my best, little sister. We can go in a moment." She shoveled another piece of meat into her mouth. "As soon as I finish eating Garth's dinner."

Chapter Twenty-Nine

The blood-soaked cloth squelched under her fingertips and Sydney gagged.

Marla's whisper cut through the night. "Syd, keep it down."

"Sorry, I'm still not used to this part."

"You didn't even kill anyone."

"Hardly the point."

She waddled backward, dragging the Con's body into the alley. The lightstone lamps in the street glowed on their dim overnight setting, so she could not tell if she recognized him or not. For that, she was eternally grateful. When she had the Con's body fifteen feet back from the alley's mouth, she lowered his feet to the pavement.

Beside her, the willowy Drith-an-Bidi hauled the other Con under his shoulders. Her voice was a string of low curses. She dumped her burden on the body Sydney had been hauling. "There. Two less of the bastards."

"Sure," Sydney said, "that only leaves like seventy or eighty of them. At this rate, we only need to keep skulking around alleys for another six weeks and ambush them every night to wear them out. Brilliant."

Drith gave her an unfriendly look. "Marla said you were a smartass. I think she understated it."

"She told me all Dryads are complete jerks. Maybe she let us both off gentle."

Marla raised a fist. Her voice was no louder than a soft breeze. "Knock it off, you idiots. Patrol coming."

The trio froze. A moment later, a troop of ogres tromped past. One said, "Day after tomorrow, I hear."

"Yeah, in Bayberry Square," another answered.

"Already got my money on the Cons," a third said. "Those faeries are going to get carved up."

"I wouldn't be so sure," the second objected. "They're pretty tricky."

"You're drunk," the third said with a harsh laugh.

The second shoved him. "We'll see."

The voices faded as the patrol moved away. Marla scuttled to where Sydney and Drith stood. "Okay, they're gone. Choy's shop is only two more blocks. Let's go."

Sydney motioned at Drith. The dryad nodded and slunk after Marla. Sydney brought up the rear. At random intervals, she stopped, looked behind, and listened. With the Cons down, she could not hear or see any signs of pursuit.

If the Nightshade shows his ugly face, I'll never see him until it's too late.

Her lip curled. *Of course, now that I think about him, he'll probably turn up.*

She had not seen any sign of the black-winged faery since the confrontation in Beechwood Hall. After she and Marla returned to Woodhollow, events had proceeded at such a breakneck pace that Sydney had barely had time to breathe. Now that thoughts of their lurking nemesis surfaced, Sydney found it hard to excise them.

Get out of my head, whoever you are.

She collided with Drith, who had come to a halt. The Dryad glared at her but held a single finger to her lips. Angry at herself for not paying attention, Sydney only nodded.

Get it together, damn it.

Marla crouched a few feet in front of them. She edged to the corner, slid a fraction of her head around, looked for a moment, then retreated to where the other two waited. "We have a problem."

"We have lots of problems, Marla. What's this one?"

"Urgon Thunderhand is standing in front of Choy's shop. He's wearing full plate armor and is carrying a pair of double-bladed battleaxes. She must have hired him to guard the place."

Drith snorted. "No wonder she felt safe leaving the store untended."

Sydney's spirit sank. "Do we retreat?"

"No, Syd, we need this too much. You were right when you said we needed the Dryads on our side. Drith, you need this too. This is your one chance to wipe out the power of your rival."

Drith licked her lips but said nothing.

"But Marla—"

"But nothing, Sydney. You're the brains. How do we do this?"

Sydney's mind raced. She poured over what little she knew of the dwarven mercenary, from both his reputation and her brief interaction with him. "We can't fight him. Even three to one, he'd easily kill us all."

Marla and Drith both nodded.

"And magic is too risky. He's partially immune, which means anything we do might fail and get us killed. We can't even trick him with some fancy illusions. He'd either see through them or not see them at all.

"I don't think we can lure him away, he's too smart for that." Sydney's mind kept churning. "And I don't think we can offer him anything to break his contract. I don't think we can bribe or coerce or blackmail him."

An idea dawned and Sydney's eyes widened. "We're going about this the wrong way. If we can't go through Urgon, we should go around him. I know there's no back door to Choy's shop—"

Drith nodded as if to confirm it.

"—but nothing says we can't make an entrance in the back alley. A little crumble and we can carve a hole in the back wall, traipse downstairs, and do what we need to do."

"No good," Drith said. "The Bear shares a back wall with the bakery behind it, which faces the next street over. There is no alley between them. And that bakery is owned by a paranoid gnome, who's got the place wired with all kinds of magical alarms, so we really can't go through there."

Marla's eyes glinted with determination. "Then we do it from the roof."

"Marla, that's crazy. He'll see us for sure."

"Maybe not. We'll just have to stay low and quiet."

"How do we get up there?" Drith asked.

Marla and Sydney met each other's gaze. Sydney's stomach bottomed out. "Marla..."

"We'll have to fly up."

Sydney expected Drith to look horrified but the dryad merely seemed amused. Drith said, "Aren't you worried about the drakes giving you a little flame bath if you do that?"

"Yes, there's a very good chance of that happening," Sydney said. She glanced into the distance, where a pair of the immense winged reptiles, backlit by the half-moon, turned in lazy circles over the city center. "Marla, why can't we just do a dimensional step?"

"Because if we make any kind of noise, we're fucked. Dimensional stepping at this distance is usually accurate within a foot or so, but if you come in a foot high, you're going to make a hell of a racket when you land. Gods forbid you come in low, try to materialize inside the roof itself, and the spell throws you off the building. We're going to have to glide in from behind the shop and land with as little noise as possible." Marla's face twitched. "Which means I can't do it."

"What?"

"Syd, you know how I land. If I hit that roof with a thud, Urgon will hear. I think he's strong enough to leap onto that roof from a standing position, even with his gear, and if he does, we're finished. You're going to have to do this—and you're going to have to do it while carrying Drith."

Sydney put her head in her hands. "Oh, Gods."

Marla's voice whispered in her ear, strangely gentle. "Look, if you can't do it—"

"I'll do it." Sydney took a deep breath. "One way or the other, I want this over."

"I'll keep watch from down here. If it looks like Urgon spots you, I'll run out and engage him."

Drith's eyes widened. "That's suicide, Marla."

"Maybe. I won't make it easy for him. Even if he cuts me in half, and that lets you get in and get the Dryads out, it's worth it. All right, we're wasting time. Can we try this?"

They moved a street away. Sydney made an abortive test flight with Drith, being sure to keep below the tops of the buildings, lest she catch the attention of the drakes. The first time, she held Drith under the arms. The dryad wasn't heavy but she was long and her feet bounced along the cobblestones.

"Ow! Damn it, Sydney, you're breaking my legs!"

"Keep it down you maniac! You're too tall for me to do it that way. Try and wrap your legs around my waist and your arms around my neck."

Drith did. She placed her head next to Sydney's, resting their cheeks together.

The smell of loam and fresh-cut wood invaded Sydney's nose. She steeled herself and launched her second test flight.

They sailed a few feet and landed on the street without a sound.

"Good," Marla said. "Again."

They did it two more times before Marla was satisfied. "All right, come over here. Chicory Lane runs right down to intersect with Briar Street here. You should be able to get a running start, glide up just enough to get over this bakery and land on Choy's rooftop without Urgon or the drakes being any the wiser."

"Easy for you to say."

Marla jerked her head. "Drith, can you give us a moment?"

"Okay." The dryad wandered up Briar Street thirty feet.

Marla took Sydney's hands. "Syd, I think Drith is on the up-and-up. I wouldn't ask you to do this if I felt strongly that she wasn't. But watch out. Don't put yourself in a position where she can stab you in the back, okay?"

"Okay."

"If she tries something, you run out of there as best you can. Don't stop running until you get to Sylvan Valley."

Sydney started to respond when Drith came scurrying back to them. The dryad pointed. "Another patrol."

The three huddled in the shadows as the ogres tromped through the far intersection and disappeared.

"They're out in force tonight," Drith said.

Sydney scoffed. "I bet my wings that Burnside ordered them out here to keep us and the Cons both from getting a little preemptive strike in, which might result in productive citizens getting killed, not just the riff-raff and crooks." Her laugh was without humor. "Can't have anything interfere with the tax base."

Marla nodded. "We better take advantage of the gap between patrols and go now." She pointed. "Walk down there. Give me about five minutes to work back around so I can get into position. Like I said, if you draw his attention, I'll attack. Syd?"

"Yeah?"

"Don't draw his attention."

Marla flitted into the night.

Sydney and Drith walked a hundred feet beyond the intersection. Drith said, "You think this is going to work?"

"Hell, no. I think we're both fucked. But I don't see any other choice."

"Neither do I." She hesitated. "Have you seen Urgon in action?"

Sydney kept her expression even. "Yes. Up close."

"Sounds interesting."

"That's one word. I would have chosen terrifying."

They loitered for a moment. At last, Sydney said, "Well, Marla should be in position by now. You ready to try this?"

"I guess. Sydney, I have to ask you something."

"What?"

"Do you really think we're going to win?"

"Drith, I have to believe we have a chance or I wouldn't be doing this. You really want to lead your gang into an alliance with us?"

"I don't see that we have any choice. I sure as hell am not going to ally us with the Cons."

"Fair enough." Sydney closed her eyes and uttered a silent prayer. "All right, let's do this."

Drith wrapped her arms around Sydney's neck and legs around her waist.

Sydney looked skyward. She couldn't see any of the drakes.

Now or never.

She took two steps and sprang into the air.

Powerful flaps of her wings propelled her skyward. The buildings rushed past as she climbed. Sydney whipped her head side to side.

There. She spotted the drake patrol to their west but the beasts were turned away from them. She focused on the front edge of the building.

She glided over the roof of the bakery, so close her toe scraped against the brick edge. She furled her wings, angled down towards the next roof. Just as she was about to slam into the wooden planks, she flared her wings and stepped onto the roof as if she had just alit from a single step of a staircase.

She held her breath. So did Drith.

They heard nothing.

Ever so slowly, Drith peeled herself from Sydney's body. Staying low, the dryad moved to the back corner of the roof. She reached into a pocket of her gown and withdrew a short, crooked stick. Drith muttered something and made a circular sweep with her hand.

A glowing line appeared on the roof, in the path of her motion. When the circle completed, the section of roof inside the circle shimmered and vanished.

Drith slipped inside the hole and landed on the interior floor with the grace of a cat. She motioned to Sydney to follow.

Sydney tucked her wings and slid in the hole. She landed just as quietly as Drith had. She whispered, "Neat trick. A magic wand?"

"Rootwood, taken from my tree. Amplifies my magic."

"Nice. Okay, which way?"

Drith pointed at a thick oak portal. "Behind that door is a

ladder leading down. That will take us to the grove cavern."

Sydney squared her shoulders. "Okay. You first."

"Sure."

Drith opened the door, revealing the aforementioned ladder. The twisted wooden structure was bolted to the wall. The dryad grabbed the top rung and began her descent. Sydney peered over the edge. She thought the square shaft just big enough for a faery with folded wings to climb down. Faint lightstones lit the ladder's path. The bottom seemed very far away.

Drith glanced up and made an impatient gesture. Sydney followed.

They dropped down fifty feet before the ladder ended in a sandy-floored dirt tunnel. Stout timber frames, spaced every ten feet or so, kept the ceiling aloft. Lightstones hung from every other frame.

"Do you have to climb down this ladder every time you want to commune with your tree?"

"No, we can teleport to our trees from a short distance. We call it recalling. It works much like the dimensional stepping you faeries do, though we can only do it to our trees. Once we enter the shop, we can recall with ease and no one is the wiser."

"Why the ladder, then?"

"The ladder is for when we're out of magical power, or when we don't want someone nearby to know we're using magic, like we're doing now."

"How'd you all carve this without Lord Burnside finding it?"

Drith shrugged. "I'm sure he knows. Does he care? That's another matter."

Sydney touched one of the timbers. "I didn't think dryads would use wood from a tree to build something. Seems...I don't know, slightly cannibalistic."

"Waste not, want not, as they say. We only use wood from dead trees, never from living ones."

"Drith, you know Marla planned to burn every tree down here that was attached to Choy and her followers. Are you sure you're okay with this?"

"No, I'm not okay with it. I hate it." Her face was grim. "But if one branch is rotten, the tree will let it fall off before it infects the entire trunk. Lose a limb, save the body. That's how I am approaching this."

"Is it working for you?"

"No choice. Quiet, Sydney. I don't know how many guards Choy left behind."

They crept along the tunnel, which took a sharp turn to the right. Soft light fell around the corner. Sydney slid to the edge. She could not suppress her gasp.

The cavern was vast, over a hundred yards across. Rows of squat trees—evergreens, stubby oaks, a few birches and elms, and a maple or two—radiated out in neat lines from the center of the chamber. Fifty feet up, a network of the brightest lightstones Sydney had ever seen hung suspended in a webbing of fine ropes and chains. Grass lined the floor of the cavern.

Sydney's nostrils flared. In a clearing in the center of the trees sat a square cage of iron bars. A score of dryads languished inside. Even from the distance, she saw the misery on their faces.

"Drith, why don't they recall to their trees? They're in range, right?"

"Choy probably drained their power—siphoned it away to the point where they can't do anything until they commune with their trees again. I just hope she didn't do a debarking on any of them."

"A what?"

"Debarking is what we call it when a dryad is permanently stripped of her magic." Seeing Sydney's confused look, Drith said, "It basically involves committing certain unsavory acts on them with wood from their own trees. I don't really want to talk about it."

Sydney shuddered. "I don't think I want to hear it."

One of the captives stood and placed her slender hands on the bars. She stared into the grove and started crying. Another of the captives wrapped her arms around the shoulders of the sobbing dryad and led her back to her seat.

"That's what I was afraid of," Drith whispered. "They're starting to crack. Good thing we came when we did."

"See any guards?"

"Yes, two over there by the cage. To the right."

Sydney nodded. "I see them. Okay, how do we play this?"

"We'll have to kill them."

She glanced at the dryad and saw tears on Drith's face. "Can you? I mean, you know them, don't you?"

"Yes. Kyne-de-Marti and Palla-vo-Argan. They've both been in the Dryad Gang almost as long as I have. I like them both. Unfortunately, they're also both very loyal to Choy-na-Sal. I tried to convince both to join me and both refused. We won't be able to talk them into standing aside and we can't risk them escaping and alerting Choy and her loyalists."

Some of Sydney's skepticism must have shown on her face because Drith's own countenance hardened. "I can do this, Sydney. Marla says you're good with throwing knives."

"I do all right."

"My tree is only twenty-five feet away from the cage, and behind those two. Let me recall and carry you with me. All you have to do is hold my shoulders. We'll appear almost on top of them. If we can catch them by surprise, we'll have a few seconds." She frowned. "We dryads don't react well when we're startled and usually panic."

Remembering Marla's words, Sydney nodded.

Drith continued. "If you can put down Palla first—she's the one with the short dark hair—we should be able to overwhelm Kyne. Kyne's young, her tree is young, and her magic isn't very strong."

"All right," Sydney said. She withdrew a packet of mushroom crumble and pressed it under her tongue. Magic coursed down her limbs. Sydney shivered and flexed her fingers.

"How can you eat that stuff?"

"It's not bad. Doesn't really have much flavor at all." Sydney tapped her chin with a finger. "Of course, it's poisonous to other races and not faeries, so I'm sure that figures into it."

"Smells horrible. What can you do with that dose?"

"Enough to save my ass. I can usually get a few quick spells or one long one. What can you do?

"Plenty. I haven't expended any magical energy since I last touched my tree. I already have a spell primed. You ready?"

Sydney drew one of her daggers. Sweat slicked the suddenly-cold skin of her palms.

I have to do this. I have to...kill them. Every other time I've used a knife on someone, it was self-defense. Even then, I never actually killed anyone. But this...this is premeditated cold-blooded murder.

Drith eyed her. "You've never killed anyone before, have you Sydney?"

"That obvious?"

"The expression on your face says it all."

"No, I haven't. I've been in some fights and when the Cons attacked us on the Boardwalk, I tried to kill a few of them but I didn't. I even let you and Marla do the dirty work earlier this evening. I've never actually had to take a life. And attacking them from the shadows...it seems so unfair."

Drith's voice held no compromise. "Sydney, there's no such thing as a fair fight. Live or die, is all that matters. Palla and Kyne—they'll do it to you if you let them. So however you have to get your head around it, do it."

"You sound just like Marla."

"I'm sure. She didn't get to her position without having to make hard choices—and planning to kill your own people is one of the hardest possible." Drith sighed. "Believe me. There's no other way."

"But—"

Sydney had a sudden mental image of Lila, Markus, Garth, Robin, Gordon, and Dana laying on the cobblestones of Bayberry Square, their sightless eyes staring at nothing as blood pooled about their bodies. She heard the sobs of shackle-wearing Natasha, Patrice, and Vivian, as they were herded by the Cons into Belles as a long line of customers leered. The specter of Marla being flayed alive by a grinning McGee tore something primal from Sydney's subconscious.

Never. I can never let that happen, whatever the cost. And if that cost is my innocence or my life—or my soul—then so be it.

"You're right." Sydney balanced the knife in her fingers, ready to hurl it into living flesh. She grabbed onto Drith's shoulders. "When you're ready."

"All right. On three. One—"

Sydney twitched and yanked her hands back. "Wait."

Drith blinked. "What?"

"On three? I mean, is it one, two, three, then recall? Or one, two, recall?"

Drith stared at her.

"What?"

"Now, of all times, you make that joke?" Drith looked appalled. "It was old when I was young."

"Tension breaker," Sydney said, blushing. "Sorry. Just go on three, okay? One, two, recall."

"Very well. Ready?"

Sydney nodded and placed her hands on Drith's shoulders again. *Just like throwing at the target board. Yeah, keep telling yourself that.*

The dryad took a deep breath. "Here we go. One, two...."

Chapter Thirty

"Three!"

The world blurred. It was not like the rainbow-hued streaks that flooded past her when she did the dimensional stepping, nor was it the darkness of the Nightshade shadowdance. Instead, this was as though her eyes had misted over in the space of a heartbeat and just as quickly cleared.

That's a neat trick.

Their feet hit solid ground. Sydney's eyes focused on Palla-vo-argan. The dryad wore her dark black hair short, just above the collar. She was clad in a sleeveless pale blue gown and didn't carry any weaponry.

Her magic is probably just that strong.

Sydney fixed her target in the space of an eyeblink, raised her arm, and flung her knife. The moment it left her hand, she reached for the next one.

Palla glanced their way just as Drith and Sydney materialized. Her dark eyes widened and she opened her mouth to shout.

The diamond-shaped blade lanced across the intervening space and sunk into Palla's chest with the sound of a stick striking mud. The dryad folded in half and tumbled to the ground.

Kyne whirled at the sound. She yelled and raised her left hand.

Sydney's thought was automatic.

Shield.

The power of the albino mushrooms evacuated her blood. An arced shield of shimmering white light sprang up in front of her just as Kyne's attack arrived. The gout of flame split and hurled aside, scorching the ground a few feet to either side of Sydney.

Kyne pivoted her body and fired again, this time with her right hand. The second bolt struck Sydney's shield with much more force. Glowing cracks appeared in the barrier.

Sydney poured her remaining crumble energy into the shield just as the third arrived, deflecting the attack yet again. The crumble in her veins wavered and the shield vanished.

Oh fuck.

She tensed to dive behind the nearest tree when Kyne suddenly froze and jerked off the ground. The dryad's head canted to the left and her arms seemed to be pinned at her side.

Drith approached the suspended Kyne, her left fist held aloft. Her raised hand glowed. Fresh tears painted her cheeks.

Kyne's eyes bugged. "Drith."

"I'm sorry, Kyne."

Drith wrenched her fist to the side. Kyne's head snapped in the same direction and the sound of splintering bone filled the clearing. Kyne's eyes went slack and her entire body slumped.

Drith lowered her fist and the unfortunate Kyne tumbled to the ground.

Sydney downed another crumble packet and trotted to where Palla lay quivering. She readied a defensive spell and rolled the dryad over.

She saw in an instant that the dryad was finished. Blood gushed from Palla's mouth and crimson stained the entire front of her gown.

Palla's bleary eyes focused on Sydney. Her voice was a croak. "You...you...."

"I'm sorry."

Palla choked, gasped, and fell limp.

Sydney groped for a pulse but felt none. She sighed. *Gods, what a mess.*

Drith appeared at her shoulder. "Is she gone?"

"Yes."

Drith touched Sydney's arm. "Steady, Sydney. It had to be done."

"I know. What did you do to Kyne? I've never seen that before."

"Applied force in all directions, so she couldn't move. It's not easy but anyone that practices should be able to do it. I'll show you later. We have to free my ladies."

Drith hurried to the cage. As soon as the dryads within recognized her, they all broke out in an excited babble, demanding to be released. Drith held up her hands for silence. The dryads quieted. "Listen up, ladies. I'm going to let you out but we have to do something ugly."

"Whatever, Drith, just get us out of here!" It was the dryad Sydney saw crying at the bars.

"Not until you listen to me. This is critical. Choy-na-Sal isn't only going to keep us from siding with the faeries here." She gestured at Sydney.

The dryads glanced her way. Their looks ranged from curious to warm to indifferent but Sydney didn't think any were outright hostile.

Drith continued. "Choy plans to side the Dryad Gang with McGee and the Cons."

"No!" one said.

"Yes. She's over at the Four-Leaf Club right now, probably whoring herself even as we speak." The corners of Drith's mouth turned down. "If we all don't want to be turned into prostitutes for those green-wearing bastards, we have to stop Choy, and that means siding with the faeries. It also means we cannot allow Choy to stop us. She and the others must not be allowed to recall to this grove to commune with their trees and regain their magical strength. We must burn their trees."

The dryads shrieked, clearly disgusted and outraged by the notion. The bar-crier said, "Drith, that's monstrous! We can't do that!"

Fatigue—emotional and physical—filled Sydney's head and with that came irritability. She marched to the cage and put herself face-to-face with the speaker. "What's your name?"

The dryad stared down her nose at Sydney. "Josi-me-Klio, if it's important. Can you stand aside? This is dryad business."

Sydney thrust her arm through the bars, grabbed the front of Josi's dress, and yanked the Dryad against the cage. "It's my business too because faery asses are on the line even more than yours. Drith is giving you dryads a chance to get out of this alive but only if we all work together. If you want to stand here and cry and scratch your buttcracks, do it on your own time. Until then, get with the program!"

She shoved Josi back. The dryad stumbled into her compatriots, her wide eyes full of fear.

Drith gave Sydney a sideways glance. "You heard her. This has to be done. Look here, ladies. You know I am not an enormous fan of the Faery Gang. To an individual, they're crass, rude, and obnoxious."

Sydney's eyes narrowed but she kept her mouth shut.

Drith's eyes never left her audience. "But allying with them is our only chance. Choy is moving the gang closer to the Cons and none of us want that. If we are going to break with them, it must be done now. And if we don't cut off Choy and her loyalists from the source of their magic, they'll come after us. Once the battle is over, if we win, the faeries will protect us. Right, Sydney?"

"We don't abandon our allies."

"Exactly." Drith paused. "Ladies, this is the only way."

Josi looked around the captive group. Slowly, all the dryads nodded.

Sydney exhaled. She realized she'd been holding her breath.

"All right," Drith said. "As soon as their trees are all dead, head upstairs. Do not go out the front door. Choy hired Urgon Thunderhand to guard the front of the Dancing Bear."

"What?" Josi said. "We can't—"

"I cut a hole in the roof. Slip out and go over the back, over Lorr's Bakery and down to Briar Street. Do it quietly and no one will be the wiser. As soon as you get out, head to The Log on Bayberry Square. Sydney, will the faeries there allow us in?"

"Ask for Dana or Markus when you get there and say that Sydney sent you."

"Very well. Any questions?"

No one moved.

"Good." She pointed her rootwood at the cage lock.

The steel bolt crumpled and the door opened.

Sydney darted to the side as the prisoners tumbled out of the cage like a tidal wave. They fanned out into the grove and in seconds, dispersed to their trees. Dryads hugged the bark boles of oaks, dryads swung from pine branches like unruly squirrels, and dryads held elm leaves to their faces in dreamy contentment.

Sydney smirked at Drith. "And you were giving me crap over eating mushroom crumble?"

A rare smile lit Drith's face. "I guess we all have our idiosyncrasies. Give them a few moments and their magic will be restored."

She let the dryads cavort, then clapped her hands. "All right, enough. Get on the trees. Any dryad who isn't here with us, burn their tree down."

The group hesitated. Drith's face wrenched into a scowl. "Now!"

They hurried to obey her. Sydney followed as Drith stalked to a tree. "Is this Choy's?"

"Yes."

Even though the maple was less than twenty feet high, the trunk was a good three feet thick and topped by a dense tangle of twisting branches. Sydney felt the power pulsing from the old tree. "Kind of stunted."

"Some species grow well down here, like my oak. Maples get a little warped. I don't think they do quite as well under the lightstones as they do under the sun. Choy's birth tree is a maple. Maybe that's why she's a little bent too."

"Why do you say that?"

Drith looked down her nose at Sydney. "Humiliating herself like a common trollop? Spreading her legs for multiple Cons and who knows what else? What would you call that?"

"Slut-shaming doesn't make you look virtuous, Drith. It makes you look like a jerk."

"If you say so."

"Never mind that now," Sydney said. "What next?"

Drith aimed both hands at the base of the trunk. A gout of flame poured from her palms, forming a continuous stream. Within seconds, scorch and smoke assailed Sydney's nostrils. Within half a minute, the bark had blackened and the lowest leaves burned away. Drith kept up the attack. In less than a minute, the entire tree was ablaze.

Heat beat at Sydney's face. She took a few steps in the opposite direction, only to be assaulted by a new heat source as another tree caught fire. In the time it took her to boil an egg, half the trees in the grove were living torches. Sydney thought she heard a series of distant screams but decided she was imagining things.

Drith pointed at two of the dryads. "Stay behind and collapse the tunnel as soon as the trees are cinder. Get out as soon as you can."

The two nodded.

"The rest of you, make for The Log. Do it quickly, before the smoke from the grove's vent shafts draws a crowd."

The remaining dryads scurried for the tunnel.

"Is that going to do it, Drith?"

"Choy and all her loyalists just lost their magic. They will have to find trees, re-bond, and commune with them. They will be days or weeks recovering, or even longer if they don't have seeds from their birth-trees. In the meantime, they'll be weak and emotionally overwrought. They shouldn't be a factor in the fight."

"Aren't you worried they might sneak down here and do the same to you?"

"You heard me, right? I told Ebi-lo-Fars and Nada-ci-Pel to collapse the tunnel. It might take us a few days to dig out the grove but we can worry about that after we deal with the Cons. Without their magic, Choy and her whole cohort won't be able to get to it in time. They'll be cut off and the grove will be safe until after the battle. Trust me."

"I hope you're right. Now let's get out of here."

They scaled the ladder and climbed outside.

Smoke boiled from the twin chimneys rising from the Dancing Bear's rooftop. Sydney half-expected Urgon to be waiting for them but the hulking mercenary was nowhere to be seen. She glanced over the roof's edge. The street was similarly empty.

No Urgon. No Marla.

"Sydney, this way."

Drith hopped across the adjoining rooftop with the agility of a cat. Sydney followed, praying they wouldn't drop into a street, straight into the arms of an ogre patrol.

But the lane was vacant, save a pair of waiting dryads. One was Josi-me-Klio. Drith and Sydney landed next to the two. Josi said, "Drith, everyone else is out and on their way to The Log."

"Good."

Josi cast a nervous glance over her shoulder. "There are a lot of ogres out tonight."

"We know," Sydney said. "Go on. We'll catch up."

The dryads looked dubious but took off.

"What was that for?" Drith asked.

"Small groups are less noticeable than big ones."

"Is that something you learned running around the streets with Marla."

"Yeah, pretty much."

"Are you going to look for her?"

Sydney paused. The desire tugged at her heart—the desire to make sure her sister was safe. She shook her head. There was too much at stake. "No, Marla has to make her own way back."

They set off at a brisk pace. Sydney asked, "If you don't run around the streets, as you put it, how does your gang do business?"

"There's more than one way to run a criminal enterprise. You faeries act as little better than thugs. We involve ourselves in more intelligent activities: bookkeeping, pyramid schemes, embezzlement. Less filthy and less violent. I don't really expect you to understand."

"Drith, I understand perfectly. You have your way of doing business, we have ours. I don't care if you think we're thugs. When the chips were down, you turned to us for help." She grinned. "I suspect you'll have a hard time living that down."

"What?"

"That your high-and-mighty gang had to rely on such lowly creatures to save your asses."

Drith shot her a dirty look but only said, "The enemy of my enemy, Sydney." She motioned to Sydney to stop and lowered her voice. "Wait. Listen."

They ducked into a shadowed alley. Sydney heard the stomp of booted feet. An ogre patrol came into view. She sucked in a short breath.

Crol led the pack, moving at a brisk pace. His narrowed eyes burned and his snarl suggested that anyone in his way might be on the receiving end of his anger.

Sydney and Drith waited for them to pass, then hurried towards The Log as fast they could silently manage.

*   *   *   *   *

Sydney's eyes raked Bayberry Square for threats but the plaza was silent. She spotted Anders on the roof of The Log. He held a crossbow at the ready. Even from the distance, he looked half-asleep, though she knew from experience he was paying better attention than he let on.

But if he's in that semi-relaxed state, then no one has made a move tonight.

"C'mon, Drith."

They scuttled across the darkened square to the front door. She tried the handle and heard the lock rattle. Sydney rapped on the panel.

A muffled voice drifted from within. "We're closed, assholes!"

"It's Sydney."

She heard a slight scuffling and the door cracked open. The business end of a crossbow emerged, followed by a scowling face.

"Easy there, Lila."

"Sydney, it is you!"

The door opened all the way. Sydney grabbed Drith by the elbow and hustled her inside. Lila slammed it in her wake and applied the door bolts.

Dirty dryads jammed the tavern room. Though they were all dead-eyed with exhaustion and their once-beautiful dresses bore stains of sweat and smoke, none of them seemed injured.

Thank the Gods for small favors.

"Drith, have a seat wherever. We'll get the sleeping arrangements worked out." Sydney glanced at Garth, who stood at the bar nearby. "If you want something to eat or drink, talk to Garth over there. He'll set you up."

"Okay, Sydney. Thank you."

Sydney blinked. It was the first word of gratitude she had heard from any of the dryads.

Drith sat with a group of her gang. Sydney faced Lila, who hurled herself into Sydney's arms. "We were worried about you, buddy."

"I'm fine, just worn out. Did Marla make it back?"

"She's in her office with Dana and Markus. They're reading her the riot act."

"Serves her right for keeping them in the dark but it looks like we've got some allies for the battle."

"You can tell me about it later." Lila grinned. "I'm just glad you're back."

"Me too. What time is it?"

"Close to three. You tired?"

Sydney slumped. "Exhausted. But I better go tell Marla I'm back, then come back and work out where we're going to put all these dryads."

"Gotcha covered. As soon as Marla came back, Garth and Robin and me prepped some of the empty bedrooms. We pulled a bunch of extra blankets from storage. Robin is upstairs, making sure we have everything covered. All our guests should all have a place to sleep."

"Great. Thanks, Lila."

Lia gave Sydney another quick hug. "You got it, buddy."

Sydney made her way back to the office. The workroom was deserted. She supposed her friends and comrades were asleep. She snorted. *Big day coming up. I should be in bed too.*

Marla glanced up as she entered. "You're not dead. That's good."

"Screw you too, sis."

"Drith make it back with you?"

"Yeah, she's out front with her ladies."

"Good." Marla stood. She stretched and groaned. "Probably time for sleep."

"Lila said Markus and Dana were back here."

"They were. I filled them in, took the browbeating for acting without discussing things with them, then sent to get some rest. You should do the same. The sun will be up soon and we'll have less than twenty-four hours to get ready."

"Yeah. By the way, I saw Crol. He was heading to the Dancing Bear and he looked pissed. We might get a visit tomorrow."

"We'll deal with that tomorrow."

"What happened with Urgon?"

"He saw the smoke and made a move to check it out. I distracted him."

Sydney raised an eyebrow. "How did you do that?"

"I chucked a rock at his head. Bounced off his helmet. Then I ran like a rabbit." She scowled. "It's not fair that someone so big can move so quickly. He almost caught me several times before I finally lost him."

"I'm surprised he chased you."

"Why? He was pissed off enough."

"Maybe. From everything I've seen and heard about Urgon, he's a consummate professional. A rock wouldn't draw him away from his contract. Not only that, he's smart. He must have expected you to be a diversion." Sydney frowned. "We're missing something, and I seem to be saying that a lot."

"Whatever it is, Syd, it can wait until morning. I'm going to bed. Goodnight."

Marla left the office.

Sydney sat. She stared at the window magically showing Bayberry Square.

There was a flicker of movement on the periphery, near the entrance to Tower Street. Sydney blinked and whatever had moved was gone.

Gone...just like a Nightshade.

She stared at the window for another hour, daring it to reveal something new, before exhaustion finally overtook her.

Chapter Thirty-One

"Sydney, wake up."

Her eyes fluttered half-open. Sydney recognized a hand a few inches from her face. She shoved the hand away. The words rumbled from deep in her chest. "Lila, go away."

"Crol is here to see you."

Sydney blinked awake. A surge of fear-fueled adrenaline drove away her drowsiness. "Me? You sure?"

"You're the only Sydney here."

"Is...is he here to arrest me or something?"

"He didn't say but he's downstairs in the tavern."

"With his boys?"

"No, just him."

Sydney tossed back the blankets and reached for her clothes. She forced herself to stay calm. "What time is it?"

"Just past dawn. You've only been in bed a few hours."

"What are you doing up, Lila? You should be resting too."

"I took a long nap yesterday."

"Hmph." Sydney buckled her boots. "Well, I better go see what he wants before he gets impatient and rips the place down."

"He wouldn't do that." Lila laughed, though to Sydney, it sounded a little forced.

Sydney descended to the tavern.

Garth nodded as she entered. He loitered behind the bar, one eye on their guest.

Crol lounged in a chair too small for his oversized frame. One hand rested around a gallon jar filled with ale. His eyes locked on Sydney the moment she entered. "Sydney. Good. I was thinking I was going to have to help myself to another one or two of these while I waited."

"A little early to get roaring drunk."

"Nah. I can drink a couple of kegs of Ascorian ale at once without feeling anything." The ogre drained the jar in one long pull. "Now the sugar tree rum my mother used to brew...that was some strong shit."

"Oh yeah?"

"You're what, Sydney? A hundred twenty-five pounds? A single swallow would knock you on your ass." He set his jar on the table and motioned. Garth brought him a full gallon jar and Crol handed him a few coins. "But I didn't come here to talk about booze."

Sydney grabbed a bottle of strawberry wine from the bar.

Garth eyed her. "You gonna be all right?"

"Yeah. Give us a few moments, would you?"

"Sure, kid." He slipped out the kitchen door.

Sydney took a seat across from Crol. She popped the cork and drank from the open bottle. The tangy liquor left a warm trail as it slid down her throat. "If not liquor, what did you come to talk about?"

"What happened over at the Dancing Bear last night?"

"I have no idea."

"You have some new guests here at The Log."

"None that I know of."

Crol guffawed. "Then why do you happen to have strawberry wine standing by at the bar? The favorite drink of most dryads? Coincidence?"

"Other creatures drink it too."

Crol drummed his fingers on the tabletop. "Sydney, let's not beat around the bush. I know what happened last night. You burned down the dryad grove or at least part of it."

"Wasn't us."

His eyebrows arched. "Really."

"Look, Crol, we can't be blamed because the Dryad Gang had a little disagreement in their ranks and some rebels got out of hand. That's on them."

"And these dryad rebels...on whose side are they standing tomorrow?"

Sydney didn't answer.

"That's what I thought." He took a drink. "Well, however you did it, you really did a number on the rest of the dryads. Choyna-Sal and her pack of idiots were crying so much they were almost incoherent. I've never seen dryads lose their composure so completely. Kind of funny, actually."

"Are you here to arrest me?"

"I should. You were told to keep your little war confined to one day, and to Bayberry Square."

Sydney held her breath.

Crol let out an exasperated sigh. "But I'm not going to."

"Without admitting to being guilty of anything, may I ask why not?"

"Because I like you." Crol chuckled. "No, I don't mean that in the sense that I want to bone you, but you're one of the more interesting creatures to come to Woodhollow recently. I'm curious to see how this plays out."

"If I'm so interesting, why don't you go round up McGee and his boys and toss them out of town? Make sure I stay around a bit longer?"

"Because I'm not stupid. This is a great gig and I am not going to fuck it up."

Sydney could not repress her sneer. "Good gig? Being Lord Burnside's errand boy?"

"Sydney, do you know what the average lifespan of an ogre is?"

"No idea."

"Ogres usually pass from old age by the time they hit forty-two; at least, they would if they made it to old age. Most of us die in battle by the age of twelve."

"A little young."

"Ogres reach full maturity by the time we're seven or

eight."

Sydney whistled. "That's some fast metabolism."

"Right. Also, why we die so quick."

He leaned forward and placed his elbows on the table. It creaked beneath his weight. "Sydney, I am eighteen. I have maybe two decades of good life left in me, and I'd like to enjoy them to the fullest. Even with my size and strength, if I stayed in my people's lands, I'd lose my life in battle within a few years, tops. So, yes, answering to Lord Burnside and cracking a few heads on his behalf is a price worth paying if it keeps me here and enjoying a comfortable life."

His gaze bore into hers. "That's why I am not going to ruin it for anything, or anyone. I'm not going to arrest you. This time. You have one more day before your battle. I highly recommend you don't do anything to draw my interest between now and then. Are we clear?"

Sydney nodded.

Crol's face relaxed. "Good. I'll take you at your word on this." He paused. "If it's any consolation, I'm rooting for you."

"Have a large wager with a bookie, do you?"

"Nope. Some of my boys made bets but I can't do that. I can't be seen to be taking sides. If I placed a bet and then the Enforcers have to intervene tomorrow because things get out of control, it will look mighty convenient if I intervene on the side I bet on."

Sydney took a drink of her wine. "You're a different kind of ogre, Crol."

"I guess we're both interesting, Sydney, in our own way."

"If you say so."

"I do say so. Your presence here had made the entire criminal side of Woodhollow a little more lively. You're not quite the firebrand that Marla is and from what I hear, you can't swing a sword worth a damn, but you think fast on your feet and you're more intelligent than the majority of the thugs in town."

"That's a backhanded compliment."

"Only kind I know how to give. I know you faeries don't bother people who don't bother you and unlike that clown McGee, you rarely resort to violence. I'd rather have you all in charge of Woodhollow's underworld than the Leprechauns. It would be more peaceful for everyone and make my job easier."

"You could help us."

"You could all flee, too."

Sydney opened her mouth and closed it again.

He stood and hefted his club. "Good luck, Sydney, and I mean that."

Crol headed to the door. Sydney said, "What about Urgon Thunderhand?"

"What about him?"

"Did he get that notice too, about not starting trouble?"

Crol frowned. "What are you talking about?"

"He was...I mean, I understand he was standing guard at the Dancing Bear last night, out in the street."

"If he was, I didn't see any sign of him. And it all depends on whether he was acting on a legitimate contract or not."

"How so?"

"If he was hired to guard the shop, okay. It's Choy's money, she can spend it however she wants. If he was involved in something else...well, if we find that out, he'll have to answer for it."

"You think you can handle him?"

Crol laughed. "Only one way to find out."

He pushed through the door and departed.

*   *   *   *   *

Sydney found Marla on the roof of The Log, The gang leader leaned against the roof wall and stared out over Bayberry Square. The stub of her cigar smoldered.

She followed Marla's gaze. Groups of ogres erected wooden barricades at every entrance to the square save one. Woodhollow citizens who approached the ogres did not tarry long; Sydney was too far to hear any of the Enforcers' words but a few grunts followed by a raised weapon was enough to persuade curious onlookers to move along.

"See what they're doing out there?" Marla asked.

"Looks like they are blockading all the entrances except for Tower Street."

"Yeah, making it damn sure none of tomorrow's fight leaks out of the square."

"That actually simplifies things for us, Marla."

"How so?"

"It means that the Cons can only come at us from one angle." Sydney pointed. "When we set up tonight, we can focus our attention there."

"That sounds good. What did Crol want?"

"How did you know he was here?"

Marla frowned. "Jeez, Sydney. I've been up here for thirty minutes and I just watched him walk away. Since he didn't ask for me, I assume he talked to you."

"He did."

"And?"

Sydney chuckled. "He wished us luck."

"Is he going to help us?"

"Uh, no."

Marla spat the stub of her cigar over the edge. "Then he can cram it."

There was a brief disturbance at one of the barricades, followed by harsh shouting and swearing. Grumbling ogres hefted a half-built barricade and set it to the side. Several dozen short men and women in chocolate-colored clothes marched into Bayberry Square. A smattering of red dotted the sea of green stocking caps. To a soul, their faces were set in a scowl.

Sydney pointed. "The Browns are here."

"Thanks, Captain Obvious. I guess we better go down and greet them before someone says something wrong and there's a fight."

They shimmied down the ladder and trotted downstairs just as a harsh banging erupted at the front doors. Sydney looked around. "I thought you had Markus keeping an eye on things."

"He's there but Wychia is in that group and as soon as someone so much as mentions her name, he starts getting stupid. Kind of like he was doing with you."

Sydney didn't know what to say to that.

Marla caught the look on Sydney's face. "Look, try not to think about it."

"Sure."

"Did Gordon and Patrice head out for Salmonkia?"

Sydney nodded, glad to focus on something other than Markus. "As far as I know, they left before dawn. I hope they strike a deal. It might be just enough of an edge."

"Yep." Marla opened the door to the tavern. "Cost us a fortune to have it done on such short notice."

"We'll take it out of the Cons' hides if we win. And on that note, let's see to our guests."

"Open up in there." Even through the thick timbers of the doors, the voice carried an unmistakable hint of irritation. "It's Wulf son of Warth."

Lila still manned the door with her crossbow. "How do we know it's you?"

Sydney could almost hear Wulf grinding his teeth. "Look, jackass. Open the door or the Browns walk and you idiots can fight the Cons, Rats, and Hobs on your own."

"It's them," Marla said. "Better open it before they rip the hinges off."

Lila unbolted the doors and opened them. Without pause, Wulf stomped into the tavern, followed by a troop of brownies. They immediately took seats and looked around, as if expecting drink service.

Wulf himself paced directly to Marla. "Can we get something to drink?"

"As long as you don't reduce yourself to incoherence. We have a battle tomorrow."

"Yes, yes, *mother*."

Markus wove through the tables until he was face-to-face with Wychia. He bowed low. "Welcome, dear lady."

She glared at him. "Come to try more of your useless flattery?"

"I did."

"You could at least get me a drink first. Ascorian ale, with a brandy chaser."

"Coming right up."

Markus straightened, a wide grin on his face. His eyes met Sydney's and his smile faltered.

Wulf glanced around. "So where are we sleeping?"

Marla said, "We're pretty full at the moment, Wulf, but I think we can find all your people a bed to sleep in tonight."

"Filled up? You get reinforcements or something? More faeries come up in from Sylvan Valley?"

"No, I have half the Dryad Gang here. The other half has been—" Marla smirked. "—been rendered ineffective."

"Dryads?" Wulf scratched his chin. "I guess we can work with them. Buncha snotty bitches most of the time."

"That they are," Sydney said, "but they're on our side, so take it easy on them."

"Fine. Now, about those drinks."

Sydney nudged Marla. "You might want to get Garth and Robin. They'll get this all sorted out."

Marla gave her a grateful nod and left the room. Garth and Robin returned a few minutes later and took charge of the room full of grumbling brownies. Sydney thanked him. "Where did Marla go?"

"As far as I know, she went back to the roof."

Sydney returned to the roof. Marla was not there. Dana was, however. She saw Sydney and motioned towards the tavern. "The Browns get settled?"

"Garth has them in hand. He really is a hell of a quartermaster, you know."

"I know, he does a good job. We live through this, we should make his title official."

"I think that's a great idea." Sydney moved alongside the old woman. "What's on your mind, Dana?"

"Same old, same old. Wondering how fucked we are."

"Moderately, I'd say." Sydney watched the ogres assemble their barricades. "There are forty of us. Looks like about twenty-five Browns, plus Wychia and eleven other redcaps. I counted twenty dryads. Against that, there at least sixty Cons, as many Rats, and....shit, I don't know how many Hobs. We're going to be outnumbered around three to two. It could be closer to two to one if Choy can get the remaining Dryads organized to stand with the Cons."

"They won't have any magic."

"Even if they simply show up with bows, they're bodies on the battlefield."

Dana nodded. Her face was grim.

Sydney surveyed the square. She recalled all the discussions she'd had with Jacob on strategy and tactics. "So we have to cut down their advantage."

"I think your ideas on that front are about as good as we can do."

"Thanks, Dana. You and Marla and Markus and Garth had great details to add."

"But the core is yours, Sydney." Dana patted Sydney on the shoulder. "If we win this, you're going to be known as a tactical genius. You know that, don't you?"

"Maybe. If we lose, I'll be remembered as a bonehead."

Dana smiled. "Even if we don't win we're going to bloody the hell out of them. They'll never forget it, and neither will the rest of Woodhollow."

"That's the idea. Well, the idea is to win."

"You know what, Sydney? I think we just might."

"If the Gods love us."

Dana's laugh was a short bark. "Well, in that case, we're dead faeries walking. Have Gordon and Patrice made it back yet?"

"No, but they should be back soon."

"Is it something the ogres will let them bring through?"

"I sure hope so, especially since they won't know what the cargo is capable of. I told Gordon to just remind any Enforcers that the fighting hasn't started and we plan to keep it in the Square, and the devices he's carrying are for post-battle celebration. Most of them are simple-minded enough that they should be fine."

A crash erupted from below, followed by loud brownie and faery voices. "I'm not worried about Gordon and Patrice. I'm worried that I'll be able to talk the Browns into this. They're...." Sydney trailed off.

"Stubborn?"

"To say the least."

Dana snickered. "If anyone here can convince them, you can."

"Gee, thanks."

"All right. I think I am going to stay up here a bit." Dana gave her a wistful smile. "You should probably get some rest, Sydney. You've got a long night ahead of you."

"Okay, Mom."

"Laugh all you want. Someone has to keep you kids in line. By the way, do me a favor."

"What's that?"

"Draw your sword."

Sydney frowned but pulled her short sword, which was little more than a long dagger, and held it in front of her.

Dana stepped forward and peered at Sydney's hand. "That's what I thought. You're holding the hilt wrong. Here."

She moved one of Sydney's fingers and adjusted her thumb. "There. You think you can remember that?"

"I think so. Wow." She cut the air with the blade. Her grip felt ten times more secure than before. "Is this why Markus was always able to knock my blade out of my grip while we were sparring?"

"It didn't help."

"Why didn't he catch this?"

Dana snorted. "Too busy thinking about screwing you, I'm sure."

"Thanks, Dana. But I hope I don't have to pull it. Everyone in Woodhollow knows I can't handle a sword."

"I understand. But if you do, maybe now you'll at least hold onto it. Now go on and let an old woman enjoy her last peaceful morning."

*   *   *   *   *

Sydney waited in the gloom by The Log's rear entrance. None of the lightstones in the Square were lit. All of the windows in The Log sported thick wooden slats and consequently, it was quite dark. Even the other shops around Bayberry Square had been tacked shut.

She smiled to herself. Some of the shopkeeps had complained loudly about the boarding. One bootmaker gnome with a shop opposite The Log, when he was told by the Enforcers that his store was also going to be sealed for the upcoming fight, had reacted with unusual vigor. One ogre hobbled away with a sore shin. The gnome himself got an unconscious ride to the Woodhollow Jail.

Her amusement tapered off. She needed to stick to business. Patrice and Claire were due back any moment.

That thought made her scowl. Markus was supposed to join them on this raid but they couldn't find him. She suspected if they checked the room where Wychia was lodged, they would have.

Let it go, Sydney, before it burns you up.

She nodded and pushed him out of her mind for good. Things with Markus were never meant to be and as she accepted that, she found a measure of peace.

Where are they?

Sydney shifted her weight back and forth. She wanted to grab her work team but they couldn't start preparing the Square until the other two returned. Anxiety and stress chewed at her mind.

A roaring cheer erupted from the tavern room. She knew Marla had the faeries, the dryads, and the brownies all crowded together and was giving a last rousing speech.

I hope it's enough.

A light breeze tickled her skin. Sydney rubbed her forearms. The simple friction brought a little warmth to her flesh. The sensation was welcome, yet fleeting.

Amazing how much we take for granted, she mused. *A little light rub on the skin for warmth, the pleasure of a swallow of ale, the cool sensation of a breath of crisp morning air, a hug in the arms of a loved one....tomorrow it could all come to an end.*

Sydney faced death any number of times since she came to Woodhollow. There had been moments of terror, during which she hadn't felt the cold clutch of her own mortality until well after the actual danger passed. When she thought about it, she never really thought she could die.

But I can. And likely will.

The thought did not frighten Sydney as much as she thought it would. She contemplated the idea of her vision dimming, her hearing fading, and the finality of a cold sensation creeping over her body as her spirit slid away into oblivion. She didn't fear it.

She feared what was left behind without her.

Marla. Brigid. Lila. Vivian. All of her friends.

I'll miss them. Whoever lives, I hope their lives are full and safe from here on out.

Except, they wouldn't be. Aside from Brigid, whoever survived the battle would be in danger from the Cons. And even Brigid. The Nightshade wouldn't leave her alone. Maybe Edmund could protect her, maybe not.

Sudden anger boiled to the forefront of her mind. Her fingernails dug into her palm.

It's not fair! This shouldn't be happening to us! We— She took a deep breath and fought down the hammering of her heart. She closed her eyes.

Do your best, Sydney. Fight until you've got nothing left. After that...whatever happens, happens.

She opened her eyes and exhaled.

A bulky shadow broke away from the shade a few feet away, more distorted and heavier than any faery should have been. Sydney reached for her knives but she halted when she heard

Claire's husky voice. The big faery limped towards her. "It's me, Sydney."

"Why are you walking funny? You didn't get hurt, did you?"

"Not me. But them? Maybe." Claire dumped the two bodies at Sydney's feet.

Sydney knelt. The telltale aroma of the sewers rose from the dark fur of the two corpses.

"That's two of the Rats. Where's the third?"

"Patrice has his body."

"Good. As far as I know, that's all three of the spies they set to watch the Square. I couldn't spot any others."

"Us either. We looked but nothing."

"You didn't let the ogres see you, did you?"

She couldn't see Claire's face in the dark but Sydney sensed the scowl pointed her way. "No, Sydney. We've done this kind of thing before, much more than you. We know what we're doing."

"All right, all right. If the watchers are down, we can get to work. Let the others know."

"Right." Claire slipped inside.

Patrice appeared from the shadows, dragging a third body, which she added to the pile. Her ebullient tone drifted through the night. "Well, that was fun."

Sydney nodded to herself. "All right. McGee just lost his eyes and ears on Bayberry Square. He won't know what we do for the rest of the night. So let's make him pay for that."

Chapter Thirty-Two

Dawn broke over Woodhollow. Bright yellow sunlight filled Bayberry Square. It glinted off the few uncovered glass surfaces still visible and poured from the cloudless sky to bathe every cobblestone.

Sydney glared at the rising sun.

Marla elbowed her. "What's your problem?"

"A nice sunrise seems inappropriate for the morning. Red skies would have been more fitting."

"That's an old wives tale. You know that, right?"

"What is?"

Sydney eyed her sister. Marla wore a leather jerkin lined with bronze metal scales, plate thigh and shin guards, and etched vambraces. A winged helmet adorned her head. Sydney wondered when her sister acquired a suit of traditional faery war mail.

Sydney herself wore a heavy leather shirt laden with rows of interweaving metal rings sewn into it. She'd been offered a helmet but declined after setting the thing on her brow and having it fall down over her eyes.

Marla rolled her cigar to the other side of her mouth and clenched it in her teeth. She said, "That red skies in the morning is a dire omen of some kind."

"Yeah, I know. Still, the day looks a little too cheery for busting heads."

"Any day is a good day for busting heads." Wulf sauntered to where they stood. The four-foot-high brownie still wore his dyed brown leathers from head to toe. A conic steel helmet replaced his normal green stocking cap. He carried in one hand a three-foot iron mallet with a hammerhead on one side and a thick spike on the other. Even as he spoke, he twirled the weapon as if it was light as a twig.

"You look ridiculous holding that thing, Wulf."

His answering grin was vicious. "More than one person has laughed about this hammer, Sydney—right before I brained them with it."

"Okay, works for me."

Marla rubbed her chin. "Wychia is in position, with the redcaps?"

"For the last time, yes. Stop worrying, would you?"

"Maybe once I'm dead." She glanced at Drith-an-Bidi as the dryad leader joined them. "How are your ladies this morning, Drith?"

"Ready to do our part." Drith wore one of her elaborate lacey dresses, though beneath a knee-length coat of overlapping leaf-shaped leather plates.

"I hope so," Marla said. "I think—" She paused. "Wait. Do you hear that?"

Sydney heard it: the sound of many stamping feet mixed with bellowing war cries.

Marla nodded. "This is it."

Wulf stuck out his hand and glared at Marla.

She looked at his palm, back at Wulf, then placed her hand in his. They both looked at Drith.

The dryad placed her hand on top of theirs.

"To the death," Wulf stated.

Marla nodded. "To the death."

"Err, yes," Drith replied, without enthusiasm.

They broke their handshake. The leaders of the Browns and Dryads trotted back to their ranks.

Sydney stepped out of the line and surveyed their position one last time, looking for any last-minute improvements they could make.

The three gangs spread out in a battle line in front of The Log. The Faery Gang stood in the center. Most of them carried swords and were dressed in a variety of metal-covered leather armor. A few veterans of numerous fights, like Markus, bore looks of bored impatience. Others, like Lila, looked scared but determined. Vivian alone displayed an expression of vapid indifference.

To their left arrayed several dozen Browns. The brownies all wore leather breeches and jerkins, dyed in shades of chestnut, chocolate, and taupe, with iron caps similar to the one Wulf wore. The Browns carried various hammers, mauls, and maces.

The Dryads took up position on the faeries' right. Like Drith, they wore plated leather jackets over their intricate dresses. A few carried thin knives but most waited with glowing hands as they primed their powerful magic. A couple batted a glowing ball of energy back and forth.

Sydney raised her eyes. Anders, Natasha, and a recent recruit named Louisa crouched behind the wall at the edge of The Log's roof. If she hadn't known they were up there, she wouldn't have seen them. Since they had eliminated the three rats the night before, perhaps the Cons and their allies wouldn't know they were there either.

That's the plan, anyway.

A second glance told her that Garth, Robin, Trish, and Gerry clustered to the side of their line, hidden behind a derelict cart. Worry gnawed at her; if something went wrong, those four would be cut off and horribly vulnerable.

Nothing to be done about it now.

She flicked her eyes to the Tower Street entrance to Bayberry Square. Sydney wished the ogres had put up any kind of obstacle there, as they had at the other streets. Even a partial one would have funneled the Cons into a tight spot where only a few at a time could advance...a "bottleneck," the volumes on strategy had called such a situation.

But there was no barricade. The street entrance yawned open, ready to disgorge their attackers.

I guess that would have defeated the purpose. Burnside isn't our ally. He doesn't want this to be easy for us. He really wants them to get in here and have it out with us.

"There they are," Marla said.

The Cons stomped into view, marching in formation ten-wide across Tower Street. When they saw the faeries and their allies, their shouts doubled in volume.

"Damn, there are a lot of them," Lila muttered.

Sydney patted her on the shoulder. "Just stay calm, buddy. Stick to the plan and everything will be fine. I hope."

Markus laughed. "Your optimism is overwhelming, Sydney."

"Just keepin' it real."

"Crumble," Marla said.

Each of the faeries consumed two packets of mushroom crumble. As always, Sydney welcomed the familiar jolt of energy that bolted down her arms and legs.

"Again!" Marla called.

Sydney devoured another two packets. She had never consumed quite so much together. Her fingers trembled. Her vision and hearing felt suddenly acute. The pall over her emotions lessened and Sydney fingered one of her daggers, wondering if the Cons' blood would feel hot on her skin, or cold.

The Cons entered the Square and immediately spread out into their own battle line. She had heard there were as many as a hundred Cons in the gang but as expected, there appeared to be about sixty present. They wore no armor but carried a motley variety of clubs, cleavers, and hatchets.

To their right, the Rats scurried forward on all fours. Each wore a belt adorned with knives and darts.

On the Cons' left, the Hobs came forward in a stone-faced block. Sydney hadn't dealt with them much; the Hobs resembled goblins, but taller, heavier, and less jovial. They were also reputed to be more warlike and savage. The Hobs wore mail coats and horned helmets. They carried spears and other polearms.

The Con line halted maybe a hundred feet from the faeries. They hollered, jeered, and shook their fists.

Sydney shivered. She did not see fear or hesitation on a single Con face. All she saw was bloodlust and excitement.

Maniacs. At least they stopped where they did, and not on this side of our little surprise.

The rank of Cons parted and McGee emerged. In his right hand, he clutched a heavy chain of thick steel links.

He raised his other hand and at once, the rest of his warband fell silent.

"Well, well, well. Look at all these wingers lined up for the taking. Looks like quite a feast, doesn't it boys?"

A rumble of assent rippled through the Cons.

McGee said, "Where are you, Marla? No point in hiding."

Marla took two steps forward. "I'll never hide from a piece of shit like you, McGee." She held her hand over her brow as if she was scanning the enemy. "I don't see Choy-na-Sal or her pack of traitorous sluts with you. You guys wear them out or something?"

A cruel smile appeared on his face. "Brave, to speak me to that way. Foolish, but brave."

"No one ever accused me of being smart."

"Well, here's your chance to prove otherwise, and believe me, Marla, I'll only offer once."

"What's that?"

"Walk away. You and your little winger bitches walk out of this square, with your allies, and leave Woodhollow. Today. Do it now and I'll let you live."

Marla's tone was incredulous. "You would let us all just leave?

"Of course."

"No attacks? No revenge?"

McGee grinned. He held up one hand and placed the other on his chest. "I give you my word."

Marla spat on the ground. "There's what I think of your word."

The faeries and browns yelled and cheered. The dryads remained stoic.

McGee's grin widened. "Good. I was hoping you'd be too dumb to accept. We're going to enjoy this. Boys?"

The Cons bellowed in response.

Sydney motioned to Drith, who nodded. She took a deep breath.

Here we go.

McGee pointed at Marla. "Bring me that bitch's head. Kill 'em all!"

The Cons cheered and flung their hats in the air. As one, they charged, the Rats and Hobs at their sides.

"Now, Drith!"

The dryads raised their hands. From each palm, streaks of fire seared fiery paths through the air and struck the cobblestone thirty feet in front of the faeries and their allies. The oil soaked-ground erupted. Gouts of flame burst skyward, separating the two groups. A pair of Rats, who had been too close to the conflagration, squealed in pain as their fur ignited. The two flopped to the ground and rolled about, while their companions beat at them with their paws.

Thick clouds of black smoke billowed up, obscuring their vision. Even as it happened, Sydney's skin prickled and a shiver shot up her spine.

The flames shrank.

The Cons are trying to put out the blaze with their magic.

She glanced at the dryads. All twenty stood rigid, their eyes narrowed and jaws locked. Beads of sweat appeared on the dryads' foreheads. Sydney knew they fought to keep the fires burning but even with their individual strength, they were outnumbered. The barrier dwindled as the Cons poured their magic into quenching it.

Just like we thought they would.

Sydney waved to the roof with both hands. Natasha waved back and disappeared from sight.

A dozen crossbow bolts lanced from the rooftop and penetrated the smoke. Shrieks of pain echoed over the crackle of flame. A few seconds later, another volley flew overhead and elicited another series of screams.

"So far, so good," Marla said.

"They only have five sets of the of multi-crossbow-rigs assembled," Sydney replied. Her gaze scanned the wall of fire. "At most, we're going to drop ten or twelve of them."

"They'll try to reload but it's gonna take time."

"Too much time, Marla. We move on to the next step and
—"

A spear lunged through the flame wall, skewering a dryad, who fell with a cry. It was followed by others, darts, and throwing axes. A few more found their mark. Lucy, a Thistle-Clan faery a year older than Sydney, screamed as a thrown cleaver gashed open her thigh. Noah threw her arm over his shoulder and helped her hobble to the doors of The Log. Two Browns also fell back, seriously wounded.

Sydney ground her teeth as another round of bolts arced overhead. She heard a series of *dinks* and rattles. "They're shielding from the crossbows."

"Good, we're making them burn their magic."

"Right." Sydney raised her voice to a shout. "Now! Hit them from behind."

As she yelled, the fourth round of bolts flew through the smoke. Cries of pain told her that some had found their mark.

She grinned. *I knew some of them would turn their shields when I said that.*

A flicker of motion caught her eye. From the roof, Louisa waved a flag—an appropriated pillowcase, really—emblazoned with several bands of color.

Rainbow. They're using the marbles.

Sydney took a deep breath. She raised her hands over her head with her wrists crossed.

Louisa disappeared from view and reappeared with another flag.

Marla yelled, "Are they doing it?"

"Yep. Keep your fingers crossed."

A sheet of darkness descended on the other side of the flames. Cries of outrage echoed from the ranks of the enemy. A moment later, the darkness faded.

Four faeries soared through the smoke. All four tumbled to the stones, hacking and coughing.

Sydney grabbed Garth's arm. "What happened?"

Garth smiled and coughed. His voice was weak. "McGee gave the order and almost all of them threw up the marbles at once. As soon as the dark hit, their rainbows vanished, along with their caches. They blew an entire round of recharges."

Trish lay on her stomach, retching smoke from her lungs. Marla slid her hands under Trish's arms and hoisted her. She motioned at Robin, who also lay coughing. "Help her up. Get more crumble, all four of you."

A final volley of bolts plunged through the smoke. Sydney's grin faltered as the flames shrunk yet again and the smoke started to dissipate. "Wulf, now!"

The Browns dropped their weapons and each hefted a sling. Sydney all but wept with relief.

Wulf had been adamantly against the use of the slings. 'Weapons for wimps,' he called them. It had taken Sydney an hour to convince Wulf that saving his gang's lives wasn't cowardly, and another to convince him to actually practice with the damn things. Even after his grudging acquiescence of her point, Sydney hadn't been one-hundred percent sure they would bring the slings to the battlefield, so seeing the Browns load the slings with metal balls gave her hope.

As one, the brownies whirled their weapons and fired, about where the massed Rats would be. Even through the smoke, the bursts of blue static and cascades of sparks were clearly visible. The air crackled and despite the smoke, Sydney smelled ozone and sizzling flesh. Squeals and shrieks echoed from the other side of the flames. She cheered. "They're working!"

"Damn right," Marla shouted. "For what we paid, they better have."

The Browns loaded another round of the balls Gordon and Patrice purchased at the Salmonika forge the day before. Each ball contained a tiny powder charge. On impact, the powder detonated and fired a copper tube into a set of foil-lined chambers filled with an electrified fluid. The result was an electric discharge that was loud, hot, and fatal.

The Browns fired a second volley, then a third and a fourth, finding more and more targets.

Sydney held her breath.

The Rats were the enemy's weak link. Though they would fight and were happy to attack when they had the advantage of numbers or surprise, they were cowards and known to flee when the odds turned against them. If the mass sling assault—something no one would have expected from the Browns—broke their morale and the Rats fled, that would deplete the Cons' numbers by over a third. Between that and the attrition of the arrows from the roof of The Log, the odds would be evened, with the Cons having expended a lot of their magical energy to suppress the flames. Stationing the quartet of faeries behind the cart, to cast a darkness spell the moment the Cons tried to recharge their magic, had been risky but had paid off, weakening the Cons even more.

Sydney's optimism surged. *This might just work. They're depleted and off-balance. I imagine the Cons are all but frothing at the mouth in frustration by now. They'll be careless. And we still have the redcaps to hit them from behind and—*

All at once, the flames along the line sputtered and died.

Sydney's mouth fell open. "Oh shit!"

"Sydney!" Panic covered Drith's face. "I can't feel my tree! My power is gone!"

Wails broke out in the dryad ranks as the realization hit them all. As one, the tree-women cried out. Some sobbed. Others screamed. Several fell to their knees.

"How? You collapsed the tunnel!"

"I don't know! Someone got to the grove." Drith's hollow eyes darted back and forth and tears painted her cheeks. "My tree, my tree!"

Sydney's heartbeat accelerated. "Drith, don't—"

"Ladies, run!"

Drith and the other dryads fled Bayberry Square. They scrambled over the north barricade and disappeared.

The smoke cleared, revealing a pack of perhaps fifty angry Cons and thirty-five or so Hobs. Eight or ten of each lay dead on the ground, riddled with crossbow bolts.

About fifteen Rats sprawled lifeless on the cobblestones. The survivors were nowhere to be seen.

Sydney swallowed hard. Her plan worked, at least as far as it had gone. She had not counted on losing the Dryads and their magic. There were about sixty-five faeries and brownies left facing eighty or ninety Cons and Hobs.

McGee locked eyes with Sydney. All trace of his prior humor had vanished and his lips pulled back in a savage snarl. "No more tricks, you stupid cunt. Now we're going to carve you up so bad your fucking mothers won't know you."

Her own temper flared. "Oh, shut the fuck up!"

Sydney yanked a knife loose and jetted it at McGee. He whipped his hand to the side and deflected the blade. It struck the Con standing next to McGee in the shoulder. The man yelled and stumbled.

McGee shouted, "Damn you, woman!"

With a collective roar, the two sides fell on each other.

Chapter Thirty-Three

Sydney lurched to her left as a Con raised his shillelagh in both hands and swung. The club whistled so near Sydney felt the rustled air of its passage on her cheek. She kicked the side of the man's knee. He fell off balance but she shrieked as a thudding pain lanced up her foot. She staggered a few steps back.

Was like kicking a brick wall. Oh, right, their magic.

The Con recovered and made an arcing backhanded swing. She ducked and thrust both hands out, shoving with her magical power.

The Con tumbled over, colliding with a Hob struggling with two Browns hanging on him. All four went down in a heap.

She whipped her head left and right, trying to find a friendly body to put on her flank.

No good. The battle lines disintegrated, on both sides. It's one big melee now.

Sydney's heart fell; in such a fight, without coherent organization, the side with fewer numbers was in serious trouble.

And that's us.

To her left, a big faery named Caleb dodged a spear thrust from a Hob and ducked underneath to stab at his attacker. His blade pierced the Hob's arm. Before Caleb could press his advantage, a grinning Con appeared, pointing both hands at the faery. Fire erupted from the Con's fingertips. Caleb howled as flame burst from his skin. In less than a heartbeat, he was a faery torch. His skin charred, his hair dissolved to ash and even the membranes of his wings melted and popped. Mercifully, he fell after only a few seconds.

Her stomach heaved. Sydney pulled a knife but the Con disappeared behind other combatants.

A hand fell on her shoulder. She whirled, dagger in hand, but it was Marla. "Marla, what—"

"Where the fuck are those redcaps? I lost track of Wulf and he was supposed to summon them. We need them here now."

"I don't know." Sydney dodged a random thrust by a gibbering Con. Before he could recover, Markus leaped on the Con's back, wrapped one arm around his neck, and slit his throat. Scarlet covered the Con's chest; he fell to his knees, clutching his torn jugular.

Markus yelled, "Where's Wychia?"

"We were just wondering that." Marla put her back to Sydney's and parried a Con's hatchet blow. She swung at her attacker's legs but the man danced out of reach. "Call her."

"Do what?"

"Use a spell, be loud. Tell her you'll give her a spanking. Infuriate her so she attacks."

"How?"

"Figure it out, asshole, you infuriate me enough." A Hob slashed at her; Marla dodged and was lost to Sydney in the swirling melee.

Markus took a deep breath and closed his eyes. Another Hob moved behind him, spear raised. Sydney flicked a knife at the Hob, catching him in the arm. The Hob staggered back.

Markus opened his mouth. Sydney winced as his crumble-amplified voice thundered across the Square. "Wychia, you worthless slut! Stop fucking around and get your stupid ass here right now!"

Magical energy expended, Markus slumped to his knees. A Con raised an ax to strike the unsuspecting faery but was tackled by the bulky Charley. The two rolled to the ground, pummeling each other.

Markus grinned at Sydney. "If that doesn't get her attention, I don't know what will."

"Get up, you idiot." She grabbed him under the arm and hauled him to his feet. "Crumble, now!"

"Yep." He dug in his pockets.

A crossbow bolt arced a few feet over Sydney's head. It pierced Henry in his left shoulder. The Con yelled, gripped the bolt, and pulled it from his flesh. Henry wavered, took one step, then toppled to the ground as a mace-armed Brown landed a glancing blow on the back of his skull.

Sydney glanced to the roof of The Log. She spotted Natasha, pulling back the arms of her crossbow to reload. Sydney could not see Anders but her spirit sank when she saw Louisa hanging limp over the edge of the roof, streams of scarlet staining the wall beneath her.

An unearthly screech reverberated from the Tower Street entrance. Eight fast-moving streaks of crimson charged into the fray. Even as Sydney watched, a Hob leveled his spear and thrust it into the stomach of one of the newly-arrived redcaps. The Hob smirked—which changed to astonishment as the redcap grabbed the spear in both hands and pulled himself down the shaft, drew a knife and stabbed the Hob in the chest four times. The Hob slumped to the ground. The redcap spun, still skewered by the spear and lurched towards another enemy before blood loss finally overcame him and he fell.

Wychia bashed her way through the melee, screaming incoherently. She clutched a heavy hammer in both hands and swung at everything within reach. After a second, Sydney realized the tiny berserker yelled Markus's name again and again.

She risked a quick scan of the fight. The arrival of the redcaps had stemmed the onslaught of the Cons and Hobs, though only just. All about her, outnumbered faeries and brownies fought against two or three opponents, slowly giving ground. The cacophony of metal on metal, curses, and cries of the wounded filled the air. Stray bursts of magic skittered overhead or assailed combatants, though not as many as she'd expected.

The only thing saving us is that the Cons depleted so much of their magic fighting the fire. If they hadn't, they would have already run us over.

Sydney dodged a thrown hatchet from a Con and made a backhand flipping throw of a knife in return. The Con ducked to avoid it and engaged a nearby Brown.

A faery named Brianna knocked a Con's cleaver from his hands, reversed her stroke, and eviscerated her opponent. Entrails tumbled loose and the Con fell screaming. Before she could recover, a spearhead burst from Brianna's chest. She went rigid. The Hob behind her wrenched his weapon free, just as a baying Garth knocked him to the ground. Garth landed on top of the Hob. He stabbed the Hob once, twice, then a third time. The Hob's eyes bulged in agony and his mouth moved but no sound emerged.

Brianna's gaze met Sydney's. A single tear trickled down Brianna's cheek before her eyes rolled back in her head. She slipped to the cobblestones, spasmed once, and went still.

Sydney tripped over a downed Con and almost fell. The cobblestones were slick with blood and bodies lay everywhere. Many of them moaned and writhed but just as many were still.

Nausea assaulted her gut. Too many of the fallen bore colored wings.

Sydney's eyes filled with tears.

We're getting cut to pieces.

Marla reappeared from the melee. Her sword was bloody, as was her now-helmetless brow.

Sydney shouted, "You all right?"

"Yeah."

"Marla, we're getting our asses handed to us."

"I know."

Markus emerged again, supporting a wounded Lila. Crimson covered the young faery's ribcage and her eyelids fluttered, as though she hovered on the brink of consciousness.

Sydney's vision dimmed. "Lila! Markus, how bad—"

"Real bad, we have to—"

A heavy strand of metal links slammed onto Markus's wing, just where the joint met his back. Markus shouted and fell to one knee. His wing folded, crumpled and hung askew.

Lila toppled to the side without a sound. Her chest rose and fell erratically.

McGee appeared behind Markus. His blood-splattered jacket gave mute testimony to his morning's work. The business end of his chain was equally-stained red and to her revulsion, Sydney could not help but notice a tuft of black hair lodged in the links.

McGee placed his boot in the gang lieutenant's back and shoved, sending Markus sprawling. "Good. Just the bitches I was looking for."

Visceral rage and hatred all but pushed coherent thought from Sydney's head. She fought to resist flinging herself at the Con, to rend his skin with her nails and teeth. She pulled another knife. "You that eager to die?"

Marla circled to McGee's left. Her sword slashed the air. "I'm going to cut your fucking heart out."

McGee smirked. "You took the words right out of my mouth."

Marla charged.

McGee spun and shoved his hand at her. A wave of force pulsed from his fingertips.

Marla rolled to her left, the magical attack passing over her head. She came to her feet and hacked at him. He shifted to his right to avoid her attack and punched her with his free hand. Marla staggered and nearly fell.

The move exposed his back to Sydney. She pointed at McGee and focused. A bolt of lightning lanced from her fingertip, striking him between the shoulder blades. He lurched but instead of screaming, he merely glared over his shoulder at her.

Sydney's head swam. Her best magical attack and it had not only failed to kill McGee but hadn't so much as knocked him from his feet.

Shit, I didn't even singe his jacket!

A Hob moved at Marla, only to be cut down from behind by Dana. The old faery's clothes were covered in soot and splatters of crimson though she did not appear to be injured. She held a short curved sword. Dana saw McGee and thrust at him.

McGee caught her arm, wrenched the sword loose, and stabbed at her with her own weapon. Dana twisted but was not fast enough. The sword pierced her side. She gasped, took two steps back, and fell across Lila.

Blood streamed from Marla's nose. She thrust both hands out, palms up, and yanked her arms towards the sky.

McGee rose six inches from the cobblestones. He laughed.

"What do you think you are, a dryad? No, you do it like this."

He squeezed his left hand into a fist. Marla jerked off the ground, her hands pinned to her sides. She struggled but could not free herself. The color drained from her face and her breathing faltered.

McGee threw his arm back to strike. The chain snapped like a whip.

"No!" Sydney hurled her knife at the Con's back. The blade grazed his shoulder, opening a bloody gash.

Marla tumbled in a heap. She clutched at her throat.

McGee grunted and whirled on Sydney. "You motherfucking backstabber!"

He barrelled towards her, cracking his chain from side to side. Sydney threw another knife. It ricocheted off the Con's forearm. She tried to evade but he was too close.

The chain arced from above and slammed into her thigh.

Shattering pain bolted up her hip. Sydney screamed. She tried to put weight on the leg but the agony was so intense her vision dimmed to pinpricks.

It's broken for sure.

She hobbled backward. Her fluttering wings helped her stay standing. The sheer torment of every step threatened to overwhelm her thoughts. Only the power of the crumble in her veins kept her conscious.

"Poor Sydney." McGee leered at her. "That winger with the black wings said to keep you alive but you know what? Screw him."

Sydney's knees buckled and she would have fallen has not a random Brown careened into her and shoved her upright.

The Nightshade? What—

McGee didn't wait for her to sort through the revelation. He lashed his weapon against the ground. Chips of cobblestone sprayed from the impact.

"This might make your teeth ache a little." His face twisted in a savage sneer. "But don't worry: they won't be anywhere near your head!"

She reached for a throwing knife but they were gone, depleted. Her bandolier was empty, as was the pouch at her waist. She still had her long dagger on her belt but that was ridiculous. She could barely hold the thing without dropping it. McGee would slap it away with ease.

Is this how it ends?

Her eyes fell on a knife laying on the pavement, just a few feet away.

Sydney concentrated. The knife rose from the pavement and hovered, blade level with the ground.

McGee snorted. "That all you got left?"

She sped the knife towards him, going wide on purpose. McGee turned his head to watch it pass. "Pathetic." He hefted his chain and started towards her, murder in his eyes.

Sydney angled the knife up and arced it over the fight. It swung in a wide loop, increasing in speed, hurling towards McGee's unprotected back.

The power of the crumble in her veins hiccupped, nearly expended. Her magic was a heartbeat away from failing. She poured everything she had left into the knife's speed.

Darkness descended around the edges of her vision as the last of the crumble flickered. Sydney's throat constricted. *This is gonna be close.*

The crumble expired. The knife wobbled in mid-flight and slowed. But it was still fast enough. It zoomed towards McGee's neck.

Just as it was about to plunge into his flesh, McGee whirled and plucked the knife from mid-air. "This again? Don't you ever learn? Now I'm gonna—"

When McGee pivoted to grab the knife, Sydney yanked her long dagger from her belt and threw her body at him. Her broken leg screamed in protest. She ignored the pain and focused on the hilt of her weapon.

Thumb there, like Dana said.

McGee's eyes widened.

Sydney's body collided with his. Driven by the force of her impact, the dagger sank into his chest.

They fell to the stones together. Sydney's vision blurred. She panted, fighting to stay conscious just a few more seconds. Every breath was a burning needle in her lungs.

McGee stared at the quivering blade stuck in his heart. He coughed; blood spurted from his mouth. "W...what..."

"You asked me if I ever learned. I did. I learned not to get distracted in a fight." She grinned through her fatigue. "But then, that's all women are—a distraction, right?"

McGee's eyes bugged out. He gasped and sank lifeless against the pavement.

Sydney summoned her last reserves of strength. She spread her wings and grabbed McGee's lapels. With three powerful flaps, she shot into the sky. Her leg shrieked in anguish and her face contorted. She hefted McGee's corpse and with all the voice she had left, she shouted, "Run, you bastards! McGee's dead and you're next!"

She dropped his body. Her vision dimmed again and this time, she could not stave it off. Sydney spiraled to the ground. She scarcely felt the cool stone against her cheeks or the tickle of wind in her hair. Rough hands grasped her arms and she spun into darkness.

Chapter Thirty-Four

The voice penetrated her consciousness and would not cease.

"Syd! Syd!"

She waved her hand. "Leave me alone, Marla."

"Damn it, Syd, wake the hell up."

She blinked one eye open. The concerned face of her sister filled her vision. "Marla, what are you doing?"

"Trying to get your dumb ass conscious."

"What? Where—"

Everything rushed back into memory. Sydney tried to sit up but Marla put her hand on Sydney's chest. "No, stay down. You've got a broken leg."

"But—"

"Garth will be over here in a moment to set it."

"Marla, what happened?"

Marla sat on her haunches. Dried blood plastered her lips and chin. A tuft of reddened cotton protruded from each nostril. Her forehead was crusted with blood, dirt, and sweat, and an angry gash creased her hairline. Sydney realized her sister would bear a sizeable scar for the rest of her days.

"What happened? Well, we won."

"We did?"

"Yep. After you ventilated McGee and flipped his corpse in the air, all the fight went out of the Cons. To a man, those still standing fled. The Hobs too."

"Really?"

"Yeah. We knew McGee was the glue holding the Cons together but I didn't know it was that extreme. When he was killed right in front of them, they all panicked." Marla's face hardened. "They left behind a lot of Con and Hob wounded."

"You didn't—"

"Damn right we did."

Sydney thought she should have been more repulsed by the idea but nothing came to the fore of her mind. Just a few months before, the idea of such slaughter would have filled Sydney with horror. But she couldn't muster the empathy.

Is this how seasoned veterans feel? Why they so often seem callous and cold? Maybe they're just always too tired to care.

She gazed at the blood-slicked cobblestones and had a sudden thought. Sydney said, "Marla, is Lila okay?"

"She took a pretty nasty stab wound to her abdomen, just under the right side of her ribcage. We thought it might have gotten her in the liver, which would have killed her for sure, but she lucked out. It looks like she's going to make it. She's already in The Log. We filled her with crumble and knocked her out. Garth accelerated her healing a bit. I put her in my room so you won't bother each other. Give her a few days and she should be better."

"Thank the Gods." Sydney hesitated. "How...how bad is it? How many?"

"Syd, you don't need to get yourself all stressed. Wait until —"

"Marla!" Sydney clenched her fists. A sense of growing dread gnawed at her gut. She kept her voice level. "How many did we lose?"

The corners of Marla's mouth twitched. Sydney was shocked to see tears in her sister's eyes.

"Ten."

"Oh." Sydney's voice was subdued. She knew there was no good answer to the question and she dreaded hearing it but she had to ask. "Who?"

"Syd—"

"I saw what happened to Caleb and Brianna." Sydney swallowed hard. "Who else? Marla, please."

"Louisa died on the roof. I'm not sure what happened but her throat was torn out. I guess it was Con magic."

Sydney nodded.

"Brandt took a Hob spear to the chest. He didn't make it."

Sydney hadn't known the taciturn faery from the Ivy Clan very well. He had mostly kept to himself but seemed a good sort, who didn't shirk his duty or complain. She sighed. "Okay."

"Allie and Charley both went down at some point. I didn't see what happened to either. Both were dead before we could get to them."

Sydney thought of the hulking, dumb Charley and the quiet, competent Allie. Despite their foibles, she liked them both. Her throat felt dry. "Oh, Marla."

"It gets worse." Marla's eyes focused on something distant. "The twins."

Sydney's eyes watered. "No."

"Yes. They tried to stand against McGee. They weren't up to it."

Sydney wiped her eyes. Lucian and Lucas were fixtures in The Log and in the workroom. It would never be the same without them.

Tears meandered down Marla's cheeks. "Patrice."

Sydney choked back a sob. An image of the smiling, brown-haired faery flashed through her mind. "Oh no. She and Gordon—"

"I know."

Sydney snuffled quietly for a moment. Then she jerked her head up. "Marla, that's only nine."

Marla's lips quivered. "And Robin."

"R-Robin?" Sydney erupted in tears. She cried for a moment before wiping her eyes again and trying to stem the sniffles. "Poor Garth. Is he okay?"

"No. No, he's not. He's devastated. He cried over her for ten minutes. Then he got up and started helping. He's working with Kent and Vivian and Trish and Gerry to get everyone bandaged up. I told him to go inside but he won't. I guess he wants to do something to keep his mind off it." Marla sighed.

Sydney took a deep breath and let loose one last hiccuping cry. "What else?"

"About half the Browns went down, along with all of the redcaps save Wychia and three others. I hate to say it, Syd, but they saved our asses today."

"Wulf?"

"Gone." She glanced northward, at the nearest barricaded street. "It looks like only the one dryad bought it before they fled. I'm going to have words with Drith."

"Later." Sydney wiped her eyes. "How is everyone else?"

Marla shrugged. "Fucked up. Almost everyone is wounded. Yours and Lila's are some of the worst. Dana got opened up but a few stitches and she'll be fine. Claire has a broken wrist but she's more mad than injured. Thom lost the little finger on his left hand. Noah got burned on the leg by a Con spell and will need some help getting around until he heals. A lot of things like that."

"Markus?"

"His wing is toast. Severed tendon. Even after it's reattached, it won't hold weight anytime soon, if ever. He'll probably never fly again." Marla glanced at the roof. "Anders and Natasha are okay. Anders caught some shrapnel from a spell but it's mostly a flesh wound. He'll have some scars on his shoulder but it's nothing life-threatening. Thankfully, Natasha managed to duck behind the wall. She wasn't hurt."

"Can't put the stage shows at risk," Sydney said, her voice laden with sarcasm.

Marla ignored it. "Exactly."

"What about Vivian?"

Marla snorted. "She wasn't even scratched. I thought someone might step up in the heat of the moment and show themselves to be a natural warrior but she was about the furthest one from my mind. Despite her injury, she killed five Cons and Hobs on her own, including Grak-salk, the Hob leader. She was an absolute cyclone of death, and she had the most deadly serious expression on her face the whole time. I am starting to think her dumb blonde act is just that."

In spite of herself, Sydney smiled. But her smile quickly faded. "Marla?"

"What?"

"Was it worth it?"

Marla looked away. "This is always the wrong time to ask that, Syd, in the aftermath of the battle. Looking out at our dead and wounded, it never seems worth it, even if it is."

Garth arrived. He took in Sydney's condition and probed her leg with gentle fingers, ignoring her grunts and moans. "Broken thigh. Sydney, I have no easy way to say this, but I am going to have to set it."

"Okay." Sydney touched his arm. "Garth...I'm sorry."

His lips pressed into a thin line and he gave her a clipped nod. "Thanks. Now, this is going to hurt."

"I know."

"It's going to hurt like a mother."

Sydney gritted her teeth. "Do what you have to do."

"Take a deep breath." He placed his hands on her leg. "Remember, you told me to do this."

He shoved.

Pain engulfed her. Sydney's last thought as she faded into unconsciousness was, *Why the hell did I tell him to do that?*

*   *   *   *   *

Sydney sat in the bed, scowling. "Damn it, Natasha, how much longer are you going to baby me?"

The singer fluttered her eyelashes at Sydney. "As long as Marla tells me to. I'll be back soon."

Sydney glowered but said nothing. Natasha smiled at her as she left.

Of all faeries she could have assigned to tend to me, Marla had to choose Natasha. I am going to kill her.

For her part, Natasha had done nothing untoward. She brought Sydney her meals and checked on her every hour. She'd been considerate and gentle, just as always. Her eyes conveyed to Sydney even more adoration than before and Sydney was waiting for Natasha to give up restraining herself and just leap on Sydney. Fortunately, that had not happened.

She shifted her weight and received a sharp poke in her leg. Sydney frowned and ran her hand between the sheets. Her fingertips encountered something metallic. She withdrew the object.

It was the plain copper medallion she'd found in her mom and dad's footlocker on her visit to Brigid's shop with Lila. Sydney scrunched her brows.

I wondered what happened to this. Never figured out what it did. Oh well, time for that later, I guess.

She stuffed the medallion in her nearby trouser pocket.

The door opened. Sydney said, "Natasha, I—"

But it was Marla who entered, followed by a bandaged Lila. The latter grinned as she laid eyes on Sydney. "Hey, buddy."

"Lila! How're you feeling?"

"A bit better. I can walk for a little while now but I'm still sore and wear out too quickly. You?"

Sydney huffed. "You'll pardon me if I don't get up. Marla, I'm getting ornery here. How long are you going to keep me laid up? It's been two days and I am already getting stir crazy."

"Until you're ready to move on your own, Syd." She sat on Lila's bed. "Garth did a good job of setting your leg and magically accelerating your healing but you still need at least one more day of rest to let the bone knit itself back together. What's the matter? Isn't Natasha taking good care of you?"

"And that's another thing. Why did you assign her? That's just cruel."

"She volunteered." Marla lit her cigar. "The Log is still shut down and she's not singing, so she's bored. She wanted to help."

"Even so...."

"Sydney," Lila said gently, "Natasha knows you don't feel the same way she does. She's not stupid. But even then, she still likes you and if she can do something nice for you, it makes her feel good. Okay? Just be nice to her, thank her, and it will be fine."

"You're supposed to be on my side."

Lila grinned. "I am on your side, you big dope."

"Lila, can you make it back to my room by yourself? I want to stay here a bit and discuss our news with Syd."

"Yeah, I think so. Be good to get off my feet again." Lila waved at Sydney and left the room.

Sydney struggled to sit up straight. Her bound leg complained at the movement but it was not the sharp pain it had been just a few hours before. "What news?"

"Well, I had an interesting audience with the head honcho this morning."

"Lord Burnside?"

"Yep. He was quite satisfied with the way everything turned out."

"I bet he was," Sydney said, her voice tart. "He didn't have to do any of the bleeding."

Marla nodded. "Anyway, he basically offered us the chance to go semi-legit, to keep all the operations we run now but to do it under the umbrella of the local governance. So we'd be the official organized crime in town."

"Sounds like you're considering it."

"Considering it, hell. I already accepted. Just think, Syd." Marla got up and started pacing. "We now have the controlling interest in the underworld for the whole city, with the de facto blessing of our immortal ruler to pretty much do as we want."

"I don't understand why Burnside would agree to that. Why doesn't he just wipe us out?"

"You know, I had the same question. As he explained it, he said we 'vermin' would always have a need to lie, cheat, and steal, and that no amount of brutality would ever suppress it altogether. He said he would rather it be kept to a dull roar and was prepared to accept a certain amount of vice, so long as it didn't interfere with his tax revenue."

Sydney pondered that. "Okay, then. So we're the gang now."

"Yes. We'll have to share the city with the Browns. Wychia had a rare moment of lucidity. She said the Browns would follow the faery lead, as long as we left them alone to do their own thing in their territory. I'm inclined to let them."

"She must have been tired or drunk or something."

"I think the reality is starting to sink in for her. Since Wulf died, she's in charge of the Browns now, and it's a lot to take in." Marla sat again. "Don't get me wrong; I think she would still go murderous at the drop of a hat. She is a redcap, after all. Do you know why she and her lunatics were late showing up for the fight?"

"No."

"They ran into the retreating Rats. The Rats attacked them."

"And?"

"And the redcaps pretty much butchered the entire Rat gang. By my count, they lost four and killed over thirty Rats, including Dominique. The rest of those furry bastards ran and haven't been seen since. I bet they're hiding in the sewers. Crol ordered the Enforcers and drakes to arrest them all on sight since they started trouble outside Bayberry Square."

Marla took a deep drag on her cigar. "Between the Enforcers and the Browns, I suspect we won't see a Rat show their face above ground for a very long time. Wychia already said she wants to tear the genitals off every last Rat in Woodhollow."

Sydney shivered at that image.

"I told Wychia we'll keep supplying them with Shroom and keep the same deal we had with Wulf. She seemed amenable to that and suggested they might be willing to share some of their gambling rings. You were right, Syd. The brownies turned out to be good allies."

"You catch up with Drith-an-Bidi yet?"

"Not yet. None of the Dryad Gang have been seen on the streets since the battle. I suspect they're hiding, afraid of retaliation." Marla snorted. "I haven't decided what I am going to do about those traitorous bitches yet. They aren't getting a piece of the action for a long time, if ever, that much is sure. Drith is on my shit list."

"Don't be too hard on them. When they lost their magic, they panicked."

"Yeah, and left us in the lurch."

"I know," Sydney said. "They don't have to be equal partners, like the Browns. Maybe once everyone settles down, we can integrate them into our operation somehow, even if they have to give up some power to do it."

"Maybe," Marla said. She folded one leg over the other. "Got some other changes to make. With us assuming a more 'official' capacity, I think we're going to add onto The Log and build some nicer office space and maybe a conference room off the south end of the tavern. I already asked for estimates from two goblin construction firms."

"How are we going to pay for that? I've been over the books. We don't have that kind of cash reserve."

"The Cons and Hobs are paying for it. Me, Dana, Garth, Wychia, and one her boys named Arnolf already looted the Four-Leaf Club, and we're going to Grak's old shop this afternoon."

Sydney folded her arms. "I can't believe they even let you in the door."

"They're gone, Syd. Every last Con in Woodhollow packed up and left town. I checked with Crol and he confirmed it. All of the surviving Hobs left too. There are still hobgoblins in Woodhollow, of course, but all the ones in the gang are gone. There *were* no leprechauns in town that weren't in their gang, so there are literally none of them left."

"I guess that only makes sense," Sydney said. "They probably thought that we were going to do what they would have done if the situation was reversed—namely, kill off every one of their enemies still standing."

"Probably. Doesn't matter though. I'm just glad they're gone." Marla took a light draw from her cigar. "Anyway, the cost wasn't an issue. If I'm going to move us up in the world, I need the right digs to do it in."

"I don't understand."

"There's a whole dimension of Woodhollow we've never been able to tap into, except around the fringes. Crafters unions, the big shipping companies, the conglomerates like the Salmonika forges. This is a chance for us to become a major power player in the city. To do that, though, I'll have to give up running the day-to-day operations of The Log and the gang."

"Oh? Who's going to fill in for you? Markus? Dana?"

"I was thinking about you."

Sydney jumped. "Me? Marla, I'm no leader."

"Shut up, Syd. Maybe you're too blind or dumb to see it but every faery in this gang looks up to you. Dana already said she will back you all the way. She'll advise you and be a sounding board, just like she was for me."

Sydney's mind raced. *Me? A gang leader?* "What about Markus? He was your next in line."

Marla sighed. "I don't know what to do about him. I told you his wing was crippled, right? Well, he's been drinking nonstop ever since the battle. He may recover physically but mentally? We both know faeries that lost the ability to fly. Some of them never shake the depression."

Sydney nodded.

"We can't afford to wait to see if he recovers his mojo. So you're not only the clear choice, you're the only choice. And just so you know, I will probably take Lila with me when I shift positions, so you'll have to find someone else to keep your records."

"I can do that."

"As you said to me a moment ago, it sounds like you're accepting."

"What did you expect me to do?"

Marla laughed. "I expected you to whine, dither, go back and forth, and finally grudgingly accept. I'm glad to see you cut out the intermediate steps."

Her laugh faded. "I'm glad you did because we need to move on some things quickly. We're pretty depleted, Syd."

"Supplies, you mean?"

"Yes, that, but I really meant members. We were forty-two before all this started. Will fled after killing Donovan, we lost ten more in the fight, and Gordon left this morning."

"He did?"

"Yeah," Marla said. Her expression showed her dismay at the fact. "He said everything here at The Log reminded him of Patrice. He said he was going back to Sylvan Valley."

Sydney suppressed her disappointment. *Another trusted friend gone.* Aloud, she said, "I guess I don't blame him."

"Yeah, I understand where he's coming from," Marla replied. "Still sucks. Regardless, we're down to about two-thirds of our former number. We have to re-staff your lieutenants, find a secretary for you, put someone in charge of collections, and get someone with experience on the lab for the Shroom trade. It will take time to rebuild our numbers, so that will have to be your number one priority."

"If I am going to run things, shouldn't I be able to name my number one priority?"

"You haven't taken over yet."

An idea occurred. "Marla, you haven't told Brigid about all this yet, have you?"

"Not yet."

"She's going to hear about the big brawl here in town soon enough."

"You're right," Marla said. "I'll get word to her. When I brought up the demon tube, Brigid hinted that Edmund knew of it. I'll send a message to him today. That probably won't stop her from charging down here to check on us but at least we'll be able to say we told her."

"You think she will? She was pretty disappointed in us."

Marla grinned. "Remember what Edmund said? He said she loves us in spite of our wicked ways. She'll come, Syd."

Edmund's name triggered another memory. "Marla, did you hear what McGee said before I killed him?"

"No, what?"

"He said the black-winged faery wanted me to live."

"He was talking out his ass, Syd."

"Was he?"

"Of course he was. Sounds like disinformation to me. I mean, why would a Nightshade confide in a leprechaun crook?

Who knows what the hell that assassin really wants."

"I don't know, Marla. What are the odds we'll find out, and sooner than we care to?"

Marla's face was calm. "Pretty good, I imagine."

Silence fell over the room as the two sisters receded into their own thoughts, looking for answers they knew they wouldn't find.

Epilogue

"Anything else, sugar?"

The faery shook his head.

"Well, if there is, you just let me know right away, 'k?" The green elf barmaid gave him a suggestive smile and sauntered away, swinging her hips.

Though his eyes lingered on her ample backside, he remained in his seat. The maid would be a welcome addition to his evening bed but that would draw far too much attention and he didn't want his passage noticed.

Not that I am going to be able to hide it very well, he thought.

He glanced around the common room of the Green Pines Inn. Despite being right on the north road from Woodhollow, towards the elven republics and Gorn, the historic home of the trow, the inn was all but deserted.

The barmaid deposited her burden on the bar. An older male elf wiped the already-clean counter and acknowledged her with a nod and fond smile.

Her father, I suppose.

A pair of unsmiling dwarven merchants huddled in the corner by the hearth fire. Each clutched a mug of ale. Neither so much as glanced at him.

Across from them, a cloaked *landvaettir* sat by herself. She was dressed as a noblewoman but he knew that didn't mean anything. She could be a baroness or a whore. Either way, her eyes never left the book before her, which meant she wasn't looking at him.

Still, with so little traffic, someone there was sure to say that they had seen him. That would be fatal.

He fingered the three packets of albino mushroom crumble in his pocket. He could ingest it and kill everyone in the common room before they could react.

Well, in theory. I'd probably screw it up.

He had never been much of a fighter. In the gang, he'd gotten by on his charm, his gregarious nature, and his affinity for spellcasting and the demon tube. In a fight, he'd almost been as useless as that skank Sydney.

His lip curled at the thought of her name. Everything had gone downhill since she had arrived.

If it hadn't been for her, I'd be running that gang now. If I could get just two minutes alone with that bitch and a couple of long knives....

Lost in his thoughts, he didn't even notice exactly when the hooded figure sat across from him. When he did, he sat straighter in his chair. His pulse quickened and his throat went dry. "Hello?"

The other figure did not answer.

It's him.

He said, "I didn't expect to see you here."

"You failed me, Will."

The man's tone was soft but the menace was unmistakable.

Will shivered. He'd know that voice anywhere. Speaking became a conscious effort. "Are you here to kill me?"

"Not just yet." The new arrival continued. "Why did you flee Woodhollow?"

"With the Cons crushed and McGee dead, it seemed like a good idea. My life wouldn't be worth shit in Woodhollow with the whole underworld following Marla's lead."

"Marla got the plans back."

"Yes."

Will braced, wondering if that fact would seal his fate but the other man only shrugged.

"Inconvenient, but that will be dealt with. What is your

intent now?"

"Run, as far away from Woodhollow and Sylvan Valley as I can."

The man shook his head almost imperceptibly. "No."

"You're the second person to tell me that. The last one died."

Will couldn't see his table-mate's face beneath the folds of his hood but he got the impression that the other man was laughing. "And you think I'll die as easy as McGee?"

"No."

"Good. You retained some brains after all."

"What difference will it make in the end?" Will said. Bitterness crept into his tone. He figured he was dead either way. "Someone will have seen me come this way. Marla will never stop looking for me. All the brains in the world won't help me evade her vengeance forever."

"Maybe, maybe not."

"I'm tired of the riddles"

The man tossed back his hood, revealing the middle-aged face Will knew well. The man's eyes glimmered like coals in a just-stoked fire. "No riddles, then. You're still drawing breath because you may yet be of use to me. When that ends, so do you. In the meantime, I will see to it that Marla never finds you. Just keep your head down and be discrete and everything will be fine."

"Can I get you something, darlin'?" The elf-maid returned. She winked at Will and bent over the table towards the older man, giving him an easier view down her low-cut top. "Anything t'all?"

He didn't even glance at her. "Nothing for me."

"I suppose you'll be wanting a room then?"

"No."

The elf's flirtatious mood vanished in the blink of any eye. "The tavern is for paying customers, mister. Buy something or get out."

He ignored her and stared at Will. "We have business to discuss, young lady. Leave us."

Her lip curled. "Dad!"

The tavern keeper came around the bar, clutching a cudgel.

Will noted that the two dwarves and the landy now watched the spectacle unfold and he groaned. *So much for discrete.*

The proprietor stopped behind Will's companion. He smacked the oak club in the palm of one hand. "Some trouble here?"

The barmaid folded her arms across her breasts. "Deadbeat, who don't want to buy nothin.' "

The male elf nudged the sitting man in the back of the head with his weapon. "Friend, you need to leave right now before—"

To Will's perception, the man was just a blur. One instant, he sat at the table. The next, he was on his feet, behind the tavern keep. Steel flashed and a gout of red sprayed from the elf's neck.

The barmaid had time to widen her eyes. She inhaled, as if to scream.

She never had the chance.

A blade glinted in the firelight. The maid stared at the knife buried to the hilt in her chest. Her dress darkened about the wound. She glanced at Will, blinked and sank to the floor without a sound.

Shouts erupted behind, followed by the scrape of chairs. Will slammed his eyes shut, though he could not avoid the grunts, the smash of a broken table, and the single scream from the landy that ended in a thick, syrupy cough.

When he opened his eyes, his companion was back at his place, seated across the table, as if nothing had happened. He had dispensed with his hooded cloak and allowed his wings to stretch.

His black wings.

"Did you have to kill them all?"

The man shrugged. "You were the one worried about being seen. No witnesses now."

Will took a deep breath and tried to control his trembling hands. "Now what?"

"Now we move onto the next plan."

"I don't like it. Sydney...leaving her alive is too risky."

"I didn't ask your opinion." The Nightshade's eyes narrowed. "And if you have some hair-brained scheme to go behind my back and cause her harm, you'll regret it. Trust me on that. I came damn close to pulling your guts once already."

"Why?"

"I gave you those blackteeth blades for a reason, and it wasn't to hand them off to Rat thugs."

"I didn't—"

"Of course you did. You think I didn't know what you were doing? A slight wound can fester for weeks and it's even odds anyone injured will die a wasting death. Her companion came damn close. It's just sheer dumb luck—good luck for *you*—that Sydney didn't get hurt then."

"She could have died in the brawl with the Cons."

"I wouldn't have let that happen. I was ready to stop McGee but she handled it herself, as I suspected she would. She ended up with nothing but a broken leg." The Nightshade smiled. "The pain is good for her. It will harden her soul without corrupting her."

"So you let the faeries win?" Will's eyes narrowed. "You didn't have to stop with burning down the rest of the Dryad Grove. You could have helped the Cons. They would have put me in charge of the Faery Gang and I would have handed Sydney over to you."

"Will, do you think I'm an idiot?"

Will's hold on his anger was strong enough that he answered with the only response he knew would let him go on breathing. "No."

"I would have intervened had Sydney been about to die. But that was the only reason. To do what you were suggesting would have required a sustained use of my strongest skills. As soon as I did that, Burnside would have sensed my presence and being the inquisitive sort he is, he would have started asking questions as to why a Nightshade was in Woodhollow and why that Nightshade was involved in a gang war. He's smart—too smart. That worm will destroy everything I have planned if he chooses to get involved."

Will took a sip of his drink, trying to loosen his dry throat. "You could kill him."

The man sighed. "We were discussing the possible, idiot, not fantasy. Without the Hearthglitter in my hand, such action would be suicidal folly. Even with the gem, it would be no easy task, and an unnecessary risk."

The corner of his mouth turned up in a mocking grin. "If that was your attempt to get me killed, it was pathetic."

He continued. "Anyway, I let it play out and the Cons lost. McGee was overconfident. The fool underestimated Sydney and Marla. It cost him. Me? I will simply move on to my next plan."

He folded his hands on the table. "And you're going to help, Will."

"No. I never should have gotten involved in this. I want out."

"I don't care what you want."

"This is pointless," Will yelled and slammed his fist on the tabletop. He supposed that the Nightshade could not help but interpret his outburst as a threatening act—then just as quickly realized the man could kill Will whenever he wanted and likely wouldn't feel threatened.

The assassin didn't so much as flinch at the impact of Will's hand and the confirmation of his second thought only made Will angrier.

"Pointless! Why all the intrigue? Why all the plots? You could just grab her, you could—"

The Nightshade moved his hand from left to right. Will shut his mouth.

"Sydney will never leave Woodhollow of her own volition. I understand that now. She's tied too tightly to Marla and the Faery Gang, and they to her."

He smiled again. "Even those cretins recognize how special she is."

Will bit back a retort.

The black-winged man went on. "If I 'grabbed her,' as you said, they'd come for her. I might be able to kill them all but that would only alert the dragon. No. My only hope is to either break the gang or to maneuver Sydney into driving herself from it. It didn't work this time. I'll keep trying until it does. It's the only way she'll see reason. If Sydney doesn't join me of her own free will, she'll fight me every step of the way. I want her safe—and after the unpleasantness in Beechwood Hall, I believe I am going to need her innocence and cooperation."

The Nightshade fixed Will with a burning gaze. "And as I said, you're going to help me. If you refuse, I'll kill you. I don't care if you're my kin. Betray me and try to harm her again, and I'll make your death last three days."

"I could go to the Octagon," Will blustered.

"You could? How? Do you even know where to find it?"

Will opened his mouth and closed it just as rapidly. It was a hollow threat and he knew it.

The Nightshade nodded as if acknowledging Will's recognition of that truth. "Exactly. The Nightshade Elders know what I need them to know. You can't find them and tell them otherwise. Even so, don't ever threaten me again. Period. You understand?"

"I understand." Will hesitated. "And your...other informant in the gang?"

The Nightshade smirked. "Still there."

"And?"

"And Marla and Sydney won't see that betrayal coming until it's far too late." He stood. "Now, come on. Time to move to the next stage. We're going to Tharsis. One of your old friends is expecting us."

The Nightshade strode to the exit.

Having little choice, Will followed.

END

GLOSSARY OF MYSTICAL RACES

Brownies (and Redcaps)

Hot-tempered to a fault, brownies are somewhat short. Both men and women tend to be about four feet tall and weigh less than a hundred pounds. Despite this, they are incredibly strong, falling behind only ogres among humanoid races in terms of physical power. Brownies have various shades of chocolate, dun, or nut-colored hair and skin, and varied eye color. Brownies are quarrelsome and quick to anger, though this means they fight well and ferociously. As a rite of passage to adulthood, they don green stocking caps. Certain brownies can develop berserker tendencies; those switch their green caps for crimson ones and are known as redcaps. Redcap brownies are noted for their battle prowess and lack of fear, and will often fight on after appalling wounds that would immediately kill another race.

Drakes

Drakes act as the aerial enforcement arm of the Woodhollow constables. The undersized dragons are approximately ten feet long and weigh well over five hundred pounds each. They have silvery scales and black eyes. They are temperamental but are sticklers for laws, orders, and regulations. Drakes are powerful combatants; in addition to their strength, speed, and savagery, they are fire-breathers and are known to use their breath weapon when confronted with even mildly uncooperative criminals. They are fast fliers but are not as agile in the air as faeries. They are feared by the residents of Woodhollow. The drakes themselves look at all other races, save the ogres, as beneath them.

Dryads

Tall and thin, dryads are one of two unisex races in Woodhollow, being all female. All dryads are about six feet tall, though slender, and seldom weigh more than one-hundred-twenty pounds. They have pale-to-dark green skin, dark brown or black hair, and the solid green eyes broken only by black pupils. All dryads are connected to a tree, though they can sever their tie and connect to a new one. Because of their trees, dyads can live hundreds of years. Dryads who commune with their trees (spend time in contact with it) can effect some of the strongest magic, outstripping other mortal races. Despite that, they are not expert fighters and generally react poorly when surprised. Dryads are haughty and arrogant, believing themselves above most other races.

Dwarves

Dwarves are the entrepreneurs of Woodhollow, running the banking, moneylending systems and other major businesses. Dwarves are around five feet tall and tend to be broad in the shoulders. Most have bronzed skin, dark hair and eyes, though both hair and eyes fade to lighter tones as they age. Dwarves hail from Kroven, southwest of Woodhollow. Their capital of Tharsis is the sight of many bloody battles between rival merchant houses. Male dwarves tend to grow long beards, marking their success with their beard ornamentation. Female dwarves grow their hair long for the same reason. Dwarves fight bravely but generally prefer to resolve differences off the battlefield or in court, where they tend to be be litigious and greedy. Dwarves have the least magical attunement of any Woodhollow race and often ruin any magical device they touch just by picking them up. They live about two and a half centuries.

Elves, General

Elves are tall and muscular, and are marked by their pointed ears. Most males are around six feet and close to two hundred pounds, females about the same height and one-hundred fifty pounds. They are usually light-skinned, though hair and eye color vary. Elves have a strong sense of honor and duty. They tend to be high-strung and quick to defend their honor—elven women even moreso than the men. Duels to the death are not uncommon in elven nations. Elves are also very militaristic and despite their nations having representative governments, conflicts and civil wars are common. Elves live around five hundred years.

Elves, Green

The green elf nation of Dylia is one of the more populous of the land, lying to the northeast of Woodhollow. It is also the scene of many terrible battles as the green elves war among themselves. Green elves are excellent strategists and warriors and—of all things—musicians.

Elves, Wood

Wood elves hail from Ascoria, north of Woodhollow, and are the most rigid and least compromising of the elven subraces. They are excellent farmers and vintners, and some have taken to brewing beer for export. Wood elves have a notable rural accent.

Elves, Dark

Unlike other elves, dark elves have ashen skin and black hair. Legend says that dark elves are wood elves who were cursed with a powerful talent. They have a magical ability on par with that of faeries but each use costs them decades from their lifespan, which means they are reluctant to use it unless the situation is extreme. The curse makes dark elves more philosophical and less prone to violence than their cousins.

Faeries

Faeries are winged humanoids, standing between five and six feet tall and weighing one-hundred-fifty to two hundred pounds (males) and a hundred to a hundred-fifty pounds (females). Most have white to olive skin. Hair and eye color varies. Faeries can fly rather gracefully and with remarkable endurance, sometimes staying aloft for an entire day. Faeries hail from their traditional homeland of Sylvan Valley, where they live in clans, denoted by the colors of their wings. Some faeries have randomly-colored wings; those subjects are usually called "unaffiliated" and are often treated as outsiders by the Clans. Faeries are often sarcastic and quick-witted, and most have a wide streak of hedonism. They are not the strongest of races but are typically agile and fast, and naturally-skilled fighters. Faeries consume white albino mushrooms—usually dried—to acess their magical talents. Their magic is middling—weaker than that of leprechauns or dryads, stronger than *landvaettir*, *vilas*, or werevixens—but perfectly servicable in and out of combat.

Gnomes

Most gnomes grow to no more than three feet tall; as such, most develop a massive inferiority complex when dealing with other races. This tends to make them aggressive and paranoid. They are excellent craftsmen and women. Male and female gnomes both have light-colored skin, hair and eyes.

Goblins

Goblins are green, warty-skinned humanoids who are all around five feet tall and a hundred-fifty pounds, with black hair and dark eyes. Both goblin men and women are frequently regarded by other races as the ugliest race Woodhollow has to offer. Despite this, goblins are intelligent, strong-willed and often have a fierce sense of humor. They are skilled workers and with their high tolerance for heat, they are excellent smiths and tinkers who can all but stand in their forges to work. Goblins love dabbling with mechanical devices. They are slightly more long-lived than most Woodhollow races, tending to last a little more than a hundred years.

Hobgoblins

Hobgoblins (sometimes known as "hobs") resemble goblins, though taller, heavier, and slightly more belligerent. Unlike goblins, they are good fighters and are often involved in criminal, mercenary, or security work.

Landvaettir

Also known as "landys," *landvaettir* are earth spirits. Both male and female landys are around six feet tall and very slender. They have hair so blond it is often almost white, with very pale skin and blue eyes. *Landvaettir* are talented with numbers and have significant math skills; unfortunately, they also tend to be weak of character and use their inherent skills to gamble and commit fraud. They are physically inept but possess a weak form of inherent magic that they can use for very minor probability-altering incantations. Most use this to supplement their illegal activities.

Leprechauns

Leprechauns are one of the two unisex races of Woodhollow, being all male. They are typically over six feet tall and above two hundred pounds, though certain larger specimens are known. Leprechauns are usually ivory-skinned and redheaded, and tend to wear beards and dress in green and black. Most are bullies and can be sadistic and cruel, though it means they usually follow the strongest among them out of fear. Though physically strong, they are often rash and quick to anger to the point of acting impulsively.

Leprechauns charge their magic through making physical contact with their personal cache of treasure, which can be accessed in the presence of a rainbow. Their raw magical strength and endurance is significantly stronger than that of a faery. Other races in Woodhollow often refer to them as "Cons" for short.

Ogres

Ogres are large. Most are seven feet tall or more, and weigh over three hundred pounds. They have olive skin, dark eyes, thin dark hair, and two short mouth tusks. Ogres are the shortest-lived of the Woodhollow races, reaching full maturity before age ten and passing in their fourth decade. They are monstrously strong and are also, through training and heritage, excellent warriors. Often mistaken for slow, most ogres simply don't worry about what other races think. They are employed in Woodhollow as peacekeepers and are generally feared, if not respected, by the other races.

Trow

Distantly related to gnomes, trows are short and broad, often being about three feet in both dimensions. Female trow seldom venture out of their homeland; all the trow in Woodhollow appear to be male. Trow have dark eyes and dark hair, and usually grow beards that nearly reach the ground. Trow are instinctive builders and are commonly employed in construction. They tend to be dirty compared to other races, and their beards are often filled with straw, food, and other debris. Trow are contemptuous of other races and will steal from and rob them as often as possible. In spite of this, they are not brave and will often choose to flee rather than fight.

Vilas

Vilas are house spirits and are routinely found engaging in cooking, baking, cleaning, or other domestic trades. Males and females both stand around five-and-a-half feet tall, and because of their frequent (and enthusiastic) eating habits, all *vilas* have a tendency to be rotund. They are usually happy, generous, and laugh a lot. *Vilas* are seldom involved in crimes or trouble and seem content to live their lives in peace. They are poor fighters. They use their minor magical skills in ways to enhance their domestic chores, such as allowing a rolling pin to flatten dough on its own power.

Wererats

Wererats are small and thin, with both males and females no more than five feet tall and a hundred pounds. In appearance, they resemble faeries without wings. Wererats can alter their form, becoming an upright humanoid rat that is capable of wielding weapons. The fur color of their rat-form matches their hair in humanoid form. Rats are intelligent and agile but are cowards who like to attack their opponents from ambush or overwhelm with superior numbers. In the face of strong resistance, they usually retreat. They are most comfortable in sewers and subterranean tunnels and often appear nervous or skittish while above ground.

Werevixens

The svelte, golden-haired werevixens are women who can take the form of a yellowish fox. Also called foxwomen, werevixens are about the same size and appearance as female faeries. They have striking yellow hair and gold-colored eyes. Little is known about their society or activities. They are standoffish and uncommunicative, even with each other. Werevixens can cast small spells but are known to avoid combat if at all possible. When confronted, they usually change to their fox forms and flee.

Wingless Worms

Little is known about the dragons of the realm, also called wingless worms. They are ancient, solitary beings, living for millenia. Wingless worms typically reach a length of greater than sixty feet in their first thousand years. Besides their physical strength and power, which is considerable, each has an inherent command of the strongest known magic, which they can use to great effect. Worms are intelligent and acquire considerable knowledge and wisdom over their lifespans. Despite not having wings, they are known to magically fly. Worms are capable of decimating entire armies. Their colors and personalities are widely disparate. In dealing with other races, they typically use the terms "Lord" and "Lady" to describe themselves, and often assume aristocratic names. Their true names are known only to themselves.

Rumors of their cousins, greater winged worms, who reputedly were even more powerful, remain nothing but legend.

Follow Sydney's adventures in Book 2 of *The Holly Sisters. The Mauler*, coming soon....

The door to the workroom banged open and Sydney stomped inside, her face a thundercloud.

Her auburn hair had come loose from its customary pony tail and was now matted with sweat and dirt. Scratches and splotches of mud adorned her face and arms. A thin trickle of dried blood clung to the corner of her mouth. Her hose was ripped, her boots muddy, and her favorite tunic--once a clean snowy white and embroidered with crimson thread--hung in tatters. She plucked at the garment, realizing it was nothing more than a handful of fabric scraps held together by the stitching.

At least I wore an undershirt or else half of Woodhollow would have gotten a look at my chest.

Curious faery heads turned in her direction. Sydney saw more than one smile. A few of the newer members gawked at her.

"What are you staring at? Get back to work!"

Faeries snickered and returned to their projects.

An older faery waited by the door to Sydney's office. She was slightly taller than Sydney and wore a rose-colored gown and matching slippers. Her gray hair, healthy and shiny despite its shade, hung loose down her back. The faery's silvery wings, adorned with scarlet circles, marked her as a member of the Foxglove Clan.

She smirked as Sydney approached. "Looks like things went well."

Sydney grunted and stepped past her, pushing open the door to her office.

A young faery sat behind the desk. Her midnight blue wings perked up as Sydney entered and the youngster jumped to her feet. Her wide eyes took in Sydney's appearance. "Sydney! Are you okay?"

"I'll live."

"You sure?"

"Emma, I'm fine," Sydney said with more conviction than she felt. Her limbs sagged with fatigue. "Any messages?"

"Just one from Gerry. He wanted to talk about the new

formula."

"All right."

The secretary hefted a folder. "And here is the file you asked for, about Dillon's Shroom sales."

"I'll come back and get it in a bit."

"Okay. You need a water or ale or anything?"

"Not right now." Sydney glanced at the exterior door, where the old faery stood waiting expectantly. Sydney motioned to her. "Give me and Dana a few minutes."

"Yes, Ma'am."

Sydney entered her interior office. A plain desk sat in the center, facing the door. On the wall behind the desk, a wide panel displayed a second-story view of Bayberry Square. Out of habit, Sydney glanced in the magical window. As usual, she saw nothing amiss.

Yeah but sooner or later, you will see something and you'll be glad you got in the habit.

"Dana, come in."

Sydney's lieutenant entered and shut the door behind them. She sat and folded one leg over the other. "I guess the sprites wanted to argue with you."

"Is it that obvious?"

"Just a little."

Sydney collapsed in her own chair. "Yep. They do the same song and dance they always do. They don't know why the mushroom shipment was light. They don't know why the field count was low. They don't know why we would accuse them of something so heinous as stealing from us. Plyfft acted very outraged over the whole thing."

"She always does. It's just like dealing with children."

"That's about what they are."

Dana cocked her head. "Do you wish someone else had gone with you now?"

"Absolutely. I feel like shit."

"Look like it, too."

"Thanks, Mom."

Dana smiled. "Someone has to keep an eye on you kids. Okay, so they wanted to fight. How'd that go?"

"Well, I won, but they didn't make it easy. Ever have a

flock of sprites attacking you at once?"

"Yes. I know they're only the size of sparrows but a whole group is a lot to handle."

"My only consolation is they are probably hurting worse than I am right now. When it was over, I put my foot on Plyfft and told her if I had to come back anytime soon, I was going to squash her."

"I'm sure that did the trick."

"It did. She begged for mercy and swore up and down that they wouldn't steal anymore and that they'd have the full shipments ready on time. I asked for her word and she gave it."

"Of course she did." Dana flipped her hand in a dismissive motion. "Just like she always does. Then she'll forget and in six months we'll be out there again."

"Yeah, I know." Sydney raised her voice. "Emma!"

Her secretary popped her head in a moment later. "Yes?"

"Would you mind going to my room and getting me a fresh tunic and a pair of trousers? And a towel too, if you don't mind?"

"Of course." She closed the door.

Dana jerked her head at the door. "How's she doing?"

"Working out fine. She's young but Lila trained her well."

"Sixteen, right?"

"Yeah."

"I wonder how the Bluebell Clan would feel about her running away to Woodhollow to join a gang."

Sydney gave her head a slight shake. "I doubt they'd care. She said her father was a drunk who used to beat her."

Dana sighed. "Some faeries are just assholes."

"No question." Sydney hoisted herself from her chair. Her body hurt--not in any serious way but though she'd overused every muscle between her brow and the soles of her feet.

Dana raised an eyebrow. "You sure you're okay?"

"Yeah, just feel like ass."

Sydney dug in her desk drawer and pulled out a pair of small paper packets. Each was filled tiny crumbles of dried albino mushroom. Sydney placed the two packets on her tongue. The filmy paper dissolved in her mouth and in an instant, the power of the mushroom soaked into her bloodstream. The fatigue in her muscles faded to a mute ache.

She took a few steps to the corner of the room, to a tiny booth with no door. The tile floor, which stood in stark contrast to the hardwood of the rest of the office, sloped to a corner drain.

Sydney concentrated. A miniature stormcloud appeared just above head level. A torrent of steaming water gushed forth.

She peeled off her filthy clothes and stepped into the booth. The hot water cascading over her skin brought immediate relief. Sydney angled her head back, placed her face under the water, and brushed her hair away from her forehead with both hands.

"Dana, having this built in here when The Log was renovated was one of the best decisions I ever made."

"If you say so."

"I'm not opposed to using the showers in the living space. But on days like this, it hurts to climb the stairs."

"That's fine, Sydney. You give so much and take so little from the gang no one is going to begrudge it to you."

She tilted her head from side to side, enjoying the warmth on her neck. "I take my stipend, same as everyone else."

"You know what I mean, Sydney. When was the last time you took a day off?"

"I don't know."

"You're turning into as much of a workaholic as your sister."

She's right, Sydney thought. "Yeah, well, family. You know how that is."

To be continued....

Acknowledgements

Oh, man, where even to begin....

First off, thank you readers for making it all the way to the end. This first book was a blast to write and these characters, more than any other work I've done, really came alive in my head. I hope it's been fun and enjoyable, and you were entertained enough to keep reading about Sydney's adventures.

I am sure there are folks I will overlook here, and apologies in advance for that.

I'd like to acknowledge all of my friends from my online communities, who have given me invaluable advice and guidance, offered support, or just encouraged me indirectly: Petros, Rita, Michael, Lindsey, and Sarah. Special thanks to Mihir, for being one of my biggest boosters and supporters.

Thanks to Brian, who re-invigorated my writing passion at a critical moment when it was flagging, through just a simple ten-minute conversation.

Thanks to Jeff, Robb, Brant, Rob, Sue, Carla, Christine, Andrea, and Thom, and all the others who just put up with my inane banter on the subject.

To my local writer's group--Paula, Conni, Sean, Nico, and Kaye--thanks for always providing a good sanity-check on my work and for the comaraderie we've had over the years.

Thanks of course to Jessica, who put together this wonderful cover for me.

Thanks to Jens, Andy, Jonathan, and Beth, for beta reads and targeted feedback. Everything y'all gave me did nothing but help.

I have to give a hearty, "Thank you," to my family: Mom, Dad, Rachel, Leigh, Levi, Kelly, and Dani. Without your love, I doubt I ever would have been in a position to get this far in life.

Last, I have to express my undying thanks and gratitude to my wife Lisa, without whose love, devotion, and whip-cracking, I never would have embarked on this writing journey. She's been part cheerleader, part drill-sergeant, and one-hundred percent in my corner. Love you, babe.

Made in the USA
Columbia, SC
21 June 2022

61980150R00250